THE
IMMORTAL

GENA SHOWALTER

THE IMMORTAL

HQN

Recycling programs
for this product may
not exist in your area.

ISBN-13: 978-1-335-45344-0

The Immortal

HQN
22 Adelaide St. West, 41st Floor
Toronto, Ontario M5H 4E3, Canada
www.Harlequin.com

Printed in U.S.A.

To Jill Monroe and Naomi Lane for the read(s),
the catches and the suggestions. Ladies, you are
two of the best people on Earth, and I love and adore you.
Obviously any mistakes in the story are your fault.

To Helen Mays and Wendy Higgins for being all-around amazing.
Thank you!

THE
IMMORTAL

PROLOGUE

Excerpted from *The Book of Stars*
Author unknown
Warning: Living text subject to change

They are ancient warriors, evil to the core and loyal only to one another. Known as the Astra Planeta, Wandering Stars, Warlords of the Skies—the beginning of the end—they travel from world to world, wiping out enemy armies. Drawn to war, they turn even the smallest skirmish into a travesty of pain and bloodshed.

To glimpse these warriors means you'll soon greet your death.

Having no moral compass, they kill without mercy, steal without qualm, and destroy without guilt. Their aim is simple, their goal unchanged. Win a blessing, whatever the cost. Five hundred years of victory without suffering a single loss. A requirement in their endless battle with a powerful god: Erebus the Deathless,

Master of the Depths, the Dark One. Without that blessing, the Astra automatically obtain a curse. Five hundred years of utter defeat.—Page 1

The next bestowing has come, each of the nine Astra charged with the completion of an impossible task.

Currently, the score stands at Astra—1, Erebus—0.

Halo Phaninon, second-in-command, First and Last of the Order, the Machine, the Ringed One—Immortal of Immortals— is the newest challenger.

He must perform the twelve labors of Hercules…in a day.

For the emotionless assassin, failure is not an option. If he must raze a world and its occupants to achieve victory, so be it. And if he must destroy the female who can bring his dead heart back to life—his fated mate? What then?

Let's find out.—Page 10,519

A faraway realm
Long ago

"Emotions are our greatest enemy." With an unhurried stride, the headmaster paced before his charges. Students of the Order. The train of his voluminous black robe dragged behind him.

The most notable acolyte—Four—stood shoulder to shoulder with nine others in a perfectly straight line. Each boy wore a colorless tunic and loose pants; each kept his eyes focused ahead, chin up, hands locked behind his back and bare feet pressed together. None dared to take more than eight inhalations per minute. The allotted amount.

Though a mere twelve years in age, Four already towered over the others. As the son of an eight-foot-tall war god, he might grow bigger than even the headmaster. If that happened…

Headmaster dies screaming.

The stern, merciless male possessed crimson skin and obsidian eyes without any whites; the instructors were exact copies of him. Their only differences came from the symbols etched into their faces. Symbols that glowed when they contemplated any kind of punishment.

Headmaster never ceased glowing. "Say it," he commanded now.

"Emotions are our greatest enemy," the boys echoed in unison, monotone.

Four meant those words with every fiber of his being. What he wouldn't give to rid himself of any softness. To no longer suffer the torment of grief and loss. Perhaps then he might finally forget his tenth birthday. The day invaders murdered his mother and carted him to the Order.

Here, orphaned children of "myth and legend" learned to assassinate kings and gods. The best executioners received rewards. Those who floundered were often used during target practice.

"Today, you will prove you mean what you say." Headmaster continued his unhurried back-and-forth stride, drawing out the suspense. Testing his students, always testing. In the empty white room, his footfalls proved silent. "Shall I tell you how?"

"If you wish, Headmaster," the boys responded, again in unison.

Four's stomach churned, bile singeing his chest. He'd felt sick all morning. Even before he was summoned from his quarters—a small cubicle containing only a bed, nightstand, and handful of books he'd received for exemplary behavior. A sparse prison he'd come to appreciate. The less you owned, the less others could use against you. But not by word or deed did he reveal his physical discomfort. He knew better.

What would Headmaster force the students to endure today? Or worse, to do?

His skin glowed brighter as he passed Four. Five, the boy to his right, released an almost imperceptible whimper.

In a blink, the headmaster returned to the lad.

Four didn't move. He willed his heart to maintain a slow, steady beat, lest a glaze of sweat dampen his skin, giving him away.

Headmaster purred, "Are you afraid, Five?"

Each student was known only by a number. A reminder of a terrible truth: *we are easily replaced*.

"No, sir," Five said, but a slight tremor proved him a liar. "I fear nothing."

"I'm not certain I believe you." Headmaster lifted an arm and snapped his fingers. "But there's a way to learn the truth."

Instructors observed the proceedings from the back wall, lined up just like the students. A lone male eased into motion, closing the distance to stand beside his superior.

Dread gave the sterile air a sharp bite.

"Whip him," Headmaster ordered. "He's to receive twenty lashes. If he makes a noise, cut out his tongue. If he sheds a tear, blind him."

No one in the room revealed an outward reaction as the instructor padded behind Five. But inside, Four waged a fierce war. He liked the boy and protected him whenever possible. Of the ten students in their group, Five was the kindest. Unlike the others, he shared his rewards, no matter what they happened to be. Food. Soft blankets. Special weapons. But Five was also the weakest among them, and he was about to suffer untold agonies. Could he maintain his silence until the end of the whipping? Could anyone?

As the instructor unhooked a barbed rope from the belt of his robe, Four fought the urge to safeguard his friend. He knew better. He'd made this mistake once before, with another student. The moment he had intervened, he'd made everything worse. At least Five wasn't being given an animal to raise and later kill.

The first strike landed with a whoosh. Relief sparked as silence stretched. The second and third strikes fell. Five did well, his face remaining a blank mask.

Headmaster leaned down, putting himself at eye level with his victim. "With every lash, you are being rid of your secret shame. Thank me for this opportunity."

"Thank you, Headmaster."

Whoosh. Crack.

Whoosh. Crack.

After the seventh strike, Headmaster slowly slid his attention to Four. He canted his head, staring hard. The symbols in his skin glowed brighter and brighter.

Four revealed nothing.

"Tell me what you think of Five's situation," the evil male cajoled.

"I cannot." The calmness—the coldness—of Four's tone chilled even him. "I think nothing of his situation."

"Is that so?"

Whoosh. Crack. Whoosh. Crack.

Calm. Steady. Breathe in, out. "That is so."

After searching Four's face, Headmaster withdrew a dagger from a hidden pocket of his robe and offered the hilt. "Kill him."

Four blinked twice. "Sir?"

"You will kill Five, or I will kill you. The decision is yours. You have one minute to decide."

As Four held the male's gaze, he knew two things with absolute certainty. If he hesitated to do this, he *would* die today. If he revealed a single emotion, he would *want* to die.

With iron resolve, he accepted the weapon, his grip steady. He stepped backward and to the right, moving between the instructor with the whip and Five. Staring at his back—at the blood wetting his tunic.

I can do this. Four had delivered many deaths the past two years, his kill list more than double the length of anyone else's. But then, he was born for this. And yet...

He felt as if a part of *him* died each time he stole another's life.

Would he act anyway? Oh yes. Without hesitation.

Four stepped forward. Mere inches separated his chest and the ravaged back of his newest target. He reached around and gripped the boy's chin, angling his head to the side. With his free hand, he pressed the tip of a blade into the upper dip of Five's sternum.

A mewl of fear escaped his friend, and the churning in his stomach intensified.

"Your time runs out," Headmaster stated.

Four blanked his mind, a grueling skill he'd worked hard to perfect. One by one, his thoughts faded to the background, his emotions dulling until he felt nothing. Only a cold, gnawing void. He calmed, and his breathing evened out. This? This was nothing. A single death among hundreds.

As the boy opened his mouth to protest or plead, Four met Headmaster's obsidian gaze—and plunged the dagger deep. He twisted his wrist at the end. Bone cracked.

Five stiffened against him, choking sounds leaving him. In seconds—an endless eternity—he collapsed, crashing to the floor.

Blood spurted from the wound, splattering the motionless body, the floor. Four...didn't care. He survived, whatever the cost.

One day, things would be different. Until then, Four could only bide his time...

Warm liquid pooled around his feet, and his inner cold thawed fast. The sickness returned to his belly.

"What is this I smell on you, hmm? Fear?" The headmaster swooped in and ran the tip of his nose across Four's neck while inhaling. "No, not fear, but *something*." He straightened and motioned to the instructor with the whip. "Give him twenty lashes."

Reveal nothing. "Thank you, Headmaster."

Already in position, the instructor struck without delay. *Whoosh. Crack.*

Pain splintered through Four, shooting across each of his limbs.

Whoosh. Crack. Whoosh. Crack.

He held Headmaster's gaze until the end—and smiled. "Thank you again, Headmaster."

Scowling, the male grazed two black claws across his cheek. "Whatever you're feeling will boil over as soon as I turn up the heat." Walking away, Headmaster spoke to the instructor. "Give him twenty more."

2

Harpina, the harpy realm
6:00 a.m.
Day 1

"Get your lazy butt out of bed. Operation Lady O Be Good commences in thirty."

The beloved but evil voice preceded the sudden ripping away of Ophelia Falconcrest's trio of comforters, leaving her with only a sheet. Although she wore neck to toe flannel, frigid air enveloped her in a hurry, and she groaned. Even the most sedate temperatures affected harpymphs like Ophelia. Not that there were many harpy-nymphs in existence.

As she roused slowly but surely, she became increasingly aware of a great and terrible hangover and groaned louder. Her head throbbed, her stomach roiled, and her mouth tasted like a broken garbage disposal. *Never drinking again. Maybe. Probably.*

"Go away," she muttered. "Let me die dramatically and in peace."

"The motto you stole from *Survivor* is outwit, outplay, and outlast. Unless you've decided to go with a new one. Give up and give in." Vivian "Vivi" Eagleshield, her best friend and favorite tormentor, clapped her hands twice and commanded with an exaggerated Russian accent, "Up, up, Lady O! Today is big day for you. Meaning, yes, it's big day for me. You *know* I take my big days seriously."

"You're the best and the worst, and I love you, but I also kind of hate you." Ophelia smacked her dry lips and whimpered. "If you have any affection for me, you'll pretend today doesn't exist."

"Up! Up!"

"So cruel and heartless," she whined. She cracked open lids as rough as sandpaper. Though her eyes burned, she did her best to focus. "Come back tomorrow. Friday at the latest." Like most single harpies, she enjoyed the luxury of sleeping on a bed only when she was safe in her home world—and she *never* parted with her luxuries easily. "Also, stop calling me by that ridiculous nickname."

Although, it certainly beat her epithet. Ophelia the Flunk Out. A title she'd earned eight years ago, at the age of eighteen. The day she'd gifted her virginity to her boyfriend, ending her fight to become harpy top dog: the General.

Once upon a time, virginity had been a requirement for any General hopeful, and even the General herself. The fact that Ophelia had willingly parted with hers for a cute smile and a false promise of eternal love was one of her greatest regrets. Especially since she was the only sister of Nissa the Great, a previous General known for her uncompromised, unwavering standard of excellence.

And what had Ophelia gotten out of the loss? Zero climaxes, a bitter breakup the next day, and a derailed future. *Lady O No.*

The worst part? The soul-crushing mistake was the first of

many made throughout her life. To be honest, mistakes had become her specialty. As her sister used to say, "If ever someone hands out an award for screwed-up priorities, bad taste in guys, or most wrong turns, you deserve first, second, and third prize, Ophelia."

She squeezed her eyes shut and moaned. "I hate my life."

"So?" the cruel and pitiless Vivi countered. "You love me, and I'm not leaving until you get up and push me out of the room."

Ugh. There were approximately zero people more stubborn than the harpy-vampire. A combination affectionately known as "harpire" and "vampy." Either Ophelia participated in her own awakening, or her friend continued torturing her.

She rapid-blinked to clear her vision, her focal point expanding gradually. Morning sunlight streamed through the lone window in her cramped bunkroom. A precious space she'd had to fight fang and claw to get, since Nissa had expected her to live at the palace.

Too bright! Her eyes stung and watered, the minimal furnishings blurring. She rapid-blinked again, finally finding Vivi. An elegant, fine-boned beauty with dark hair, darker eyes, and pale skin.

"You have two settings constantly at war. Overachiever and self-destructor." Vivi offered Ophelia a sweet grin that masked her core of iron. "Care to guess which direction you leaned this time?"

"No," she grumbled.

"That's right. Because you don't need to guess. You already know you reached rock bottom and tunneled underneath. But guess what? This is my rescue mission. You're getting up, and we're heading to the gym where you will sweat out your hangover. You aren't missing your meeting with General Taliyah."

"Don't remind me." She motioned to the empty vodka bottles on her "desk," a detachable slab of wood. "Not after I worked so hard to forget. What time is it, anyway?"

"Only 6:00 a.m."

What? Only? *What?* Ignoring her aches and pains, Ophelia eased into an upright position and stretched. The tiny, translucent wings between her shoulder blades fluttered, relieved to be free of the mattress. "The big meeting isn't until noon," she grumbled.

"I know! So we'd better start sobering you up ASAP."

Someone save me. Taliyah Skyhawk, the newest Harpy General, had demanded a sit-down with Ophelia. Her friend believed a promotion waited in her future. Maybe leading a patrol of her own or joining a higher ranked unit. Her dream. Ophelia wasn't convinced and feared the worst.

"What if she complains about me? I've served to the best of my ability, but is my best good enough?" Nissa had *always* complained.

Why didn't you throw the first punch faster, Ophelia?

Are you trying to tickle or subdue him, Ophelia?

How are we even related, Ophelia?

"So what if she does complain?" Vivi asked. "She only corrects the ones she loves. And your skill far outweighs your errors."

True. And, honestly, Ophelia *had* been an exemplary soldier lately. Mostly. Kind of. Her record shined like a freshly polished diamond. Or cubic zirconia. She'd graduated from Harpy University with high dishonors, majoring in Murder and minoring in Revenge. She'd never missed a day of class or training without an excellent excuse.

To maintain her incomparable stamina, she jogged daily upon occasion. When off the clock, she participated in countless digital combat simulations to hone her most lethal skills from the comfort of her room. She absolutely, positively *never* questioned her superiors very often. Anytime she patrolled the city, she remained almost fully alert, even when hot guys entered the picture. Even on vacations and holidays, she always sometimes avoided males as if they were a plague. Because they were!

Her first boyfriend had taught her well. Her second and final guy had served as a reminder. Romance brought nothing but heartbreak. Males desired her until they won her. As soon as they realized they couldn't satisfy her nymph side, their pride nosedived and they bailed.

So why do I continue to yearn for someone of my very own?

As if she didn't already know the answer. She was a weak, foolish half-nymph, who sought pleasure above everything. When she got turned on, her common sense switched off.

Seriously. If allowed to run wild, nymphs became single-minded with their pursuit of passion. They wanted what they wanted, and they wanted it often. Even when a lover had nothing left to give, nymphs begged and pleaded for climax, all pride erased. No man could keep up.

Thankfully, her harpy kept her nymph buried in the back of her mind, ensuring Ophelia never again forgot her life plan—taking another shot at the Generalship. Expectations for the title had recently received an overhaul, the virginity rule axed. Any contender of consenting age could bang on the daily if she so desired.

Ophelia now had a chance to qualify for the position. And qualify she would or die trying. So. Best to avoid temptation altogether and maintain her focus. Meaning, no sex for her. With near-constant hard work and unshakable dedication, she could complete the ten requirements for General in only a handful of centuries.

Did she wish to rule the entire species, as Nissa had? Yes. But also no. The thought of so much responsibility left Ophelia shuddering. But stop her? Not for a second. She *must* prove herself. And she would. Gradually. A single step at a time.

Fingers snapped in front of her face. "—listening to me?"

Great. She'd gotten lost in her head. "No. I'm thinking about my next step. I've got to make a kill, Vee." Her cheeks flamed at the lack. Everyone in her graduating class had a substantial kill list. She should too.

"You will."

"How can you be sure?" The past few weeks, she'd fought countless phantoms—mindless, soul-sucking husks intent on draining life. Or rather, she'd tried to fight them. As soon as she had approached, they'd vanished.

"Because I know you. And I know you're afraid Taliyah will banish you from Harpina. Which is ridiculous, by the way." Vivi spread her arms wide. "I mean, maybe she does banish you, but so what? You'll fight to change her mind. And guess what? What you fight for, you win. Always. That's why I lowered myself to love you, isn't it? You waged wars for my affections."

Ophelia snorted and tossed a pillow at her favorite vampy. Whether the General found fault with her performance or not, banishment was a very real possibility.

Taliyah probably expected Ophelia to retaliate against the Astra Planeta for their part in Nissa's death.

My right. Not too long ago, nine warlords had conquered the harpy realm for reasons no one had considered Ophelia worthy of knowing. And they'd done the deed in a single day! Their power seemed limitless, their tempers more so.

Their vast armies consisted of warriors of varying species. Everything from pure-blood vampires to banshees, to shifters and gorgons. Basically anything found in myths and legends.

Ophelia had never gone head-to-head with an Astra or even a soldier under their command. Before her unit had ever reached the battlefield, the fray had ended. Harpies all over the land had fallen asleep, herself included. She'd awoken weeks later, only to learn Roc, the Astra Commander, had killed Nissa.

Nissa. Gone.

Ophelia pressed her tongue to the roof of her mouth. She had every right to declare a blood vendetta against the Commander of the Astra. Among harpies, vendettas of every kind were common. And revered. As long as the punishment fit the crime, not even the General herself had a right to obstruct Ophelia's vengeance.

Though Ophelia and Nissa had been centuries apart in age and had barely liked each other, they'd been family. The last of their line. Deep down, Ophelia had loved her sister. She still did.

She hated the Commander for what he'd done. Could she beat him in a battle, though? Not at this time, no, and there was no reason to delude herself otherwise. Did she wish to spend the rest of her life attempting to harm him while merely managing to annoy him, simply to satisfy her need for revenge? Also no. Maybe? Ophelia didn't know anything anymore.

"Chop, chop." Vivi clapped her hands with more force. "Don't just sit there, staring at nothing. Get up and get dressed."

"Okay, okay. But I'm not meeting with Taliyah." If the General had something to say, she could find Ophelia and say it.

"That's a good one. Because yes, you are. Up, up!"

Grumbling under her breath, she untangled herself from the sheet, clambered to her feet and stumbled into the bathroom. As next-door neighbors, she and Vivi shared the small space. Clean freak Vivi kept things tidy, ensuring everything stayed where it belonged, even after Hurricane O, category 5 blew through, disrupting everything. The harpire even redecorated with a new theme every month. At the moment, all things glitz and glamor surrounded Ophelia.

After double-brushing her teeth for good measure, she splashed warm water on her face. Her headache faded and her stomach calmed as she dressed in a black sports bra and too tiny, matching running shorts. The same workout clothes as all the other good little harpies. Oh, how she wished full-body coverage was the style.

With her long, dark hair secured in a tight ponytail, she rejoined Vivi. They wore the same clothing, yet they looked completely different. Tall, slender ice versus short, curvy fire.

The vampy wagged a finger in her face. "You listening? You will run on a treadmill until you sweat out the very last drop of vodka, and you will remember that I do not, under any circumstances, hang out with losers. Meaning, yes, you're a winner. So do it. Win."

Friends were the worst and the best. "Why are you so terrible and wonderful to me?" she complained, swiping a pair of bespelled earbuds she'd paid top dollar for.

"Because you're even better and worse to me." Vivi folded Ophelia in a much-needed hug, softly offering, "Everything will be all right, O."

Ophelia squeezed the amazing woman with all her strength. They'd met eleven years ago, during harpy training camp, where little girls learned to master their incredible power and hair-trigger rages. One day, Ophelia had rescued scrawny Vivi from a beating via other harpies. Of course, Vivi liked to claim she had saved *Ophelia*. Whatever had happened, they'd been inseparable ever since, their loyalty steadfast.

"Fine!" she cried when she finally eased back. "I'll meet with Taliyah."

Vivi beamed at her. "See? A winner."

They made their way from the barracks to the gym, where everything from treadmills to boxing rings and weight stations abounded. In every direction, harpies worked out at level max.

Ophelia and Vivi threw elbows and exchanged a round of threats to snag the best treadmills. Ophelia inserted the earbuds. With the soundtrack of an action movie blasting, she set her machine to the highest incline and a moderate speed. Climbing. Warming up. Sweating. Thinking of everything that could go wrong today. But the more she marched, the more doubts she shed. Vivi was right. Why would Taliyah banish Ophelia? She was, in fact, a winner.

Flunk out? No! Try beast out. Ophelia cranked the speed, gliding into a steady 100 WTFs per hour. She wasn't a disappointment or a waste of space. She would not leave a legacy of disgrace and dishonor. She had worth. Her temper was just as fierce as the next harpy's. Probably fiercer! Her stubbornness couldn't be beat. Ask anyone. If a harpy requested an assist, she provided brass-knuckle backup, guaranteed, and only ridiculed the other harpy mildly afterward.

Harpies today, harpies forever.

Outwit, outplay, outlast.

But, if General Taliyah *did* banish Ophelia, what could she do? What recourse did she have?

She slowed her pace. Where would she go? Where *could* she go? She had no blood kin, no friends outside the Harpinian army. But wherever she ended up, Vivi would follow her. That wasn't even a question. Then, at some point in the future, they would sit on matching rocking chairs and discuss retribution for their exile. The torching of Harpina. Former friends would be forced to declare a blood vendetta against *them*. On her death-bed, Ophelia would realize she'd never been the good guy in the story; she'd always been the villain. The total ruination of a once great civilization rested entirely upon her shoulders.

You ruin everything, Ophelia. Nissa's voice filled her head once again. *You lack discipline.*

Though she slowed her pace, her heart rate sped up. Her breaths turned shallow. No. No! Ophelia ruined *nothing*. She had plenty of discipline. And she would prove it. *Outwit, outplay, outlast.*

She let the soundtrack wash over her. In books and movies, superheroes faced terrible odds, but they always overcame. If anyone had reason to claim superhero status right now, it was Ophelia. Well, superhero adjacent. When she fell, she fought her way back up every time, eventually. She almost never allowed an insult to slide. And she was smart upon occasion. Those hot guys she so rarely allowed herself to approach barely gained her notice anymore. Except sometimes. Or most times. But she never failed to resist!

Mmm. Hot guys.

Arousal seared her, and she groaned again. Then she groaned. *Not a needing. Anything but a needing.* A temporary but insatiable hunger without any true, lasting satisfaction, when nearly everything provoked her lusts. Not that she had ever known true, lasting satisfaction. Most nymphs didn't until they found their entwine, or other half.

During a needing, her Dumb-Dumb switch got flipped, and she forgot everything but orgasming.

Since the arrival of the Astra, she'd often felt as if she hovered at the cusp of her worst needing yet. Why, why, why did no one else seem so hot and bothered by them? Did they exude a nymph-specific vibe or something?

Whatever. Ophelia had bigger thoughts to mull. Like what did Taliyah want with her, and how did Ophelia convince the General to let her stay in Harpina and serve in the military? Harpies were in the middle of a war. Something she'd dreamed of experiencing since training camp. To get fired now? The horror! Especially when life had finally grown interesting again.

The Astra warred with a god named Erebus the Deathless. Father of General Taliyah. Biological son of the god Chaos. And creator of phantoms—vile creatures able to ghost or embody at will, raining destruction upon anyone in their path.

Every night on patrol, Ophelia yearned for another chance to strike at phantoms. Just one more. Perhaps two. If she sprinted a little faster or swung a little harder, she would totally accomplish her goal.

Movement at her right. She whipped her head— Huh. A freshly showered Vivi stood beside the treadmill, holding a thin, black cord and a squeeze bottle. No longer in workout gear, she wore the harpy uniform: a metal and mesh breastplate, a pleated leather miniskirt, arm and shin guards, and combat boots.

Her friend casually yanked the cord—the machine's plug. As the treadmill screeched to a halt, Vivi drank from the bottle.

When Ophelia regained her balance, she plucked the buds from her ears. "Seriously?"

"You've been running for five and a half hours. You now have half an hour to prepare for your meeting with Taliyah. Just enough time to shower, dress and not overthink. But you'd better hurry or you'll be late."

What? Thirty minutes to shower and change and hustle to the palace? Her wings rippled with the challenge. Ophelia rushed off.

"I guess I'm supposed to clean the machine for you?" Vivi called.

In the locker room, Ophelia cleaned up and donned a uniform, then raced from the barracks. The palace was a mere mile away, an easy sprint through wooded terrain and beautifully manicured gardens. Past a marble water fountain and up a hundred steps, the only path to open front doors.

The opulence of the royal lodgings never failed to dazzle. Priceless vases. Gold-veined marble. Plush rugs and gilt-framed portraits of past Generals. Treasures acquired throughout the ages.

Ophelia avoided Nissa's portrait, hanging just over the mantel between a set of dual staircases, and rounded a corner. The large, arched throne doors loomed ahead. Picking up speed—whoa!

She slammed into a brick wall of a male who hadn't been there a split second ago. As she bounced back, he shot out muscular arms, capturing her in a hard grip and yanking her against him.

Their gazes met, and she gasped. For a suspended moment, the rest of the world ceased to exist for Ophelia, as if eternity's time clock had just stopped. Well, why not? Her heart certainly had.

He was a brute with a faint smoked cherries and sandalwood scent—in other words, pure lust to her. His eyes were extraordinary, his brilliant gold irises circled by spinning jade and umber striations.

Hypnotic. She did her best to concentrate, her mind tossing out random particulars. An Astra. The second-in-command. Halo something. Supposedly the "kind" one. Never raised his voice and sometimes smiled. Gorgeous. Built. Sexy. *Hot.* Mmm. *Very* hot.

Generates heat like a furnace. Her entire body responded, going liquid.

Her gaze dipped to the plethora of tattoos that covered his upper body. Images she couldn't make out as they vaulted from one place to another in his skin. Wait. Information clicked. The moving tattoos weren't really tattoos but *alevala.*

When an Astra made a kill for his cause, the action stained his soul, which stained his skin. If anyone else peered at one of the images, they relived the Astra's memory of the deed in full detail.

General Taliyah had recently issued a new realm-wide rule. Never study the *alevala* without permission.

Taliyah. Meeting! Late! With a scowl, Ophelia scrambled from the warlord's embrace. "Next time watch where you flash, douchebag." Flashers—teleporters—never considered the non-flashers they impeded.

Not waiting for his response, she dashed away. *Can't be late, can't be late.* What if Taliyah had already given up and left?

Lose the opportunity to explain all the reasons Taliyah was wrong to believe whatever she believed? No!

Ophelia flew into the throne room. Scanned. Thank goodness! The General hadn't vacated her seat. The pale-haired goddess wore a gossamer ice-blue gown. A delicate creation at odds with her fiery glare. Her second, Dove, stood at her right. A harphantom with silver hair and white skin. The embodiment of an ice queen who had no softer side. A handful of harpies flittered about.

"Someone find Blythe *now!*" Taliyah bellowed. Blythe the

Undoing, the General's widowed sister. The second Ophelia was spotted, the General pointed an accusing finger her way and snapped, "You're late."

Ophelia cursed the Astra. "My apologies, General." She offered a respectful incline of her head rather than excuses. "It will never happen again. You have my full assurance."

She expected a rebuke. Something. Anything. She got eerie silence instead. Wait. Her gaze darted. Everyone had frozen midaction and gone eerily quiet.

"General?" Heart thudding, Ophelia darted through the capacious room. She checked every occupant for a pulse but found none. She refused to panic, though. She could figure this out. She could.

She was Ophelia Falconcrest, and she could do anything.

3

Halo Phaninon, Immortal of Immortals, wrapped a towel around his waist and exited his private bathroom. His concubine was naked and bent over the bed, reading a book. Excellent. He paid the Amazon well to service him each morning at this exact time.

Be here. Be ready. Expect nothing in return. Why use his hand on himself when he could easily afford a warm, soft receptacle? Though he didn't like touching or being touched, he functioned best with at least one physical release a day. A small measure of relief from the relentless pressure inside him. The constant squeeze of a spiked, gauntleted fist around each of his organs.

Sometimes he imagined his chest filled with metal gears and pullies, fueled by memories of his years at the Order, ever tightening.

"Good morning, Halo." Andromeda flipped to another page,

not bothering to glance up. They'd been together for one year, three months and eight days.

Today, the sight of her agitated him, and he drew up short. Frowning, he rubbed the center of his chest. What was this he was feeling? Because it wasn't consuming desire or frothing passion. Not that he'd ever experienced those things.

He thought he might recognize remnants of…guilt? But why would he feel guilty? Andromeda was here of her own volition and paid handsomely for her troubles.

Just get in and get out. No hint of weakness was to be tolerated. Ever. Halo might disdain the lessons he'd learned at the Order, but he never hesitated to employ them. Logic and precision colored his decisions, not emotion.

Determined, he positioned himself behind the Amazon, clasped her hips and kicked her feet apart.

Page flip.

He pursed his lips. She was the fourth concubine he'd ever employed. Beautiful beyond imagining. Tall and leanly muscled with pale hair and golden skin.

Most Amazons were known for their strength, bloodthirst, and total lack of a softer side. Females utterly unbothered by his detachment. Halo's ideal companion. Andromeda teetered somewhere between sharp steel and melting butter.

The guilt intensified. *Don't do this.*

"Got a busy day ahead?" she asked when he continued to stand behind her, motionless.

"Yes." Deep breath in. Out.

"That's cool."

Perhaps it was time to select a new concubine? "Enough chatter."

"Sure thing, boss." Page flip.

Gritting his teeth, he removed the towel, tossed the material next to the Amazon, and placed the tip of his erection at her core. *This isn't right.*

He reached up and gripped the rail above the bed. *Just get it done.* With a hard thrust, he sank inside the Amazon.

Pleasure surged, and he breathed easier. All right. Yes. This was nice. Exactly what he'd needed to properly start his day.

He pulled out a little, then thrust again. And again. Faster. Faster. He frowned. Not as much pleasure now. Faster still.

She moaned and gasped and continued to read. The glide grew slicker. Better. And worse. The gears in his chest tightened, any lingering pleasure quickly morphing into pain.

Beads of sweat popped up on his brow. He pumped even faster, hammering into her. But the gears increased their speed too.

Muscles tensed, turning to stone. Tendons pulled taut. *Ignore the ache.*

Hammering… He would empty himself, and he would reset. As always.

Come on, come on! He just needed a minute of ease. Even a few seconds would do.

Andromeda said, "You want me to change positions or maybe—"

"I said no more chatter," he grated. In. Out. In, out. Faster. Faster…

"Ahhh!" Halo wrenched free of her, severing contact. He was panting, almost wheezing, throbbing from head to toe. "Go. No, say nothing else," he snapped when she straightened and met his gaze. "Just go."

Leaving the towel behind, he returned to the bathroom, where he showered and dressed in a black T-shirt, leathers and boots. His motions only grew more and more clipped as his frustration sharpened. He desperately needed *some* kind of reset today.

Adjust course as needed. Why not hunt down a phantom or twenty and pour himself into combat? Yes. Halo sheathed a three-blade at his waist. A weapon forged from trinite—a combination of fireiron, demonglass and cursedwood. The only substance able to kill a phantom in any form. The more phantoms he killed, the better he protected his brothers. The Astra Planeta. Skylords who had forever altered Halo's fate, the day they were brought together by the god Chaos to serve, for a time, as his royal guard.

Though centuries had passed before the other Astra managed to build a bridge between the empty vessel Halo had been to the worthy male he might become, they had persisted until they succeeded. By example, they taught him the joy of protecting what belonged to him and the value of trust. The sweetness of believing in someone other than himself. Again and again, they'd earned his loyalty. He loved *nothing*—except those males.

Together, they fought to ascend. A moment an immortal reached a new level of power, gaining abilities and strengths.

If the Deathless managed to ascend before them…

I will lose more brothers.

Halo rubbed the spot above his heart. Every five hundred years, the Astra participated in a series of "blessing tasks." Individual challenges with army-wide consequences. If one failed, all failed. This time, the ultimate winner would ascend. Erebus or the Astra.

Only days ago, Commander Roc had successfully completed the initial task. Now the second task loomed, set to begin any moment.

Halo was ready to do his part, whatever it was.

He flashed to the Tree of Skulls, an important landmark in the realm of Harpina. The land of the harpies, and his current home. The colossal tree marked the epicenter of the town square, where shops abounded. Thick branches stretched in every direction, blooming with red, skull-shaped flowers that perfumed the air with a sweet scent he didn't dislike.

On the lookout for Erebus and his mindless puppets, the phantoms, Halo stalked the cobblestone streets.

The stores had yet to open, few harpies in the area. He wasn't disappointed by this. Harpies liked to prattle about everything and fight about nothing. If they weren't snickering at you, they were leering at you—on both occasions, they were plotting your murder. They liked to say and buy the most ridiculous things, exhibiting pure emotion and little control.

He passed eight door-to-door karaoke bars, six happy-ending massage parlors, a lone "hard-wear house," whatever that was, and a neon sign that displayed the words *ANYTHING GOES!* Odd creatures, harpies.

Soldiers on patrol sprang out of his way, because they knew two things. Never approach an Astra without permission unless absolutely necessary—and it wasn't ever necessary.

No sign of the enemy. How disappointing. It was only a matter of time, however. When the second blessing task kicked off, the god would wreak havoc hourly.

Halo prowled the streets for hours, scouring every inch of everything. He stopped only when his internal clock buzzed: 11:58. Upcoming meeting with the Commander.

He sheathed his weapons and flashed to the palace. Specifically, a conference room Roc reserved for such briefings. A spacious area with a long desk and ten chairs. One for each Astra, one for Taliyah. Notes littered a wall. Some featured a harpy's phone number, others crude suggestions. A handful offered a lewd sketch.

Roc already occupied his seat at the head. The seven-foot-tall Commander with cropped black hair and a beard in need of a trim reclined, deep in thought, stroking his chin.

Halo had overheard many harpies refer to him as "serial killer dreamy."

The familiar sight loosened some of his gears. This was a new day to serve his brothers to the best of his abilities. And so he would.

"My apologies if I kept you waiting, Commander."

Without missing a beat, Roc motioned for him to sit. "The lost weapon is in play."

He eased into the chair at his leader's right-hand side, asking, "Do you know what it is?" Roc's blessing task had come with three parts. A thirty-day marriage. The sacrifice of his bride's life. And the maintaining of her virginity.

The two had "fallen in love" and copulated often. But, despite the nonexistence of the General's hymen, Roc had been crowned the ultimate winner of his task, putting the entire Astraian army one step closer to group ascension. However, deviation from the mission had cost them all dearly. A mysterious weapon was given to Erebus, putting *the god* one step closer to ascension.

"I know its name now," Roc said, "but little else. The Bloodmor."

The Bloodmor. Halo searched his mental files but found no information. No matter. "Someone somewhere knows something. Soon, we'll know it too."

"Agreed." Roc drummed his fingers against the tabletop. "Chaos offered a warning. He says the Bloodmor will do more damage to us in one day than the Blade of Destiny has done in centuries. To you in particular."

The Blade of Destiny. A weapon somehow able to peer into the many paths the future might take, allowing Erebus to plan someone's downfall accordingly. Another weapon given to Erebus in times past. That infernal blade had caused the Astra countless devastations for centuries, and this Bloodmor was worse?

Halo gripped the arms of his chair. Voice tight, he asked, "Do you doubt my ability to succeed, Commander?"

"Not at all." Roc pinched the bridge of his nose. "I'm stewing in my own guilt. The second blessing task begins today. A to-the-death battle of wits and weapons. Erebus was given his choice of opponents this time. He selected you."

Face the Deathless on a battlefield? Halo *seethed* with eagerness. "I have killed him on twenty-three separate occasions." The god had always come back to life, but a kill was a kill. "I will deliver the twenty-fourth without fail." Nothing would stop him. He—

Halo leaped to his feet, every muscle in his body suddenly alive and humming with challenge. What was that scent?

He sniffed. Sniffed again. And again. The perfume filled his nose, his lungs. Rich. Sweet. *Very* sweet. Like pleasure itself. His head fogged, the gears in his chest loosening. His eyelids grew heavy.

"Is something wrong?" Roc asked, his brow furrowed.

Everything. Nothing. He didn't know *anything* just then. No, not true. He knew he must find the scent's source. *Hurry!* "I'll return soon."

On a new hunt, Halo stalked from the room. Aggression hardened his muscles, and he removed his shirt, dropping the garment without a thought. His *alevala* jumped about. Following the ever-strengthening fragrance, he traveled to the other side of the hallway, rounded a corner, and stopped at the edge of a balcony overlooking the foyer. Blood heating, he dropped his chin and narrowed his focus.

Below him was a wide-open area overflowing with harpies both coming and going. Scanning... *Can almost* taste *the sweetness.*

There! Her. The one who'd just flown through the entrance. A growl erupted in the back of his throat. Short and curvy, with light brown skin and long sable hair, the top plaited, the bottom tumbling in glossy waves.

Halo acted without consent from his brain, appearing directly in front of her— Impact! She plowed into him. As she bounced back, he snagged her and yanked her close.

Gasping, she slapped her hands on his chest, her adorable pink claws curling and cutting his skin. Fancied herself a predator holding on to her prey, did she?

Her touch…didn't bother him. Which bothered him greatly! Then their gazes connected, and *nothing* bothered him. His thoughts dimmed, the rest of the world blotted out, forgotten. Gears ceased grinding. Pressure eased as sizzling heat poured out of him, as if stored for such a time as this. Her eyes. *Exquisite.* Light green, framed by a fan of jet-black lashes and topped by thick raven brows. A smattering of freckles. A plump upper lip with a plumper bottom boasting the sexiest little dip in the center.

He opened his mouth to demanded answers: Who was she? Where had she been hiding since his arrival? How dared she smell so intoxicating?

Must have more!

"Next time watch where you flash, douchebag," she groused, wiggling free and sprinting off.

He watched, shell-shocked, as the little harpy headed for the throne room. She was equally spectacular from behind.

Must hold her again—will *hold her again.*

The thought seized him. He tensed to flash—

A frowning Roc appeared in front of him. "I would appreciate an explanation."

Right. Their meeting. Halo shook his head, his blood cooling. As the perfumed fog dissipated, calm enveloped him. Mostly. The gears cranked on. "I am unsure what happened. There was a harpy."

"Ah." Roc reached out and patted his shoulder. "Say no more. I—" He went silent. Still. Too still. Was he even breathing?

Confused, Halo tapped the Commander's cheek. "Roc?"

No response. Not even a blink.

He looked left, right. The harpies had stilled as well. In fact, some of the females had frozen midaction, their feet hovering inches over the floor. Every conversation had ceased. Quiet ruled the palace.

"My apologies for the theatrics." The voice drifted from

everywhere at once before Chaos, Ocean of the Dark, materialized a few feet away. "My new oracle Neeka has a flare for the dramatic. On that note, she has bid me to ask if you are ready to play."

The god looked the same today as he had centuries ago, when he bought Halo from the Order. Wild, curly black hair, skin a shade darker and eyes like the night itself. Chaos stood at seven feet tall and wore a dark robe. Typical garb for a certain generation of deities. The strength of his power nearly drilled Halo to the ground.

It was the kind of power he would inherit with his next ascension.

He resisted the drive to sink as long as possible. In the end, he hit his knees. While he respected the male, he didn't like him. Their interactions rarely ended well.

"I'm ready for battle," he grated. The level of power lessened, allowing him to rise.

"Are you?" Chaos arched a brow. "You don't even know whom you are to fight."

"I am to fight Erebus. Who else?"

"Yes." The god walked forward and circled him, the hem of his robe dusting Halo's boots. "Who else?"

"Am I to slay his phantoms too?" Halo could think of no other being Erebus might control.

Chaos stopped in front of him and offered a smile of challenge. "You are to fight Erebus's chosen champion, whoever it may be. You, too, are free to select a champion, of course."

No need. "I choose to fight for myself." Always.

The god inclined his head in acceptance. "In the coming weeks, you will go head-to-head with your opponent twelve times. Each battle will be inspired by Hercules's labors. Consider the first eleven tests...of sorts. Learn from each. Grading counts. The twelfth decides the prize winner. The loser dies and will not be resurrected with outside aid of any kind."

Halo absorbed the details and nodded. So far, he'd heard nothing alarming.

"The first battle begins tomorrow," Chaos continued, "and also today and a week from now. But only after the freeze. Between one and the other, seven days will pass. The cycle ends only with the final death. No need to worry for the other Astra. They are off-limits."

Another freeze? The first battle occurred today *and* tomorrow? Could the god be any more confusing? At least Halo wouldn't have to divide his focus between duty and protection. "I will be ready."

"Will you?" A grin, there and gone. Then Chaos threw more information at him. "Harpina is the battlefield. A trumpet signals a new clash. A single blast, and a kill must be made. Two blasts, and there's a puzzle to solve or a feat to complete. Before you begin, shout the name of your champion. At the end of a labor, you'll hear another trumpet. Tonight, you will meet Erebus at the harpy coliseum. A greeting of rivals. There shall be no bloodshed among the two of you."

"I won't kill him...yet," Halo promised.

"Exactly what he said about you." The god studied him for a long while, curious and silent. It was something Chaos had done the day they'd met. The day he uttered the words that forever changed Halo's life. *You will be my crowning glory. My Halo. I'll teach you a better way to hate.* "Fight well. In the end, you won't succeed otherwise."

"I never fight any other—" Chaos vanished "—way."

Halo's mind whirled as he tried to make sense of everything he'd heard. Twelve feats, fought by Erebus or his champion. Twelve opportunities for the god to torture Halo in some way. Beginning tomorrow, but also the day after. And yet the day wouldn't end until Halo won or lost the twelfth battle.

What was Chaos telling and not telling him? Halo thought he understood the instruction about Harpina at least. He wasn't to leave the battlefield—the realm—for any reason. A warrior persisted until the end of the war. No retreat and no surrender.

A noise caught his attention. A high-pitched voice. Female. Panicked. Coming from the throne room. Someone else was aware of the events?

He flashed inside the palatial chamber...where he found the dark-haired beauty with the luscious body rushing from harpy to harpy, chanting, "Don't freak out, don't freak out, don't freak out." She shook someone, then slapped another. "Wake up! I mean it. The joke is old."

At the sight of her, his blood boiled and pressure eased, as if already programmed to do so. He curled his hands into fists. Did the sweet-smelling female play a part in his task? Was she a tool Erebus hoped to use against him? She must be. Even the General was suspended in time upon her throne, half-standing, appearing to have stopped in the middle of a sharp rebuke.

With the Blade of Destiny, the god could have easily predicted Halo's unprecedented reaction to a certain female. For all he knew, his enemy had used this mysterious Bloodmor to manufacture the response. Either way, this harpy was dangerous to him. So what was he going to do with her?

4

Ophelia sensed a presence. A familiar warmth layered with the scent she'd dubbed *pure lust*: that not-even-fair infusion of smoked cherries and sandalwood. It was *his* scent. The Astra's. With the slightest whiff, different parts of her tingled to startling life. She buzzed with anticipation and curdled with dread.

Trembling, she spun to face him. Oh yes. It was Halo, the douchebag who'd made her milliseconds too late for her meeting, earning her the beginnings of a severe and completely undeserved scolding.

He stood near the doors, roughly twenty feet away, his hands opening and closing into fists. Had he stalkered-up and followed her in without her knowledge?

Super flattering and uber annoying. But, um, the picture he presented...did something to her. He was all hard strength and savage determination, with a body built for war—her most favorite kind.

Her heart thudded as if she'd just finished another five-hour sprint on the treadmill.

Focus! Right. Surely the "nice" Astra would help her figure this out.

Speed walking closer, she blurted, "Do you know what's going on?" Where was Vivi? Was she okay? Had the entire realm gotten stuck in time like this?

He narrowed his eyes. The slightest lowering of his lids that was somehow terrifying. "You don't ask questions, harpy. You answer them."

Whoa! Not so nice, after all. She bristled. "First of all, dude, chill out. Final answer. Lock it in and send me home with my prize money."

"I will have what I want." He clasped her wrist, and she gasped, a total body fever spiking in an instant.

The heat! Had there ever been anything more delicious? Humiliatingly docile, Ophelia allowed the big, bad wolf to flash her to a bedroom. *His* bedroom, no doubt about it. The potency of his scent heightened exponentially. In other words, pure lust saturated her being. She teetered at the edge of a needing.

Panicked, she wrenched from his grip. The heat cooled. Okay. All right. Better. She scrutinized her surroundings. A large suite usually reserved for a decorated leader; someone who served directly under the General. Ophelia recognized the array of weapons hanging on the wall. Things the previous owner had taken from her conquests.

She had entered this hallowed chamber only once before, when a superior officer had debriefed her concerning a skirmish with rogue berserkers. Despite Halo's move-in, the chamber was unchanged. A crimson comforter draped the canopied bed. A plush bear-shifter rug stretched before an unlit hearth. Beside each row of weapons hung a gold framed portrait of a late, great harpy.

With an easy tone, Halo asked, "Would you like more time

to catalog all the exits and weapons you can use against me or may I begin my interrogation?"

"This breaking story just in. I finished five seconds before we ever arrived. Now I'm debating your endgame. You say *interrogation*. I say *Astra, please*. You brought me to a bedroom to repopulate the world. Admit it."

He blinked while emitting more of that delectable warmth. "We will not be having sex, harpy."

"Yeah, that's right we won't. As if you could be so lucky."

He crossed his arms over his chest, like he'd practiced the favored power pose in a mirror before deciding to unleash it upon the world. Not bad. Look at the way those tattooed muscles flexed. The way those images moved. Especially that one. A gorgeous female with crackling eyes, beckoning her closer...

No! Not tattoos. Alevala. *Focus.* But it was too late. A link between Ophelia and the image solidified, a memory that wasn't her own filling her head...

Suddenly she was peering into another bedroom. Bigger than this one, with gold furnishings. A female—the beauty inked in Halo's skin—sprawled over a plush mattress, naked. A glorious mane of red curls tumbled around delicate shoulders as white as snow.

"You are the immortal who slays other immortals," Red purred, unafraid of the fully clothed warrior who lurked nearby, an ebony dagger clutched in each hand. "The warlord who has chased me across galaxies for weeks."

"I am." Halo's voice was as cold as his expression, as if he were utterly removed from the situation. There, but not there as the female smiled and spread her legs.

"Are you here to kill me, then?"

"You are the goddess Succubia, are you not?" A deep chasm of nothingness; that's what he was. The bawdy sight affected him not at all.

A true shock. This was the original goddess of lusts. Ophelia had studied the star of myriad wet dreams in college. A powerful enchantress who had existed eons ago, said to be the mother of all succubi, incubi, and nymphs, with an ability to inflame anyone's passions to desperate, unfathomable heights.

The ultimate superheroine. Almost. Kind of. Mostly, Succubia had been pure evil and a blight on humanity, feeding on those she bedded. But honestly, there were worse things to do, right?

"I am," Succubia said, mimicking Halo's coldness even as she beckoned him closer.

"Then yes, I'm here to kill you."

"And yet you haven't struck. Because you can't stop wondering what it feels like to be inside me." Eyelids hooded with invitation, the goddess traced a blunt-tipped nail between her breasts. "I can give you pleasure beyond your wildest imaginings. Surely you've heard the rumors."

"What need have I of pleasure?" Halo said as other Astra appeared around the bed. "And I hesitated only because I awaited our audience." He acted, moving too quickly to track. At first.

Shock sent Ophelia reeling inside. Such savagery! He showed not a drop of mercy as he sliced, hacked, and shredded the goddess into too many bits to count. He never hesitated, never broke a sweat or lost his breath. When he finished, he calmly gathered the edges of the bloody comforter together, creating a death satchel as his fellow Astra patted him on the back in a job well done and he blushed, almost sheepish.

What Halo did with the goddess's remains, Ophelia might never know. The memory faded, the present—real-life Halo—returning to her awareness. He hadn't adjusted his position in the slightest. No, he towered mere feet away, his muscular arms still crossed over his chest, his expression impassive.

Tremors cascaded down her spine, and she gulped. If Halo was heartless enough to harm the goddess of lusts, how much more would he harm Ophelia, a descendant?

Wait. Had he finally frozen up like the others? He wasn't blinking.

"Not you too," she groaned. Racing closer, she slapped a hand over his heart. Wait again. *Thump, thump, thump.* It beat. Oh wow. It beat quickly. And hard. Like a hammer. And his skin...so hot. Mmm. Like a cozy blanket you snuggled against.

A growl rose from him, and *she* blushed, hopping back. Okay. Not frozen. Good to know.

He narrowed his eyes ever so slightly, and it was just as terrifying as before. "Which memory did you witness?"

Should she apologize for manhandling him? No, no way. Earlier, he had clasped her wrist. What he'd started, she'd finished. She would express regret after he did, and not a moment sooner. The fact that he wasn't chastising her for getting snagged by an *alevala* without the required permission was the first point in his favor.

"Harpy," he snapped. "I asked you a question. You will answer."

And there went his point. "I saw the death of an almost galactic treasure, the goddess of lusts."

He thought for a moment, nodded. "One of my more difficult blessing tasks."

Difficult? Hardly. "You slayed her so easily." Like a supervillain gathering inventory for a body parts store. *I'll take this organ and that limb.*

"Yes, but I had to chase her for weeks, while being attacked by legions of lovers willing to do anything to please her."

Oh, to have a stable of playthings, all her own.

No! Bad Ophelia. No messing around with pleasure. "How could you hurt an unarmed opponent like that? I mean, I get that she was evil incarnate and all, and that you had to end her for your task or whatever, but you showed no mercy."

His brow wrinkled, as if the question perplexed him. "Why would I show mercy to an obstacle in the way of my victory?"

Good point. "Did you have to turn her into confetti, though?"

The wrinkles deepened, as if he'd grown *more* perplexed. "And give her an opportunity to revive?" He flashed away, only to return seconds later wearing a shirt. "Enough of your queries, harpy. Answer mine. Why are you aware right now?"

Uh… "Why are *you*?"

He ran his tongue over straight, white teeth. "What's your name?"

"Ophelia." No harm in telling him that much.

"The rest," he commanded, his biceps flexing beneath the material. Which she hardly even noticed, thank you.

"I'm Ophelia…Falconcrest," she admitted with gritted teeth. "And don't you *dare* mention the TV show by the same name. I'll only want to binge it again, and there's no time."

She scrutinized his face for any change of expression. Had he pegged her as General Nissa's sister? Yes? No? Would he care when—if—he did? He gave nothing away, yet her nerve endings pinged with aggression, as if he emitted a low-level charge of *something*.

"What is your father?" he asked.

Okay, that one hit her like a punch, and she flinched. "Why does my father matter?" No way she would share that little gem. Males forgot her personal boundaries the second they heard the word *nymph*.

"My reasons aren't your concern. Only the act of responding to my words."

Did Halo believe her current cognizance stemmed from her father's origins? "You should read my file," she quipped, refusing to give in.

He popped his jaw. "Stay put. If you leave, I'll hunt you, and I will find you. You won't enjoy what happens then. That, I promise you." His threat lingered, chilling the air as he disappeared.

Shivers racked her, born of fury and *not* arousal. Not even a little. Where had he gone? And when would he return? Wait.

Why did it matter? When the big, scary bad man ordered you to stay put, you bolted at the first opportunity. Of course she was bailing right this second.

Ophelia hustled to the door. Only, she stopped short with her hand on the knob. Hold up. She knew the dangers of acting on emotion—the key to any disaster. Cold, hard logic would be a better guide with a better destination. So. She would take a sec and think this through.

The Astra had lived a long time. He comprehended things she'd probably never heard of. If anyone could figure out and fix whatever had happened, it was Halo. Did she really wish to make an enemy of him right from the start?

So far, he hadn't attempted to harm her. And he wouldn't. All Astra obeyed Roc and Taliyah, and Taliyah considered her soldiers off-limits. Ophelia was one of those soldiers. Ergo, Ophelia was 100 percent safe in Halo's presence. For the sake of the realm, she could table what he'd done to Succubia. And his curtness with Ophelia herself.

Okay. Yes. She would "stay put" for five minutes. If he took longer than that, she'd bail. Her time was precious, too, or whatever.

Resigned but unable to just be, Ophelia wandered about the chamber. In her tiny bunkroom, she had enough space for a bed and a nightstand. But she made up for the lack with the handmade comforters she'd stolen and a wealth of awards Vivi had given her. World's Second-Best Friend. Most Amazing Almost Kill. Recognition for Miraculous Selective Hearing. Most Wrecks in a Week. Most Disasters in a Month.

Ophelia peeked inside the dresser drawers. Plain black shirts, perfectly folded. Black underwear, also perfectly folded. Socks. Black. Folded. *I'm sensing a theme.*

Feeling petty, she reopened the underwear drawer, looked left, then right, then knocked over a stack. Ohhh. Hold up. What soft material. How decadent it felt against her skin.

"You cannot be only twenty-six years old!" he exclaimed from behind her. "You're practically mortal."

Oops. Caught with her hand in the pervert's cookie jar. Cheeks burning, she withdrew and pivoted to face Halo.

He held a file in his big, masculine hands, staring at her with something akin to horror. To her relief, he made no mention of her peeping as she closed the drawer with a bump of her hip.

"Your father is a nymph." His extraordinary eyes pinned her. "A species known for playfulness and insatiably high sex drives. Rumors suggest a nymph's climax causes days of euphoria for a lover."

She smiled with saccharine sweetness. "It's weeks of euphoria, thank you." And from her experience, it was an absolute lie.

"Your kind produces a pheromone known to lure unsuspecting prey into your clutches."

Had his voice roughened at the end? Did he blame Ophelia for his attraction to her? And he *was* attracted to her. Her nymph side suddenly pinged with the knowledge.

"My clutches?" Voice dipping low, she said, "I assure you, I'm not luring anyone with a pheromone. You want me all on your own, big boy. And for the record, I'm one hundred percent, grade A harpy." The same was true for all harpykind. Though, yes, they exhibited different abilities that were dependent on their father. "So? What else you got?"

"You currently have no known consort."

"Again, so? Lots of harpies have no known consort." The equivalent of a nymph's entwine and the only calm to her storm. "For all you know, no one's been good enough for me."

"Every teacher, trainer, and superior has bemoaned your stubbornness."

"I'm passionate about my belief that I'm right." Needing to do something with her hands, she picked up a knickknack. A small crystal vase filled with rings. *Ohhh. Diamonds. And sapphires. And rubies. And emeralds. And pearls. Mine, all mine!*

No. Wrong. Harpies enjoyed pretty things, yes. And they enjoyed stealing pretty things even more. But they did not steal behind another harpy's back. Only her front.

Ophelia set the vase aside, then lifted a trinket box brimming with teeth. A safer option to study. Except, she kind of wanted to swipe these even more. Back the trinket box went.

Halo continued to scan the pages of her file. Every so often, he tensed.

Did he really have to be so gorgeous? *Look at him.* All that thick, shiny dark hair probably felt like silk. And that huge, muscly body, with its broad, capable shoulders might feel incredible on top of hers.

What are you doing? "So, um, what's *your* father?" she asked. Fair was fair. If he opened a subject, she had a right to sail through its door.

"He was a god of war, and I killed him." He offered the information easily, as if the detail carried no significance to him. He flipped his gaze to hers. "Designation—the Flunk Out. Nicknames—Phel, Fifi, Lady Orgasm, Lady O, Lady O No, Lady No O, Lady Go O, Lady No Go O, the Big O, the Big O No, the O Spot, the O No Spot, Hurricane O."

So harpies liked to drag each other. So what? "You forgot Mistress O, Mistress No O, and Mistress O No."

He continued reading. "You have zero kills."

"Your mom has zero kills!" The *nerve* of this male, throwing her biggest flaws in her face this way. She had done *nothing* to him—but that could change on a dime. "If you want your mind blown, check out my maiming and pillaging stats. Yeah. That's right. They're off the charts."

"Known to be volatile, with a hair-trigger temper. As proven by a hundred and eighteen write-ups for quote, unquote episodes, ninety-eight citations for uncontrollable rage, and two thousand and twelve recommendations for promotion." Again, his gaze flipped up. "What constitutes an episode?"

"Your face! But, um, did you say two thousand and twelve?" No big deal, but a couple thousand harpies had pulled their recs for some reason. Whatever. Onward and upward. She hiked a shoulder, as if she hadn't a care. "Maybe I should study another *alevala*. You shouldn't get to learn my life story while I'm forced to cobble together fragments of information about yours."

"Your mother isn't listed," he said, disregarding everything she'd said. "Why?"

"To maintain my privacy. Why else?" And to hide her connection to Nissa from outsiders. "You should try it sometime. Five stars. Highly recommend."

He closed the folder with a snap. "What did you flunk?"

"Tolerating irritating males." Patience at an end, she lunged, attempting to snatch the file from his grip. The paperwork vanished.

Before she could backtrack, Halo snaked an arm around her waist and dragged her closer. Her breath hitched. The desire to wrench free...did not spark. The multicolored striations in his irises spun, luring her closer.

The air thickened with sandalwood and smoked cherries. Her inhalations quickened, but so did his.

"You will cease using your pheromone on me, Ophelia." His modulated tone persisted, but his intensity jacked up another thousand degrees. A warning of incoming danger; she knew it.

She wanted to care. She *needed* to care. But he was cocooning her with that incredible warmth. A sensation she'd craved her entire life. To finally feel no hint of cold? The stuff of dreams.

"I told the truth before, *Hay-low*. I'm not using my pheromone on you." She didn't mean to purr the words, but she freaking purred the words. And she'd spoken true. Her harpy side constantly battled her nymph side, making the release of the infamous pheromone difficult for her. She had to work to do it. So unleash it by accident? Not likely.

Besides, she loathed the result. A heartsick sap willing to commit any deed, if only to be near her, or a sociopath determined to own her, no matter the cost. Sexy, yes, but *so* annoying.

"I didn't believe you before, and I don't believe you now." He stared at her lips—and licked his own. Was he...could he be considering...kissing her? "Stop it."

"Sorry, warlord, but truth is truth. No pheromone." Did she sound smug? "You want me because you want me." Yes, she sounded smug.

Tension poured off him. "You *will* stop this." He maintained his hold and stalked forward, forcing her to backpedal, until they reached a bedpost. "I will make you."

Her every pulse point fluttered, leaving her breathless. And angry. Mostly angry. Surely! Smirking at him, she asked, "Are you planning to club me with your meat stick, Astra? I feel it expanding, even now."

The barest hint of a scowl. He adjusted his hold, clasping her wrists and anchoring her arms over her head. "You are using your pheromone. Admit it. Do *not* lie to me again, female."

"In order to lie to you again, I'll have to lie to you a first time. Which I haven't done."

"You will stop, or I will... I..." The scowl returned and stayed put. He gave a quiet growl before flickering in and out of view.

An icy sensation registered on her upraised wrists, and she frowned. She dragged her gaze up— *Douchebag!* He had shackled her to a metal beam.

Fury defeated her desire with a brutal slash. Ophelia yanked up her knee to nail the Astra in the groin.

He fled striking range, smoothing his shirt as well as his features. "I have much to do today. Until I know what part you play in my task, you will stay here and consider the dangers of attracting a male like me."

She barely heard him; her mind got stuck. He'd chained her, and she couldn't chase him.

He thought she had episodes? She would show him episodes.

With a shriek, she lunged in his direction, willing to rip off her limbs if only to headbutt his face. But the links had little give. When the tendons refused to part with her shoulders, she rammed into air.

"I'll gut you for this," she hissed at him.

"Behave," he commanded, unperturbed. Then he disappeared.

Shrieking louder, Ophelia spun and attacked the bed with crazed fervor. But the initial round of punches and kicks knocked some sense into her, random strikes turning into a planned ambush. If she could break the bedpost in half, she could slide the shackle free. But any time she made a dent, the wood mystically reinforced.

Bones cracked and shattered. Muscles tore. Refusing to surrender, she kicked and punched harder. Surely the column would splinter. Any second...

No one kept Ophelia Falconcrest bound to a bed without permission. No one! *Punch, punch, kick.* She threw her entire body into the beam, different wounds throbbing in protest.

"I must say, you are even better than I expected." The sinister voice registered at the same time as a frigid breeze enveloped her. "Brava, harpy. Brava."

Ophelia whirled around, the chains rattling. Two realizations gelled at once. Erebus looked just like his sketch—and the enemy was here, within her reach. She crouched, preparing to attack while taking stock. He was taller and wider than she'd realized, with a mop of pale curls. An obsidian robe draped a muscular frame, with very little of his pale, frost-glazed skin revealed.

His craggy face boasted an array of prominent features. Arresting black irises and obscenely long lashes. A large, hooked nose. Full lips. A strong jaw covered by a braided beard.

Adrenaline surged to new heights, dulling the searing pains throughout her body. "Why don't you come a little closer?" she asked, batting her eyes.

"I will. Soon." He watched her as her breaths pitched. Unlike Halo, he smiled a little. "The warlord can do anything... but resist you. You, my darling, will give him everything he's never had and everything he's always wanted. And then I get to take it all away."

She didn't know what the god referenced, but icy foreboding pricked her nape.

Then he said, "You're going to die, Ophelia Falconcrest. Again and again and again."

Panic rushed in, an ice storm threatening to overwhelm her.

"I can make these deaths easy for you, or I can make them not easy." His smile grew wider. "Don't take offense if I root for the latter."

He swooped in, shoving her to the mattress.

As she and the god grappled, a thousand thoughts rapid-fired. *Trapped like a lamb at slaughter. No match for someone as powerful as this. Going to lose. Soon to die. As promised, he's enjoying it. Fight! Too much to do. Too much to prove. Leave Vivi? Never! Still going to lose. Will perish on a field of battle at least. Every harpy's dream. The stuff of legends. Just not the kind of legend I hoped.*

Here lies Ophelia Falconcrest. Basic damsel in distress.

Fight harder!

In the end, Erebus succeeded, driving a rigid dagger into the hollow above her sternum. Cold metal sliced her airway, and searing pain consumed her. Blood rushed up her throat and into her lungs, drowning her. Her vision blurred. *So dizzy.*

"Poor harpy," Erebus cooed, tenderly smoothing hair from her brow. "You feel your life slipping away. How terrible it must be to realize you aren't as indestructible as you once believed. Immortal, but not. The younger you are, the swifter death sets in before an injury can regenerate. But I'm sure you know that."

Fighting...

"Don't hate me for loving this. You are magnificent." He

kissed the tip of her nose. "You're making me even more excited for what comes next."

Fight...

He twisted the blade, giddy as he announced, "Get ready, little girl. Your second ending will not be as tame as this. But then, I'm not the male who will wield the blade—Halo is."

Figh... Death came as Ophelia expelled her final breath.

5

The little beauty might be a big problem.

Halo stalked through the torch-lit catacombs beneath the coliseum, determined to root out any traps his enemy might have readied.

A mission had never been more vital, yet again and again his thoughts veered to the harpymph he'd trapped in his bedchamber. A room with walls fortified by trinite, thereby limiting a phantom's abilities. Ophelia wasn't a phantom, the substance nothing to her—but Erebus was.

Did she align with the god? Was the curvy seductress tasked with Halo's distraction, perhaps?

He narrowed his eyes. Though the bundle of energy struck him as a walking contradiction—defensive but inviting—Halo had enjoyed her company far more than he should have. Somehow, he'd tasted both the ease he'd sought for so long and a tension far worse than any other, and swung between the two.

When she'd told him she wouldn't bed him, she'd eyed him as if he were a slice of warm honey cake fresh from the oven. He'd throbbed then. He throbbed now, remembering.

Despite her denials, the nymph pheromone *must* be responsible. No matter how powerful it was, Halo would not succumb. Rather, he would learn more about Ophelia Falconcrest and build stronger defenses against her allure.

Return to her. Now. The unexpected, instinctual command jolted him, and he stumbled. Return to his distraction before the meeting with Erebus? Hardly. Halo wasn't so foolish.

He poured his energy into his mission, taking note of his surroundings. Eternal torches hung from posts on cracked stone walls, casting muted beams of golden light over high, arched ceilings and dirt floors. Different aromas layered cool, damp air. The metallic stench of old blood. A tinge of smoke and burnt wood. A collage of fading perfumes.

Finding no sign of foul play, he flashed topside to the center of the battlefield. The sun was in the process of setting, painting sections of the sky with streaks of azure fire.

Before invading Harpina, the Astra had spent a year traversing the realm, invisible to all. He'd observed hundreds of violent matches in this stadium as harpies settled their disputes in front of a roaring crowd. If Ophelia had attended, he would have scented her.

What did she do in her spare time? Sex? As a nymph, she must have an insatiable sexual appetite.

A fire of...something burned his chest, unnerving him.

Recall your training or lose everything. The stark command had the deserved effect, and he snapped to attention. The other Astra counted on him. He would not let them down.

A trumpet boomed from the stands. Frowning, he palmed two daggers and looked about.

In a flash of light, Erebus appeared on the other side of the battlefield, wearing his customary black robe. The hem billowed in a soft breeze. Fresh blood wet his pale curls, splattered his face, and coated his hands. Behind him stretched an army of phantoms. Females dressed in widow's weeds, slumped over and motionless, their feet hovering several inches off the ground. Eerie silence permeated the masses.

With a single command from their creator, those lifeless phantoms would attack with mindless fervor, desperate to feed. To suck Halo's soul from his skin. A revolting act that drained even an Astra's strength.

"Hello, Halo," Erebus said. "Our first solo face-to-face in centuries."

The god's deep voice inspired a tidal wave of hatred. An emotion Halo had *never* forgotten, no matter his training. "Consider pleasantries exchanged. Meeting adjourned." He poised to flash to his bedroom—

"I know what the harpymph is to you, and why she isn't frozen like the others."

The words stopped him cold. A terrible suspicion rose inside him. The god had evinced the same satisfaction after Roc met Taliyah, the course for their defeat already well established. "Do tell."

"With a little effort, I'm sure you can put the puzzle pieces together on your own."

Instincts dinged. *Say nothing. Reveal nothing.* He knew better than to converse with an adversary. Especially this one. But he said something. "Why should I bother? We both know you're happy to do it for me." If there was one thing the god enjoyed more than inciting an Astra's misery, it was taunting him with the truth—a nugget of information Halo desperately wished to confirm.

Why did her intoxicating scent coat the breeze, even now? He tensed. Had she escaped her chains?

Oozing satisfaction, Erebus grinned. "She is your *gravita*. A part of you and therefore exempt from the freeze. Consider it a loophole."

He bowed up in pride as much as denial. Ophelia, the female made for him alone? The treasure he was to protect with his life? The sun able to hold him in orbit?

No. He shook his head. Someone as emotionally stunted as Halo wasn't meant to have a *gravita*.

Was he?

He shifted from one foot to the other. An Astra recognized his *gravita* when he produced stardust for her. A powder released by his hands, and a claim no other warlord could refute.

"Oh, and before I forget," the god added, gleeful. "Allow me to thank you for restraining your female. The little filly is all fury, isn't she? Without those chains, I might have gotten hurt. I wonder if she'll tussle harder tomorrow."

He recoiled inside. "You lie. You are unable to enter my bedroom."

"Am I? Let's just say there's wiggle room and leave it at that." The god laughed at his own joke as he and his army vanished.

Heart banging like a war drum, Halo flashed to his bedroom. Ophelia wasn't dead. The Astra's master strategist had not left an innocent female vulnerable to an enemy's attack.

His muscles felt like rocks he was attempting to smuggle underneath his skin as he scanned the chamber. A coppery tang tainted the air, no sound forthcoming. Oxygen congealed in his throat when he spotted her, choking him. Her mangled body was sprawled on his bed and shockingly still. *So much blood.* A dagger protruded from the top of her sternum.

His own chest constricted. Erebus had done it. The god had entered the bedroom despite its defenses, and brutally murdered a little beauty with soft curves and a delectable scent—and he'd done it the same way Four had once killed Five.

Inhale deep. Exhale slow. He expected a measure of calm,

but the breathing exercise did him no good. Embers of rage created flames. Fuel. Coils and gears cranked tighter than ever.

He yanked his gaze to Ophelia's face, to the delicate features now fixed in an expression of fierce determination. Work with Erebus? No. This female had fought for her life with everything she had.

No doubt she had died cursing his name. And he had deserved it. *Gone forever.* Halo stumbled back.

Something the god said prodded at his mind. *I wonder if she'll tussle harder tomorrow.*

The dead couldn't do battle. Had Erebus hinted at a possible resurrection? Or something else? According to Chaos, tomorrow was also today—and today Ophelia had lived.

Halo's heart leaped. Would the day repeat until he completed his labors? Like a game.

Are you ready to play?

Would he have a second chance to protect the harpymph? To figure out their connection, whatever it was? Would Halo remember her in the morning? Would she remember him?

So many questions, and only one way to obtain answers: wait.

He trembled as he lay beside the body. He clasped her cold, limp hand and closed his eyes, willing sleep to come...

6:00 a.m.
Day 2

"Get your lazy butt out of bed. Operation Lady O Be Good commences in twenty."

Ophelia's eyelids popped open as soon as Vivi ripped away her comforters. Survival instincts roared to life before thought. *Fight!*

Heartbeat emanating to her throat, she came up swinging.

"Whoa, whoa, whoa," Vivi said, ducking. Straightening, she raised her hands in a gesture of innocence. "I expected resistance, not insta-combat. Although, yes, this might deserve a new award for your wall of accomplishments. Woke Up Wearing Big Girl Panties."

Ophelia was panting as she searched the bunkroom. *Her* room. Hers. Not the Astra's. There was no sign of Erebus. No dagger being shoved into her airway.

Okay. All right. But what did this mean? She'd merely dreamed—vividly—of dying? She hadn't met either male?

Stomach roiling thanks to her hangover, she scooted to the edge of the bed and met Vivi's curious stare. "What happened last night?"

Her friend approached, dressed exactly as before and ready for another early morning workout. "You mean the part where General Taliyah called you personally to schedule a meeting? Or the part where you panicked and stole my secret stash of vodka?"

"Uh, I've already met with Taliyah. For all of three seconds. Then everyone froze in time or something." Ugh. She'd dreamed that too, hadn't she? She hadn't woken up, sweated out her hangover, and smacked into Halo. "Never mind."

Too bad his furnace-like heat wasn't real. She'd kind of enjoyed him. Or it. *Only* it. Before he'd chained her up, earning her eternal hatred, of course.

Vivi pouted for a moment. "Why can't people do cool things in *my* drunken reveries?"

She rubbed the spot she'd been stabbed. Maybe the dream was a warning. "I should probably skip the meeting."

"No way." The harpire hauled Ophelia to her feet, jostling her brain against her skull. "You're attending, and that's that."

"Then I guess I gotta sober up," she grumbled, stumbling into the bathroom.

"Look at that. My baby *is* wearing her big girl panties today! She knows when she'll be out-stubborned and it's best to give up."

"Oh, my gosh, shut it," Ophelia mumbled, earning a snort. As she washed and dressed, a sense of déjà vu plagued her with increasing fervency. A sense that followed her to the gym, where the same harpies occupied the same machines. How in the world had a drunken dream predicted her day so accurately?

Just as she remembered doing before, Ophelia threw elbows and exchanged insults to claim the perfect treadmill.

She plugged in her earbuds and ran for an hour, but she failed to focus her thoughts. Again and again, her brain returned to the subject of Halo. Just how precisely had her dreams portrayed *him*?

Why not ask others about him and find out? Assuage her curiosity and shutdown this line of inquiry.

As she jogged at a slight incline, she muted her music to ask, "What do you know about the, um, nice Astra?"

"Halo?" Vivi asked with a frown.

"You guys talking about the Machine?" The girl on Vivi's other side inserted herself into the conversation. "He's the one who gives good hello, right? Sometimes smiles, and never raises his voice?"

"If he's so great, why does everyone call him the Anaconda?" another said. "Those things are mean, yo. Unless he's the proud owner of a wild trouser snake, and it's time for a good old-fashioned hunting expedition. I'll report my findings tomorrow."

Comments rang throughout the gym.

"I bet he drills his females until he hits liquid gold."

"Have you seen those arctic blast eyes? The only thing he's drilling into is permafrost."

"Do you think he knows my legs make amazing earmuffs or should I tell him again?"

The tiniest glimmer of irritation, well, irritated Ophelia. They were treating Halo like a piece of meat being carved up and served on toothpicks...and she should totally do the same. So why wasn't she?

"If you plan to make a move on the Ringed One, you'll have to get in line," a girl named Reshma called from the other side of the room, chugging away on an elliptical machine. She was a patrol mate and someone Ophelia greatly admired. If Reshma got in your face with a beef, you might as well disembowel yourself to save time. "There's already a list. First come, first served. Next up is three hundred and sixty-eight."

"Dibs on three hundred and sixty-nine," someone called.

Ophelia's treadmill shook as she slammed her feet down.

"Why the sudden interest in an Astra?" Vivi asked, jogging at a sedate pace. "I know you're not going to bag and tag him. Wait. You're not going to bag and tag him, are you?"

"No fair," another cried. "You can't put the Flunk Out on the list. Once they go nymph, others make them limp."

Kill me now.

"Have you seen Halo's concubine?" asked the harpy next to Reshma. "She's a genuine Amazon."

"Do you think she'd, like, sign my chest or something?"

Ugh. The Astra had a paid for perma-lover. Meaning, he was completely off-limits. Not that he'd ever been *on* limits for Ophelia. Nope. There would be zero lovers for Lady O No.

Another hour passed, music cranking. This time, she stayed in a zone...until a new round of thoughts and worries surged. If her real life followed her dream—or whatever—she would smack into Halo on her way to see General Taliyah.

How should she handle it? Forget what the imaginary Erebus had claimed? The Astra wasn't going to kill her. That, she knew. One, never trust the prick who brutally slayed you. Two, Taliyah. Three, why would real-life Halo ever notice Ophelia?

Great! She'd started slamming her feet into the treadmill again.

Movement at her side drew her attention to a showered Vivi, who pulled the plug on the machine. Dang it! This part was a repeat, too?

Ophelia freed the earbuds and glanced at the clock. Argh!

"You've been running for five and a half hours," her friend began.

"I know, I know. I now have half an hour to prepare for my meeting without overthinking." She darted from the treadmill, shooting out of the gym.

"I guess I'm supposed to clean the machine for you?" Vivi called.

How many other details had Ophelia correctly dreamed? Or not dreamed? Would she smack into Halo or not?

In the locker room, she trembled as she zipped through a shower and donned her uniform. Taking the same path as before, she cleared the garden. The same impediments caused the same problems.

Halo won't flash into me. He won't.

But what if he did?

Her breath hitched, and her tremors doubled. She soared up the palace steps, past the gold columns, across the wraparound porch and through the double doors, only then noticing there were no other harpies about today.

She pumped the brakes, her feet stopping as her heart picked up speed. Halo. Here. He stood in the foyer, alone, his arms crossed over his chest as he showcased his terrifying narrowed gaze.

He was here, waiting for her. Because she had *lived* the dream. But...

How was that possible?

Get ready, little girl. Your second ending will not be as tame as this. But then, I'm not the male who will wield the blade—Halo is.

She backed up a step, caught herself, then lifted her chin. "Did you wake up this morning expecting to lose your nut sack, or will my next actions be a surprise?"

"Harpy," he intoned, "we need to talk."

6

The harpymph lived. The day had indeed repeated.

More and more of Halo's strain eased, relief and hope rising from the ashes of his fury. Until his gears wound tighter, ruining everything.

Erebus's scheme was so clear now. Distract Halo with an alleged *gravita*, leading him to bomb his labors. A good plan. Let her die again? No. Halo would go to great lengths to protect her from further harm. What he wouldn't do? Lose sight of his ultimate goal.

Unfortunately for his enemy, he was an excellent multitasker.

So far, the day both had and had not proceeded like yesterday. At 6:00 a.m., Halo had come to awareness in his bathroom, draped in a towel. Andromeda had been bent over his bed, reading her book. He'd asked her a few questions before sending her on her way. While he'd dressed, intending to hunt Ophelia, he'd used a telepathic link with the Commander to explain what was happening.

He should have known Roc would summon him, ending the hunt for the harpymph before it started.

Halo had then spent several hours debriefing the Astra. An astonishingly torturous experience. Every minute—every second—he'd wondered about Ophelia. Would she remember him? Would she forgive him for his part in her death? Harpies were not known for giving second chances.

Now, here she stood. The little beauty in the flesh. Alive and well, her sweet fragrance saturating the air and heating his blood.

"How is this possible?" Shock glazed her stunning green eyes. Cherry lips parted as a flush brightened her cheeks. "Wait. Did you just invite me to another chat? Because the last one worked out *so* well for me?" Her lids slitted. "Consider this a blanket eternal refusal."

So. She remembered him, and no, she hadn't forgiven him. "I won't chain you again unless it proves necessary." He rubbed the center of his chest. "You have my word."

"Unless it proves necessary? How comforting for me." She gave a near-hysterical laugh. "It happened. All of it. Everything I thought I dreamed, I lived. I don't...this is...you are..." She sucked in a breath, rage pulsing from her. "You left me to die!"

He expected an attack, welcomed it even, but she remained in place. "You are alive now. That is what matters. However, I will allow you to punish me. Go ahead. Get it out of your system. Then we will move on."

"Move on? There's no moving on from this! In fact, consider me your worst enemy. You go your way and I go mine. I'll figure out what's happening without you. Now good day, sir." She extended her middle finger, turned on her heel, and bolted out of the palace.

With a curse, Halo tore off after her. Outside. Down the hill of steps. Across the front lawn, deeper into the fragrant, sunny warmth of the new-old day. The garden. Running toward the town square. Never missing a step, she wove around frozen harpies.

The freeze had occurred right on time, then.

Halo flashed directly behind her, close enough to see the rapid flutter of her wings through slits in her armor. He reached out...

He snarled as Ophelia expertly evaded his grip and he clasped hold of another female.

The harpy moved quickly. Swifter than he'd anticipated. Noted. More than that, she knew the terrain. Every tree and bush to avoid. Every divot to leap over. To catch her without harming her, he needed to predict her decisions.

He flashed around her, cataloging her reactions to his instant appearances. Tells revealed themselves. A plan of action formed. When she geared up, as if to shift right, he teleported to the left.

She slammed into him like a cannonball. As he flew back, he clamped her tight. Halo absorbed the bulk of the impact with only minor aches and pains. When they skidded to a halt, a cloud of dirt and debris surrounded them. He lay on his back, with the harpy draped over his chest.

The moment the dust settled, she attempted to scramble off. Too bad. He flipped her over, trapping her with his much heavier weight.

"Oh, no you don't." She clawed, bit, punched, and bucked, a living grenade—but she didn't free herself. "I won't be a good little prisoner."

"You'll be whatever I tell you." His control nearly burned away, torched by a flashfire of arousal. To restrain her arms above her head and disarm her, Halo had to work against her as much as his treacherous body. Pressure ebbed and pleasure flowed, until something inside him threatened to snap.

Sweat beaded his brow. Her softness...her curves... Her *passion*. This female felt *everything*. For a moment, he longed to bask in it all.

Snapping... "Harpy. Be. Still," he grated. *I will not thrust my hips.*

"Make me." She bucked harder.

I will not thrust.

She ground against his throbbing length, and he sucked in a breath.

Halo bellowed, "You will *mind* me, Ophelia."

To his surprise, she did, finally going still. Also panting and glaring. "You are *such* a douchebag. Now do us both a favor and put your chub club away. This isn't happy ending hour."

Inhale. Exhale. "Trust me. I would put the...club away if I could." Rational thought flickered on and off. "We will return to my bedroom, and I will explain what's happening to us."

"Thanks, but no thanks. We can talk here. Who's gonna eavesdrop?"

A measure of calm trickled over him. She could be reasonable at times. A surprising development. "The palace offers better defenses against Erebus."

"Does it?" She smiled with pure malice. "Rumors suggest innocent harpies get chained and slaughtered in there."

Or not so reasonable. He closed his eyes. Tried to center. Failed.

He needed to not touch her, but he also needed to not risk another chase. Focusing on her, he said, "We'll chat in your bedroom." Though her file hadn't listed an address, he figured she lived in the barracks. "You weren't harmed in there."

"Give you my address so you can pop over to borrow a cup of my sugar, wink-wink? Hard pass." Defiant and beautiful, she scowled at him. "Now, if you don't mind or even if you do, get off me, freak."

Halo ground his teeth and flashed her to the palace library, landing them both in an upright position. "I will let you go, and you will stay put. Understand?" He pried one hand from her, then the other.

When she remained in place, he breathed easier and scanned the room for threats. Books, artifacts and priceless treasures filled the enormous, three-tiered chamber. No shifting shadows. No odd scents.

"Well? What's going on?" Ophelia issued the demand as if she'd waited weeks for a response. Unwilling—or perhaps unable—to stand in place, she paced between two tables. "I deserve to know. Or did you already forget today's headline? Harpy dies due to foolish Astra's mistake."

He flinched. He would never forget the horror of her death. *Erebus will pay.* "I'm not sure what you've heard, but here's the full story. Every five hundred years, each Astra must complete a specific task, one after the other. If we succeed, we receive a blessing from Chaos. Five hundred years of victory. If we fail, we are cursed with five hundred years of defeat. This time, we fight for more than the blessing. We seek to ascend."

"Keep talking. I'm listening." Pacing, pacing. Graceful. Fluid. *Carnal.*

Halo tracked her with his gaze, increasingly...hungry. The way she moved. His palms itched, eager to explore her curves and hollows. "In the past, I've always been tasked with the hunting and killing of a specific god. This time, I must complete twelve feats or labors of strength and cunning. This started yesterday. Which is also today. The day will continue to repeat until the final battle concludes."

"Sure. A typical Groundhog Day situation." She rubbed her wrists, as if remembering the shackles, making him flinch anew. "Why am I aware of what you're doing? No one else is."

"Erebus hopes to use you against me."

A humorless laugh erupted from her. "That's ridiculous. How can he use me against you? Why would he bother? We're strangers. I'm nothing to you, and you're nothing to me."

Those words. *I'm nothing to you, and you're nothing to me.* Hmm. They scraped Halo's nerves raw. Something he didn't understand. What did her opinion of him matter? His *gravita* or not, her admiration had no bearing on the situation.

"What did the god say to you?" he demanded.

"Before he plunged a knife into my airway? Sorry, but you don't get info from me until I get info from you. Tell me why he hopes to use me against you."

Admit that she might belong to Halo, body and soul?

He ran his gaze over her curves once again and pulled at the neckline of his shirt. "When you collided with me yesterday—"

"Hey!" she interjected. "I didn't collide with you. You collided with *me* when you flash-landed. Get your facts straight."

"—the interaction caused my scent to coat you. Now, Erebus believes you are...mine."

"Yours?" Her jaw went slack, and she halted, gazing at him with something akin to horror. "He thinks I belong to you because you suck at flash-landing? Did he forget you have a concubine?"

"There's a difference between a lover and a mate."

"You're right." The horror faded. Thoughtful, she tilted her head. "And I *am* a harpy. *Of course*, Erebus pegged *me* as the cherished mate and the Amazon as the forgettable lover. Yes, this logic fully tracks." Seeming to forget his presence, she kicked into another pace and mumbled. "Think this through. Erebus wants to destroy the Astra. He'll slaughter innocent, hardworking harpies to do it. He's a foe, no ifs, ands or buts. The Astra are now allied with the harpies. And Halo didn't *mean* to serve me up for murder. The poor guy is probably just as dumb as a box of rocks. Erebus is bad, no matter how you slice it. Halo might have a sliver of potential. Honestly, this might be my big break."

Every word lashed as powerfully as the Headmaster's whipping.

Ophelia faced him, determination etched into her exquisite features. "Fine. You talked me into it. I'll do you this enormous favor and help you complete your twelve labors. But in return, you're writing me a glowing recommendation letter. And ensuring I get my first kill."

She thought to...bargain? "A recommendation letter? To what end?" A harpymph with no kills would not be taking down her first victim during a blessing task.

"A promotion. I'm due. And I expect gold embossing on the letterhead. Flowing script. A poem extolling my amazing amazingness could be a nice extra. But I'll totally deserve it. I'll let you decide how lyrical to be after you've partnered with me awhile."

Put her on a battlefield with the Dark One and his phantoms? No. Halo did not lose what belonged to him, and a possible *gravita* most certainly belonged to him. But where was he supposed to stash his Lady O No while he handled things? Where would she be safest?

Only at my side. Where she could be a distraction to Halo. The very dilemma the god had intended to cause.

He worked his jaw. There was one thing he knew. The Astra—the blessing task—came first, always, a *gravita* second.

"Hear me well, Ophelia." He kept his tone balanced between command and threat. "We aren't partners or teammates. I am fighting for my brothers. I won't bow to your dictates or make bargains. I will give orders, and you will obey without hesitation. You won't even speak a word without permission. Do you understand? Say it. Say the words."

"Do you understand?" Ophelia mocked behind Halo as he stalked through the palace, pride forcing her to follow. A good soldier obeyed a superior's orders. "Oops. I didn't have his highness's permission to repeat the words a second time. Bring on the punishment. Or is my time with you punishment enough?"

She might not be a good soldier.

He offered no response, just marched ahead, checking different rooms. He'd done this for hours, seeming to catalog everything but Ophelia's direct location, wherever she happened to be. He seemed to have forgotten her presence altogether.

Why not remind him? "Roc won his challenge by doing the opposite of what he normally does," she said, trying to sound reasonable. "Have *you* considered doing the opposite, Halo? You know, doing the *right* thing and not ruining everything for everyone else?"

A muscle twitched beneath his eye.

Another hour passed in utter quiet.

"Ever wondered if people admire you?" she grumbled. "Let me save you the trouble. They don't. You're the literal worst! I mean, nymphs admire everyone, but I would rather bury myself in ice for the rest of eternity than spend another minute in your presence. I'm not even being dramatic right now."

Silence.

Hanging out with a legendary Astra sucked so hard. But guess what? She. Said. Nothing. Else. Instead, Ophelia bottled up the remainder of her speech. Outwit, outplay, outlast. Tough times never persisted, but tough people did.

When they found an Astra frozen in a compromising position, she almost broke her silence. The one named Roux Pyroesis. Also known as the Crazed One, and the sixth ranked in the Astrian army. He was the torture master, known for excelling at his job—both with others and himself.

He was a big guy with pale hair and golden everything else. Seated on a pillow in front of a coffee table, he held a pink teacup. At his side was young Isla, daughter of Blythe the Undoing.

A tea party for two.

Wearing a pink leotard and tutu, Isla was in the middle of pouring the tea.

The rumor mill claimed Roux had killed Isla's father—Blythe's consort—the day the Astra invaded Harpina. Was the girl learning to poison her enemies early? Because why else would she invite her dad's murderer to tea? And how absolutely, utterly adorable was that?

Wow. Kids maybe weren't so terrible all the time.

"I'm unsure what I'm seeing," Halo muttered, circling Roux as he might a caged animal.

Ophelia held her tongue.

He glanced her way at last. His hands curled into fists—as if he'd just spotted something he wanted to grab. Had he?

Nymph senses said, *Oh yes*.

Heartbeat speeding up, she waved to the door, a silent command to move on. Might be better to encourage more snubbing.

He slitted his eyes, but he obeyed.

Again, she followed. Yeah, being ignored was best. She was part of a mission to defeat the great and powerful Erebus. What better opportunity to showcase her combat skills, proving she was a soldier worth keeping? That she was loyal to the cause, able to see past a personal wrong in favor of aiding harpykind. In other words, perfect General material.

If she resisted the urge to maim or sleep with Halo as warranted—often and in equal measure probably—this blessing task could mark *her* chance to ascend to a higher rank.

The problem was, he blasted all that delicious warmth.

He stepped into a beam of sunlight, muscles rippling with his movements. On his forearms, *alevala* jumped from here to there, attempting to lure her gaze and trap her in another haze of memories.

Look away!

She managed it—barely. A dozen times or so, she allowed herself one last fleeting glance at the *alevala* to glean as much info as possible without getting snagged. Most of the images were faces, and most of those faces watched her, tracking her every move. It was as eerie as it was sexy. What? She was part nymph, and she liked what she liked.

Mmm, mmm, mmm. Would the images taste as different as they looked?

Ophelia combated the urge to curl up against him and find out. To rub, just a little. Or a lot.

"Tell me what you're thinking about, harpy." He whirled to face her, stopping her cold. And hot. Strong fingers wrapped around her biceps, trapping her body only inches from his.

Fight the needing.

Standing at attention, Ophelia broke her silence. "Sorry, sir, but that information is classified. Only halfway decent friends and above have clearance."

The glorious muscles in his shoulders bunched beneath his shirt. "Do you have any other questions for me?"

Wait. He was huffy. Had he *wanted* her to ask stuff, despite his order to the contrary? "Should I respond or be silent, sir? Your orders are increasingly unclear."

He released her and scrubbed a hand over his face. "Just do one thing I've requested and tell me what Erebus said to you before he killed you."

For a moment, she almost considered debating feeling sorry for him. But onward and upward. To cop to it all or not? The same logic she'd used before applied now. If Erebus was her enemy, and he was, and Halo was her ally, which he might be, she owed him the truth. Or some part of it, anyway. He should get the benefit of the doubt, not the other guy.

"Fine. The POS told me you'll be the one to kill me next time," Ophelia admitted.

Halo's chest puffed up, the tendons in his neck pulling taut. The rings in those incredible irises spun. "He. Said. What?"

Man, the Astra was sexy when affronted. "Look. I'm sure he was just trying to make me paranoid or whatever. So you don't have to worry that I'm spending every minute imagining all the ways I can rip out your spinal cord. I stopped doing that thirty minutes ago."

He double-blinked at her. With a shake of his head, he marched off. Next stop? The theater room, where a handful of harpies lounged, most in the process of throwing popcorn at a mega screen.

The place for relaxation and entertainment made Halo's rigid intensity a thousand times more noticeable, and the contrast was smoking hot. Of course, a slobbering troll would light Ophelia's wick right now. But come on! When would the urge to throw herself into this male's arms fade?

He surveyed the scene, stiffened, and swung his gaze to Ophelia. Spinning… "Do you have a sibling in Harpina?"

Careful. "No." Not anymore. "Why?"

"You've been in this room before," he continued. "Recently."

"Yeah. So." His point? "Even lowly soldiers get to take breaks."

"But your scent. It's the same but different now." He canted his head slowly, his focus sharpening. "I think I comprehend how you were in the palace, close to me, and I didn't know it."

"Okay. So?" she repeated. "Dude, you're making me tired. Just state whatever conclusion you're failing to point at and put us both out of our misery."

Unfazed, he stated, "A nymph's scent is known to change so quickly for a single reason. A needing." His gaze dropped to her lips—and he licked his own. "Are you in the midst of one, Ophelia?"

Breath lodged in her throat, a spike of searing arousal catching her off guard. But anger wasn't far behind it. Was the douchebag considering taking advantage of her weakening morals?

"Slow your roll, Immortal." She brandished a condescending tone like the weapon it was. "I'm not that desperate yet, so you have no chance of getting lucky."

The insult landed, and he flicked his tongue over an incisor. "Do you currently have a male?"

Would he keep his big, beautiful hands to himself if she did or would he feel challenged and up his smolder? Why risk either outcome when she could shut him down with a single question? "What does it matter to you?"

He bristled, somehow appearing angrier and softer at the same time. "Whatever I ask, you *will* answer."

Swallow your retort. Be a (genuinely) good soldier. Too late. "Counterproposal. I answer only what I wish to answer. Which is nothing now. Because yes, you did it again. You made the wrong call and ruined everything for everyone else."

"Harpy." Expression thundering, he stepped closer and snarled, "You will give me what I want."

"I thought we'd gone over this." She squared her shoulders and stepped closer too. Furious, she snapped, "If you keep staring at me like that, I just might." Wait. Those were not the words she'd planned to say.

They must have surprised him as well. He did that double-blink thing again. He was just so delicious. All powerful and growly. And at this particular moment in time, she kind of... wanted him. But she also didn't want him. Except she did. Except she didn't. Did. Didn't. The tug of war never ceased.

His brow furrowed. "Are you asking me to...touch you, Ophelia?"

"I don't know." She was still snapping at him; she couldn't stop. "Are you wanting to touch me, Halo?"

Blink-blink. He took another step forward, his countenance softening. "I want—"

Agony flared dead center in her chest, a sharp cry exploding from her.

"Ophelia?" He flashed to her side and—nothing. Halo and the theater room disappeared.

Suddenly cool, damp air chilled her skin, but her pain was fading. Fighting for breath, she looked around. The catacombs beneath the coliseum. Torchlight provided dim illumination of familiar dark walls—stationary phantoms hovered all around.

Danger! Ophelia reached for a weapon she didn't have.

Too late. Phantoms awoke and swarmed, clasping her arms and legs. Living-dead chains.

A grinning Erebus materialized only a few feet away. As he approached, he twirled the hilt of the death dagger.

Ophelia fought the urge to shrink from him. Reveal a hint of fear? Not this girl. She lifted her chin. "Well, well. I see some evil villains can't be trusted anymore. You said Halo will kill me next. Not you."

"I'm wounded that you doubt me. Especially since I'm your best ally during this labor. A detail you will realize soon enough."

Foreboding seized her. "Erebus. An ally. That's rich."

"Allow me to prove myself. Today, I happily give you what you seek most. Incredible strength. Unfortunately, it won't be enough to win tonight's battle." He winced, as if he felt sorry for her. "But take heart. The more we do this, the stronger you'll grow. We'll charge you like a battery and you'll overflow with every creature. You'll be unstoppable. Yes. Soon, you'll be ready, and we'll do what's needed. You and me. Together."

What did he mean, *every creature*?

As she struggled to no avail, he pressed the weapon between her breasts, the blade flat. As the jewel-encrusted hilt glowed red above her sternum, he said, "The primordial Nemean lioness with certain augmentations." He prattled on, listing things like "a mouthful of daggers" until his voice faded from her awareness.

A loud ring erupted in her ears, and she attempted to gather her thoughts. The Nemean lion she'd studied in history class. A beast Hercules once choked out. A terror of teeth and claws, with an invulnerable hide nothing could pierce. And the *primordial* Nemean lion, at that? The original, with defenses its progeny lacked?

Why— A high-pierced scream ripped from her being. No, not a scream. A roar. Golden fur sprouted from her pores as bones melted and re-formed.

A final thought registered before an insatiable bloodthirst consumed her. *I'm becoming the lioness?*

7

For the second time in one day, Halo chased after the harpy. Following her scent, he alternated between sprinting and flashing. Outside the palace. Into fading sunlight. Across the royal garden once again. Colorful flowers blurred at his sides.

All the while, the truth clamped his throat in a vise grip. Erebus was responsible for this. Somehow, the god had exploited an ability he shouldn't wield—the flashing of another person without contact.

If something happened to the harpy... A growl brewed.

Astra mattered, not the female. She'd been a nuisance today. A thorn in his side as he'd searched for signs of phantom possession among the frozen. Erebus specialized in using the living as Trojan horses to sneak his puppets into specific locations. But Ophelia had also been a help, her presence a natural soothing balm occasionally. He'd loved and hated every minute in her presence. If Erebus harmed her again...

The growl escaped.

Whatever happens, she'll recover. The day will repeat.

The reassurance failed to calm Halo. She would recover, yes, but she would be forever stuck with a headful of memories. Every pain the god had visited upon her. Those kinds of recollections accumulated and festered, leaking poison into your thoughts. Halo's female—his *potential* female—shouldn't have to deal with such things. He was the Immortal of Immortals, *and he did not lose what belonged to him.*

A trumpet blasted from somewhere in the distance, and he went cold. The first labor had started.

"Halo Phaninon," he called, naming his champion as instructed. He never slowed his pace, running, flashing, scenting and searching.

A second blast didn't come. Very well. To win this round, a kill must be made. This was only a test but grading mattered.

Where was Ophelia? As he continued charging forward, seconds ticking past, no attack was forthcoming. His chest squeezed. *Duty before dishonor. Win the labor, find the female.*

Unsure of what he might need, he summoned different weapons into his grip with only a thought, sheathing them as they appeared. Spear. Whip. Bow and arrow. Sword. A three-blade. More daggers.

On the horizon, the sun was beginning to set, streaking the sky with those azure flames. Those flames congregated above the coliseum, creating a halo effect. In that moment, he knew. There. Of course.

Claws lengthening, muscles hardening into slabs of granite, he flashed to the far end of the battlefield and skimmed the area. Alone. Empty stadium.

"Show yourself," he bellowed.

A fierce, ear-piercing roar sounded, rippling the dirt. Halo stiffened. His challenger? *Bring it.* He unsheathed two daggers. Nothing would derail his victory.

Another roar. Throughout the stands, flames burst to life atop torches, casting amber beams over a sea of phantoms. The females floated in place, as boneless and silent as dolls.

A grinning Erebus appeared on the royal dais overlooking the stands. He stood at the rail, a soft wind lifting his pale curls and whipping against the folds of his robe.

"Let the first battle commence," the god called. "A test of ferocity. The primordial Nemean lioness against Halo the Ringed One. Cheer, everyone. Cheer."

"Whoo-hoo," the phantoms said in their monotone voices. "Whoo-hoo."

With a third roar, the ground shook. Ophelia's sweet scent amplified, sparking protective instincts. *She is nearby.* Perhaps even hidden among the phantoms.

Halo stiffened, his instincts growing frenzied. He resisted the urge to charge after her, thereby overseeing his own downfall. The attempt at distraction wouldn't work; he wouldn't let it. She was alive. She could be saved after the battle.

He shut down any other thoughts. As expected, all emotions faded. *Kill or be killed.*

At the other end of the coliseum, 350 feet away, poles exploded from an entrance to the catacombs. A creature the size of an elephant surged onto the battlefield, charging in Halo's direction. A grotesque feline face with wild red eyes and daggerlike fangs. Foam bubbled at the corners of its snout. Bulging muscles were packed beneath a sleek, golden hide. Needle-point talons tipped massive paws.

According to legends, the pelt was impenetrable, nothing sharp enough to pierce it. Hercules had to choke out his opponent. An impossibility for Halo. This she-beast wore a collar made of firstone. A powerful substance able to prevent Astra from flashing.

A hundred feet away...

He shed all weapons but a bow and brimming quiver. Ophelia's scent drifted closer, now mixed with blood and—Halo's eyesight redlined. The beast carried the scent.

The beast had killed Ophelia.

She was dead. No doubt used as an appetizer before the main course at Erebus's behest.

Halo's emotionless shell cracked. He nocked two arrows, drew back his elbow and released the string. Target: the she-cat's eyes. The missiles whistled across the distance.

The feline blinked, nothing more, and the arrows pinged off her lids, bent and useless. Crimson irises leveled on Halo, feverish bloodlust crackling in their depths. A snarl, a faster pace, and a leap...

Halo braced. Fourteen tons of raw power slammed into him, flinging him into a wall. Broken stone rained. Organs burst on impact but swiftly re-formed. Bones shattered and mended. As he hit the dirt, he never lost his hold on the bow.

The second he emerged from the rubble, the lioness swooped down with a clear intention: bite off his head.

He maneuvered, her metal teeth shredding different parts of him. Ignoring the waves of pain, he unleashed a new volley of arrows. Rolled away from a swipe of those paws. Unleashed new arrows. On his feet. More arrows. Nothing stuck to her.

He dropped the bow and quiver and changed course. Running across the field, he swept low to grab three of the bars that once graced the entrance.

As expected and hoped, the bundle of rage followed him. The creature closed in, approaching from behind. A roar signaled her next strike. Halo twisted with blurring speed and rammed each of the poles into her mouth. She stumbled as she struggled, shaking her head, attempting to work her jaw, but the metal held.

Enraged now, she batted at Halo with those razored paws. He darted this way and that, dodging every blow. But so did she. He tried and failed to spear her open throat.

"Encourage our champion," Erebus called from the dais. "Tell our lioness she can win this."

With their awful voices, the phantoms chanted, "You can win this. You can win this. You can win this."

Halo disregarded the noise, keeping his focus honed. The beast possessed only three vulnerabilities—open throat, open eyes, and her ear canals. The canals couldn't be closed or guarded as well as the others. Better odds of success.

Creaking sounds testified to a break in the bars... *Crunch!* His opponent spit the trio at Halo's feet. Dropping her chin, baring those savage teeth, she shot forward, slinging dirt from her paws.

Protect her. The urge jolted him. Protect...who? Ophelia? But she was dead. Unless he'd miscalculated and she lived? What if she needed him? What if—the lioness sliced into his chest with her claws, sending him flying.

Concentrate! Halo popped to his feet, already healing. He swiped up his spear and charged the beast. Rather than attack, he grappled for dominance and climbed onto her back. Though she fought to buck him off, he shoved the metal into her ear, and her next roar ended in a mewl of pain.

He jumped down and rolled, collecting two more spears. She teetered, off balance. He wasted no time, throwing one weapon, then the other, nailing each of her eye sockets. She crashed into the ground, and she didn't rise. Didn't move.

A trumpet declared the labor's end.

Panting, bleeding, Halo wiped the sweat from his face and pivoted toward the royal dais. He'd won, but he felt as if he'd lost the battle. He wanted to vomit, not celebrate.

"Where is the harpy?" he demanded of Erebus.

"Dead." The god showed no remorse. "You know this. Sense it."

Yes. Despite Halo's earlier hope, he sensed the truth deep down. *Gone.* So even though he'd won, he'd lost. He'd failed to protect her. Again.

He opened and closed his fists. "Better luck with your next champion." How he longed to flash to the dais and shred the god.

Erebus laughed, gleeful. "Perhaps I wanted this one to die, eh?"

6:00 a.m.
Day 3

"Get your lazy butt out of bed. Operation Lady O Be Good commences in thirty."

Ophelia awoke with a pained cry as her friend ripped away the bedcovers. But she felt no pain. Only rage. Already it kindled in her bones, boiling over the fresh cauldron of memories that simmered in the forefront of her mind. Erebus had turned her into a monstrous lioness and pitted her against Halo.

The god hadn't lied, after all. The Astra had indeed killed her. Brutally. Pitilessly. But in Halo's defense, the transformation had cursed her with an uncontrollable bloodthirst; she had existed only to tear into him. But still! The male hadn't recognized her. Unless he had, and he just hadn't cared?

Either way, he'd slain her as effortlessly as he'd once slain Succubia. Ophelia despised him with the heat of a thousand suns for it. But she also might not despise him. She might not even blame him. Argh! How was she supposed to feel right now?

He'd fought to protect himself. As he should have. If their situations had been reversed, she would have done the same thing. But oh! She was still so...so...livid. She'd died and now someone needed to pay for it!

"Um. Phel?" Vivi asked.

"I just need a minute more. I'm in the middle of a cataclysmic decision about my current mood and the one to blame."

"Oh. Well. Carry on. If you're taking suggestions, I have a list of mortal enemies I'd love to see suffer."

Why was Ophelia flip-flopping between crazed ire and total

understanding, anyway? Halo had *murdered* her. And what had she gotten out of the deal? Nothing. Except. Hmm. She wasn't hungover. She kind of felt, well, good. Better than good, actually. Amazing. Different parts of her hummed with power, as if she'd plugged into an outlet.

The more we do this, the stronger you'll grow. We'll charge you like a battery and you'll overflow with every creature. You'll be unstoppable. Yes. Soon, you'll be ready, and we'll do what's needed. You and me. Together.

Intrigue blossomed. Had Erebus told the truth about that, too? Would Ophelia continue to strengthen if she allowed him to transform her? Better question: Exactly how strong could she get?

Dying wasn't exactly the worst thing in the world, she supposed. She— No! She absolutely could not travel down that road, even for a dream. Endure more deaths? What if she failed to revive at some point? A boatload of newfound power couldn't help a corpse. Better to avoid the next battle altogether.

Did Halo know he'd annihilated her or not? Did he comprehend how ruthlessly he'd stripped her of her defenses before that?

They needed to discuss it. But should she wait for their official meet and greet or track him down?

Why not wait? Give herself a chance to burn off some of this newfound energy. Because wowzer! She kicked her legs over the side of the bed, stood and bounced for a minute. "Give me ten, and we'll head to the gym. I want in a boxing ring with anyone willing to take me on. But they better not whine when I mop the floor with their faces."

"I gotta say. I'm really digging your can-do attitude today," Vivi remarked.

"Thanks." Dying twice and mystically resurrecting with a new superpower could change a girl.

How much to tell her friend? Or should she keep quiet? Yeah, definitely keep quiet for now. At least until she figured out a rock-solid plan of action. Tales of gods and Astra and res-urrections would only spread. Not because Vivi blabbed—she wouldn't—but because the walls had ears.

Ophelia power-walked to the bathroom, where she cleaned her face and brushed her teeth while jogging in place. Dude. Had Nissa felt this unstoppable all the time?

A new thought stirred, refusing to die down. What if Oph-elia had nixed the dying thing too quickly? *More strength for the taking...*

And what if she could *help* Halo win his blessing task? To be-come the opponent he fought over and over, ensuring he won the match, she had only to transform and willingly die. Some-thing she could endure once more. Even twice more. As long as she avoided the twelfth battle—which she could absolutely do, if she were strong enough—she could come out of this blessing task with a new life and a stellar resume.

—good soldier
—died repeatedly for a cause
—helped defeat Erebus
—almost solely responsible for the salvation of Harpina, harpykind and the Astra

Think about it. The fate of the Astra and harpies were for-ever tied. What happened to one happened to the other. General Taliyah might not be Ophelia's biggest fan, but she could be, with the right incentive. And Ophelia might not be the Com-mander's cheerleader, but she wasn't willing to condemn her sis-ters to five hundred years of defeat simply to strike at the male.

Forget her infusion of strength. Forget the glory. Couldn't she withstand the torment of a few more deaths for the sake of her sisters?

Well then. What more was there to dissect? The decision was

made. Ophelia would beast out and power up. She grinned—until she frowned. Halo was going to protest.

Although, he couldn't protest what he didn't know. Had he realized the truth about the lioness or not?

"Something's happening in the hallway," Vivi called from the room. "Girls are going wild. Imma pop out to check out—" Glass shattered.

Threat! Still in flannels, Ophelia rushed from the bathroom—she drew up short. Her friend crouched on the dresser, her fangs bared. The photos that once decorated the surface lay in pieces on the floor.

Halo stood in the center of Ophelia's cramped quarters, wearing the same T-shirt and leathers as before. He peered at her with chilling eyes—and still managed to heat her blood.

So annoying. "Vivi, meet Halo. He's the Astra we haven't discussed yet." Not today, anyway. "Halo, meet Vivian Eagleshield, my best friend."

"Leave us," he commanded the harpire, never shifting his attention from Ophelia.

Does he know, does he know? Or at least suspect?

Vivi smirked at him. "Sorry, warlord, but I'm not leaving until the babe you're eyeing like the last sliver of meat at a free buffet tells me to beat feet. Fifi?" With only a nickname, she asked a hundred different questions.

"I'll be fine," Ophelia promised. "He isn't going to harm me." Yet.

Waggling her brows, Vivi said, "Here to do some wet work then, Astra?"

"There will be no wet work," Ophelia said in a rush. An assurance for her friend as much as herself. The blueprint for more strength did not involve a sexual distraction. No matter how tasty he looked, standing in her home. Seriously. Halo was a total thirst trap right now, pulsing with raw intensity.

Her knees trembled. *I might be in a spot of trouble.*

At last, he deigned to glance in her friend's direction, slowly craning his head. It was a deliberate power move. Intimidating and as sexy as it was terrifying.

The harpire went sheepish, holding up her hands in a gesture of innocence. "No, no," Vivi told him with a wink, vaulting to the floor. "There's no need to toss me out of my best friend's bunk, where I'm always welcome. I'll see myself out. You two obviously have big things to discuss. Huge. I'll mosey on out now and get all the details later." She exited through the bathroom, shutting the door behind her with a soft snick and louder snicker.

Halo found Ophelia again, his muscles seeming to expand. More heat emanated from him, sizzling hotter by the second, and she swallowed a groan.

Resist! Her word of the day. "What do you want?" she asked, wishing she were wearing armor.

"Tell me what happened yesterday," he demanded.

Well. There it was. Confirmation. He *didn't* know. She was cleared to proceed as planned. "I'm not telling you anything anymore. We aren't partners, remember?" Another reason to keep her secret close. "Do us both a favor and flash yourself out of my space."

He rooted in place, as stubborn as she was. "When you were taken from me, you appeared before Erebus, did you not?"

Why did the Astra have to smell so good?

What was he getting at? That she was working with his enemy? She spread her arms wide, announcing, "This is me, not telling you anything."

"I believe he has a mystical tie to you," Halo persisted. "Something he gave you after your stabbing. If I'm correct, there's a way I can stop him from taking you from me a second time."

A mystical tie—to Erebus? Oh…balls. A part of the equation she'd ignored. The Deathless could summon her on command, the same way Halo summoned weapons. Bile singed her throat.

Give an enemy so much power over her? That, she wouldn't allow for any reason. Not even for strength.

Ophelia tweaked her plan. *Severe the connection to Erebus. Become a beast again. Grow stronger on my own terms.*

"Do it," she said. "Whatever it is."

"Very well." Halo appeared grim, and yet his irises spun with excitement. "Take off your clothes, harpy."

8

Halo struggled to retain his calm facade. *By a thread...*

He had failed this female—supposedly *his* female—twice. At noon, everyone but Ophelia and Halo would freeze, marking the official start of the blessing task. There would be no more labors for the next seven days. But. After the freeze, Erebus could steal the harpymph from Halo yet again. Maybe. It was probable.

Muted emotions? No longer. For the first time in his remembrance, a pot of rage simmered in his mind, spiced with other things. Guilt. Shame. Concern. Relief. Desire. Oh, the desire. At times it eclipsed everything else, making him as restless as a caged animal.

Every time he imagined tossing this female onto a bed, an avalanche of other images invaded. Putting his hands all over her. Having her hands all over him. Kissing and rubbing. Things he'd never hungered to experience with another. But he hungered now.

Touch her. Mark her. Claim her. Save her.

How he loved and hated this. His strain grew worse by the minute, everything in his torso tight and stinging. And yet, as he breathed in the harpy's luscious scent, the promise of relief had never seemed surer.

What if she'd told the truth yesterday? What if she drew him like this *without* the help of a pheromone? If she *were* his *gravita*...

What then?

"You did *not* just tell me to take off my clothes." She sputtered for a moment. "Unless you assume you're getting laid right now?"

"I do not." But maybe he should try. Why not give them *both* a reset? He'd never attempted to pleasure his concubines, but he didn't think he wanted to release the nymph until she had reached her own end. To *see* her climax...

Yes. At the very least, he should learn Ophelia's full effect on his body as soon as possible. An uncompromised strategist would insist on it. How else could he mount a proper defense against the constant distraction she presented?

Rationalizing your way to defeat?

Perhaps. But he didn't think he cared right now. "Take off your clothes, Ophelia," he said. A softer request. "I'm going to check you for a brand."

She sputtered a bit more, then pointed an accusing finger at him. "I'm perfectly capable of using my own two eyes and a mirror to check *myself*, thanks. There's no reason for you to—"

He flashed a whisper away, crowding her personal space. Her scent saturated his being, razing already fried nerve endings, and he rationalized even more. Having sex with her would not equal defeat. It would be a temporary distraction, nothing more. The long-term results could sway in or out of his favor, but he wouldn't know until he knew.

"Some brands can be etched into muscle or bone. So. I will peruse every inch of you, harpy, and you will let me." With a quiet but lethal tone, he vowed, "One way or another, your clothes are coming off before we leave this room."

Ophelia glowered at him...but she also exuded excitement. "You're a secret pervert, aren't you, H-bomb? You come in here, swinging front tail, thinking you can command a peek at my goods. The nymph is easy, right? Well, you picked the wrong nymph. This one is future General material."

H-bomb? "Nothing about you is easy." He traced his fingertips along a lapel of her flannel top, the action unstoppable. "Why is so much of you covered?"

Some of her animosity faded, and she shivered. "I'm cold all the time," she admitted, leaning into his touch. Then she narrowed her eyes, raised her chin, and revved back up, stepping away and tearing at the buttons on her top. "You want to see what you'll never have? Fine. Go right ahead. Take a good, hard look, Astra. Because I *will* resist your allure."

His allure? His? He went on instant alert, determined to get answers about his...about her...about... The top slipped to the floor, revealing plump mounds with amber peaks, and his thoughts derailed.

Those magnificent beauties jiggled as she shimmied out of her bottoms and kicked the material aside, revealing lacy black panties. As she straightened, those long sable waves danced around her delicate features. Exquisitely prideful, she put her nose in the air and rolled back her shoulders.

She should be proud! He almost couldn't comprehend the perfection of her body. This female was flawless. A masterpiece of peaks, dips, and hollows. Miles of the lightest brown skin offered a visual feast.

Carnality in its purest form.

He met her gaze, and his breath caught. Emerald irises glittered, daring him to reach out. To take whatever he desired.

Heat collected in his muscles, forging his bones into steel. Pressure magnified, gears cranking in the opposite direction.

"The panties," he said, almost embarrassed by the huskiness of his tenor. "Remove them."

Head nocked higher, she hooked the fabric in her fingers and wiggled. The garment slid down her legs. She kicked, sending the material flying. With lightning-fast reflexes, he caught the panties midair.

Damp. With arousal. For him. The knowledge robbed him of sense. Perhaps the reason he stuffed the panties into his pocket.

"Told you," she said with a smirk. "Secret pervert."

"Perhaps I am." His eyelids grew heavy as he followed a flush down the elegant column of her throat...over those mouthwatering breasts. Lower... A tiny thatch of dark curls held him enthralled.

Temptation itself...

"Well?" she prompted with throaty command. "Do you see any brands on me?"

"Still searching." Because he hadn't started. "The process takes time."

"I'm sure."

He focused on her adorable toes, with their pink nails, peering past the natural dimension, into the mystical. He raked his attention up one leg, then the other. One arm, then the other. Up her abdomen...between her breasts—there. The spot where she was stabbed. There was a faded star-shaped smudge, like spilled ink she'd tried to wipe clean. Not a brand, exactly, but definitely something.

In that moment, Halo *burned* to end his enemy once and for all. And he would. Soon. Once he ascended, he would live only to deliver the god's final demise.

For now, he thought he knew how to preclude Erebus from summoning Ophelia a second time.

—*How quickly can you forge a trinite collar?*— He projected the question into the mind of Silver Stilbon, a gruff Astra that history touted as the Fiery One. When Silver reached *anhilla*, a mindless state of violence achievable by all Astra, literal flames crackled over his skin.

The dedicated metalworker responded within seconds. —*For a harpy? Not too long. Roc requested one for Taliyah only to change his mind before I finished. I need only to etch runes into it.*—

—*Add a two-inch chain in the center and attach a coin-size trinite disk.*— That disk would adhere to Ophelia's skin, just over the smudge, preventing Erebus from reaching out with spiritual hands and latching on to the harpymph. In theory.

In reality…the thought of Ophelia wearing a special band Halo secured around her throat proved shockingly gratifying.

He told Silver —*I require it as soon as possible.*—

The warlord asked no questions. —*Give me ten minutes, and I'll flash it to your hand.*—

He licked his lips. Ten minutes? He might as well search Ophelia for more marks…

"Turn around," he croaked.

A husky chuckle teased his ears. "Can't get enough of me, Astra?"

He could not. Later, he would not let himself even consider her. He would scrub this image from his mind. He *would*. Until then… "Turn around," he repeated, a little too eager for his liking.

Another, softer chuckle. With languid grace, she obeyed.

"Your hair. Move it." *Let me see every inch of you.*

"Are you always this bossy with naked females?" Again, she obeyed him, sweeping the glossy mane over one shoulder.

Look at her. Made for pleasure. Made for my *pleasure.* Those small, delicate wings fluttered; as they shimmered in the morning sunlight, they looked like cutouts of lace. She possessed an elegant spine. The most sublime curves.

The firm body of a harpy paired with the lushness of a nymph. A combination clearly lethal to his common sense.

"Halo?" she purred.

Her question. Right. "I'm always this bossy, period," he said, pulling at the neckline of his T-shirt.

"Well. That is very good to know." Her tone and scent deepened. "Very, very good."

His nostrils flared. Had she grown *more* aroused? Halo wiped his mouth with his palm. "Yes. Very, very good."

With her face in profile, she smiled as if they were playing a game, all feminine power and seduction. "Do you like what you see, Halo?"

Perhaps they *did* play a game. "I do." He couldn't deny her beauty, and he didn't want to. "Do you like me looking, Ophelia?"

Her smile widened, pure confidence. Maddening. "I might. I might like a hands-on inspection, too. Best to be thorough, don't you think?"

"Thorough," he echoed. To maintain strength, nymphs required regular orgasms. The reason many of the species worshipped pleasure. Did this one?

When I get her into bed, I won't stop until she collapses from exhaustion.

The thought jolted him. When? Not if?

Halo swallowed. As he'd proven time and time again, he failed at nothing, because he stopped at nothing. Though making a female climax had never mattered before, something inside him *demanded* he please this harpy better than anyone ever had. But he had to wonder. Which path did Erebus hope Halo traversed? Resistance to Ophelia's charms or utter indulgence?

And if Halo did indulge? Claiming the harpymph during a blessing task, making her come and come and come? What then?

Would he only want more? Consider nothing else? Would his tension ease, granting him greater focus? Or would he lose his edge?

"I'm waiting for that inspection," she goaded, the words as luscious as the rest of her.

"You want my hands on you, Ophelia?" Halo flashed directly behind her. "Then let's get my hands on you."

"Yes. Let's."

He shook as he glided his fingertips down the ridges of her spine. Goose bumps spread over her skin, as if to greet him.

She is sensitive. Responsive.

"Mmm. Your skin is so hot," she breathed, inching closer to him. "You make *me* hot."

A hint of satisfaction stirred within him, fierce and wild, promising more. He remembered what she had admitted. She hated being cold.

Confidence grew in *him*. He could pleasure her. And he would.

Halo cupped her backside and squeezed. Soft. Giving. Perfect.

She moaned, and his control frayed. Yesterday, he'd fought a monster. Right now he felt like one, aggression agitating the *alevala*. Images changed places, jumping to different parts of his body.

The lioness had already made a place for herself over his heart. A spot usually reserved for a warlord's most guilt-inspiring act. A spot that had remained bare on Halo, no matter the number of atrocious acts he had committed. Why the exalted placement now, for a mindless beast? And why had he vomited after the battle? Why had he battled protective urges against an opponent? Simply because he'd smelled Ophelia?

He suspected he was missing an obvious answer.

"Hey, Halo?" she said with a little pout. "I have a front too, you know?"

"Oh, I know." More resistance crumbled. He wrapped both arms around her and tentatively clasped her breasts. The feel of her! The mounds overflowed in his grip.

She moaned her approval as he kneaded. When the distended crests tightened beneath his palms, he sucked air between his teeth. Had *anything* ever felt this good?

"Oh, by the way," she said, panting when he nuzzled her cheek with his own. "I should probably mention I'm currently running a sample sale. The first examination is free. The second will cost you dearly."

"And you as well. But which of us will pay more, hmm?"

"You, Astra. Definitely you." She tipped back, resting her head on his shoulder, exposing the elegant line of her throat. Sinking one set of claws into his scalp and the other in his thigh, she rasped, "But please, do continue."

Continue. Yes. Need battered him with increasing fervor. "I think you are enjoying this, Elia." The shortened nickname flowed from his lips without thought. "I think you are enjoying it greatly."

"Whatever you gotta tell yourself, Hay-low." A full-body shiver led to slow undulations. "Just don't stop."

Drawing on centuries of iron control, he merely kneaded her breasts with a firmer grip. "I think you love this. I think you *need* this."

"Wrong. I need nothing." She rubbed her backside against his shaft and gave a soft little chuckle. "Mmm. Excuse me while I correct myself. I might need more of *that*."

Desire choked him, dulling his thoughts. The pressure was good and only getting better.

What is she doing to me?

Halo nipped her earlobe and pinched her nipples. "Will you let me do anything I desire to you, harpy?"

"I'll let… I'll…" Her broken cry filled the room. "Give me more." The pulse at the base of her neck raced. "Don't flip, don't flip, don't flip," she chanted beneath her breath. Then, at a louder volume, she commanded, "Give me more."

Flip? *Can't think.* Her scent was changing again, becoming richer. Every ragged inhalation fogged in his head. Muscles flexed, and tendons stretched.

"Are you wet for me, nymph?" He glided his knuckles down

her belly, and she moaned his name. The sounds she made. The silkiness of her skin. The soft cascade of her hair. "Tell me, *I'm wet for you, Halo*. Then I'll give you more."

"I'm not wet. I'm soaked," she admitted without shame. Then she groaned and muttered, "And I *demand* more, Halo. Face it, you kind of owe me."

His lips twitched. Different impulses surged, demanding he take what he'd been denied for so long now, now, now. The pleasure and the release. The relief. But he forced himself to go slow. "I will make you feel good."

"Yes. Make me feel good. That's all I've ever wanted."

Halo grazed her tuft of curls, and a mewl escaped her. "Like this?" His body jerked when she rolled her hips to send his fingers lower.

"Just like this."

Soaking wet, as advertised. New impulses overshadowed the others. Cage her. Never let go. Bend her over. Or flip her to her back. Feast. Pin her down. Pound inside her again and again and again.

"When I remove Erebus's mark from you," he growled against her skin, "I might add my own."

"Wait. What?" She went still. "I have a brand?"

"Yes and no." Halo licked her racing pulse and—nothing.

She had spun to face him, pulling from his embrace. Those light green irises spit fire at him. "Remove the brand-not-a-brand, Halo. *Now.*"

He barely stopped himself from snatching her back. "I will but not today. I believe its removal will be complicated, requiring immense amounts of power." Let himself be drained mere days before the next test? Was that Erebus's hope?

Hands balled, she lunged to beat at Halo's shoulders. "Why even bother examining me, then?"

"I can neutralize the link with trinite." He fit his hands on her hips, thinking to set her away for good. To end their interaction. Too late. Now that he held her, he couldn't bring himself to release her a second time. "In a few minutes, Silver will provide you with a necklace." A more palatable descriptor than "collar." "The simple act of wearing it should prevent Erebus from flashing you. Until then…"

Halo walked forward, forcing the harpy to walk backward. As he pressed her against a wall, he flattened a palm near her temple. Bending down, he put himself at eye level with her.

"Shall I continue with the inspection now?" With his free hand, he lightly pinched her chin and tilted her face up to his. "I believe you commanded me to give you more."

To his delight, the temptress melted against him, winding her arms around his neck. "Will you be kissing me this time?"

She craves my kiss? His gaze dropped to her lips. Plump and red. Parted. A slight dip in the center of the bottom filled his head with ideas. *Will lick her right there.*

"Oh yes. I will be kissing you this time, harpy. I will be doing *everything*."

"Everything? I— No. Wait," she said, shaking her head. "We can't have sex, even if I beg you for it. And just to be clear, sex means putting your penis inside my vagina. Okay?"

The thought of this female begging him for anything, especially pleasure… Yes! Halo needed her to do it. He wasn't sure he'd ever needed anything more. But he drew on centuries of discipline and said, "Very well. No penetration."

"Can I trust you to keep your word?" She toyed with the ends of his hair, flushed and pliant, but somehow also unbending.

"Always. I never lie." The language of weak-willed cowards. More than that, a single untruth enslaved your will to another's opinion, no matter the reason for it. He applied pressure to her chin, keeping her gaze steady on his. "Here's a second vow for you. One day soon, I *will* have you."

"I make no promises." Need darkened her features. "Now kiss me, Halo. Kiss me quick before I change my mind."

Yes. He swooped down and slanted his mouth over hers. Eager, she opened for him. Their tongues thrust together, the sweetness of her taste registering, and his eyes flared wide. Then his lids slid closed, too heavy to hold open. He lost himself in the moment.

He feasted on the female, a starving man who'd somehow stumbled upon a banquet. An animal reduced to raw need.

The strain inside him both eased and worsened, gears stopping, starting, and squeaking. But he hardly noticed. For so long, he'd known only toil. The harpy was introducing him to sensation after sensation, each a shock—and necessary. And he'd thought he couldn't get enough. Fool! He'd merely glimpsed the possibilities before. Now...

A long-buried spark of *something* revived. Something the Order must have failed to extinguish. Whatever it was, it triggered other emotions, fueling unquenchable flames.

Halo throbbed for relief. The slightest bit. He shoved one hand in Ophelia's hair, tangling his fingers in the silken strands. He returned the other hand to her breast, plumping the generous mound. A groan escaped. He hadn't won any relief, but he couldn't regret the action. Nothing had ever felt this good.

"Halo," she cried in between kisses, a sharp pang of arousal nearly gutting him.

He needed more of *that*. His name on her lips.

—*Report to the palace foyer in five. We'll talk.*—

The Commander's voice filled his head, and Halo had to swallow a roar, the words a lash of cold amid the sultry heat. Though he would slay thousands to continue this kiss, he would not, should not ignore Roc during a blessing task.

Something must have transpired. The first and second day of the repeat, Roc had requested Halo's presence only after he'd reported in. Which he hadn't done this morning.

Was Erebus causing problems before the appointed time?

Astra first. Halo lifted his head, but he didn't sever contact with the harpy. A mistake. He breathed her in. His head fogged again. His gaze returned to her lips. They were parted, red, and glistening. He nearly dove back in for a second helping.

With a desperate curse, he flashed several feet away from temptation. But he could still scent her; need clawed at him. Desire *ravaged* him, and he fought for calm.

"I wasn't done." Ophelia panted, peering at him with a riotous mix of arousal, confusion, and hurt. "Why did you stop? And when can we start again?"

Gears tightening... "I've been summoned to the palace foyer, and you'll be accompanying me. You have two minutes to dress. The countdown starts now."

9

Ophelia's Dumb-Dumb switch flipped again, from On to Off. She snapped out of her sensual haze in an instant. Well. From almost getting lost in a needing to ticked.

"That's all you've got to say after pawing at me?" she demanded.

First Halo had the gall to turn her on beyond distraction. Then he'd made all kinds of demands—extreme flirting to nymphs like her apparently. *Then* he'd done this ultra-sexy chin pinch thing that wasn't even fair and kissed her as if he couldn't live another second without learning her taste. Finally, he'd dismissed her as if she were of no importance to him.

A familiar page in the story of her existence. Desired for a moment, forgotten soon after. But no big deal. Whatever.

"Pawing?" he grated.

She hiked her shoulder in a breezy shrug. "I call it like I see it. But no worries. It's fine. Everything is fine." Everything was not fine!

She wasn't some weak-willed nymph who faltered at the first sign of affection. Not all the time. She was a cruel, vicious harpy with a heart of iron and a spine of steel. A fact she had proved every day of her life. Well, almost every day. Or some days. Every so often.

Still! Very few beings comprehended the strength of will required for a nymph to deny her body's urges. Even fewer realized Ophelia always felt like a powder keg set to blow. The very reason she had enacted her only rule. No men. That was it. Simple, easy. No. Men.

After years of hard work and self-denial, she'd had the audacity to lean into a needing. To allow her desires to turn on and her mind to shut off. She knew better. To cave to her desires for someone, anyone, especially an Astra—argh!

A moment of weakness often led to a lifetime of regret. Nissa would have *drowned* in disappointment.

When will you learn to control yourself, Ophelia?

Her shoulders rolled in. For most of her life, she had pretended to mock the dream of making her sister proud while longing for it with every fiber of her being. To know, finally, that she was worthy of the Falconcrest name. To hear a lone sentence of praise. To see one smile of encouragement. Or to at least gain equal bragging rights. *See, Nis. I'm not a failure. I did what you did.*

Now Ophelia had only the dream, an eternal longing, and a headful of childhood memories that left her conflicted.

She figured Nissa had, in part, hated her because their mother had died of complications soon after Ophelia's birth. Nissa had been a busy General back then, but all reports claimed she hadn't hesitated to seize the reins of control and raise Ophelia until her tenth birthday. From there, she'd ventured off to training camp like every other harpy her age. Then Harpy High, Harpy Academy, and the military.

Though she'd made no real progress with her end goal over the years, she'd almost always given her everything to every duty. That had to mean something, right? At least a little? The barest smidge?

At some point, she would prove herself worthy of Nissa's approval—if and only if she stopped letting males sidetrack her. The pattern had to end sometime, right? Why not now?

And really, resisting Halo shouldn't be a problem anymore. He sucked. Before he'd oh, so abruptly ended the kiss, she had teetered at the verge of begging for sex, as feared. And what a humiliating realization. Especially since he'd been the one to pull the trigger.

How could she forget he was a path to promotion? A means to an end. One should not bang their boss.

Yet still I crave more.

Cool air brushed her exposed skin, and she shivered. Ugh. How long had she stood statue-still, while a silent Halo glared his fill at her naked form?

"Nothing else to say?" She grabbed a bra and pair of panties from a dresser drawer, uncaring that they didn't match. Seriously. She didn't care. After yanking on each piece, she gathered a tank top, cashmere sweater, and leathers from hangers in the closet.

Fur lined the inside of the pants, a true luxury item for a soldier. They were her favorite pair—proof she didn't need Halo's warmth.

"You relished my so-called pawing," he grated. "You *requested* it. Bargained for it even."

"Are you wearing your listening ears, Halo? Here goes. I'm part nymph. I would've bargained for nookie with a zombie."

He canted his head, studying her as if he'd just discovered a map of enemy territory. Voice dipping, he said, "So you like to be eaten. Good to know."

Ophelia gaped at her companion. Had the Machine just made a crude joke?

How sexy was that?

Resist! "You're just another mistake in a string of mistakes," she snapped at him. "FYI, I never make out with the same mistake twice."

A muscle jumped beneath his eye. "You have one minute, four seconds."

So Halo was her own personal brand of catnip? Nymphnip? So what? Her goals hadn't changed. Make Nissa proud, and maybe save harpykind along the way. Ophelia loved her sisters in arms. They were her family. Her coming actions would prove that, too. No more forgetting the future in favor of a moment. No more getting turned on and veering off course. This time, her navigation was fixed. Full steam ahead.

"Just enough time to explain you are *not to* get physical with me again." Chin up, back straight. "You aren't my type, and you have a concubine." A concubine she'd forgotten about.

Selective memory loss was a genuine disease she must have inherited from her father.

"What is your type?" Halo narrowed his eyes and gave a clipped shake of his head. "Never mind. Forty-two seconds. Do you wish to traipse about bare foot? Don shoes."

"You are so annoying." Ophelia stuffed her feet into socks and combat boots, then shoved her arms into a jacket. Problem: the clothing failed to lessen the Astra's visual appeal.

Well then. She would just have to batten down the hatches, if ever her nymphy lusts fought her harpy determination. And she thought she knew just where to start.

Look away from the smoke show of a male immediately.

Think an unsexy thought. Think another unsexy thought to be safe.

"Time's up. Dressed and ready, sir," she said, giving him a mocking salute. Expecting him to perform a swift grab and go, his usual MO, she braced. Only, he crossed his arms over his chest. A stance she officially dubbed Ophelia's in Trouble.

"You must be curious about the concubine, since you brought her up."

Her claws sharpened. Had he slept with the Amazon, then

kissed Ophelia? *Douchebag!* She tried for a casual tone, saying, "Nah. I'm good."

"I didn't bed the Amazon this morning or the other. I won't. I have ended her service to me." He threw the words at her, as if she'd spent the past hour demanding to know.

Do not rejoice. "You hoping for an award or something?"

"The" Amazon, he'd said. Not "my." A significant detail or a mere slip of the tongue? Not that it mattered.

"I hope for nothing, but I demand a response." His narrowed gaze pinned her in place. "Did *you* bed anyone this morning? Someone you see on a regular basis, perhaps. One of several?"

Why did he care if she had a roster of current lovers...unless a part of him intended to sign up and join the rotation? "What do you think? Nymphs *are* known for their stables of boy toys." She'd never kept one, but there'd been interest a few times, probably.

The striations in his irises spun with dizzying speed. "You will not be with another male while we're together, Ophelia. I'll kill anyone who touches you. Do you understand?"

He...she...*what?* Was he *jealous?* Proprietary toward her? And had he said *together?* As in *together* together? Uh... Maybe he did want on that roster.

Her blood quickened, and her limbs trembled. Neither of the two losers she'd slept with had been possessive of her, so this was a brand-new experience. The perfect time to engage her three-step program.

She averted her gaze and welcomed an unsexy thought. *A spear slicing inside your ear* hurts. Not something she'd known pre-Halo.

Second unsexy thought. *Halo has seen my body, but I haven't seen his.* Though there'd been something bafflingly exciting about standing naked before a fully clothed male.

Red alert! Abort thought! Not unsexy. I repeat, not unsexy.

Okay, so her three-step program needed tweaking. "Look," she said and sighed. "We shared a brief kiss and some light petting. We dislike each other. Why would you care who I'm with?"

"That answer is above your pay grade," Halo snapped. Subject closed, then.

Good! "My sexual arrangements are above yours."

He stood there for a long while, slowly powering down to his emotionless default setting. "Your…necklace has been completed." A half circle of thin, dark stone appeared in each of his hands. He marched over. "Each piece is marked with mystical runes. No matter how many times the day repeats, I'll be able to flash them to you first thing in the morning."

A ribbon of his heat caressed her, and she shivered. The abilities this male wielded…intoxicating. No. Annoying. "I hope you're not expecting a thank you," she said, lifting her mass of hair out of the way.

"From you, I'm expecting nothing but trouble."

He fit the pieces above the neckline of her sweater. A round disk hung from the edge of one of the halves, dipping underneath the top, adhering to the spot where Erebus had stabbed her as if it had been glued there.

"There will be at least seven days between each labor." Halo tugged the sweater aside and traced a fingertip around the disk, his knuckle brushing her skin. "I fully expect Erebus to cause trouble in the meantime. This will help."

His hot skin was a tantalizing contrast to the cool stone. She closed her eyes, fighting the aftereffects. A mistake! His smoked cherries and sandalwood scent registered. Mmm.

Okay, so, Ophelia tweaked the third step. *Stop breathing.*

She pried open her lids and stepped away from her companion, patting her new accessory, learning it through the cashmere. More of a choker than a necklace, without being too constrictive. Lightweight. Not bad. Of course, she would've driven a hundred-pound spike through her heart to block Erebus.

Halo watched her, seemingly fascinated by what bling he

could see. As his eyes grew dazed, the striations in his irises began spinning again, mesmerizing her. Maybe one more kiss wouldn't— Nope. Not doing that.

"Don't we have somewhere to be?" she asked. "I'm pretty sure my two minutes expired two lustful stares ago."

The striations halted. Another blank mask fell into place, colder than the last. Icy even. What had the harpy in the gym said? Oh, yeah. Arctic blast. *Check.* This man desired *no one.* Ophelia mourned the transformation, feeling as if she'd lost out on something special.

More nymph foolishness, that's all.

He clasped her wrist and flashed her to the palace foyer. Hundreds of harpies congregated in the area, gossiping in whispers as they stared at the hearth between the left and right staircases, where Nissa's portrait hung. Degrees of confusion shone on their faces. She followed their gazes...

A hand fluttered to her mouth of its own accord as she stumbled back. Nissa's portrait was gone, replaced by a severed head. The lioness. Both of her—*my*—eyes were gouged out, thanks to Halo. Blood stained her muzzle. Pieces of Halo clung to her many, many metal teeth.

I looked like this? No wonder Halo had ended her as hardcore as possible.

Struggling to maintain a steady attitude, Ophelia said, "You, uh, killed your first beast, huh?"

"I did." He offered no more. He barely even moved. But he couldn't mask a slight twitch from his fingers.

Curiosity got the better of her. "Was the battle a challenge for you?" *Careful.* "I've heard the Astra are impossible to kill."

"Not a challenge, and not impossible." He pointed to the beast's throat, where fur appeared flattened. "During the battle, the creature wore a collar made of firstone. A poison to Astra."

Not a challenge. Wow. Okay. A bit harsh, in terms of feedback, but good to know. She pressed her tongue to the roof of her mouth. *Say nothing. Offer no response.*

"Maybe the next monster will do major damage to you," she blurted out.

"Maybe. But probably not."

That one stung. A silly reaction. She wouldn't be seeking his elimination when they battled. Not purposely. In that regard, the joke was on Erebus. *Gonna get another infusion of strength, overcome the bloodlust and accept my slaughter.*

If not next time, the one after. If she gained enough power, she could take down the god himself.

Ohhh. Now there was a heartwarming idea; a little beauty of a thought that grew legs and ran for miles. Killing Erebus was the absolute best possible ending for this blessing task. Halo would win, while Ophelia did what no one else had been able— destroy the Deathless. *My first kill. A god no less.* What a bucket list accomplishment!

"So who displayed the head?" she asked. "Do you know?"

"Chaos, I'm sure. At the end of a task, I always present a piece of my opponent to him. This task is different, however, and being done in stages. This must be a way to track my progress."

"Makes sense, I guess." In a sick way.

His fingers flexed against hers again—why hadn't she tried to free herself yet? "I'm sorry I allowed Erebus to throw you to the beast before the battle," he said.

He thought she'd served as beast bait? Guilt slithered through her, a snake with venomous fangs. "Oh. Um. There's no reason for you to feel guilt." Truth. "You aren't responsible for me."

"I am responsible. For now."

Wrong. "I take care of myself."

Beside them, two harpies launched into a quick back-and-forth conversation, cutting into theirs.

"It just appeared," the first said. "What do you think it means?"

"Taliyah hired a better decorator? She has a secret admirer?"

"Check it! Some of the Astra are here."

"No, *you* check it. I think Halo is boning the Flunk Out. Look! They're holding hands!"

The discussion tapered, others following suit. Silence descended upon the crowd, and Ophelia's cheeks flamed. If harpies didn't turn to leer at the warlords, wag their brows and give suggestive winks, they gaped at her as if she'd sprouted a second head.

She would absolutely, probably give everyone lip about their rudeness just as soon as she finished her study of the other Astra. Before this, she'd only seen the members of the infamous nine at a distance. Up close and personal, they wowed.

Silver, the metalworker, possessed straight black hair, bronze skin and irises like mirrors; his intensity rivaled Halo's while his ferocity equaled Roc's.

Then came the one named Ian. He had black eyes and skin a shade lighter. His dark hair was styled in thick braids. Rumors suggested he had a warped sense of humor and a temper far more lethal than any of the other Astra.

Roux, the sexy tea-drinking brute with pale hair, golden skin, and molten eyes—whoa! He was glaring at Ophelia as if he'd locked on a target for elimination, a thin red circle backlighting his enlarged pupils. Aggression thrummed from him.

Threat! She wrenched from Halo at last, positioning for attack. Or she tried to. The Immortal held on tight and yanked her closer before slinging an arm around her hip, pinning her to his side.

Oh, no, no, no. This wouldn't do. Fused with him, she felt naked all over again. Warmed from head to toe. Needy.

"Let me go," she snapped, planning to fight her way free. But he smelled so good, and his muscles were so big... Mmm.

She melted into him, running her hands over his chest. Other parts of him were big, too, and they were only growing bigger.

And what a heady development. He might have been the one to stop their kiss, but he still desired her. Greatly.

Ophelia dragged her gaze to his face—and flinched. Now *Halo* was glaring at her as if she were a target for elimination.

"What'd I do?" she demanded, un-melting. Had she committed a grave Astraian faux pas or something?

"Roux has informed me you are General Nissa's sister." He raised a brow. "That information wasn't listed in your file."

Oh. That. "Yeah? So?" Why deny it now?

The muscle twitched in his jaw once, then again. On any other man, a double twitch meant nothing more than increased irritation. With Halo...*huge mad.*

"So," he grated. "You have a reason to sabotage my task."

"Like Nissa is the only one I've got," she quipped. "Exhibit A, your sparkling personality."

Jump. "I want to know why you kept this detail from me."

"First of all, you never specifically asked if I had a sister or who she might be. That's on you. Second, I don't need a reason not to tell a stranger I don't like a personal detail about my family. That's on me." Let him stew over the real justification. He deserved it after that sabotage crack. As if she would *ever* endanger harpykind. On purpose.

A line of blue bulged between his eyes. "You compromised my task. Those who do so usually die screaming."

"Well, thank goodness I'm covered then. Been there, done that." *Already bought my ticket for round three.* "You remember my stabbing, right?" She buffed her fingers on her sweater, over the disk. "The night your bedroom bondage fetish prevented me from defending myself against your enemy? Ringing any bells or should I go on?"

The slightest vibration registered, as if he'd trembled. But that couldn't be right. Halo the Machine did not tremble. Did he?

"We are supposedly allies." He bent down, putting them nose

to nose. "Tell me the real reason for your silence of your own volition, harpy."

Was she sensing a pattern to his use of nicknames? Did he call her "nymph" when he wanted some O and "harpy" when she irritated him? "Or what?"

"Or I will be forced to extract the information another way."

"In that case." She smiled sweetly. "Extract the information another way."

He inhaled, exhaled. "Have you aided Erebus in any way?"

Okay, so, she rethought Operation Let Him Stew in a hurry. They had just entered super dangerous territory for her, the truth both a danger and a shield to her cause. If Halo believed her to be an enemy, he would convince Roc of it, who could convince Taliyah, who could label Ophelia a traitor. Banishment might be the least of her worries.

"Look." Sighing, she eased back. Distance—smart. "Am I seeking a lifelong friendship with Nissa's killer? No. Will I destroy all Astra for a chance to strike at the Commander? Yes. One day. Maybe. I'm still debating it. But here's what I know beyond a doubt, now and forever. I will never purposely harm my fellow harpies. Since their fate is linked with yours, you and your task are kind of important to me."

Halo pinched her chin in that gentle but firm clasp— *Help me!* It was only the sexiest hold in the freaking world. Her heart raced.

"You love your sisters. I believe that. But Erebus is persuasive. If you decide to aid him... Do not aid him, Ophelia."

"I won't, Halo." She meant that. For her sisters in arms. For Nissa. For herself. Which solidified her decision not to blab her end game to Halo, risking a counterplay on his part.

Cat calls sounded around them, and he released her to palm a three-blade. But there was no threat. Harpies were simply doing their thing, backing up in unison to form a wide circle around

Ophelia, Halo, and the handful of other Astra while chanting, "Bone. Bone. Bone."

Commander Roc appeared nearby, and the cheers instantly ceased.

Ophelia snapped to attention. The Commander. Here. This was the closest she'd ever been to him. She expected a rise and crash of emotion. Rage. Grief. Resolve. Her mind merely tossed out useless observations. Stalwart. Cropped dark hair. Gold irises encircled by rings of varying shades of gray. Proud, patrician nose. Soft lips. A thick beard. As usual, he'd forgotten to wear a shirt. The muscles packed beneath his bronze skin put highly agitated *alevala* on display. If she searched long enough, would she see Nissa's face?

"Halo," Roc said, ignoring her.

"Commander." Halo wrapped an arm around her waist, not to hold her in place but to...comfort her?

No, no. Of course he didn't seek to comfort her. What a ridiculous notion. Halo, offer anything other than cold disdain or the promise of an orgasm without the actual delivery? Please!

Wait. He and the Commander had lapsed into silence. Roc was studying her now. Really looking her over. His gaze got stuck on the muscular arm that shackled her against his second-in-command.

Halo stiffened, as if Roc had said something he didn't like. Roc probably had.

The Astra possessed the amazing ability to speak telepathically, and it was the bane of harpy existence. Assuage a girl's curiosity already. But, okay, fine. This conversation she thought she understood. No doubt Roc had asked three questions. *Who is she? Who is she to you? Where did you find such an exquisite creature?*

Or just two questions. Whatever. They could have their secret mind-meetings. She couldn't deny the time-out had incredible perks. More warmth. That scent. The majestic view couldn't be beat; it trapped her gaze once again.

Halo's body had been built for war. Utterly jam-packed with strength. A shadow of stubble graced his strong jaw. And look at those broad shoulders. His biceps remained flexed. Ohhh. Was he tense, preparing to cause damage to something? How utterly delicious.

Mmm, mmm, mmm. He had a chest *made* for her hands, didn't he? So many ridges beneath his shirt. And the heat of his skin…she slipped her fingers beneath the fabric, touching sizzling flesh. A mewl left her. *Will never get tired of this.*

"Ophelia," he snarled, waking her from a stupor.

Oops! She had a palm on his shoulder and a palm on his abs as she rubbed all over him. In front of everyone. Needless to say, there was a lot of staring.

Cheeks burning, she eased away from the Astra, and he let her. She needed to give herself a stern talking to about what had just happened. And she would. After she ditched her companion.

"Very nice to meet you, Ophelia," Ian said. He flashed off, clearly trying not to laugh.

The other males ranged in emotion as they disappeared on his heels. Two warlords maintained their stations, however. Roux, and the one named Vasili. A quiet, brutish Astra who wasn't always sane. He had more harpy-fans than any other.

The two scowled at her without cause.

She bristled at them. "What? You want to say something?" *Superior officers. Allies. Right.* She pasted on a smile and added, "Because I'd love to listen, sirs."

Halo muttered something under his breath, then flashed her to the royal library, where a handful of harpies loitered. The kindest, most caring harpies of them all—the readers. Woe to anyone who disturbed their force field of quiet, however. Ophelia shuddered inside.

Thankfully, no one paid her and Halo any heed.

He didn't release her right away. No, he held her against his body, once again enveloping her with his scent, and he stared, hard. She gulped, remembering the way she'd rubbed all over him only moments ago, losing herself. Why, why, why did she yearn to do it again?

"Yeah. Um. Thanks for the exit." This man was an ally to her harpy but foe to her nymph. A temptation like no other.

Self-preservation propelled her to an abandoned table two shelves over. "So what else did your friends blab about me?"

Okay. All right. Yes. The distance helped. She paced between the tables. Oh, look at that. A copy of *1001 Ways to Torture an Enemy without Breaking a Claw*. A must read.

Focus! Get it together—keep it together. Clear mission objective, clear path to victory.

"Well?" she prompted.

"They told me different things. Facts." He crossed his arms over his chest. His power pose. "Suppositions, really."

What did that even mean? "Such as?"

"Such as. You are a complication."

"And you aren't?"

A sharp noise preceded a sudden chill she recognized, ending the conversation. *Phantoms.*

Halo extended his hand, and a three-blade appeared in his grip. No other weapon would help against the embodiments of death.

On the other side of the library, a phantom floated through a wall and walked forward. Head bowed. Dragging feet. Dressed in the usual widow's weeds; the material bagged over her emaciated frame. She winked in and out of view, a spirit one second and embodied the next. She bypassed reading harpies as if they weren't there. The harpies didn't notice this disturbance, either.

The phantom chanted, "Find Halo, tell Halo, eat the girl. Find Halo, tell Halo, eat the girl."

No better time to make my first kill. "Throw me a three-blade, man!" she commanded, waving her fingers. Because of Halo, she currently carried no weapons of her own.

He ignored her, flashing to the phantom and gripping her throat.

"Don't you dare," Ophelia called, running for the pair. "That target is mine!"

Halo didn't bother glancing over his shoulder as he pointed the tip of the three-blade in Ophelia's direction. "You will stay back, harpy. You do nothing but obey me during this blessing task. Which means you will do *nothing*." To the phantom, he intoned, "I am Halo. Give me your message."

Incredulity yanked Ophelia to a halt. What did he mean, *do nothing*?

The phantom tilted her head to an unnatural angle as she flipped up milky white eyes. With no intonation, she told him, "I killed your *gravita*, yes. Do you think a bit of *trinite* will stop her next death? Oh, warlord, I can't wait to prove otherwise. She'll scream so loudly." Master's order completed, she swung that white gaze to Ophelia and screeched, stretching out her arms and attempting to fly over.

Halo stabbed her thrice in quick succession. Throat. Heart. Gut. The phantom crumpled to the floor and slowly evaporated.

"You suck *so* hard," Ophelia muttered, even as her mind whirled. *Gravita*. A word she'd heard before. An Astra's fated mate. Like a consort or an entwine. But worse. An Astra's obsession and possession of a mate supposedly fed on a steady diet of steroids, testosterone and *anhilla*. And Halo had found his? And this mysterious paragon currently wore trinite? And Erebus had killed her at some point. *And* the god hoped to arrange her next death?

Ophelia tried not to wheeze as the oddest question popped into her head. Was *she* Halo's *gravita*?

No, no. She couldn't be. The very idea! It was the most far-fetched thing she'd ever heard. Ophelia and Halo had nothing in common. How old was he? Too old for her, guaranteed.

He was moody without being emotional, and she didn't like it. Not one bit.

But what if, maybe, possibly, she wasn't just some amazing but random innocent bystander who'd gotten hit by an Astra during a flash-land gone wrong? Stranger things had happened.

But. Halo and Ophelia? The Astra and the harpymph?

No. Absolutely not. She couldn't be Halo's other half.

But what if she was? At times, he practically frothed at the mouth with desire for her. And she *was* the only other unfrozen individual in the palace. A match wasn't totally outside the realm of possibility.

Her knees threatened to give out, so she plopped into a chair at the table closest to her. If she were Halo's *gravita*, he might be her consort or entwine. Or both! That was how these things usually worked. Which might explain her unprecedented reaction to him. The constant needing.

But what would the status of *gravita* mean for her life? Her career? Her goals?

He had insisted she do nothing but keep him sated and happy before the message. He must have known what she might be to him, or at least suspected; why else would he have sought to protect her so stridently?

Okay. Not telling him about Erebus's scheme had been the right call. Halo might attempt to remove Ophelia from the equation entirely.

Although, if anyone could get through to him and convince him of the error of his ways, it was his *gravita*.

No immortal male could resist his fated mate; they lived only to please the object of their fascination. It was practically science. And Halo was the Immortal of Immortals, more science-y than most. When he learned the only way to make her happy was to put his mammoth ego aside and let her help orchestrate their enemy's defeat, he would backpedal.

If she confessed all—after their victory—he would have to

forgive her. Hold a grudge against your cherished female? Not for long.

Ophelia pressed a hand over her fluttering belly. So. Was she or wasn't she? Was he or wasn't he?

To find her consort and entwine this young? Was it even possible?

If so, could she have power, success *and* a lover?

No, no. She didn't want a perma-bang. Except, she thought she maybe kind of, sort of…did. Secretly. Sometimes desperately.

Ophelia ducked her head. This. This was the real reason she'd avoided pleasure. To want it and lose it…oh, the pain. But to break her rule a third time and bomb…

No, she couldn't risk it. She wouldn't be so weak. What if she lost herself in the needing?

On the other hand, pleasure kept nymphs strong, and she needed to be as strong as possible for the task. And contenders for General *could* take a lover nowadays. They could have a career *and* a side slice.

On the other, other hand, Ophelia wasn't like most contenders. She wasn't fighting for the title alone but her sister's respect. No sex for Nissa—no sex for Ophelia. No reason to let herself tangle with her true kryptonite: being needed in return.

But. Gah! Always there was a *but* nowadays. She and Nissa weren't the same, either. Different strengths, different weaknesses, different requirements. What if Halo could fully satisfy Lady No O, ending the threat of the needing altogether? He didn't strike her as a male who *ever* gave up.

Trembling, she locked her sights on him. Extra strength, tougher defenses. No needing, no near constant arousal. Possible rewards: helping Halo take down Erebus and total satiation. The risks: greater distraction and the total loss of everything she'd built. It would be one or the other.

No risks, no rewards.

Think of it. Her, the youngest contender for General in harpy history to take out a big bad, win an Astra *and* be satisfied sexually. Shouldn't she go for it? Shouldn't she find out if she was the Astra's *gravita* or not?

The answer seemed fairly obvious to her. And, really, for all she knew, her first relationship had been a rookie mistake. The second might have been an anomaly of some kind. A third failure—or first success—should provide the full truth, nothing but the truth, once and for all.

Could Ophelia Falconcrest have it all?

10

Halo gathered multiple tomes. Some featured Hercules's labors, others provided information about different species. Ophelia was quiet and pensive, reminding him of himself when he tracked a specific target, scheming all the different ways to strike. He felt the hot ping of her focus and knew her plans revolved around him. He did his best to avoid looking at her. No more temptation. No more distractions.

He prided himself on performing his duty, no matter the situation. He may not have much to offer his brothers in terms of affection, amusement, or excitement, but he always excelled at his assignments. The Astra could count on him to push through any hardship and succeed on their behalf.

He needed to prepare for the second battle. His enemy continued to run circles around him. Erebus had overcome the palace defenses installed by Halo himself, sneaking in a phantom, simply to deliver a message.

Things must change—so he would change them.

But what had the god meant when he'd promised to strike at Ophelia *in other ways*?

Fury hard-boiled Halo's muscles. What other ways?

So much for no distractions.

He dropped his selection of books on Ophelia's table. *Thud.* He didn't care if she noticed the titles referencing nymphs or consorts, didn't care if she supposed there was an eternal tie between them. But...

More and more he suspected she did, in fact, belong to him. The way his body reacted to her. This preoccupation with every part of her. Erebus's delight in the circumstances. At the mere mention of a "stable of boy toys," Halo had *longed* to geld each stallion. That longing hadn't faded. This possessiveness...this jealousy. How was he supposed to shed them?

He eased into a seat next to his companion. Something the Commander had suggested earlier returned to Halo's mind. Rearrange his priorities for a week, as an experiment. Seven days between tests meant he had time to explore diverse routes to triumph. One of those routes, according to Roc, included making Ophelia his primary concern. Roc suspected the harpy influenced Halo's task the same way Taliyah had influenced Roc's. For better or worse.

The argument made sense on multiple levels. Change had the ability to facilitate growth; growth carved out more room for more power. More power led to ascension. Catering to a *gravita* might be the biggest change of all for someone like Halo. In terms of numbers and odds, the Astra had lived eons without finding a fated female. Now, when the whole army hovered at the cusp of ascension, the leader discovered his mate and won his task with her aid. It stood to reason Halo, the second-in-command, would receive a similar opportunity to grow and rise.

Change. Growth. Power.

Maybe the harpy influenced the outcome of Halo's task,

maybe she didn't. But she absolutely played a role in it. When they'd stood in the foyer and she'd fondled his chest in front of his brothers, seemingly oblivious to the rest of the world, Halo had felt as though she played a role in his *everything*.

Inhale. Exhale. The Commander had also mentioned stardust. For Roc, the powder hadn't come until he'd gotten Taliyah into bed.

"Okay, you've pretended to ignore me long enough." Ophelia popped to her feet and anchored her hands to her hips. "Forget your no questions from a subordinate rule. I'm asking stuff and you're answering. How does an Astra recognize his *gravita*?"

Oh, yes. She suspected their connection. "No stardust, no *gravita*."

"The powdery substance produced by your hands, right, safe only for the woman wearing it?"

"Correct." He offered no more.

She persisted. "The stardust is that important to a pairing?"

"Yes." Her sweet scent hit him anew. *Control*. He leaned back in the antique chair, increasing the distance between them, and regarded her warily. "Sit." He motioned to her seat, the chair at his right. "You may ask me about anything else. Just know I'll be asking you anything in return."

"An equal exchange? Yes. Agreed." Chin lifted, she sauntered around him and claimed the chair at his left.

He very nearly rolled his eyes. "You asked if this will be an equal exchange. My answer is yes," he said, and she groaned a weak protest. "Now it's my turn to ask and your turn to respond." There was something he must know. "What happened to you before yesterday's battle?"

Shifting repeatedly, cheeks pallid, she told him, "I died. What more do you wish to know? No! Don't answer that. It wasn't an official question."

He rubbed his stinging chest. *Failed her*. Had she lingered? Suffered?

"Here's my first official question," she said. "What is your plan for me? Like, what are you expecting from me, exactly? What do you want?" She traced a blunt nail over the spines of his books, mouthing the titles. At *How to Be an Unmurdered Consort*, she arched a brow at him.

He held her gaze, unflinching. "I will answer each. My plan is to keep you safe while I successfully complete my task. I'm expecting you to not be foolish enough to make me choose between your safety and my victory. To always tell me the truth and to never disobey my commands." Hot blood rushed to his groin. *Ophelia, eagerly doing everything I desire...* He gripped the arms of his chair. "Until the task ends, I want what I want when I want it for reasons. You need to know no more than that."

As she balked, Halo canted his head and arched a brow in challenge. *Something more to say, harpy?*

Bristling, she told him, "I get it. I'm worthy of your protection only as long as I'm your puppet. Well, how about this for a little honesty? I have a task of my own to complete, and more and more I'm thinking you aren't worthy of *my* protection."

"And what task is that?"

She lifted her nose. "I told you already. I will qualify for General, or I will die again trying."

He flinched at the reminder of her death. Negate her claim, however? No. Halo could trust only two things. His brothers, and a harpy's loyalty to other harpies. Especially those contending for the title of General. They put their people first, always.

Right now, those people happened to need the Astra. When it counted, Ophelia would do whatever Halo commanded, if only to safeguard harpykind.

"You owe me another answer. Two, actually." He flicked his tongue over an incisor, thinking. "Why are you known as the Flunk Out?"

She made a crude motion with her hand. "Just had to go there, didn't you? Whatever. Here's the crux of it. At the age of fifteen, I vowed to stay a virgin and fight for the title of General. At eighteen, I believed I fell in love and slept with my boyfriend. No virginity, no hat in the General's ring. I thought I would be okay with that because I'd have my male. But the boy who'd spent months winning me bailed the next day. At twenty, I decided to try again with someone better. Only, he wasn't better. He bailed the next day, too. I wasn't worth a war with my sister."

A defensive inflection couldn't hide her hurt—a noticeable chink in her armor. A chink she shouldn't have. For the two males to have her within their clasp and give her up? The sheer lunacy of it staggered Halo. Her nearness alone inspired a near-constant frisson of pleasure.

She glared at him, daring him to comment on her tale. For once, he had no idea how to respond. Offer a gesture of comfort? But how did one do so? His hands caused pain, not pleasure. Though she *had* enjoyed his touch earlier. Very much.

The same thing she could have done for a zombie. He gripped the arms of his chair—the arms split apart in his grip.

Ophelia looked at the decimated shards of wood that littered the floor, then Halo. The shards. Halo. A hint of a smile teased the vixen's mouth. Had she guessed his thoughts? Sensed his raging desire?

Was she learning her strange power over him at the same time he did? Probably. He should care. But he only wanted to kiss her again.

"What's your big beef with Erebus?" she asked. "Why is he extra revengey with you?"

Revengey? Halo eased up as if an exploding piece of furniture was a common occurrence. "Long ago, the Astra served as royal guards to Chaos. When we ascended in the past, we became gods of our own territories. Erebus ascended around the same time and became the god of his own territory as well—ours. What one controls, the other forfeits. Now his failures are our successes and vice versa. Another ascension looms, Erebus versus the Astra. One of us will increase while the other decreases."

"Yeah, but like, he *really* hates you, I think."

What exactly had the male said to her? "I killed his twin brother, and the male did not revive." Next question. "Did you hope to achieve your first kill today, even though no one will remember tomorrow?"

"Yes! I'll remember. And you blew it, by the way."

"Be grateful I did. The phantoms who come after me are aged and starving. Far stronger than the younger phantoms you find on the city streets." Risk Ophelia's harm a third time? No. "The older phantoms can pull you into their orbit, holding you without contact while they feed."

"Well, the more I practice fighting them, the better I'll fight them."

True. And a fighting harpy was a safer harpy. "Once the Astra have completed the rest of the blessing tasks, I'll train you myself." Yes, he liked this idea. A legitimate excuse to put his hands on her. To rub against her. Could he make her beg for sex, as she'd suggested during his inspection?

Her vivid gaze sharpened on him, calculated and cunning. "Why use your precious time to train one of thousands of soldiers?"

"Because I can. Now, enough conversation." He had revealed more than he'd learned. A first for him and not an experience he hoped to continue. "I intend to study. While I do, you will sit there and be quiet."

"Sure, sure. So, so quiet." She slid *The Care and Feeding of Your Nymph* from the pile and tossed it his way. "I recommend you start with this. So far, your review is stuck at zero stars."

Holding the harpy's glittering gaze, he picked up a journal written by a scribe who'd witnessed Hercules's labors firsthand.

She gave a negligent shrug, not seeming bothered in the slightest. "You do me a solid and be quiet, too. Before this whole thing started, I had myself a wild night. I could use some beauty z's." She kicked up her feet and got comfortable in her chair, closing her eyes before he had a chance to respond.

A wild night. What had she done? With whom?

Halo's claws sharpened, nearly shredding the five-thousand-page tome. Inhale, exhale. Better. He flipped the pages, tearing one. No big deal. Tomorrow would repair any damage.

Concentrate. He read about the first labor quickly, skipping over nothing. Chaos had told him to learn something from each feat. So what had Halo learned with the lioness?

She'd had weaknesses, even though she hadn't seemed to have weaknesses.

And what about Hercules's second labor? A nine-headed water beast. The hydra. A species Halo knew well. Cut off one head, and two more grew in its place.

Was he to face another beast? Or something else? The labor must only be inspired by Hercules.

"Ugh! This horrid seat should be burned." With a huff, Ophelia climbed atop the table, stretched out, and got comfortable, but she didn't attempt to sleep. She tossed a crumbled ball of paper into the air.

Concentrate. To defeat the water beast, Hercules and a partner had worked together. Hercules did the head cutting while the other male cauterized the wound, preventing any regrowth. Their weapons were described in minute detail, with sketches and an examination of their histories.

Halo had an assortment of armaments at his disposal, many able to seal a wound while causing the injury. Daggers. Swords. Sickles and axes. According to task rules, he could use any or all, no partner necessary.

A strange rumbling sound drew his gaze up. A quick scan. Nothing seemed amiss. Ophelia continued to throw her paper ball, as if she'd heard nothing.

The sound came again, bringing realization. He cringed inside. His companion required nourishment. How long had he allowed her to suffer with hunger?

He checked the clock in his mind: 11:59. His brow furrowed. Hours had passed since they'd last spoken. Now, the freeze was due to begin. In less than a minute, the kitchen chef would be unavailable to prepare a proper meal for Ophelia to steal or earn. A necessary part of any harpy's diet; otherwise, they sickened.

"You should have told me you were hungry." He closed the journal with a snap.

"Yeah, because you were *so* welcoming of my commentary before this?"

"I've been more welcoming with you than anyone else."

"Why?"

He pursed his lips, stood and offered her a hand. "Come. Let's get you fed."

"Food, yes. Aid, no." She slapped his hand aside and scrambled to her feet. "Ophelia Falconcrest, reporting for duty, sir, yes, sir."

This female. Somehow, she took everything and nothing seriously, and it was both maddening and charming. He clasped her wrist and flashed her into the kitchen, intending to gather items for her to confiscate.

The chef and her helpers manned the stoves. A thick veil of steam curled around them as they chopped and stirred different pots, despite the time. A minute past noon. He didn't understand. There was to be no freeze today?

The group stopped what they were doing and faced him and Ophelia, their expressions highlighting different degrees of shock.

He must wear one too. Had he misunderstood how things worked? Had the day ceased resetting? Did the freeze only occur on the days Erebus challenged him?

"Did you happen to notice that no one's frozen?" Ophelia asked with a frown.

"I did." He didn't like that he didn't have answers. "Tell the chef what food I'd like to eat. I want all your favorites. A male my size has a big appetite, so order accordingly."

"Really?" A bundle of excitement, she rushed to sit at a long marble counter overlooking the chopping station. A spot usually reserved for the General or her highest ranked officials. "The Astra is starved. Ravenous! He wants a seven-course feast featuring the best of everything the palace has to offer. He's willing to punish anyone who serves a subpar dish."

"He is *very* willing," Halo said, sitting next to her and doing his best to return his focus to the journal. The more he learned, the surer his victory.

Though he never looked up from the pages, he couldn't shake his awareness of the harpy. He knew the moment she received her buffet of food. Knew when she took a bite and what she selected.

For the time being, the gears and coils inside him were frozen, even though the citizens of Harpina were not. Once again, desire overshadowed his tension. He was hard and throbbing. But he thought she might be throbbing, too. Any time he leaned toward her, she leaned toward him.

Hadn't Roc all but ordered Halo to put his desires before his duties for once? *For the sake of the task.*

Could he do it, though?

"Your meal is amazing, Halo. You should try something." She brandished her fork in his direction, flashing fangs. "But only after I'm done. Mine!"

He'd never reacted to food in such a way. Had never really cared what he ate. Had rarely even chosen his own meal. Most days, he consumed whatever was served to the Astrian army. The soldiers kept beyond the trinite wall that surrounded the palace grounds.

Without thought, he snagged Ophelia's fork and tasted. Hmm. Not bad. Creamy.

"Hey!" she groused when he shoveled in several more bites.

Then she surprised him. She patted his shoulder in encouragement and told the chef, "Halo demands dessert. The Immortal
of Immortals gets cranky without his daily dose of sweetness."

The more he ate, the more his hunger intensified. He cleaned
Ophelia's plate. But it wasn't enough. He felt like a bottomless
pit…and all he wanted was that dessert. Or something even
sweeter…

He dropped his gaze to her breasts. Her nipples drew tight
beneath her sweater.

Would she give him what he craved?

"Uh, Halo?"

He tried to meet her gaze. He stopped at the trinite collar.
Up her throat. Along her jaw. How easy it would be to close his
fingers in her hair and keep her where he desired her—where
she might desire to be.

Will you be kissing me?

"Halo!"

"What?" he snapped, blinking and lifting his gaze. "I hope
there's a good reason for interrupting my studies."

"Your studies. Right. Maybe look around at your surroundings once in a while." She scanned the kitchen, and he mir-
rored the action.

Well. Another question answered. The rest of the world had
frozen again, including the flames that crackled under the pots.
He checked the time: 1:02.

Hmm. Halo closed the journal and stood. This freeze had
occurred an hour later than the others. Did Erebus lose an hour
on the battle clock after every completion of a labor?

Speaking of, there'd be no labor today. With the choker, there
was no looming threat to Ophelia, either. Why not obey the
Commander? No need to go the whole week. The experiment
could begin and end today. Desire before duty.

Would he produce stardust as soon as he got Ophelia into bed?
He should find out. Knowledge equaled power.

Halo snagged her and whisked her to her feet. Gasping, she flattened her palms over his pectorals. Her scent strengthened—sweetened.

"What?" she demanded, backing away as if she'd just come face-to-face with a dangerous bear. "Why are you looking at me as if you're going to eat me?"

"Because I am." He shot out his arm, clasped her nape, and flashed to his bedroom.

11

Oh, no, no, no. The Astra had a hungry gleam in his hypnotic eyes, his irises spinning faster than usual. Ophelia's resistance was crumbling just as speedily. But. Thankfully the Dumb-Dumb switch hadn't yet flipped. As out of control as she currently felt, she also felt *in* control. Far more than ever before.

Courtesy of her newfound strength? *I am lioness. Hear me roar.*

Shocker of shockers, she was able to think past her desire. She knew she fancied Halo, but she also knew she should wait for the stardust before she accepted his advances. The coveted powder was her only guarantee that he was worthy of the trouble he caused. That he wouldn't bolt as soon as he won her, forcing her to pick up the pieces of a ravaged future once again.

Problem was, her attraction to him wasn't snuffed at the moment. Oh, how she burned for him. For hours, she had watched him pretend to read while simmering with arousal. He'd seemed so absorbed by the pages of his book. So serious and intent.

The way other guys often beheld the "articles" in nudie magazines. And yet Ophelia had never doubted Halo's awareness of her. He'd clocked her every movement, tensing any time she'd shifted. The knowledge had stoked her inner fire again and again.

He clamped his fingers around the collar. When he gave a determined yank, she slammed against him. Chest to chest. Hardness to softness. A sharp spike of excitement left her trembling; she could do nothing but melt against him.

"You want me between your legs, don't you, Elia?" His voice was made of gravel and smoke.

Shivers rocked her. That nickname on those firm, sensual lips... "I think I should get out of the bear's cage ASAP. I'm no dummy." Not all the time. But did she really have to sound as gravelly and smoky as him? Did so many parts of her have to tighten while a thousand others fluttered?

"Too late. The bear has you in his clutches, and he demands his honey." He released the collar to grip her backside and lift her to her tiptoes, grinding his erection between her legs. "Give it to me."

Aches erupted here, there, everywhere. Breathing became impossible. "Why don't you go get honey from your concubine?"

"I told you. I ended her service. I have no concubine."

"Yeah, but that's just a thing guys like to say when they're horny." Ophelia slowly slinked her arms around his neck, an action she couldn't prevent, no matter how hard she fought. Hoping to stay engaged in the conversation, she did not rub against him...more than a little.

Maybe she'd have better success making *Halo* rethink this? She just had to remember: whatever she boasted, she must follow through. Otherwise, he would never take her seriously.

Here goes. "If I let you do this," she said, toying with the ends of his hair, "it will be as a favor to you. Because *you* need it. But you'll be responsible for doing all the work. I've done a good job lately, and I really deserve a reward. I only hope I get to enjoy it, too. I'm really rooting for you, champ. Just don't expect reciprocation." She so did not need to know how incredible it felt to master his powerful body with the softest strokes of her hands.

He kneaded her backside before shifting his grip, resting the tips of his fingers against her core. Despite her leathers, she felt his heat. As she panted for more, he grumbled to himself, "If we reap what we sow, this is my harvest." With a huff, he turned the conversation back to her. "Very well. There will be no reciprocation. I'll take whatever I can get."

Wait. He would? That was sooo not the response she'd expected. That he would agree to this...

A sense of vulnerability washed over Ophelia. "How can I make out with the guy who expects me to sit on the sidelines during the most important war of my life? I mean, I might be a nymph but I'm a harpy, too. Conquering is what I do. And turning down admirers. Seriously, you have no idea who I've rejected. Kings! Emperors!" An elderly king. A teenage emperor. Whatever. Truth was truth.

"The blessing task is mine and mine alone. But perhaps we can find a skirmish or two for you."

Well. That was certainly a step in the right direction. Everything he was doing was a step in the right direction.

"Am I to be your secret plaything?" What happened in the time loop stayed in the time loop? "Yours to command?"

His eyes blazed. Spinning, spinning. "No secret, some playing, countless commands. Though I have little experience with pleasure, I'm quickly learning *you*. Your heart races whenever I tell you what to do."

Little experience? Halo the Smolderer? Despite having a former concubine? But why? Some kind of sexual hang-up? A species thing? An ancient vow? What! And he was *learning* her? *Why is that so sexy?*

He brushed the tip of his nose against hers. "I've never tasted a woman."

Her lips parted on a gasp. "Never?" But...he'd lived so long. "Just to be clear, you're, um, curious to try oral? With me?"

A slow dip of his chin. "Very much so. *Only* you."

Gulp. *I mean, if he's just handing out free orgasms...* She glided her hands over his arms, pausing to squeeze his biceps. Such intoxicating strength. "You must desire me greatly," she said softly.

"Exactly as you desire me." He pressed his forehead to hers. "You desire me *specifically*, and I'll hear you admit it."

Her "anyone will do" barb bothered him even now? Guilt swelled and pitched. "I do desire you, Halo." Why deny the truth when she was oh, so slowly grinding against him? "You specifically."

Triumph lit his expression, and he nipped her bottom lip. "I will taste you today. Now. You'll wear the collar and nothing else. You will scream my name."

A ragged puff of air left her. *I will?* "You'll keep our bargain? No penetration besides fingers—and please do feel free to use your fingers vigorously...and often—even if I beg for it?"

"Nymph, you will beg me. That, I promise you. Though your virtue isn't safe with me, your will and body are. Protecting you is a priority for me."

Her. A priority. *I might be his gravita, after all.*

"Let's make you more comfortable."

"Let's," she breathed.

Irises spinning faster, *alevala* trading places, he walked her toward the side of the bed. The warlord and his battle prize. His intensity razed more and more of her control.

The flash of a wicked grin. Because he knew. With one hand, he cupped her jaw...with the other, he unzipped her leathers. He traced a thumb over the rise of her cheek at the same time he fingered the elastic band of her panties. Sensation rampaged what little remained of her control, and she groaned.

"Do you want my mouth between your legs?" His voice was pure silk, the needle-point edges of his strain blunted. He returned his grip to her backside—inside her panties. Skin to skin. Wild, searing heat. Kneading the generous mounds, he rasped, "Should I stop?" The kneading stopped. He removed one hand, then the other. "Or is there something else you'd like to say to me, nymph?" Triumph dripped from his voice. Possession darkened his expression.

Did he sense his victory? Trembling, Ophelia clung to him. "Yes. Taste me, Halo. Yes, yes, yes."

In a blur of motion, he clasped the back of her thighs and tossed her backward. She hit the bed and bounced. Only after he'd discarded her boots and placed her feet where he wanted them—at the edge of the mattress and spread—did he slow and straighten.

Her heart thundered.

"Let's get this out of our way." All lethal grace, he clasped the neckline of his shirt and pulled. The garment slipped over his head, revealing more muscles and *alevala*.

Careful. Now wasn't the time to view a memory of his past. Miss a moment of this? No! Skipping her gaze over the expressive faces, she noted every sculpted ridge of strength and line of sinew. A dark happy trail led to the waist of his pants, where a massive erection battled the leather, and her mouth watered.

"I like having you at my command, Elia."

This was Halo at his most primal.

With slow precision, he removed her socks. A flick of his wrists, and her leathers whooshed from her, baring the full length of her legs.

Ophelia tore off the sweater, the tank top, leaving herself in the mismatched bra and panties. The different patterns didn't seem to bother him as she reached for those, too. On the contrary, he appeared fascinated by each piece.

He leaned forward and stilled her hands, his gaze roving over her. "Will never get enough of your body."

Undulating, panting, she rasped, "You think me beautiful, Halo?" His warmth swathed her, scenting her every breath with smoked cherries and sandalwood. The most intoxicating fragrance in the world.

"I think my Elia is a revelation."

His Elia? Her lids sank low.

"I can scent your honey, nymph. I'm eager to sample it, but too much am I enjoying your unwrapping." He wedged his legs more firmly between hers, forcing her to spread wider, then he unhooked the center clasp of her bra. His hand trembled.

The male who revealed no weaknesses on the battlefield quaked for her? Ophelia Falconcrest? The Flunk Out? A plea for more, for everything, brewed on the back of her tongue.

He parted the bra's cups gradually, deliberately, as if he were indeed unwrapping a gift. At the sight of her breasts, he ran his lower lip between his teeth. "More perfect than I remembered."

Her heartbeat turned frenzied when he hooked his index fingers into her miniscule panties and tugged. Rational thoughts faded when he pocketed the undergarment. His second pair that day.

"A banquet of need," he praised, peering at her tuft of sable curls as though dazed. "My banquet. Look at how much you desire me." He reached out and slicked an index finger through her wetness.

Upon first contact, a rapturous lightning strike whipped over Ophelia. Her spine bowed, and she cried out.

A growl rose from her companion. "My sweet little nymph is teaching me what I enjoy. Topping the list is the sound of your pleasure." He brought that wet index finger to his mouth and sucked, his eyes closing for a moment. When his lids parted, he was staring straight at her. Hunger frothed in the depths of his irises. "There is *nothing* better than your taste."

Emotionless? Hardly. This male *seethed* with desire.

He dipped the finger to her again—inside her. Crying out, arching, she welcomed him. But he didn't thrust in a second time like she wanted, needed. No, he withdrew and licked himself clean, stealing another sampling.

"I want this every day, and you will give it to me." Dip. Lick. As if she were a bowl of candy.

She should protest the "every day" thing. And she would. Just as soon as she could think. Which she would do just as soon as he stopped turning her on and on and on and on.

"Halo! Do *more*."

Holding her legs open at the knees, he sank to his. His lids dropped to half-mast as he studied her aching core. Finally, when she could stand it no longer, he leaned in…close, but not close enough. His lips hovered over the spot she ached. One flick. Just one. Maybe a few dozen.

Did he fear he'd reached a point of no return with her? That he'd approached his final opportunity to retreat?

More and more desperate, she croaked, "Do it or don't." She almost begged him for sex, as feared. But she didn't. And she wouldn't. She wouldn't, she wouldn't, she wouldn't. Either he wanted her enough to proceed or he didn't. "Halo? Which is it?" The waiting was agony.

"Yes, Elia. Yes." A hoarse sound left him, and he dove down, licking her. His eyes rolled back. "More delicious straight from the source."

He licked again. And again. He *devoured*. Ophelia writhed, moaning and groaning. Though his control frayed before her eyes, right along with hers, he was a dedicated student, learning what she liked. What she responded to loudest, he repeated most.

"Can feel you swelling for me." He did something amazing with his tongue.

Ah! She undulated faster, crying, "More, Astra!"

Halo set in like a madman finally untethered. Ophelia

thrashed, getting lost in the throes. Her good sense? Gone. She wanted...*she wanted!* So, so, so, so badly. Nothing but climaxing mattered.

When he drove his tongue into her core, mimicking the motions of sex, she thought she saw stars. Then he brought his fingers into play, a digit penetrating her slowly.

"Yes! Yes, yes, yes, Halo." She rolled her hips, trying to grind on him. Cupping her breasts. Tugging at her nipples. Her pinned wings fluttered, vibrations racing over the ridges of her spine. "More!"

"Greedy harpy. I'll give you all the more you can handle." Savage need darkened his expression as he plunged another finger inside her. "When I reciprocate myself, you're going to watch me."

What a tantalizing thought. If only she could think past... he...she... Too many years had passed since she'd experienced fingers and stretching and pressure. But never had she experienced sexual banter, challenge and fevered commands at the same time. Never had she been with an ultra-intense warlord who looked like he'd found his new favorite toy.

"You think I'm a decadent treat, Immortal?" she asked between panting breaths.

"Never sampled anything better, nymph," he growled against her slick flesh.

Nails scraping through his silken hair, hips rising to meet his seeking tongue. "Don't stop. Need this. Need this so much."

No, no. She didn't *need* anything. She... *Can't think.* Was this...was she lust-drunk? Her mind was fogged, every fragmented thought branching into another. *More. Don't stop. Give me. Need. No. Want. Yes, yes, yes!*

He sucked on her at the same time he plunged those fingers deep and...bliss! Pressure broke, pleasure flooding her entire body.

"It's even sweeter now," he said, growing more frenzied with every swipe. Driving her from satisfied to desperate in a blink.

Not enough. So empty. "Maybe...maybe let's have sex, after all. Okay? All right?" The words left her, her newfound strength and confidence no match for this deluge of rapture. *Won't beg, won't beg, won't beg.* "We can play just the tip. What do you think? That's a good plan, isn't it? Just the tip? I'll make you feel so good."

"No sex." Features stark, he leaped to his feet. His body seemed to have doubled in size, his skin taut over muscle as he tore open his leathers.

Her jaw dropped when his erection sprang free. The size of this male. "Let's definitely have sex immediately. Yes?" She reached for him— No?

The Astra avoided her grip. "Will feel you against me, nothing more," he told her, his voice practically inhuman. He *looked* inhuman as he hooked his arms under her knees and spread her legs wider. Desire had removed any filters of humanity.

He rolled his hips, rubbing his shaft against her, male to female, without penetration, and hissed in a breath.

He resisted his own desperate needs in order to keep his word to her? Ophelia moaned and thrashed, erupting beneath him, coming again with a scream...but still wanting more. Needing it. "Don't stop, Halo. Please, please, don't stop."

"That's right. Say *my* name. I make you feel this way. Me and no other."

Frantic need ruled Halo. He struggled to maintain his iron control, but the pleasure... He'd never encountered its like. The female was *affecting* him. An unwanted internal softening. A jagged ache. A clawing desperation to possess someone, body and soul.

His usual tension had dissipated completely, replaced by all-consuming desire. Arousal burned in every inch of him, and he could not get enough. Not of this, and not of her. The nymph was a wild thing beneath him, thrashing over the covers, hair like tangled ribbons around her delicate shoulders. A hot flush lent her flawless skin a darker undertone. Her nipples were hard little points, her sex drenched with the desire he'd drawn from her.

How had he *ever* settled for subdued trysts? He was…this… *nothing* compared to it. Because of her.

Can't give this up.

"Halo, Halo, Halo," she chanted, hooking her legs around him to yank his muscled weight atop her. Brilliant green eyes glazed. "Kiss me."

At her nape, he fisted a length of her hair. He angled her head and took her mouth, because he couldn't not do it. Tongues tangling, he glided his shaft against her wetness, pressing, tormenting, but never entering. Could his fragile control *handle* penetration? Not yet, not yet. Not until she was ready.

"Halo!" Another scream of rapture broke from her. Another climax achieved.

The sight of her, lost to the pleasure, left him nigh mindless. He wrestled with the urge to follow her over the edge. *Not ready.* Here, now, he wasn't simply without strain; he had no gears. They'd ceased to exist, and it was *ecstasy.* But as he rubbed and thrust and ground against her, his body didn't care if he was prepared for the end or not. Seed erupted from him, lashing over her belly. Ribbon after ribbon after ribbon, as if he'd saved a lifetime supply.

When he had emptied himself, he collapsed and rolled to his side next to her. As he panted, his heart racing, he expected the gears to return. Instead, bliss cascaded over him. He couldn't think. Could only smile. Euphoric state? *I'm there.* But what was that strange feeling in his chest?

"Halo?" A soft entreaty with a hint of vulnerability.

With effort, he blinked into focus and realized a good amount of time had passed. Ophelia was mostly cleaned up and pliant, her body curled into his.

Magnificent female. He reached out to smooth a lock of hair from her cheek, a beam of sunlight striking his palm. He frowned. No stardust. Why? It made no sense. She *must* be his *gravita*. The way he had reacted to her...

He *wanted* her to be his *gravita*.

Crrrrank. The gears. Not gone, just hidden. Now they chugged into action, everything in his chest pulling tighter. In seconds, the strain was nearly unbearable.

She noticed his preoccupation with his hand, paled, and jolted upright. "Well. I'm gonna clean up for real. Alone. I mean it. Enter the bathroom, and I'll straight up murder your future children. And there's no need for us to talk about what happened. In fact, let's pretend it didn't. Okay? Yes. Good plan. Okay, bye for now."

Naked, she scrambled out of the bed and raced to the bathroom, where she sealed herself, leaving Halo alone and floundering.

He flopped to his back and rubbed his aching chest, scowling at the ceiling. What was he going to do now?

12

What have I done?

Ophelia's wings fluttered so swiftly they buzzed. The rest of her trembled. She was hornier than ever and wildly adrift as she twisted different knobs in the shower. When water finally rained from a spout, already steaming, she dunked under the spray. A good washing should free her of the most powerful flood of pleasure she'd ever experienced, this awful vulnerability, and the remnants of Halo's spunk, all at the same time.

Halo, the Astra who had rocked her world *without* producing stardust for her. No stardust, no *gravita*. She'd hoped…she'd taken a risk…she'd crashed and burned.

Satisfaction waltzed with contentment, the two seamlessly entangled and farther out of her reach than ever before. On top of that, she had a third set of relationship woes to cart around for the rest of eternity. Remembering, hungering, comparing everything and everyone to the Astra, and finding them all lacking.

The Immortal had warmed her from the inside out—he still did. A low-grade fever continued to heat her from the inside. Her constant chill? Gone. But soon, the heat would fade and the chill would return. She couldn't, wouldn't, allow herself to seek more. She wasn't his *gravita*; someone else was. The moment he met that someone, Ophelia would be tossed aside. Forgotten. No reason to try for something romantic.

The saddest part was she had known better than to do this. She wasn't like other harpies. She couldn't take a lover here and there without consequences. Arousal short-circuited her brain, reducing her to a ravenous state.

Her goals hadn't changed. Although, now that she thought about it, she was recovering from the quote, unquote most powerful flood of pleasure she'd ever experienced much faster than she'd ever recovered from an everyday, average orgasm. She shouldn't be coherent until morning. At least!

Another benefit of her transformation and death? The ability to snap out of the "nymph haze" and control any residual desires. That…didn't suck. And really, the abstinence thing didn't need to last forever now. No, Halo wasn't her male. But someone else was. One day, she would find him and rediscover heat and passion and satisfaction.

Ophelia used the shampoo, conditioner, and body wash. The sugar scrub, too. And the previous owner's jasmine-scented oil. Basically, a spa treatment. Because what else was she going to do? Snuggle with Halo?

Tremors invaded her limbs. When the water chilled, Ophelia abandoned the stall and raided the spacious walk-in closet with rack after rack of clothing in an array of styles. Gorgeous gowns. Slinky man-bait bodysuits. T-shirt with slits for wings. Shorts. The jeans looked miles too long.

T-shirt and shorts it is. Going without underwear, Ophelia shimmied into the top, the material pulling taut over her plump breasts. The soft cotton abraded sensitive nipples. New aches bloomed.

Ignore. Shoes. She needed shoes.

"I'm a few minutes too late for the reverse strip show, I see." The familiar voice came from behind her, every word laden with smugness.

Erebus.

Aggression rippled through her wings, and she whirled. He stood mere feet away, wearing his patented evil overlord smile and a black robe. His bulky frame consumed too much space.

He might not get to transform her into another beast for the rest of the week, but he could certainly cause trouble, as predicted by Halo. Though part of her demanded she alert the Astra, she stayed silent. This god was the golden ticket to victory. Halo's task. Ophelia's dream. She wasn't taking *herself* out of the game.

"As the wheels turn in your mind, let me help your common sense win the debate," Erebus said, amused. "No, you shouldn't call for the Astra. He can't sense me or hear us. I've soundproofed the room." His craggy features brightened. "Or perhaps I'm wrong and you *should* invite him into the conversation. You can expound upon your adventures as the lioness and explain you're soon to become a hydra."

Ophelia readied her claws for attack. "Don't think to call my bluff. You don't want him to know what you do to me." Otherwise, Erebus would've gotten his brag on long before now.

Or he merely bided his time…

Foreboding prickled her nape.

"Why didn't *you* tell him?" he asked, thoughtful.

"I don't need to share my reasons with you."

"True." His gaze slipped past her, looking somewhere she couldn't see. The cold draft kicked up, infiltrating her bones. Her teeth chattered. Appearing a bit unhinged, he muttered, "I can see only the what, never the why. Move the pieces. Complete the puzzle."

Pieces? Puzzle? "Um. Would you like a moment alone with your insanity?"

He blinked into focus and smiled. "Nice collar. It stops me from summoning you properly. But there are two inherent flaws with this form of personal protection. Today, I'll demonstrate the first. In person, the disk can be forcibly lifted. I'll have no trouble overseeing your transformation tonight."

Whoa, whoa, whoa. She was to battle Halo *tonight*? Mere minutes after rolling around with him in bed? But...she didn't want to battle him right now. There were too many feelings left to conquer.

"Aren't you supposed to wait seven days between labors?" she demanded.

"Yes and no. Seven days from now is also today." His smile widened, slightly maniacal. "Loopholes are fun, aren't they? But don't worry. You're going to be a far better opponent this go-round. A hydra with the savagery of a lioness."

"You can't do this," she grated. Halo wasn't ready.

"On the contrary. I can do anything. But you...you'd like to. You already feel the creature's effects on you, do you not? Imagine the power at your fingertips when you are imbued with *every* beast."

Dread warred with eagerness. Nine of Hercules's twelve labors had involved beasts. Strength that was hers for the taking.

You're so weak, Ophelia.

Not anymore, sister. She had a plan, and she was sticking to it. No matter what. Collect as much strength as possible, turn on the god, save harpykind, win Halo's task, and bask in the glory. "What do you expect from me?"

"Cooperation, harpy, nothing more."

No. There was absolutely something more. Because honestly? He didn't exactly need her cooperation. Did he seek bragging rights? A tidbit to later lord over Halo? The old, "I won over your girl" trick.

"You'll find I make a wonderful ally," he continued, giving her the hard sell. "Oh, I may strike you as pitiless upon occasion—and in the coming minutes—but you'll thank me for it one day. I've peered into the future, you see, and selected the best paths. I *will* win in the end, I promise you."

"And if I refuse to cooperate?" she asked, knowing she shouldn't appear too eager.

He shrugged, unconcerned. "I'll use you, anyway."

"Yeah. I figured that." To beat this god, she needed to learn his weaknesses and tells. The way Halo had learned hers. The best way to do that? Attack. And there was no better time.

Ophelia didn't spend precious moments debating what to do. She leaped, raking her claws over his throat. Skin and muscle tore, hot blood pouring. He evinced no reaction, however. Just smiled wider and wrapped a stalwart arm around her waist, locking her against him. As she struggled, he tightened his grip, cracking her ribs.

"Wrong choice," he told her, sounding delighted. "But don't worry. I won't punish you for it. I understand your reluctance. To prove my goodwill, I'll even ensure you suffer no heinous deaths for the full week after this. A time to get to know your new lover better. For now..."

As phantoms appeared, grabbing her arms and legs to hold her in place, he withdrew a dagger. *The* dagger.

The two sides of her warred. Fight harder—or carry on? What was this weapon, exactly? What all could it do? How did it change her?

"Ready?" He shoved the tip of the dagger under her skin, beneath the disk—and carved.

Searing pain swamped her, and she screamed. Black dots swarmed in her vision. She nearly vomited.

When he finished, a gaping hole decorated her chest, a jagged circle of raw muscle on display. He grinned, his white teeth penetrating her veil of pain. "There. That's better." He pressed the blade flat against her chest, no disk in the way.

Blood gurgled from her mouth, speech beyond her as she wheezed.

As a soft red glow shone brighter and brighter, he announced, "The primordial hydra, with augmentations."

Her pain escalated, rolling through her like thunder. No part of her was unaffected. On her shoulders, skin tore, something growing from her body. Rising. Snapping teeth at the air.

Boils appeared on her skin only to burst open and hardened into steel-hard scales. Bones lengthened and reshaped. Muscles ripped, sprouting new ones.

The god backed away from her as the instinct to kill hit. But not Halo. Erebus. All twelve versions of him.

Twelve? Comprehension dawned. Twelve sets of eyes—twelve heads. Twelve mouths. She licked her tongues over shockingly sharp teeth. *Kill.*

"More magnificent than I dared dream," Erebus said, clapping. "Now be a good girl and do your best to kill our man. Kill Halo Phaninon."

Kill Halo. Yes. Halo must die. She caught a whiff of his scent. Sniff, sniff. There.

Ophelia launched forward and barreled through some kind of an obstacle. In the back of her mind, she heard a trumpet blare. The perfect melody for her mantra. *Kill Halo. Kill. Kill...*

Three minutes earlier

Awaiting Ophelia's return, Halo paced through the bedroom. He'd righted his clothing, but not his mind. They had things to discuss.

He glanced at the doorway that blocked the female from his view. This separation from her...he didn't like it. He wanted his gaze on her always. If Erebus made another play for her...

What was she doing in there, anyway? Avoiding him? The water had shut off five minutes and thirty-four seconds ago. Did she regret what they'd done together? Did he?

He hadn't produced stardust. The harpymph had climax and bolted. His strain hadn't lessened for long…but he wanted to do everything again.

How was any of this helping him?

He scowled. He'd be better off pondering Erebus. How would the god strike next? What was the Bloodmor and what could it do besides harm Halo more than the Blade of Destiny? Had the Bloodmor *summoned* the lioness, perhaps? Would the weapon summon the other beasts? There must be a link between the two, considering those beasts would help determine whether or not Halo won.

Apprehension skittered down his spine, and he cast another glance at the bathroom door. "Ophelia?"

No response. Unacceptable. Halo had waited long enough. Muscles swelling with sudden aggression, he palmed a three-blade and prepared to enter.

Outside the palace, a trumpet sounded, and he went still. The second test? Now?

Impossible. Not enough time had passed between labors. Not without a loophole.

Halo cursed. When no other blasts sounded, he shouted, "Halo Phaninon." Another battle to the death.

The foundation shook. No, not just the foundation. The entire room quaked. Something was coming, and it was close.

He braced—a monster rammed through the bathroom door, pieces of wood flying in every direction.

"Ophelia!" he shouted, cataloging a wealth of details in a split second. A hydra. From an all-female species, like harpies and Amazons. A smallish she-dragon merged with a massive serpent, making her the size of a shire horse. Twelve heads, each with a mouth full of metal teeth. One body, with two arms and two legs tipped by razored claws. Firstone bands circled her wrists.

She smelled of some kind of venom and— Roaring, Halo attacked. The harpy's scent coated this creature.

Rage surged anew, flooding him with unparalleled strength. Erebus had gotten to her. And Halo had let it happen. His little beauty, dead again. Killed by this hydra after he'd promised to protect her.

The first sparks of *anhilla* threatened to torch his control.

Heads attacked him from different angles, dagger-teeth snapping in every direction. Up, left, right, down, and every space in between. He flashed—no. The firstone. No flashing and no summoning new weapons.

Very well. Halo fought his way to the wall, where artillery hung. Not swiftly enough. Teeth sank into each of his calves, the metal laced with saliva. Venomous? Though the Astra were immune to most poisons, this one registered as *not right*. Almost as...sexual desire? A mating drug, then?

Disgusted, he swiped a sword from its hook. Ducked and dodged, moving from spot to spot as the she-beast chased him. He avoided cutting off her heads but stabbed her any chance he got. The eyes. The belly. The throat. Her limbs.

She was a fast healer. Her scales proved tough but not impenetrable. Small horns ran the length of each neck. Well-defined musculature protected vital organs. A single tail split into twelve barbed whips.

Her biggest tell: those barbs twitched a split second before a head struck at him.

Like now. Barb twitch. He ducked, swooping in to remove a horn.

An agonized howl burst his eardrums. As warm blood leaked from his ears, he launched into action before she had time to heal, plunging the blade through the meaty center of the severed horn. Another howl rent the air.

Protect. The urge surfaced, stronger with this hydra than the lioness. Again, he resisted, knowing the sensation stemmed from Ophelia's scent.

Had she died screaming?

Another spark of anhilla. He struck with more force. The hydra snapped at him there, there, there, and also there, there, and there and flung him across the bedroom. Furniture exploded upon impact. Sections of the wall came tumbling down, dust coating the air.

Halo returned to her and sank his sword into her gut. Thicker, blacker blood gushed from the wound. The pool foamed as it ate through the wood floor. Even his blade began to disintegrate.

A plan formed as he exchanged the weapon for another. He barreled through the hole in the wall, leading his opponent into the hallway. While he enjoyed close quarters combat as much as the next Astra, he preferred wide-open spaces and distance from Ophelia's...from her body.

The hydra gave chase. Down a flight of stairs. In a sitting room, where a multitude of swords hung. Ignoring the harpies frozen in time, she kept her sights on Halo.

Ophelia's scent only intensified, and new suspicions arose. What if the lioness and hydra were somehow *linked* to the harpymph? That would mean Erebus had, what? Stabbed her with the Bloodmor and used her blood to resurrect the monsters? Summon them, as Halo had first supposed? Build them from scratch? Open a portal for them? A blood sacrifice wasn't uncommon among those of their ilk, the power of it renowned.

He slowed his strikes. The she-beast huffed and puffed, spraying spittle from her many mouths, but she too slowed.

Interesting. They circled each other, around and around. Twelve sets of eyes tracked his every movement with ferocious intent. How he wished he possessed Silver's ability to read minds.

"You want a piece of me? Come and get it."

Tail twitch. He dodged and brawled his way behind her,

grabbed a log from the hearth—for some reason, the flames had not frozen. A gift from Chaos?

Halo pressed the blazing log against his sword. The flames licked the metal as he ducked and dodged the next series of strikes. At the first opportunity, he thrust the white-hot metal straight into a horn, hilt-deep, severing one of her spinal cords. The attached head immediately sagged to the floor, useless.

He left the weapon in place. She only fought harder with her remaining heads. Fangs tore through his abdomen, shredding organs. Other fangs sank into his calf, more lust-inducing venom invading his system. Muscles seized. Sweat beaded his brow. His heart galloped, and his vision blurred. He'd never felt worse. Or better. He took down a second head. And a third. A fourth.

No mercy! Again and again, Halo claimed and heated a sword, then plugged the blade into a horn. Soon, a single head remained.

In a frenzy, the hydra charged him. She tripped over those flopping necks but didn't stop. With the force of a rocket, she slammed into him, taking him to the floor. Her final mistake.

He had only to thrust his sword up, cutting through the underside of her snout to her brain. As she flopped over, a trumpet signaled the end of another battle. Another victory.

Once again, nothing felt right. Halo hunched over and emptied the contents of his stomach.

When he finished, he flashed to his bedroom closet. He would collect Ophelia's remains. But, as he searched the blood-splattered rubble, he found no sign of her body. The trinite collar lay in shambles, bits of the harpymph's flesh stuck to the edges of the disk.

A terrible thought occurred to him. Had she removed the necklace herself, allowing Erebus to ambush Halo?

His hands fisted. He worked his jaw. Tomorrow, he and Ophelia would have a chat…

13

6:00 a.m.
Day 4

Ophelia sensed movement and opened her eyes, every inch of her crackling with energy. As her morning visitor attempted to whisk off her bedcovers, she caught the edge and held the blankets in steady claws without much effort.

"Get your lazy butt out of—oh. Good morning, sunshine. I guess you can keep those." Bright light streamed into the window, highlighting Vivi's surprise. "Time to start our day. We've got things to do."

"Oh, yes. We do indeed." Ophelia eased upright and took stock. No sign of a hangover whatsoever. Excellent. No lingering battle pains either. Full battery charge, defenses on high alert.

Try to take me down now, Erebus. Dare you.

"Wow. Okay. You look scary intense," Vivi remarked. "Not

hungover at all. Honestly, I expected an all-out war with you this morning."

"Let's just say I lost my heads over a guy." A mountain of a male who had pleasured her senseless, ratcheting her vulnerability to new heights, only to brutally murder her minutes later. From sensual caresses to stark realization—no stardust—then agonizing strikes.

The incongruity screwed with her head. She didn't know whether she wanted to run to him or from him.

During this most recent battle, Halo had been utterly methodical, purpose steeping his every action. He'd watched and he'd learned. He'd patiently worked to weaken her. Any time he'd focused on her, she'd hurt. Even worse, he had projected all kinds of suspicions before rendering the death blow. Had he realized the truth? Did he know Ophelia was the hydra?

Her claws grew, slicing through the blankets. Halo had questions, no doubt. Questions she wasn't prepared to answer. Not until she'd pondered everything without a haze of arousal or a looming threat of death. New developments—loopholes—meant new paths to consider. And what about the dagger Erebus kept using on her? It had taken total control of her will, complicating her original plan.

So. Should she tell Halo the truth, the full truth and nothing but the truth? Or should she forge ahead?

Ophelia was done making mistakes. *Gotta get this right.* A good outcome had never been so important. Like Halo would really give her a time-out, though. For an emotionless hulk, he lacked patience.

He's coming for me. Soon.

Her heart thudded. If she were lucky, he intended to visit the palace foyer to see if the hydra's head hung next to the lioness's, granting her time to, well, buy herself more time.

"Yo. Lady O." Vivi clapped for attention. "I'm still here. Ignoring me won't make me go away."

Right. "I need a minute to prepare, then we can head out."
She sprang from the bed and rushed to the bathroom to brush
her teeth and change. Today struck her as an armor-up day.

"So. Listen," she called while changing. "This day has been
repeating. Basically, Groundhog Day on steroids." The walls
had ears, yes, but she had to risk it. There were things Vivi
should know.

"Oookay."

Now. How to tell her the rest without alerting others? Oh!
Duh. She stepped into the bathroom doorway to sign her next
words, a skill they had acquired at training camp. *Twice Erebus
has morphed me into a monster and an Astra has killed me.*

Did you say an Astra killed you? Twice? Vivi signed back.

"I did. Oh, Halo might believe I'm his fated mate." She didn't
mind speaking that part out loud. But *was* she his mate? Forget the stardust. No immortal—especially *the* Immortal—had
ever wittingly or unwittingly slain his fated one. Right? Unless he lacked a heart. Which was a distinct possibility in this
situation. She ushered her friend into the hallway. "I'll explain
everything else in town."

"Town? And did you say *mate*?"

"Yes and yes. Now come on."

They ran out of the barracks, away from the palace and toward
the training grounds. A cool breeze rolled past, fragrant with
morning dew. Harpies practiced with an assortment of weapons while a group of Roc's soldiers hung around and drooled.

Seeing the vampires hanging with the shifters and trolls,
Ophelia remembered just how unstoppable the unit was. To
face the full force on the battlefield? Certain death.

She and Vivi reached the town square. The shops had yet to
open, but it hardly mattered. Considering the number of harpies and consorts who had walked the streets every day for centuries, muddying the scents, Ophelia would be harder to track
here. So far, so good.

"Well?" Vivi demanded. "Start talking. Leave nothing out."

She spilled everything. By the time she finished, her friend was agog.

"Time loops, monster mashes, and sexy times. Oh my!" Vivi jumped over a fallen branch from the Tree of Skulls. Best friends rocked. You didn't have to waste valuable moments with disbelief. "You get to add your new, special skill to your résumé. Something no one else can *ever* claim. You've died saving the Astra *three* times. Do you know what this means?" She nudged Ophelia's shoulder as they power walked the abandoned streets. "I get to be proud of myself. I picked the winning horse the day I saved your life and let you become my best friend. You'll spit out a brood of ginormous Astra babies, and I'll be the amazing aunt who pretends to hate babysitting while teaching the little fiends how to make their father's life miserable. And don't try to talk me out of that. He deserves it for killing you."

Her wings fluttered with…something. The thought of kids. With Halo. A family of her own. More pleasure. Deeper connection.

Her cheeks burned as they turned a corner and slipped down an alleyway. Considering making babies with the guy she'd known for a millisecond—who'd killed her twice—was too much, even for her. Right? Yes? Maybe?

"What's the plan?" Vivi asked.

"For you, a trip to the library. Grab a book that details Hercules's labors." Lion, hydra and then…hind? "And, I mean, since you're gonna be there, you should probably pick up something about how to properly train a house-robot. It's information I need for the task, and that's all I'm going to say on the matter. I'll be waiting for you in Haronly."

Harpies—only. A pocket subrealm newly created by the Astra at Taliyah's insistence. The garden oasis was touted as a refuge for harpies. An Astra-free zone. An unauthorized entry served as a declaration of war. The sole entrance was located on the outskirts of the town square, near the trinite wall. Ophelia had never desired to go. Until now.

"Um, defensive much?" Vivi asked.

They turned another corner—and drew up short. The dark-haired, mercury-eyed Astra loomed ahead, on patrol with a unit of soldiers. Silver noticed them. Because of course he did.

A hulking tower of disapproval, he sent the unit onward and flashed closer. "These streets are closed to citizens this morning. You will leave, or I will make you."

"Will you use your words to make me or your big, strong muscles?" Vivi twirled a lock of hair and smacked her lips. "No pressure, but my response kind of depends on yours."

Silver's scowl downgraded into a frown rife with confusion. Not used to dealing with harpies? Helpful hint: *always expect the unexpected.*

He focused on Ophelia, then canted his head with inhuman grace. Something Halo did as well. A learned trait? "You match the description of the one Halo searches for," he said. "Your friend will leave, and you will stay."

Stupid telepathy. No doubt Silver had already informed Halo, who would arrive—

Halo arrived. He was a live wire of aggression as he materialized beside his comrade. No blank mask today. He glared at Ophelia, the trinite collar dangling from his grip.

Her heart kicked into overdrive, her inhalations shallowing. Smoked cherries and sandalwood. Heat. Her downfall. Familiar tremors set in.

"We have much to discuss, harpy." A muscle jumped in his jaw, his biggest tell. *Huge mad.*

Too bad. "Sorry, sport, but I'm taking a breather from you today."

Silver glanced between them. "Perhaps I should take the female—"

"The female is *mine*," Halo snarled, and oh, wow, he looked close to drawing a sword on his friend.

Okay, how hot was that?

He reached out to clasp her hand, and she flinched from his touch, despite her low-simmer of arousal. An automatic and instinctual reaction as her mind shouted, *Attack!*

His brows dropped low, and his body tensed up. He fisted his hands.

"I see why you admire him," Vivi said, fanning her cheeks.

That's my cue. "Don't forget my books," Ophelia called, shooting off faster than a bullet.

Big surprise, Halo gave chase. "The farther you run from me," he bellowed, "the worse your punishment will be."

She almost laughed. "You gotta catch me first."

He reached out. She sensed and dodged. He flashed, but she detected a disturbance in the air before he landed and evaded. Any time he made contact, she slipped free. Something had come over her. A burning force. The strength she'd earned with each transformation?

Was this how the Astra felt every moment of every day? Unstoppable? How liberating!

Why would she not want more of this?

They passed different units on patrol. Halo barreled through them all, unwilling to let anyone or thing get between him and his target. Man, that was sexy.

More soldiers. More collisions.

"Ophelia!"

A glance over her shoulder. Silver materialized just ahead of Halo, and the two slammed together. *How do you like it, douchebag?*

Oops. Halo didn't take the brunt of the impact; Silver did, flying across the street, flipping end over end. Her Astra never slowed.

She pumped her arms with more force. *Just a little farther.* Destination ahead. A flowery archway seeming to lead to nowhere.

With single-minded determination, she dove…yes! Ophelia entered Haronly, leaving Halo in her dust.

Halo paced the sidewalk near the door to Haronly, his mask of civility nearly frayed beyond repair. Hours had passed since Ophelia's disappearance inside the subrealm. A mystical veil concealed her scent, and he almost couldn't cope. The frenzy inside his head…

Growls rumbled in his chest without cease. He just needed to see her. To hold her, perhaps. To spank the fire out of her backside, definitely. Or not. Why had she cringed from his touch, as if she expected pain?

He pulled at hanks of his hair. Checked the time. Half-past 1:00 p.m. There'd been no freeze. Erebus had lost another hour then. Since the loophole removed all hint of rules, the god might attack anytime after 2:00 p.m.

Halo rubbed a raw spot on his chest. If he didn't lay his eyes on the harpy soon, heads were sure to roll.

From now until the completion of the task, he intended to keep Ophelia close. Within his eyesight, without fail. Roc was right. She was involved in the task, an influence for the ultimate showdown.

Halo had a thousand questions; she had all the answers. Some queries singed deeper than others. Why had she hidden herself in Haronly? Why had she cringed from his touch? Did she aid Erebus? Was her blood linked to the beasts? Did she blame Halo for her suffering?

Inhale. Exhale. A crazed sound left him. *Is she my gravita?* He hadn't ruled out the possibility. How could he? He had nearly attacked a brother over her handling. That wasn't something "the polite one" did.

If he must have a fated mate, it might as well be the female who smelled like paradise, made him forget his struggles and come so hard his entire world spun out of orbit before he'd even gotten inside her. Most of all, he thought he might *like* the wily, cagey temptress.

"Be at ease, warlord."

A familiar voice penetrated his awareness, even as Halo continued pacing. Celestian "Ian" Eosphorus. The kindest and cruelest among them. A powerful male with dark skin and black eyes. For some reason, he had shorn his dark braids this morning, and many Astra enjoyed teasing him over the lack.

Centuries ago, tradition stated an Astra should cut his hair when he was open to receiving offers of romantic affection. Ian was the only warlord who ascribed to the ancient custom.

If the warlord craved a fated mate, Halo had some advice for him. *Don't!*

Ian moved in front of him, blocking his path. "Be. At. Ease." An unmistakable command.

Halo's response was automatic. "Yes, Commander." As the greeting echoed in his head, he pinched the bridge of his nose. "Sorry. Ian."

In the very beginning, Ian had served as head of the Astra. Commander of the twenty. But he'd failed his first blessing task, refusing to sacrifice his bride. She had died anyway, the moment the Astra were cursed with five hundred years of defeat. That very day, Erebus and his brother, Asclepius Serpentes, waged a savage battle against them. They lost several warlords. When the dust had settled, Astra rankings had been rearranged, with Ian slated at the bottom.

A male named Solar had assumed command, with Roc as his second. They'd ruled the army for centuries. But everything had changed when Solar wed his *gravita*. Like Ian, he'd refused to sacrifice her. And like Ian's bride, she had died anyway. A second curse came down and more Astra were lost in battle. Just as before, the survivors received new ranks.

"You're doing it again. Losing sight of what's in front of you." Ian patted his cheek twice. If *patted* meant the same thing as *slapped*. "I have a lock on the friend, Vivian Eagleshield. Do you wish to speak to her or not?"

Halo gave a clipped nod. "Bring her to me."

In a blink, Ian flashed the female to his side without the aid of touch. A skill he had always possessed. Unlike Erebus.

The dark-haired beauty materialized, holding books with one hand and swinging the other. Her claws raked across Ian's throat. Blood welled from the jagged grooves, dripping out before his flesh wove back together.

Ian merely nodded a greeting at her.

"Oops. My bad," she said with a lazy grin. "Next time you force-flash me, sugar, do us both a favor and land me straight into your arms." She winked at Ian in a sultry invitation Halo didn't believe for a moment.

Indecision tore at him. How was he to proceed with this harpire? He knew what he preferred to do—threaten her in order to draw out Ophelia, showing no mercy to accomplish his will. But he also knew what he couldn't do—threaten the friend in order to draw out the harpymph, showing no mercy to accomplish his will. She would never pardon him; her loyalty wouldn't let her. Though he shouldn't care.

"How much has Ophelia told you about our situation?" He plucked the books from the harpire's grip, even while holding her gaze, silently demanding a swift response.

"Only everything." Another lazy smile bloomed. "Guess how much I'll be telling *you*?"

"You realize your refusal is a detriment to her, yes? If you are not aiding me, you are aiding Erebus, and he wishes to kill her. I wish only to protect her."

Delicate features scrunched with confusion. She scratched her temple. "Correct me if my math is off, but hasn't Lady O died, like, three times on your watch?"

Guilt and shame collided, those invisible gears cranking on.

Needing a moment, Halo glanced at the harpire's tomes. A

highlight of Hercules's labors and a manual titled *How to Tell if Your Robot Lover Catches Feelings*.

The labors. Because Ophelia knew she was linked to the monsters? Or because she still planned to aid him and earn her kill? The other book... Hmm.

"I will not let her die again." He pushed the statement through clenched teeth.

"Let's make a deal. Return my property and send me into Haronly with a message for our dear Lady O. Or..." Vivian ran a fingertip down the center of Ian's chest. "You can feel free to torture the information out of me. FYI, I have a particular aversion to tongue-lashings."

The corners of Ian's mouth twitched. "I've known Halo for thousands of lifetimes, and I'm confident of his will in this matter. He wishes me to get started with that tongue-lashing *immediately*."

How easily the male swayed from enforcer to seducer; a talent he'd always possessed. For once, Halo was envious.

He slid his gaze to the doorway blocking him from Ophelia. "Give her a message," he told the harpire, handing over the books. "Tell her I...request a meeting. There will be no more mysteries between us." He'd never stooped to bargaining before. But what other choice did he have? "In return, I'll give her anything she wants." *I will?* "Anything within reason that doesn't jeopardize my task. Or any Astra's task." Best to be clear. "But she has only five minutes to come out and respond—or I will go in and get her." The truce be damned.

Vivian winced with embarrassment for him. "She is *sooo* gonna outwit, outplay, and outlast you." After blowing him a kiss, she pivoted and sauntered off, strolling into Haronly.

As he awaited a response, he paced anew. Ophelia would agree to his terms. She must.

"I've never seen you so flustered," Ian said, watching him with unabashed curiosity. He'd always been an observer, the wheels constantly turning in his head. "I shouldn't be surprised. Roc acted the same way with Taliyah."

Halo quickened his stride. "The harpymph is a…shock." Her irresistible pull kept him on edge—until he got his hands on her. Then, the treasured ease came for a bit. A time he stopped fighting everything he felt, his past no match for his desire.

"I suggest you handle the female with care from now on, my friend. To qualify for ascension, Roc had to win Taliyah's heart. What if the same is true for you? For all of us? As I am learning, there is no greater force in existence than love."

He stopped. Winning Ophelia's heart. Her love. Yes! He liked this idea. She would cease running from him. Wouldn't flinch from his touch. Best of all, the female of his most fevered fantasies would *mind* him. He would regain his focus, pass his tests, and do his part for the mass ascension.

Why hadn't the harpy responded to his message yet? Ten seconds of the allotted time remained.

"I will do it. I will win her," he vowed. Nine. Eight. The fastest and clearest path to success? *Getting her into my bed.*

Yes! This. Seeds of anticipation planted in the rich soil of his mind.

Five. Four.

He cast his gaze to the subrealm's doorway, his heart racing. Three. His hands curled into fists. Two.

One.

The seeds withered, and up sprouted frustration, anger, and disappointment.

"Judging solely by Roc's courtship of Taliyah," Ian said, "your greatest chance of success is impromptu feasts your friends must rush to throw together, imprisoning your female for a short time and fingering her in public often."

Another minute passed. His nerves stretched taut. Ophelia had defied him—and proven him to be a liar in the process.

He would *not* be storming the door and fetching her. He ground his teeth.

Outwit, outplay, outlast, harpy? You're on.

He was the Immortal of Immortals, and *he would have his way!*

Finally, Vivian strolled from the mist without a care. "Phel says you can't complain about the delay. I was totally on time because there is no time. Oh, and she also says yes. She'll take your anything, but with caveats. She's staying in Haronly tonight, and that's that. She'll meet you in the palace foyer tomorrow morning at 8:00 a.m. to reveal those mysteries. Or a few minutes after. Depends on how long it takes her to catch me up, since I will remember none of this. I'm invited to the meeting as her advocate, obviously. She *insists*. So. Do you agree? You have three seconds to respond, or the offer is null and void. Three. Two."

"Oh, I agree," he stated. He thought he felt his lips curl into a grin. "Until tomorrow then."

By 8:00 a.m., he would have a battle plan.

That harpymph is mine.

14

With Vivian at her side, Ophelia climbed the one hundred steps leading to the front doors of the palace. Determination welded her spine straight. She would beat Halo to their meeting. This time, she would be the one waiting for *him*. He was right. They had things to discuss.

When she'd awoken this morning, tucked inside her bunkroom, she'd had no new infusion of strength—and she hadn't liked it. Because she had *needed* more, today especially. She'd known it the instant the trinite collar appeared on her nightstand, with additional symbols etched into the bands. The very reason she hadn't donned it.

What did those symbols do? Tether her to Halo's side? Probably. He wasn't above using the collar to get his way.

More than a discussion, they had a reckoning coming.

He'd included a note.

Don't be late. This time I'll come for you, wherever you happen to be. Wear something easy to remove.
Yours, H

Her wings fluttered with excitement. Or anger. Yes. Anger.

Despite the cool morning breeze, she'd opted to wear something sexy rather than protective. And yes, it was probably super easy to remove. Not that she'd heeded Halo's suggestion on purpose. She'd just really felt the garment's vibe. Whatever. It wasn't important. The sheer, cotton-candy-pink dress provided ample cleavage. A short, slitted skirt allowed peek-a-boo glances at her panties when she moved a certain way. Eight-inch stilettos with ribbons wrapped around her calves completed the outfit.

Halo had offered her a payment of her choosing, and she'd wanted to look her best when she informed him of the cost.

"I've never visited the palace this early in the morning, but I kind of expected a crowd flying in and out, not a ghost town," Vivi remarked. "You think the Astra ordered everyone away?"

More excitement—anger—trickled through Ophelia. Halo had beaten her to the foyer and driven everyone else out, hadn't he?

"Oh, yeah," she said. "Let's hustle."

"Dressed as a tasty snack *and* in a hurry." Vivi tsk-tsked. "What's becoming of my dear Lady O No. Is she catching feelings too?"

"My intentions are a hundred percent calculating, I swear!" After studying Hercules's labors and those shockingly sexy robot lovers, she'd come to a firm, unshakable decision. Better to leave Halo in the dark and continue on her current path. Die, strengthen, and override the god's control of her will, saving everyone. Her...fate. No copping to the truth. She wouldn't lie to him, but she wouldn't spill every detail about her association with Erebus either. No matter what Halo did or did not suspect or know.

What did he suspect? What did he know?

One thing was certain: He considered her an underdog, incapable of defeating such a powerful opponent. But he was wrong. They were all wrong. Ophelia could do this. She knew it; *felt* it. She needed only a chance to prove it.

Did guilt prick her, ever so lightly? Yes. His task, his rules. She got that. But what if her repeated deaths were a necessary part of his ultimate victory? A sacrifice they must both make? Hadn't Roc and Taliyah won *their* blessing task with a sacrifice?

"Explain your masterful calculation to me," Vivi said.

"The dress is my armor, okay?" she admitted. "In this situation, my best defense is my confidence." Halo would come at her one of two ways. Big boss man or eager plaything. Either way could prove fatal to her resolve to resist him.

No longer fresh from an agonizing death, Ophelia was having trouble shaking her desire for the Astra. But there would be no more making out. No more mind-shattering orgasms. Unless she decided to give the whole stardust thing another shot? And she probably should, if she were being honest. Finding her consort and entwine would only help her cause. Natural strength for the taking, independent of the beasts!

Once without stardust didn't equate to twice without stardust. The first time might have been an aberration, right? And had she even given Halo a genuine chance to mark her? Maybe she had to do some reciprocation first.

Mmm. Yes. Reciprocation. That seemed perfectly reasonable. Worth exploring, definitely.

"Phel, my love?" Vivi said with sunny delight.

"Yes?" Halo…naked…standing—no, reclining in a plush chair as she knelt between his legs…

"You are totally making out with yourself."

Wait. What? She blinked, only then realizing she was cupping her breasts. Her cheeks heated as she dropped her hands to her sides. "I could have been fixing my dress."

Vivi snickered. "Yeah. Sure."

They topped the steps, then soared across the front lawn and through open double doors. In unison, they halted. Oh, yes. Halo had indeed beaten her here. He stood in his usual spot, the foyer's only occupant, his arms crossed over his chest. Ophelia's In Trouble. In more ways than one.

He looked good. *Really* good. A white T-shirt molded to his broad shoulders and wide chest. Leathers hugged his tree-trunk thighs.

Built for the longest, roughest rides. Her mouth watered.

His gaze roved over her—slowly. He paused at her breasts. When her nipples drew tight beneath the fabric of her dress, he licked his lips. At her navel, he unveiled his teeth. The apex of her thighs spurred him to flick his tongue over an incisor.

Breathing was suddenly impossible for her, the air too thick. And yet still she smelled smoked cherries and sandalwood. One of her greatest weakness.

She averted her gaze before she forgot everything and hurled herself into his arms. Only then did she notice the wall behind him. The hydra did indeed hang next to the lioness. A single head graced the mount. A snapshot of horror that barraged Ophelia with, well, pride. Each death had brought them closer to Erebus's defeat.

"Dude," Vivi said from the corner of her mouth. "Is your guy always this intense when he stares at you? Because I'm getting serious side-high."

"You will leave us," Halo told her friend, never looking away from Ophelia. "I will be...gentle with the harpymph."

Oh, would he now?

"Gentle? Do you *want* to lose your personal war with our favorite harpymph?" Vivi asked. "But fine. Whatever. You command me gone, I'm gone." She kissed Ophelia's cheek, whispered, "You've so got this," and bounded away.

After a signed conversation this morning, all cards on the table, they'd agreed on the best plan of action. Leave Ophelia alone with the Astra. Find out what he knew, what he suspected, and deal with the consequences.

He flashed closer, summoned the collar to his grip and secured it around her neck, ensuring she didn't have a chance to fight.

So irritating! "What problems are the added runes gonna cause me?"

"They merely ensure you cannot carve out the disk."

Okay. That worked for her. How it rankled that Erebus was able to transform her on *his* terms. This was her origin story, after all, and she should wield her own agency for it. But, um—quick mental side journey—was her Astra radiating more heat than usual? And mmm. His scent. Was it richer?

A thin fog shrouded her mind, dragging her deeper under his spell. She acted without thought, slowly sliding her hands up his muscle-packed arms. "So powerful yet so soft."

The rasp of his breaths tickled her lips. His pupils enlarged, but the striations never stopped spinning. Smoke seemed to waft from the edges.

Resist him? Why try? She'd already rendered her decision. *Take a chance and give him another opportunity to mark me.*

He caressed her cheek, astonishingly gentle. "Did Erebus appear to you in Haronly?"

Eager plaything it is.

She didn't attempt to mask her shiver. "He did not. He maintained his distance." And talk about the shock of shocks; Erebus had kept his word and given her a reprieve.

"You weren't harmed?"

"No injuries of any kind."

"None of your blood spilled, and I completed no labor." Halo brushed the tip of his nose against hers. "Is there a correlation between the two, Ophelia?"

Okay. He did suspect the depths of her involvement. "It's possible there is, yes." She offered no more. *Careful. Ignore the newest prickle of guilt.*

"You don't know for sure?"

"I know some things, but not all things." Truth.

"Now I will know those things, too." He flashed her to a velvet settee between the two staircases and urged her to sit. She obeyed, expecting him to occupy the spot next to her. Panting a little—and growing a lot hard—he remained standing before her instead, peering down at her.

She smiled at him. *Not such a well-oiled machine now, are we, Astra?*

A muscle jumped in his jaw. "I believe we have some mysteries to discuss."

"You are correct. We do." Easing into a position of great relaxation, she told him, "First, you will hear my fee. To start, I demand a public apology from Roc for slaying General Nissa."

She could think of no better revenge for her sister. Roc would hate doing it and Nissa, wherever she was, would relish his lifelong humiliation. A blood debt would be satisfied without bloodshed. Taliyah could find no fault with Ophelia, and their talk need never transpire.

"Before you explain how you can't speak for your Commander," she said, assured of her power, "don't. You can communicate with him telepathically from any distance. Second, don't attempt to tell me payment should come from you and only you. We both know better. By sharing what I know, I'm helping you and every Astra. Therefore, payment should come from—say it with me—every Astra. Each of you will owe me a debt of my choosing, at a time of my choosing."

A good harpy General used every situation to her advantage. Collecting boons along her rise to the top? Advantage.

"No," she said when he opened his mouth to respond. "Don't try to tell me the warlords will forget their vows tomorrow. You'll remind them of their acceptance post-time-loop, and they will believe you, because they trust you."

Flames crackled in his irises as he executed the requisite head tilt, initiating a conversation with the other Astra. Minutes passed before he stated, "The Astra agree to your terms, as long as *my* terms apply. You can demand nothing that puts a blessing task at risk—and we are the ones to decide what does and does not constitute a risk. In return, you will answer my questions today and every day after, without fail. You will also agree to shackle yourself to my side."

"Wrong." She shook her head and smiled again. "I'll leave your side whenever I wish. And there might be some fails." At the moment, there were only two tidbits of information she planned to keep from him. Her adventures as Monsters Galore and the promise of more power. Those, he had to earn with a vow to work with her, not against her—a vow she expected only after she had proven her strength to him. Which she *would* do.

His eyelids went heavy, his features smoothing out. A startling reaction. She'd expected resistance. "Fails are not part of our bargain. If you refuse to answer a question, I deserve compensation."

"And what is it you want from me, Immortal, hmm?"

A cunning edge overtook his expression, and dang him, it was one of the sexiest things she'd ever seen. "Refuse my question," he said, "and receive my kiss."

Ohhhh. The plaything was upping the stakes, putting the power in her hands while still maintaining absolute control of the situation. She got to decide when to refuse a question, and he got to try and tempt her into bed. "How long will these quote, unquote kisses last?"

"An hour? All night?" He leaned down, gripping an arm of the settee. "It's negotiable."

How was he so charming right now? Goose bumps broke out, and she almost agreed to the all-nighters. But. Better to have an out in case something went wrong. "You'll get two minutes. If I invite you to continue, go for it. If not, contact ends immediately."

"Agreed," he replied without hesitation. "But I may begin at a time and location of my choosing. And *I* decide where to kiss."

Diabolical Astra. "Agreed. You must alert me beforehand, so I know to start the countdown." There would be no loopholes for Halo.

And yet, he was the one to smile this time. "Agreed."

She gulped. Had she walked straight into a trap?

They peered at each other, and she started squirming. Was he imagining kissing her even now?

Her breath caught. With an imperial wave of her hand, she asked, "What does his lord and majesty of the skies wish to know?"

He breathed in and out before returning to his default expression. "Your deaths. What happened? How did you die?"

War business first. Right. As a future General candidate, she heartily approved. The nymph wasn't quite so impressed, however. "Erebus has both flashed to me and flashed me to him."

"Without contact?"

"Yes. At some point after each flashing, I died. The end."

"Has he—" for the briefest moment, his gaze dropped to the top of her sternum "—used a blade on you? A particular blade with memorable characteristics, perhaps. Or did he feed you to the beasts?"

Not as stoic about the subject as he appears. "He has used a blade on me, yes." What, if anything, did Halo know about it?

Hesitant now, he asked, "Did he call the dagger the Bloodmor?"

"He did not." But was it? Something inside her leaped with recognition.

"Does he use your blood to summon, draw or create the beasts?"

Careful. "I don't know the mechanics of it all." Moving on. "Before he whips out the blade, he likes to ask me to work for him, then offer a beef-up for my résumé."

Halo's eyes searched hers. "There's more. He's pitched you something else." A statement, not a question.

He could read her so well? "You are correct." Strength beyond comprehension. A lifelong dream realized. A future seized.

"What?" he persisted.

No help for it. "Sorry, but I'm taking a pass on that query. I don't trust you enough to share such a personal detail. And before you insist on hearing it anyway, don't. Remember my claim to never harm harpykind? I meant it. To my consternation, that vow now extends to the Astra. I will always do what I believe is best for my sisters and our allies."

He absorbed her words and nodded. "Have your pass then." His gaze fell to her lips, and he grinned. The action should have lessened his intensity. It didn't. "I'll have my kiss."

15

Halo had the harpymph in his possession and within reach once again. She hadn't been harmed yesterday, and he wouldn't allow her to be harmed today. All was right in his world.

Glorious female. Wily enough to grind nine Astra under her thumb. Sensual beyond compare. Everything she said, every move she made, pointed to sex. Hard and wild. Soft and tender. Slow and thorough. Fast and explosive.

Already he was fighting the urge to fist those rich sable waves. To angle her head and devour her mouth, stealing the air from her lungs, replacing it with his own. Until she needed him and only him.

Eyes like polished emeralds set aflame, she exuded the most tantalizing carnality, and he could not look away. *Utterly snared.*

"Shall we start the countdown?" she rasped. Her scent sweetened, and he drank of it deeply. Was she closer to a needing?

His tension dulled. His shaft throbbed. "Not yet." He leaned closer, drawing a new flush to her exquisite skin. "I'm planning my attack." Let her keep her "personal detail" for now. He required something more important from her at this time. Her heart.

"Are you open to suggestions?" she asked, breathless.

In this? "I am."

"Start with my lips." She traced an index finger over the bottom one, then lightly bit the nail. "And, since you really, really wanted that answer, I should probably offer you more than a kiss."

A bounty like no other awaited him... "Much more."

"How about this? I won't start the countdown until you touch my breasts or slip your fingers into my panties. Astra's choice."

Hands always rock-steady on a battlefield began to tremble. She wanted this—wanted *him*. "I find your amendment acceptable."

He straightened, gripped his shirt, and eased off the material. "This is no longer needed."

"Not even a little bit."

Her gaze was rapt as he unhooked his artillery belt. Slowly. "Nor this." The weapons thudded to the floor.

"What about the pants?" The tip of her tongue peeked out to moisten the dip in her sumptuous bottom lip. "They serve no real purpose."

Though he would kill to free his erection, he tugged the harpy upright. They weren't yet done with their discussion.

Clasping her waist and lifting her off her feet, he turned them both and eased upon the couch. Then, Halo settled her on his lap. The many slits in her skirt allowed her to straddle him without hindrance, fitting her core against his engorged shaft. The pressure was...good.

She mewled, a sound he wished to hear every day for the rest of his life.

"Much better." He held her gaze as he hooked his fingers

under the straps of her dress. "Did you like keeping me waiting yesterday, nymph?"

"Very much." A languid smile bloomed. "Are you going to
keep me waiting now?"

"I am." Just not the way she might think. He had a plan. If
he could survive it.

Slowly, he traced his fingers down her arms, pulling the straps,
baring her breasts bit by bit. The perfect amber crests called to
him.

"Notice I haven't touched your breasts or put my fingers in
your panties," he rasped.

"Trust me." She flattened her palms on his pecs, her claws
curling, and undulated against him. "I've noticed."

He fisted her hair exactly as he'd imagined and gripped her
backside, forcing her to still. "You have no intention of stopping me, do you?"

She merely smiled with wicked intent. "Maybe, maybe not.
Let's find out together."

Their gaze held. Heart rate jacked, he yanked her closer. She
gasped. The next thing he knew, they were kissing, exchanging
moans. An irresistible serenade as their tongues rolled together.
Her taste, even sweeter than her scent. A drug.

He roved his hands over her nape. Her shoulders and spine.
More of her backside, urging her masterpiece of a body into an
unhurried rhythm. With her breasts smashed against his chest,
her nipples grazed his skin every time she inhaled, the friction
both a torment and a delight. A wild frenzy gripped him.

Nothing can be this good.

She wound her arms around him, clinging. The urge to move
against her...with her... *Can't stay still.*

They rubbed together again and again. The sensations... Almost too much but never enough.

He wrenched his mouth free of hers, commanding, "Keep
doing that."

She kept doing that. Rocking, rocking. Panting, she arched back, lifting her arms and mass of hair at the same time. As the silken strands tumbled down, she cupped her breasts. With her lips red, wet and kiss-puffed, she was the picture of pleasure. Passion, undiluted and pure.

Fitting, since he was pure, undiluted need.

"Do you crave more of me, Halo?" she purred.

"Why?" He bucked up, a hard glide of zipper against panties. When she cried out, clasping his shoulders for balance, he asked, "Do you want to give me more, Elia?"

"I want... *I want.*"

"Start the countdown," he croaked, grazing his thumbs over each amber nipple.

Moaning, she urged him closer. He bent his head and sucked on a pretty peak, then the other. Flicked and laved.

Somehow, Halo maintained control of his actions, mentally tracking the time as he eased the nymph from his shaft, spread her knees wider and removed her tiny panties with a swipe of a claw. His knuckles grazed the heart of her desire, and they both groaned. *Soaked.*

One minute, fifteen seconds left. No refusal so far. Good. That was good.

He thrust a finger inside her...two...again, again. The feel of this female! Tight. Hot. And wetter by the moment. Halo nearly lost his mind—and his seed!

Thirty seconds. No refusal. Would she wait until the last moment, or had he driven her too close to the edge to stop now?

"Halo! Yes! There!" she cried. As he plunged his fingers in and out, she undulated against him. "I'm so close."

A bead of sweat trickled from his temple. *Steady.* He eased the pressure—she chased his fingers, seeking more of them. Of him.

Must have her.

Fifteen seconds. He thrust his fingers deep. Deeper. Ten seconds. In. Out. Faster. Working her. Control fraying.

"Yes! Like that!" Her face tipped up to the ceiling, her eyes closed. She kneaded her breasts and pinched her nipples, and he'd never seen a more sensual sight.

He eased the pressure again.

"No," she cried, pouting. He glided the pad of his thumb over her clit, and she shouted, "Yes! Yes, Halo. Just like that."

He worked her closer to the edge…closer…determined, frantic, and desperate.

Three.

Two.

"My time is up." Though it cost him his sanity, he lifted his head…and removed his fingers from her tight sex. "What is the verdict?"

Banging his shoulders, she cried, "I want more, Astra."

He gripped her thighs. Desire boiled in his gut. "I'm not sure I believe you. Perhaps I should stop."

"No! Don't stop." Melting on him, all eager supplication, she kissed his lips. Once, twice. Licked. "I want to come. Then we can stop. No, I mean, then *you* can come. It'll be your turn. Don't you want to come, Halo?" She rubbed and caressed, drawing new beads of sweat to his temples. "If you've got enough stamina, we can do it all over again and never, never, ever stop."

"Very well. I'll grant you this boon, but you'll owe me. Which means we're on my timetable now. If you want your orgasm, you'll have to convince me to give it to you." Despite his gnawing need for release, he wasn't sure he'd ever enjoyed himself more. "Tell me why I am the *only* male you crave."

The Astra's bold demand echoed inside Ophelia's mind, and it was as sexy as everything else. He'd worked her body to a fever pitch. She was sensitive *everywhere*, only able to focus on a single goal: coming and coming and coming. She ached for him.

He oh, so clearly ached, too, and the knowledge thrilled her, feeding a yearning she hadn't known she possessed. The fact he wanted to play first...even better.

"Is someone fishing for compliments?" she asked.

"Someone is demanding them." A simple statement uttered with a voice steeped in lust.

Excitement teased her. Why would he demand such a thing unless he cared about her opinion? About *her*?

Warning! Approaching kryptonite!

"All right. I'll tell you what I like about you." Growing drunk on her power, Ophelia eased back just enough to unfasten his leathers. A slow tug lowered the zipper. No underwear. His massive erection sprang free. Her mouth watered for it, and her empty core wept. "For starters, I like the look of you. You've got a body built for war *and* sex."

Starvation sharpened the planes and angles of his features. He didn't seem to breathe as he stretched his arms over the couch-back. A casual, carnal pose, lurid and lewd. He reminded her of a predator locked on his prey. "What else?"

"I like the feel of you." She grazed a claw up his entire length. "I like remembering how good it felt with nothing between us."

Inhale. Exhale. "What else?"

She settled her bare sex over his. No penetration, just contact, and they both hissed. On the edge of the couch, his knuckles leached of color. A testament of his fierce struggle to resist the urge to touch her? Deep down, he must *seethe* with sensual ferocity.

Let's see what I can do to unleash it.

Ophelia glided her wetness up and down his shaft, again and again, until he was as slick as she was. Rubbing. The friction stole her breath.

A crack spread through the wood that rimmed the sofa. "Don't you have something to say to me, nymph? Say it."

Mmmm. "I like that this is even better than I remember."

His irises blazed. "What else?"

"I adore the way you respond to me." Unhurried, throbbing, she hovered her face over his. "I *love* your heat."

Danger, danger! She'd just dropped the L word.

His sizzling gaze slid down her throat, burning her skin. A little vulnerable and a lot angry, he asked, "Do you like running from me?"

Still smarting about that, was he? "I do," she admitted, "but I think I like being caught by you more." A whip of her hips. Desire rippled from one erogenous zone to another. "I think I'll like reciprocating best."

His lashes lifted, and their gazes locked. They breathed each other's breath. "I get reciprocation."

"Mmm hmm."

"Take it from me then," he rushed to say. "Take your orgasm."

Again, he commanded while putting all power in her hands. *Heady.* "Yes, I'll take it." Did she slur her words? "Because you *need* me to take it, don't you, Halo? Me, specifically." Her turn to play. "Isn't that right? But why? Why me specifically? Admit it."

"Look at you," he breathed, as if he hadn't heard her. Maybe he hadn't. A sun seemed to dawn in his irises. The *alevala* frozen on his skin, every set of eyes watching her.

Locks of inky hair sticking out in spikes, thanks to her many tugs. He looked like the epitome of sex itself.

She quickened her pace and nipped his bottom lip. Pleasure and pressure mounted, one feeding off the other.

"You love this. You love what my body does to yours...and what yours does to mine." He whispered the words into her ear. "You love feeling what you do to me."

The L word, used thrice more. She shook her head no, because she loved only harpies and home—but she didn't cease grinding on him.

"Feel every inch of me against you." Gripping her backside, he seized control of her motions, her pace. He rubbed them together, faster and harder, stripping her of sanity. "This is for you. *Only* you."

"Only me." More pressure and pleasure. And it was good. So, so good and only getting better as they mimicked sex. He rolled his hips so quickly, his shaft vibrated against her. All she could do was gasp his name and moan. "So close...just need... I need..."

Angling his grip, he plunged two fingers inside her from behind. At the same time, her clit grazed his shaft.

Just like that, Ophelia erupted, hot springs of pleasure flooding her, drowning her sweetly. "Yes, yes, yes!"

"You're squeezing my fingers, Elia," he gritted out, a male in pain as she luxuriated in bliss. He evinced as much agony as ecstasy.

As she floated down from her high, hungrier than ever, something superseded her own need—a yearning to ease Halo. To satisfy him. Because he mattered to her. Because he was...more?

"Elia," he croaked, still fingering her from behind as if he couldn't bring himself to stop. Thrusting the digits in and out. Rubbing against her core.

Her knees knocked against the settee, and her heart thundered. As she shot into a second climax, a hoarse sound escaped him.

"Don't want to stop this, want my reciprocation, but you're going to make me stop, aren't you? No female lovelier than—" He threw back his head and roared at the ceiling, falling over the edge with her.

She only craved more.

When his breathing calmed, he pulled his fingers from her—*not ready!*—and sagged against the cushions, panting and dazed.

Beautiful. Truly relaxed for the first time. "It only gets better," he breathed.

"Don't tell me you're done." As she sulked, his lips twitched. "Has the nymph exhausted the big, bad immortal? Or did you have a full systems crash and have to reboot?"

"Not even close to done. Just in the middle of a software update," he quipped, and she barked out a laugh.

The Astra had jokes. She kissed his lips before wiggling off his lap, standing and tossing him the discarded shirt. "Perhaps the right inspiration will help speed things along."

Sunlight streamed in from multiple windows, spotlighting him as he wiped his torso clean. He never pulled his gaze from her, his spinning irises drinking her in as if she were a fine wine. "I'm ready."

Balancing on shaky legs, she shimmied out of her dress.

"And now I'm inspired." His fly gaped open, his growing arousal on display. "Come here," he said, and stroked himself.

Sexy Astra. Eager, she stepped into that beam of sunlight to place herself between his parted legs. He sat up and lightly traced the backs of her thighs, his fingertips like mini branding irons. Warmth and goose bumps spread over her skin—skin without stardust.

Realization acted as a wrecking ball to her desire. Here she was, enjoying him, falling deeper into like with him, wanting and needing, even though she claimed to need nothing, and they might not be fated. Stinging disappointment set in, any remnants of the sensual fog lifting.

Halo noticed the change in her demeanor and heaved a sigh. "We're done for now, aren't we?"

"We are." Maybe for good. She extracted from his force field of hotness and bent to retrieve her dirty dress. Um…maybe she would be better off returning to her bunkroom naked?

"Let me guess. You don't wish to discuss it now or later." A clean dress materialized in his hand. He tossed the garment her way, and she caught it with ease.

"You are correct." Vulnerabilities were hitting her left and right. Another gamble, another loss. Things were getting complicated now, real feelings developing.

The third time might be the charm. But what if it wasn't?

He stuffed his erection behind his zipper. "What changed?"

"Hard pass," she said, donning her new duds. A sheer gown of the palest pink, with embroidered bloodred roses. Perhaps the finest, softest fabric ever to grace her body—and it fit perfectly. "I've got things to do. Namely, take a shower and study." If she had to navigate the day saturated in his scent, a constant reminder of his touch, she would not survive. "We've done enough prattling. We have a task to dominate, yes?"

"We don't. I do. And just to be clear, you are refusing to answer another question?"

"Ding, ding, ding." *We don't*, she mocked internally.

"Then I'm allowed another kiss," he stated.

Um, what the what? She reared back from him, pressing a hand over her racing heart. "Don't you dare." Her defenses required repairs.

"Don't worry. I will wait," he said, rising, somehow turning the assurance into a threat.

"I can help you win, Halo. You just have to give me a chance."

"There will be no chances. You will stay safe from this day forward." His voice hardened. "There will be no more dying for you."

Oh, there would be plenty more. He just wouldn't know it.

Glaring at him, she anchored her hands on her hips. "Regale me with what it is you expect me to do while I'm staying safe."

He spread his arms, as if he were the last sane male in the universe. "Enjoy the pleasures I heap upon you. That is your only job now, female. If you aren't fully satisfied with the company perks, we can reevaluate after I ascend. But who knows? You might love your new career path."

No need for a third try. This condescending prick *soooo* was not her consort or entwine. "I feel sorry for your *gravita*. I really do."

16

Halo braced a hand on the bathroom sink, bowed his head and fumed. Ophelia felt sorry for his *gravita*.

Sorry. For herself. Possibly.

Meanwhile, the battle to control his desire for her was proving to be the most grueling of his existence. She showered only a few feet away. Naked. Wet. A living siren's call he desperately needed to escape. Just for a moment. But he couldn't—wouldn't—leave her side.

He hadn't lied. He wanted her within his sights at every moment. Whatever he did today, tomorrow, and every day after, he did with the harpy. No matter the cost to his calm.

For the survival of his mind, however, he kept his back to her. Another new experience. He never put his back to anyone but the Astra. Never trusted anyone else enough. But here? Now? Risk stealing a peek at her luscious body? No. Listening to her was difficult enough.

First had come the rustle of her clothing as she'd stripped. Then the patter of water droplets as they sluiced over her skin. Now throaty moans of bliss escaped her. The same moans of bliss she released when he'd had his fingers inside her.

His hand quivered as he cleaned his torso with a soapy rag, removing any lingering evidence of his pleasure. He'd never climaxed so hard. And yet he still ached for the female. As if *he* were the nymph!

Each time he tasted of her desire, things inside him went nuclear. Thoughts, emotions, physical responses. Afterward, nothing ever quite returned to normal.

He examined his reflection in the mirror. Flushed, taut skin. But no lines of tension. Were his irises *sparkling*? A corner of his mouth lifted, as if he fought a smile. Which couldn't be right. Because he was furious with her. Positively steaming, like the glass walls of the stall, shielding Ophelia from his view. His *gravita*—whoever she was—would be envied. *No one* would have cause to pity her. She would be protected, safe from harm, always. He would give her untold satisfaction. *Never-ending* satisfaction. *Leave my embrace then, nymph. If you can.*

A harsh punch of self-disgust wiped his smile away. What was Ophelia doing to him? Why did she shut him out after a climax? Why hadn't he created stardust for her?

Halo licked his lips. Did he need to be inside her to do it?

Yes. Need to be inside her.

She was currently upset with him for reasons he couldn't fathom. He would have to do some soothing before she welcomed another kiss.

The wait galled, however. He wanted this thing with her solidified. Wanted her surrender *now*. The plan hadn't changed. Win her heart and then the task. Like Roc, Halo would prove victorious in the end. Then he could turn his focus to his eternal connection with Ophelia. And it *was* eternal, stardust or not. Because he would not be letting his harpymph go. Ever.

He might have failed to secure her during their last sensual skirmish, but he had gained valuable insight into all things Ophelia Falconcrest regardless. She responded to three things: his commands, her own power, and all affection. The contradictions were as thrilling as her touch. The perfect ammunition to wield against her stubborn contrariness. One day soon, she would utter the words he suddenly longed to hear. *You are my consort and entwine, Halo.*

A moan burned the back of his throat. He barely stopped himself from stroking his aching length through his leathers. If not for an upcoming meeting with the Commander, he would have stripped and marched inside that stall, then dropped to his knees and offered his next kiss.

The water shut off, and his posture went rigid. *Ophelia. Naked. Wet.*

Inhale. Exhale. He should prove he meant what he'd boasted. That his *gravita* would be the most envied female in the land. Pampered. Adored.

Something Ian told him prodded Halo's memory, and he nodded, decided. *There will be a courtship.*

—*Set up a candlelit meal in my bedroom. You have two hours.*— He projected the commands directly to Ian. With a blessing task at stake, every Astra remained at the ready. —*Make sure there's something with lobster.*— The main ingredient in yesterday's lunch. —*Go to every trouble and stop at nothing to ensure the setting is magnificent.*—

—*Aw. Is our Halo going on his first date?*—

Maybe? He worked his jaw. —*Just get it done.*—

"All clean and dry, and ready to report for duty, sir," Ophelia said with a cheery tone. Her mood had certainly improved since they'd last spoken. A surprising and pleasant shift. "What is my darling's pleasure?"

My darling? She had decided to mind him then?

He turned, watching as she exited the stall on a cloud of

steam, wearing a towel. Locks of wet hair clung to her here and there.

Though he hated to utter his next words, he did it. "You should dress." And he should don a T-shirt. The Astra only went without the garment in times of war. No better way to show off past crimes. But he didn't want to don a shirt. Let Ophelia examine him and see the male who would stop at nothing to succeed.

She knotted her hair atop her head and sauntered past him, as if she hadn't a care. Pausing in the doorway to the closet, she gazed at him over her shoulder. With smoldering eyes, she asked, "Is precious dressing for business or pleasure?"

He frowned. That tone. Those words. That body language. Everything about her screamed, *I'm eager to please.* His deepest instincts answered, *Lies!*

Perhaps her mood was not improved, after all.

"Precious is dressing for business," he said, and she scowled. No, there'd been no improvement. If anything, she had regressed.

Would he ever understand this female?

As soon as he'd awoken, he'd spoken to Andromeda. After explaining that he no longer required her services, he'd admitted he thought he'd found his mate. The Amazon had expressed genuine excitement and promptly declared herself his "wing-woman." Someone, apparently, who aided a friend in the acquiring of a harpymph.

Andromeda had promptly made space in the closet and raided the palace, picking out the best garments for Ophelia, the sizes based solely on his description of "lush and perfect." He feared his reaction to the harpy in some of the scantier gowns.

"Dude. I'm naked and draped in a towel here," Ophelia huffed. "Pay attention to me while I ask the same question for the third time. What kind of business?"

He almost smiled. He very much liked the pout in her tone. "We are meeting with Roc and Taliyah in ten minutes, thirty-

two seconds. Thirty-one." Thirty. "They demand a full ac-
counting of everything that's happened during the task so far.
Which we will *both* give them. I have other clothes for you in
the closet."

She whirled around, one hand holding the too-small towel
in place, the other anchored on her hip. "You know, before I
met you, I was nervous to meet with Taliyah. Now, a conference with the General seems like old hat. No big, you know?
The fact that you track the exact time until a meeting, down to
the second, without glancing at a clock, is blowing my mind."

His chest puffed up. "I know the exact time of everything,
to the second, always." Bragging now?

He launched forward, and she hurried off, moving deeper
into the closet—where she oohed and aahed over the eclectic
selection.

Halo tracked her every graceful movement. Eventually, she
shimmied into the sexiest gown imaginable. A sheer green stun-
ner to match her eyes, and perhaps every man's downfall.

He reached up to tug at his collar, only to remember he wasn't
wearing a shirt. "I thought I remember recommending business attire."

"Then your memory isn't faulty," she told him with a sweet
smile. With a soft pull, her sable locks tumbled around her shoulders. "Business is my pleasure, and pleasure is my business."

This female. He almost laughed, almost glowered. He wasn't
sure what he was supposed to feel with the harpymph, because
he continued to feel a bit of everything. Should he shut down?
Go mad?

"Try not to distract me during the meeting, precious," Halo
said, only half teasing as he snaked an arm around her waist and
dragged her against him.

She mumbled obscenities at him as he flashed her to the war
room six minutes early. Roc and Taliyah stood together at the
head of a long table, examining ancient scrolls. Translucent star-

dust sparkled over every inch of their exposed flesh, inciting the barest thrum of envy in Halo.

Two other warriors occupied the room. Roux Pyroesis and Dove...something. A legend among the harpies. Known for leading some of the world's bloodiest campaigns in the war against...anyone.

Long ago, she'd died on the battlefield against Erebus, and the god transformed her into a harphantom. Now one of the most vicious species in existence, able to mist between the natural and spiritual realms. They fed on souls and had few weaknesses. But, because of Taliyah, these harphantoms were not like other phantoms. They were not bound to Erebus or controlled by his will. For now, they were allies to harpies and Astra alike.

The reason for the meeting became clear. Roux and Dove were to gather information, conducting Halo's research for him, allowing him to focus on winning his harpymph.

Noticing his arrival, Roc waved Roux away. The warrior glanced at Ophelia, still wrapped in Halo's embrace, and frowned. Each day, Roux reacted to Halo's transformation—if that's what it was—more intensely, as if the change in Halo was more pronounced. From controlled to tormented to...whatever this was.

Halo offered reassurance. —*I've got this, brother. I will secure her.*—

—*She is a bit...different to your usual tastes. Be careful. The softer ones bite the hardest.*— Roux was gone a second later.

Taliyah dismissed Dove, who glanced between Halo and Ophelia before vanishing in a light, barely perceptible puff of smoke.

Still Halo kept Ophelia pressed against his body, even as she wiggled around to face their leaders.

"I'll start, since I'm short on time and required elsewhere." Unlike Ophelia, Taliyah wore the standard harpy uniform. Metal breastplate, leather vest, and pleated skirt, with accompanying protections. "I understand we're on day five of the repeat, but this is our only meeting. Which means you've waited five days to know why I demanded to meet with you in the first place. The reason is simple. I decided to transfer you to Ation, where you will—"

"What?" Ophelia yelled at the same time Halo barked, "That isn't happening."

Ation was a prison realm where many species trapped their most violent females. A world of great horrors.

Taliyah swung her gaze to him. "Are you presuming to tell me what to do with *my* soldier, Astra?"

"She isn't yours, General," he snapped.

"To whom does she belong then, hmm?" Taliyah asked. Her cold smile dropped the temperature at least twenty degrees. "Because I see no stardust on her skin. The only way I'll ever relinquish her from my command."

Working on it.

"You'll relinquish your command when I take your job," Ophelia remarked.

Taliyah shrugged. "Maybe. If you beat me hard enough."

He gritted his teeth. "This is *my* task, General. *Everyone* falls under my rule."

"Don't worry," Ophelia told Taliyah, using her cheery tone again—ignoring him, even as she curled into him, resting her head on his shoulder and petting his chest. "He won't give me any orders that contradict yours. My darling insists I ride the pine." Though she maintained a sugary tone, she scraped bloody furrows in his flesh.

His desire—his need—to safeguard her should please her. Females!

He would work twice as hard to ensure Ophelia enjoyed her safety. One day, she would thank him. He was certain of it.

"But, for future reference, maybe don't threaten to incarcerate the girl who's gonna save everyone." The harpymph plucked her nails free.

Halo stiffened. What did she mean, *save everyone*?

"Did I say I was finished speaking?" Taliyah inquired in a slow drawl. "You weren't to be a prisoner but a guard. A true honor. You learn the best tricks there. But I have since changed my mind. I will let you do as you have boasted and save everyone. Which means you will help Halo defeat Erebus in any way that proves necessary. Perhaps then you will earn your first star, and I'll take your boasting seriously."

"A star," Ophelia said, her expression going dreamy soft. "Yes. I will do this."

He rubbed the center of his chest, where pressure gathered. To qualify for the position of General, a harpy must earn a total of ten stars, each designated for a specific accomplishment.

He ran the requirements through his mind—things Ophelia planned to do. Serve the army for at least a century. Win the Harpy Games, a series of contests. Convince the reigning General to do something she didn't want to do. Present that General with the head of her fiercest foe. Oversee a victorious military campaign. Negotiate a major truce. Steal some royal immortal's most prized possession. Win a battle with her wits alone. Sacrifice something she dearly loved and lastly, defeat the reigning General in battle.

The risks she would face. Risks she would take despite already dying on three separate occasions.

"Tell me why you planned to send me away." She crossed her arms, mimicking Halo's usual stance. "Is it because the Commander killed my sister? Am I to be punished for his crime?"

Ice glazed the General's pale blue irises. "Do not lie to me again, soldier. I won't just banish you from Harpina, I'll revoke your citizenship."

"What are you talking about?" Ophelia snapped. "How did I lie?"

"Roc didn't kill your sister, and you know—"

"He most certainly did!"

"He killed your mother."

"What? No." Ophelia shook her head. "I don't know where you got your information, but you couldn't be more wrong. Nissa was General during the years of the virginity requirement. I'm confident of this because she loved to remind me of it." A tremor shook her. "She had the strength to say no to temptation. I didn't. Our mother died a week after giving birth to me."

Taliyah opened and closed her mouth. She looked to Roc, who shrugged. Swallowing, she faced Ophelia, who'd grown tenser by the second. With an astonishingly gentle tone, the General said, "I'm sorry, Ophelia. I thought you knew. Nissa is—was your mother. I found the record hidden in her room. I confirmed it with her journal. In one of the passages, she claimed she confessed the truth to you."

"No." Ophelia shook her head again. "No. The record is the lie. The journal too. Nissa would never…she wouldn't… Why would she not tell me something like that? There's no reason good enough."

Halo drew her closer, held her tighter. He didn't like this. At all. Bombs were exploding inside his chest. Or was his heart pounding against his ribs?

His harpymph calmed, at least, settling in his arms.

"I had the birth record mystically tested, and… I'm sorry, Ophelia," Taliyah repeated, "but it's valid."

"Well then." She wrapped her arms around Halo, as if she wished to be absorbed by him. An action that begged, *Don't let go.* "If it's valid."

He repositioned, crossing his arms over her shoulders, and nuzzled his cheek into hers. If he could meet her needs, aid her in some way…as satisfying as bedding her.

"I'm sorry for the pain I caused with my delivery," the General said, stacking papers that didn't need to be stacked.

"Don't, um, worry about it." Ophelia cleared her throat and motored on. "I'll never be your consort's biggest fan, but I'm not out for his blood or anything. For the record, I would have made a horrifyingly fierce adversary."

"Yes. Well. Let's set all personal matters aside for the moment." Taliyah cleared her throat as well. "I believe we all have a task to dominate."

17

Shock kept Ophelia in a daze. Perhaps the reason Halo remained at her side during the endless meeting with General Taliyah and Commander Roc.

The conclusion of the hours-long briefing came only after the freeze. Halo flashed Ophelia to a private, candlelit feast in the royal dining room. To be invited here, where only the strongest of harpykind and their loved ones dined, was a true honor.

An honor her sister—her *mother* had never extended to her.

A lump lodged in her throat, clogging her airway. At any other time, Ophelia thought she might have gawked at the furnishings. Today she just didn't care. She shuffled to her seat. Her head hung, and her shoulders drooped.

Halo held out her chair for her and claimed the seat beside her, then filled her plate with delicacies. "To earn each bite," he said, so gentle she almost couldn't fathom it, "you have only to breathe. All right?"

"I can do that, I guess," she mumbled. But she couldn't quiet her mind.

Nissa was her mother. The irritating sibling who had yelled at her again and again for oh, so foolishly throwing away her future had given birth to her. Nissa had bedded the nymph, not the dead mother the General had ridiculed on multiple occasions.

All Mother had to do was say no. N.O. It's not that difficult. Look at me. No. No!

Queasy, Ophelia used the fork to push her "earned" food around the plate. What sucked most? Despite the hypocrisy of it all, she hated that she'd upset Nissa. It was one thing to disappoint your sister and quite another to disappoint your mother.

"What can I do to help you?" Halo asked.

"I want Vivi." Her eyes burned, and her vision wavered. "Is there any way you can unfreeze her?"

"I do not think so." He leaned over, grasped her by the waist and transported her to his lap. "What would Vivi do for you if she were here?"

What *could* the harpire do? No one knew if Nissa had been too embarrassed of her nymph daughter to admit the truth, or if the General Mother Dearest had kept quiet simply to maintain her title. Either way...

I was unwanted.

Hot tears poured down Ophelia's cheeks. Embarrassed, she batted at the ridiculous droplets. Breaking down in front of an Astra? And not just any Astra, but *hers*. No, not hers. *Not yet, maybe not ever. Humiliating!* But the tears didn't care; they fell faster.

"I think Vivi would mention how amazing I am," she croaked. "Loyal. Honest. Dedicated. Rare, wonderful qualities. Ask anyone. And then she'd probably tell me that being rejected by my own mother proves nothing about my worth, only Nissa's."

Halo kissed her temple. "Vivi would not be wrong. But harpy? Amazing doesn't come close to describing you."

Ophelia sagged against him, resting her head on his shoulder. A position she appreciated more and more. "I don't believe you. I mean, Vivi knows me, so her speeches work. You know nothing."

"You believe I'm saying these things, simply to be nice?"

"I know! It's shocking to me, too." She drew an X over his heart, mourning the loss of what could have been, if only Nissa had been honest with her. The conversations they could have had. "For starters, you think I'm weak." Oops. Another tear escaped.

"Weak? Why would I *ever* think that? Did you not go toe-to-toe with an angry Astra after he shackled you to a bed?"

"Well, yes, but—"

"And did you not force nine warlords to bend to your will?"

"I did do that, yes, and it wasn't even that difficult," she said, perking up. She was practically a superhero. After the task, she would be a genuine superhero.

He traced his fingertips along the ridges of her spine. "Did you not give me the most powerful orgasms of my life?"

She raised her head, meeting his gaze. "Really? The most powerful?"

"It isn't even a competition." How earnest he appeared, those magnificent irises spinning. And his pupils…they pulsed. Like a heartbeat.

Ophelia curled up against him, soaking in his warmth. He kept saying things that pointed to his lack of experience, yet he played her body expertly. "Be honest. Am I that good or are you that bad?"

He snorted. "Both?" A little smile teased his lips as he smoothed a lock of hair from her face. "I enjoy being sexual with you."

"You didn't enjoy it before me?"

"I did not."

Wow. Just wow. "What about cuddling?"

"This is my first time to do so. Before you, I got in and got out, preferring to be alone."

What? *Never* cuddled before Ophelia? And in and out? Wow again. "I hate to break it to you, darling, but your douchebag roots are showing. You didn't see to the pleasure of your partner? The disrespect!" Never mind that she hadn't seen to *his* pleasure in the beginning. They were discussing his faults, not hers.

He combed his fingers through her hair. "I didn't enjoy touching or being touched. But for a moment, I could be free of my tension."

Hesitant, she asked, "But you like touching and being touched now?" He seemed to need contact as much as she did. "With me?"

"I do," he rasped.

Two words. Pure seduction. "Have you ever discussed your thoughts and feelings like this?"

"Never."

I'm the chosen one. The lover he *relished* touching.

The action movie soundtrack filled her head without the aid of her earbuds, and her shoulders rolled back. Well, of course she was the chosen one. She was more than amazing; she was indestructible. Strong enough to survive death thrice, with a cunning side that drove her to cross any line to succeed. Even keeping secrets from an Astra.

Ignore the guilt. Her sister was her mother, a fact she couldn't change. The shock and sting hadn't lessened, but the despondency was gone, thanks to Halo.

"I want to for real cuddle with you," she announced. "Not a gateway cuddle to sex but a no-strings cuddle where I can do anything I wish to your body, and you just have to take it."

He gripped the hair at her nape, tilting her head up to his. Spinning irises blazed with desire. "If I agree to this no-strings cuddle in a location of my choosing, you'll talk and tell me other things I wish to know?"

"I will if you will. Within reason." Always have a caveat at the ready.

He rushed to nod, as if he'd hoped for such a response. "The deal is set." After adjusting his hold, he flashed them to a couch in the entertainment room. A spacious chamber with multiple other couches set in rows. A huge projector screen hung on the far wall, next to a "Rack o' Phallus" snack machine that was mystically enhanced to never run out of fresh corn dogs, pickles, bananas, or cucumbers. A "Property of Not You" sign hung from the top.

Ophelia's stomach rumbled, her appetite unconcerned by the emotional crisis. "Ugh! Why am I so hungry? We just ate."

"No. I ate. You pushed food around your plate." He flashed to the machine, punched the glass to acquire a corn dog, and returned to her. "You can earn this by asking *me* a question," he said, stretching out. He masterfully maneuvered her into the crook of his arm. Her new favorite place to be.

She asked the first thing to pop into her head, then bit into her treasure. "Why did you kill your father?"

"I killed him the day I met him," he said, petting her hair. "I learned he had arranged my mother's murder and sold me to the Order. A school for child assassins, where I was taught to detach from my emotions. By the time I left, I'd already amassed hundreds of names on my kill list. Including friends. My father had much to answer for." He offered the information without hesitation and yes, detached from emotion.

Sympathy welled as she imagined young Halo, forced to murder friends he'd loved. How the memories must torment him.

How would he react when he learned he'd killed a potential *gravita* not once but twice?

Guilt and fear surged. Maybe she shouldn't tell him...ever. For his own good. "I'm sorry you suffered as a child. But I'm not sorry for the male you've become. He's pretty wonderful upon occasion and shockingly tempting always."

He blinked at her with surprise and cleared his throat. "All right, yes. I understand why Vivi's praise brings you such encouragement." Pause. "You like when I comfort you?"

Dude. That plaintive tone got her straight in the feels. "How could I not like it? It really highlights your obsession with me. Your best feature."

"Thank you for noticing," he deadpanned. "I've worked hard on it."

Genuine laughter burst from her. A true shocker. Amusement? At a time like this?

A smile curved the corners of his mouth. "You sound like pure joy when you laugh, Elia."

Sexy, intense warlord. She rolled onto him, draping her body over his, and crossed her arms on his chest. Resting her chin on top of the pile, she peered at him through her lashes. "You get a four-star review for your comforting. I'm deducting one star so you have something to strive for. Goals are important." If only he understood hers; he would be the perfect male.

"True." Toying with locks of her hair, he asked, "And what are your goals? Other than becoming General."

Did she even want to become a General anymore? Where did she go from here? Ophelia had sought the title to prove her worth to Nissa.

Speaking of proving her worth. "You know one of my other goals. I've made no secret of it." *Careful. Proceed with caution.* "I plan to help you defeat Erebus, the way my General commanded."

He frowned. "Elia—"

"No, don't say anything else right now. Let's do something wild and crazy. Let's relax!" So much had happened today, leaving her in a tailspin and emotionally wrung out. First had come the earth-shattering pleasure with Halo. Then learning she'd faced banishment. *Then* hearing the crime of omission committed by Nissa.

The revelation was still raw. Ophelia knew the truth of her origins, but she'd never felt less like herself. For years, she'd denied the needs of her nymph, ashamed of her "weaknesses," desperate to impress someone unwilling to be impressed.

"Very well. We will relax," Halo said. "We will…rest."

Minutes passed in silence, but neither of them drifted off. Her mind was too chaotic. More than that, a harpy couldn't sleep with anyone but trusted sisters or a consort. Halo hadn't claimed her as his *gravita*, so he couldn't be her consort yet.

Unless he was hers, but she wasn't his.

For the next six days, Ophelia stewed about her predicament. What else could she do? Every day, she was forced to occupy the same chair in the same conference room *for hours*, ignored as Halo, Roc, and Taliyah talked war.

On the plus side, the meetings turned Irresistible Halo into the Machine. Cold, callous, unbending and seemingly unaffected by her swinging moods. *Almost* resistible.

The Machine refused to relent to her request and give her a chance to prove herself. He expected Ophelia to stay out of the fight, and it was complicating everything. Her thoughts. Her emotions. Her every decision. Today especially. Their reprieve was over: she sensed it. Erebus would strike soon after the freeze.

There would be another battle. Another death.

Remove Halo's refusal from the equation, and Ophelia was ready. Become another beast? *Bring it.* She was stronger than before. And this time, she expected the god's command to kill the Astra. She knew to fight against it.

Once she overcame the compulsion to obey, she could willingly lay down her life. Halo could strike without opposition, completing the labor. No muss or fuss for him. High honors for her.

Her chance to do her part for harpykind. To ovary-up or shut up. The way heroes—or cowards—were forged. *She* refused to let Halo turn her into something she wasn't.

Maybe she played with fire, but so what? She'd rather go down in flames than live without heat.

At the moment, Halo, Roc, and Taliyah were talking among themselves at the other end of the table. The trio ignored her existence. Though, okay, yes, snacks arrived for Ophelia to steal every hour on the dot. Despite Halo's aloof demeanor, he maintained an acute awareness of her and timed her food intake to prevent hunger.

How could he be so wonderful and terrible at the same time?

His electric pull only ever amplified, drawing her scrutiny again and again. Her curiosity about his past only deepened—what had created the male he was today? Her desire for him only heated. Her admiration for him had skyrocketed—and continued to climb. It was starting to scare her.

Growing attached. Was he doing the same? Maybe? Possibly? To have him for a consort...to have sex, satisfaction, companionship, a true partner... Longing bombarded her.

Was it all too good to be true?

Would he ever mark her?

Ophelia watched him, unable to look away. He stood between the two leaders, pointing to passages in different books, his muscles flexing with each movement. Not a strand of inky hair was out of place. His expression revealed polite respect, nothing more, and yet she sensed great frustration and tension inside him.

Though the Commander and General had moderated their tones the entire conversation, Halo did not show the same courtesy.

"My task, my way. In this, my authority supersedes yours," he stated. "Soon you won't even remember we had this conversation."

How delicious. Any time Halo told his Commander or the

General what to do, pervy Ophelia got wetter. She could only shift in her seat and cross her legs to mitigate the sudden ache.

An insatiable fire blazed in her marrow, the flames reaching for Halo. No one else would do. *This* was a needing.

Both Roc and Taliyah scowled at him. They didn't want Ophelia overhearing the battle plan in case Erebus got his hands on her again. As if she would ever spill! The lack of trust in her abilities only added fuel to the fires of her determination.

Strengthen. Help win the task. Bask in the accolades.

Halo's accolades, particularly. He would have to eat his doubt and admit she wasn't just some bed bunny. Granted, she would very much like to get him into bed. The way his muscles rippled...

His gaze darted to her, there and gone. A familiar action. He'd glanced her way more than a dozen times already. Had he, perhaps, scented her growing arousal?

"Why do we have to reset?" Taliyah demanded. "Why are we taken out of commission twelve hours a day?"

"Ten hours," Halo corrected. "Sixty minutes are added to your tally and subtracted from Erebus's each time we complete a labor. I believe the day will cease repeating sometime after my eleventh victory. Perhaps the twelfth. My biggest problem is Erebus's ability to bypass palace security. He and his phantoms come in and out at will." Without looking Ophelia's way, he waved her over. "Show them where you've met with Erebus."

Called off the bench? She popped to her feet with record speed, surely, and raced over. Halo's scent infiltrated her awareness, stoking the inferno in her bones to new heights.

Do not melt against the coach, player one. Not again.

At attention like a good soldier, she examined the map stretched over the table's surface, overlaid with a transparent blueprint of the palace. Pointing, she said, "Here, here and here, sir."

As though it were the most natural thing in the world, he

wound an arm around her and cupped her hip. Her heart fluttered. Was he, perchance, imagining Ophelia sinking to her knees, tearing open his leathers, and devouring his length? Because suddenly she could think of nothing else.

"Have Silver perform a sweep of all three areas," he commanded. "Perhaps he'll notice something I missed."

"Consider it done," Roc replied.

"And now, this meeting is over. No," Halo interjected when the couple issued protests. "I have other things to do."

So hot!

The Commander and Taliyah flashed from the room.

Halo exhaled a heavy breath, some of the strain easing from his features. From the Machine to Irresistible Halo.

He met her gaze. "I apologize for the time delay. There was more to cover here than I'd realized. Every day I give Roux something else to research and every day the information leads in a new direction." A slight twitch in his jaw. "Now we have only minutes until the freeze occurs. Let's go somewhere." He smoothed a lock of hair behind her ear. "Tell me your favorite place in Harpina."

She leaned into his touch, saying, "Climax Point."

"Why am I not surprised?" The corners of his mouth curved up.

He flashed her to the infamous island cliff. The obsidian peak sat miles from the Harpinian shore, overlooking an endless stretch of purple water, where tribes of harpens and harmaids resided. The sirens and mermaids.

Afternoon sunlight streaked a brilliant sapphire sky with amber. Behind them, lush emerald foliage and gleaming silver stones towered.

Her ears twitched as a faint moan carried on a cool breeze. Then another moan came, and another. The moans never stopped, the rocks seeming to orgasm with every brush of wind.

"Listen," she prompted. "Nature's best soundtrack." Climax

Point was said to be the last body of land in the entire realm. Anyone who'd ever set sail on those rippling purple waves—and returned—had claimed the ocean never ended.

A handful of harpies loitered nearby, and word of Halo's presence spread fast. Most of the girls stared at the Astra with unabashed curiosity. Some with invitation.

Ophelia's hackles rose. *Mine!*

"Go," Halo commanded, and they beat feet. Much more subdued, he asked, "Why this place?"

Not mine. Not yet. "I get stressed after training or battle. And when I'm not training or in battle, because I know I *should* be training or in battle. I come here to channel that stress into fury."

"I see." A breeze blew a lock of hair over his brow. "No, I don't see." The flash of a wide, no-filters smile nearly stopped her heart. "How does this place help you channel your stress into fury?"

"Well." She turned into him fully, pressing herself flush against his heat. *Missed this.* Sliding her hands up his arms, she told him, "The how is simple. I listen to the rocks getting off and remember that I've spent decades denying myself the slightest pleasures, and voilà! I'm frothing at the mouth, ready to render a death blow."

He seemed to analyze every word. "Why did you deny yourself pleasure?" Analysis complete, but data inconclusive? "You were unable to serve as General."

She caressed his cheek, the action somehow necessary. "Once a nymph starts, it's difficult to stop until reaching satisfaction. But we are notoriously impossible to satisfy."

"That will not be the case for you." He nuzzled into her palm, his eyes crackling with possession. His intensity ramped up a thousand degrees. "Your satisfaction is a top priority for me. Nothing will keep me from my goal, Elia."

He was *devastating* like this. Determined, attentive, and fervent. Why hadn't she slept with him yet? He would either stardust her or he wouldn't. But either way, she would finally learn the truth. *Gravita* or not—a future together or not?

"What do *you* do to alleviate stress?" she asked with the slightest tremor.

He shrugged. "Kill the source."

Yeah. That tracked. She fiddled with the button on his leathers, saying, "Maybe we should both try a new method."

"Oh?" He traced the trinite collar. "Do you have any ideas?"

So many. Judging by his straining zipper, he entertained the same ones. "What if we make *each other* moan?"

He arched a brow. "Are you requesting pleasure, nymph?"

With a wicked smile, she told him, "I might be. But I refuse to confirm or deny it at this time." Oops. The button slipped free.

"You'll have to deal with the consequences, then, won't you?" He reached up and pinched her chin. Not the chin pinch! She had no defenses against it. "Tomorrow morning, I will have my compensation for your refusal to answer my question. You will wait in your bunkroom for me. Naked."

"Will I?" she breathed, stroking his hard-on through the leather.

He hissed air between his teeth. "You will."

"Why tomorrow? Why not today?" Right now?

"The newest freeze is set to occur in eighty-three seconds, and you will not be happy with me afterward."

Ugh. The task and her benching. "What does it matter if I help you? These first labors are only practice rounds. And you're supposed to learn stuff. Like how to work well with others." Yeah, she'd listened when Roc and Taliyah whispered their thoughts to him.

"Doubtful. I allow the Astra to aid me daily."

As if she needed the reminder. Yesterday she'd stared a wee bit too long and gotten trapped by an *alevala*, living another of his memories. In it, he'd allowed the Astra to get all up in his business. Because he'd trusted them. He did not trust Ophelia.

Which was irritatingly understandable or whatever. It wasn't like he knew she was the one who'd chewed on his liver in battle. But oh! She didn't want to be talked out of her mad when nothing was going her way.

Unwilling to give up, she said, "I know I'm untested and untried in your eyes. Good news is, that can be easily changed with testing and trying."

"I have already allowed your harm and death, chaining you for a god's slaughter," he replied, stubborn to his core. "I'll let you die no more."

"Hey! Don't use that slaughter as an excuse. Wasn't my death punishment enough?"

He glowered at her. "Why can't you enjoy staying safe?"

"Because I'm a hardcore warrior with titanium ovaries."

"We've discussed this enough." He shook his head when she prepared to issue another protest. "You aren't to interfere with my labor in any way. You are simply to stay within my sight line."

And she had wondered why she hadn't slept with him already. Exhibit A. "I'm starting to dislike you again, Astra."

"Too bad. I care about your well-being, harpy."

Disregard the thrill of his confession. "If that's true you'll let me shine, Astra!"

"You don't need a battlefield to shine." He kissed her brow and sighed. "The freeze comes in three, two, one."

An undercurrent of aggression wove through the air, her body sensing what her eyes couldn't yet verify. The freeze had indeed occurred, Erebus an imminent threat.

Would he strike early or delay?

"We should—" A trumpet sounded in the distance, and Halo tensed. He shouted, "Halo Phaninon!"

Ophelia stiffened as she scanned the area. "What's happening?" Wait. Was that *the* trumpet, signaling a new test? *Now?*

Without a secret meeting with the enemy, a tussle with a dagger, and a beastly transformation?

"A new labor has begun. A battle to the death." Halo pushed her behind him and extended his arms, a blade suddenly clutched in each hand. Impressive. But she, too, withdrew blades at warp speed. He noticed, of course. "I am the one who makes the kill, Ophelia. You will stand down. Do you understand?"

She sheathed her weapons, grating, "Yes." Victory mattered to her, too. Divide his focus in this upcoming battle? No. Unlike Halo, she knew how to play a team sport.

Twigs snapped, and leaves rattled. He braced...

The most majestic beast ambled past a thicket, chewing on a vine as it approached. The beauty of the creature left her jaw hanging. Thirty-point antlers made of pearl. A sleek raven pelt. Eyes like rubies, gleaming with resolve rather than rage.

Was this a trick? Mesmerize them and strike?

"This is your opponent?" But...

"Erebus can garner his combatants without your blood," Halo remarked, his mind working in a far different direction than hers. Swords replaced the daggers in his grip. "That is good to know."

Yes, but how had the Deathless done it? Had he used the Bloodmor—or whatever—on someone else? Someone frozen? A secret third, unfrozen person? Or had he flashed in an actual hind?

The latter seemed possible as the creature eased to the ground just outside of striking distance and bowed his head, shoving the tips of his antlers into the dirt, playing the part of willing sacrifice.

"Are you sure this is a death match?" Ophelia asked. "Hercules merely had to capture the hind."

"I'm sure. There was a single blast of the trumpet. A death is required."

But... "He's not fighting for his life. Who merely accepts

death?" Besides harpies with an endgame? "No way. Just no way. This *must* be a trick. Why not do the unexpected and let him live?"

"And learn what? That mercy comes with a high cost? No need. I already know. So. I will do this, and I will teach *Erebus* a lesson in the process. He hopes I'll regret ending such a magnificent creature. He hopes the kill hurts and distracts me. But it won't. I'll regret nothing." He sounded utterly unconcerned and completely removed from the situation. "An obstacle to victory is an obstacle to victory."

Her stomach bottomed out. Would he consider *Ophelia* an obstacle, if he learned the truth about her involvement?

Halo strode forward and rendered the death blow, severing the hind's head without hesitation. The body plopped to the ground. As blood gurgled, she halfway expected monsters to rise from the crimson pool.

A trumpet sounded in the distance—the end of the battle? Not something she'd gotten to hear before.

"No sickness this time," he murmured, nodding with satisfaction. He flashed his swords away and surveyed the animal.

He'd gotten sick after the other battles? Not that this had been any kind of battle. "The labor is over? Just like that?"

"Just like that. The physical ease of the test means nothing. Erebus clearly had no wish to win this round. Instead, the god seized the opportunity to sow guilt and regret. To harken back to the years I spent at the Order, when I was forced to end another innocent soul. But there will be no guilt or regret. I am one step closer to ultimate success in every area of my life. The ascension and safety of the Astra. A certain harpymph…"

He looked positively wicked as he swung his gaze to her. Uh… What had caused *this*?

"Erebus receives a single shot at me a day. No loophole can change that." A grin bloomed, slow and *devastating*. "He's done for now. We are not. Considering we are the only two people in existence right now, there's no reason to wait until tomorrow to claim my kiss."

Wings fluttering, Ophelia took a step back. "I'm furious with you. You put Baby in a corner. You don't get any kisses today." Although...it might not be a bad idea.

He didn't seem to hear her, anyway. "Should I start with your lips or go straight for my honey?"

The honey.

Way to hold out. But come on! Shouldn't she give him that third shot to claim her? To forge the foundation of their future interactions. To enjoy him while she could.

"You are the woman I desire in my bed. That isn't going to change. Ever." He narrowed eyes that glittered with raw passion. "Give yourself to me, Elia. Let me have you."

The two sides of her remained torn. The harpy told him, "No, I don't think I will." Not without a fight. The nymph purred, "But I'll allow you to win me. If you can."

18

By sheer strength of will, Halo rooted his feet, lest he close the distance and yank Ophelia into his arms. A good warrior only struck at the proper time...

And he would be striking. Win her? Oh yes. He had tasted of passion, and he would not, could not, go back to his emotionless existence.

A soft wind blew between them, lifting strands of sable silk before her face. She'd chosen to wear another gauzy dress today, the hem dancing at her ankles. Sunlight bathed her dusky skin and turned her pale green eyes into bottomless pools of desire. With a backdrop of jagged obsidian stone, she was a wild thing. *Temptation itself.*

Halo had hungered for this harpymph every day of his life; he just hadn't known it until he'd met her. Being near her for hours each day and not touching her had been a torture worse than any other. The only torture he could not endure. Because she desired him too. The way she melted into him...

And yet, she continued to hold him at an emotional distance, determined to participate in matters of warfare. If he was going to win her on his terms—and he was—he must show no weakness.

Having learned more about his female, he suspected she harbored a frothing fear—meaning nothing to those she loved. For the rest of eternity, he would remember her devastation as she'd spoken of her broken connection to Nissa.

Ophelia Falconcrest meant *much* to him, and he would prove it. "Shall I place the heads of your enemies at your feet?"

She lifted her chin, a beauty like no other. "I stopped collecting heads a year ago. What else you got?"

The seductress is here, and she's taking no prisoners.

He dropped his chin, excitement fizzing in his veins. Electricity charged the space between them, heightening the reactions of his body. "Perhaps you require a hands-on demonstration of the things I'm willing to do to win you," he said, stalking closer.

Halo backed her into the hard rock, caging her with his harder body. Her breath hitched. She slapped her hands on his chest, not to push him away but to hold him steady. Her claws curled, slicing his skin.

He inserted his leg between hers, pressing his thigh against her core. "Would you like a hands-on demonstration, nymph?"

Her eyelids dipped to half-mast. "Very much so, Immortal."

Where to start? He stared at her. She stared right back. Together, they hovered at the cusp of…something.

Halo marveled at their differences. The hulking barbarian and the delicate rose. He might possess the strength to crush her, but she could send him to his knees with a prick of her thorns or a caress of her soft petals.

With a forearm braced against the stone and a light grip on her chin, he stated, "Do we need a countdown, or do you wish to surrender before I begin?"

"Foolish, Astra." She melted against him, exactly as he craved, all carnal indulgence and torrid fantasies. "You think you've already won, not yet realizing you fell straight into my trap. I dangled the bait, and you came running without the promise of reciprocation. Meaning, yes. One point, harpymph."

Wily female. "I'll be earning my reciprocation." Half smiling, half scowling, he dropped a hand to her waist and gripped her collar with the other, trapping her against him. "See if I don't."

"Well," she breathed. "You're certainly off to a good start."

"I can do better."

He bent his head, claiming her mouth with his own. She opened, welcoming him. Their tongues danced together, the nymph meeting his every foray with a carnal lap. Passion fed passion.

Any vestiges of his uncharacteristic playfulness vanished. Her sweetness maddened him.

How did I ever live without this?

Needs frothed, spurring vows. Halo would do whatever proved necessary to be the best lover Ophelia had ever had. He would make her come *hard*. Again and again and again and again. She would find contentment with him. Would have no reason to miss endangering herself on the battlefield. Pleasure would be hers for the taking. Never had there been anyone more willing to fight for the joy of another. In this, Halo would not be deterred.

He ran her lower lip between his teeth as he lifted his head to meet her gaze. "If I do something you dislike," he instructed, palming her breasts, grazing her nipples, "you will tell me. Agree, Elia." Kneading her slowly. Gently...at first. Beneath her gown, those stiffened peaks teased him.

"Agreed." Moaning, she clutched at his shoulders. "I like, I like, I like!"

Craving skin-to-skin contact, he shredded the gossamer material of her dress. Mmm. Yes. Much better. Halo disposed of her weapons, sheaths and undergarments, baring her body to his reverent gaze. All that soft, flawless flesh. Those lush mounds and amber crests.

His hands returned to her breasts of their own volition. As he teased and played, she tore at his leathers. Button, gone for good. The zipper, in shambles. She wrapped her fingers around the base of his erection and stroked up, and they both hissed.

The most exquisite female in all the worlds gripped his throbbing shaft.

"I *really* like," she purred in that way of hers, gliding her thumb over the slick tip, wringing a hoarse groan from him.

Pleasure stole his thoughts. "You've missed my hands, haven't you, nymph?"

"Only because you do such wonderful things with them."

The first flames of satisfaction flickered on the horizon. "You're starved for me."

"Every panty-melting inch."

He needed...so much. Immediately. More! The tiny tuft of sable curls between her legs drew his hand like a magnet. He ran two fingers over her soaked core and massaged her swollen little clit.

Back arching, she cried out with bliss. "Yes! It's good, Halo. So, so good. Don't stop doing *that*."

No sexier female. "Will any male suffice, or do you crave my touch alone, nymph?"

"Only yours," she said, leisurely stroking him while rolling her hips, chasing her climax. The first of many for her today; he was decided.

Thunder boomed, heralding an incoming storm. A crack of lightning split the sky. Streaks of otherworldly gold painted Ophelia as he thrust a finger deep inside her. Another feminine cry pierced the air.

She pumped his erection with greater force. He fed her a second finger. Her slick inner walls gloved the digits. A tight fit. Incredibly tight.

Once, twice, a dozen times, *Halo* nearly pleaded for more. He throbbed in her grip. His muscles were knotted. Sweat dripped from his brow.

Make her desperate. No mercy. The stakes were too high.

She bends to me. Not the other way around.

He scissored his fingers, stretching her. In, out. Faster. Harder. Even lost in the throes, she matched his pace.

He set his mouth at her ear, whispering, "Your sweet little body is mine, isn't it, Elia? Mine to pleasure. Mine to treasure however I see fit."

Her body jerked. "Treasure?" She threw back her head and screamed, drowning out the moaning rocks as her inner sheath contracted on his fingers.

As she came down from the high, her features soft with rapture, his control threatened to fray. With every inhalation, her sweet perfume breeched his every defense. The inferno in his bones blazed anew, his civility burning fast. He was a madman teetering on the brink of a fall.

When her tremors faded, he set in again, bringing her to another climax. And another and another, each one stretching longer than the last. He wavered between agony and ecstasy, nothing and everything in between.

She squeezed his length as he slid his fingers free of her. "No, not done." Her eyelids popped open, revealing glazed irises. "More, Astra."

"*Much* more." He sucked her sublime taste from his skin. His need...oh, his need. *Too much?* He didn't care.

Will have all of her.

"But first." He flattened each palm against the rock and dug his claws deep, caging her in. Anchored like this, he was an unmovable tower. "I'm ready to reopen our discussion."

"Ohhhh. Are you now?" Holding his gaze, grazing his slit, she nipped his lower lip. "Is my Astra ready for his reciprocation?"

He gave her the truth. "I'm dying for it, nymph."

★ ★ ★

With her free hand, Ophelia glided her nails along Halo's washboard abs and glorious happy trail. As his lips parted, she grew as vulnerable as she was aroused. This male was destroying her defenses with only his fingers and a claim of ownership.

He can satisfy me. I know he can. But would he claim her?

"I've thought it over," she said, releasing his length to run her fingers up his arms. "I've decided to hire you as *my* concubine. On a trial basis, of course."

He arched a brow, seemingly fighting a groan or a smile or both. "Oh, you wish to command me, do you?"

Yes. No. Yes? Mostly, she wanted a reason to never stop touching him. "You'll be highly interested in my benefits package, I promise you. Talk about mind-blowing."

"Will I find it satisfactory then?"

"Again and again and again."

He pressed a soft kiss into her lips. "Do you want to know what I'll give you for this?"

She licked her lips, nodded. Her heart thudded.

Eyes fierce, he said, "Elia, I will give you worlds."

The words—the emotions behind them—jolted her. Thoughts tangled as he bent his head to brush the tip of his nose against hers, then press his forehead to hers. As if they were two puzzle pieces fitting together, his jagged edges complementing hers.

Walls she hadn't known she'd built around her heart cracked, threatening to crumble. Panic bloomed in the aftermath, but she stuffed it in a box, to be unpacked later. Right now, she wanted to taste this male more than anything else in the world.

"I'm going to love sucking you off, Halo." Eyes hooding, she asked, "Do you want me to?"

His nostrils flared. He popped his claws free of the stone and gripped her hips. "Yes! Suck me off, Elia. Love it."

He was so eager, as if everything they did was a revelation. Did he know how intoxicating that was to someone like her?

The fact that he was the coldest, hottest male forged in the depths of her deepest fantasies, well, that was the icing on the cake. He wasn't cold right now, though. No, every part of him burned. Even the *alevala*. The images had gone still again, every gaze hot on her, searing her skin.

Another crack of thunder boomed as lightning split the darkness. Cold raindrops fell, splashing all around. Though she was naked, the breeze chilled, she only continued to heat. Halo the Furnace looked as wild as the terrain around them; he was shirtless, his chest littered with scratches. Wearing only a pair of gaping leathers, he made her desperate to be filled.

Splattered with droplets, Ophelia eased to her knees.

He heaved his breaths. Pleasure and strain warred for control of his face, leaving his features set in an agonized mask.

His body was strung as tight as a bow, his massive erection stretched before her. How her poor Astra must ache.

"Do not tease me, Elia." He tangled his fingers in her hair. "I need your lips. Suckle the tip. Slide to the base. Suck hard and harder. Need this, need this." He chanted the words as if he could no longer think of anything else.

He needed it. Needed *her*. The knowledge made her hungry…

Wanting him to see the eagerness in her eyes, she flicked her gaze back to his. Tendons pulled taut in his neck as she licked from root to tip.

"Yes, Elia!" His breathing quickened, his chest seeming to rise and fall with great effort. "More. Do it."

Shivering, she fit her lips over the crown and laved his slit with slow strokes of her tongue. Animal sounds rumbled from him as he bowed up.

His potent reaction to her every touch ratcheted her desires. Down she went, taking as much of him as possible. Up. His fingers flexed against her scalp. A lick of the head. Mmm. If ever passion had a taste, it was this man, dotted in rain.

"That's the way, Elia. You're making me feel so good." He growled the last. More and more tension roiled from his body.

Up, down. Up, down. Hoarse bellows left him. Despite his great need, the fingers he kept in her hair remained gentle. Her own pleasure intensified.

"Killing me so sweetly," he told her between sawing breaths. The torrent of rain softened to a light patter.

Thrumming, aching, she reached between her legs and pressed. Yes! She moaned around his length, wrenching another groan from him. He rocked just a bit...a little more... pumping his hips, tightening his grip on her hair, pulling the strands, giving and taking and Ophelia could not get enough.

"Going to...not ready...but my nymph is *forcing* me. Elia!" With a shout, Halo shot his seed down her throat.

Ophelia swallowed, greedy for every drop. Need more... more...more... A brutal climax broke free inside her. Releasing him, she screamed and whimpered. As she came down from the highest of highs, she entered a near-euphoric state, both needier and more sated than she'd ever been in her life.

"The things you make me feel, nymph." He sank to his knees before her. "Hearing you come...knowing you loved tasting me... I am undone."

The rain shower dissipated completely. With his hair plastered to his scalp, droplets wetting his lashes, he appeared as wild as the landscape. He sat and pulled her close, those glowing eyes issuing a thousand commands and even more promises.

All she could do was sag against him, breathing, "By the way, I liked everything." Except, he still hadn't claimed her. No stardust, no *gravita*. But that was a worry for tomorrow. Here, now, she felt too good.

He wrapped his arms around her, cradling her. In this position, her cheek pressed against his shoulder and, oh wow, okay, this wasn't exactly a comfortable fit. Ophelia wiggled to politely but obviously point out that his less than stellar after-hold needed major tweaking.

"Now then," he said with a calm, businesslike tone. "We will be discussing what happened between us—and what will happen between us in the future. You will not run from me."

Whoa, whoa, whoa. "Discuss it? Out loud?" Before she'd figured out her own feelings on the matter? "You let me go this instance, Halo. I mean it."

"We climax, we cuddle, we talk. That is your life now. Best make your peace with the notion, harpy."

"Astra! I mean it. There will be no discussion about anything." She beat her fists against his shoulders. "You are so lucky I don't dislike you enough to hate you right now."

"You feel some affection for me. Admit it."

He just had to dive straight into the deep end, didn't he? "I admit *nothing*."

"Then you owe me another kiss." Without a pause, he said, "I want to keep you. Do you want to keep me?"

"I. Admit. Nothing."

"Another kiss." He didn't loosen his grip, but he didn't tense up, either.

"Just...give me time to think, okay?"

"That, I can do. As long as you are in my arms."

They lapsed into silence, leaving her to ruminate, cuddle, and stew.

Affection. For Halo. The overprotective warlord with no heart now clinging to her as if she were a lifeline. Well, maybe he owned a tiny sliver of a heart. It wasn't like he was awful *all* the time. There were moments he was downright adorable.

Oh...crap. She did feel affection for him, and a *lot* of it—she felt it without the promise of stardust.

A kernel of fear settled deep in her chest. Guilt wasn't far behind. She was falling for the domineering male, while also setting herself up for a terrible splat. Every moment she retained her secrets, she created more of a no-win situation for herself.

But nothing had changed. If she caved and told him the truth about the beasts, he would fight to bench her. Might think she was working with Erebus, then deem her an enemy, unnecessarily dividing his focus. But if she kept her secret until the end, he might not forgive her. On the other hand, she might not require his forgiveness. Couples broke up all the time. Or he might not be upset at all. For all she knew, he would thank her for helping him win. And she *would* help him. The deep-seated assurance of victory had only grown stronger.

Halo wasn't the type to back down, though. No, he was more likely to double down. There was no male more stubborn. A fact that answered a burning question for her.

No, Ophelia Falconcrest could not have it all.

19

Deserve this. I really do.

The little temptress certainly loved to keep Halo in agony after they exchanged pleasures. He ground his teeth as he redirected her slight weight and flashed her to his bedroom.

She wore her pensive face, the world forgotten as she debated something inside her head. Halo had watched her do this a thousand times the past week. The outcome usually never skewed in his favor.

He laid her on the bed and stripped out of his wet leathers, then settled in beside her and gathered her close, luxuriating in the utter rightness. Having never met a woman like Ophelia—having never even entertained the notion of such feminine perfection—he hadn't understood why other males wasted time with cuddling. Now? He understood the appeal all too well.

Beyond my wildest imaginations. She was teaching him to crave *every* carnal indulgence. *I will win her. Nothing will stop me.*

During their briefings with the Commander and the General, Halo had gathered much information about Ophelia. She was defensive but vulnerable. Secretive, and always in survival mode. Soft and hard. Eager to laugh or argue, and sometimes both at the same time. Playful. Impish. Relentless.

The conclusion? He coveted both her mind and her body—and he would have them.

Every complaint she'd voiced had revolved around the task. She wished to participate and "pad her résumé." Though it was clear her sights were no longer set on becoming General, she sought more power. Despite the dangers to her life, he thought he could get on board with the quest—after the completion of the task. To keep her, he would have to. He was wise enough to reason out that much. But then, he would be taking extreme measures to ensure her safety.

Erebus and his phantoms would not be taking the harpymph from Halo. *Guard what's yours or lose it.*

She didn't seem to understand that he wished to partake in her joy, not leach it from her.

As he recalled her hoarse bellows and screams, he grinned up at the ceiling. He loved the way her scent fused with his, becoming theirs. Loved how her breaths fanned his sensitive skin. Loved so many things about their time together.

Why hadn't he produced stardust?

"I'm not taking a nap with you, so don't even think about it," she muttered, reminding him of warm honey slowly poured over a hot cake as she roused from her musings and melted into him. "But, to thank you for services rendered, I'm willing to stay for a short chat about nothing. Your heat is my kryptonite." A grumble.

He kissed her brow. "Other females would *kill* to use me as a scratchpad and discuss their day. My first and second concubines tried, and they lost their positions."

"Yes, and I'm sure they cried *buckets* of tears when you fired them." Ophelia rolled her eyes. "By the way, you're about to get fired from the same position for the same reason. Mistress O No prefers her men less talky."

He remembered her defense of her nicknames the day they'd met. Knowing her better now, he thought she might have been embarrassed of them. "Do you desire a new moniker, Ophelia? If so, we will get you a new moniker. Whatever you wish."

"Uh, not likely. Other people get to pick our nicknames for us, always. It's an unwritten rule. Isn't it?" She dug her claws into his pectoral and gasped out, "Halo, can we pick nicknames for ourselves?"

"Harpy, we can do whatever we want. When we tell someone to use a certain title, they will use a certain title. There will be no exceptions."

She rewarded his honesty with an infectious laugh as earth-shattering as her touch. "From now on, I'm Ophelia the...something. I need a moment."

"Our deal still stands. As long as you are in my arms, you may take as much time as you require."

As she muttered ideas under her breath, Halo cast his gaze over the room. A candlelit lunch—attempt two—had been prepared by Ian before the freeze. The food waited untouched on a small round table near the crackling hearth. A bottle of vodka chilled in an ice bucket. He'd noticed the twenty empty ones in her bunkroom, figured she enjoyed the beverage, and made a special request this morning.

"Perhaps you'll think clearer with a full stomach," he suggested.

"But I'm not ready to leave the cocoon of your warmth." She plucked her claws free and rested a palm above his heart, tentative, as if trying out the new pose.

He wasn't ready to leave, either. "Have you watched any memories of my *alevala* lately?"

"Only the elfin goddess with the pet unicorn. You were so cold and callous to her."

Ah, yes. Halo had been unable to kill the elf as easily as his other targets. The powerful female had possessed the ability to blend into her surroundings with such seamlessness, he'd been unable to find her. And he could find anyone. To draw her out, he and the other Astra captured and trapped her favorite pet, creating a transparent doorway before it. The moment she had slipped through that doorway, she had entered a duplicate realm, allowing Halo to track her every movement from then on, blending in or not.

"She stood between me and the well-being of my brothers," he explained.

"And all obstacles get obliterated. Yeah. I remember." Bitterness tinged her words, confusing him.

"Had I not defeated her, I would not be here with you." He would have done much worse to get here.

"Yes, but at the time, you didn't know someone as glorious as me would ever cross your path."

If he wished to win this harpy, he must share something of himself. Give and get. Sow and reap. An unavoidable fact of life. "You resent my coldness. But I would not have survived the Order without it."

"I'm listening."

"The instructors used pain to teach me to shut down. To forge ahead, no matter my thoughts, feelings, or desires. That kind of training is difficult to shed." He waggled his jaw before admitting, "If ever a hindrance kept me from reaching a goal, I lost something precious to me."

"That sucks. I'm sorry." As she petted him, he decided sharing wasn't so bad, after all. "It explains a lot. You equate punishment with emotion and fight what you feel."

Until you. Everything she elicited, both the good and the bad, came with rewards. Excitement and ease. Effortless pleasures. Anticipation…

"The same can be said of you, eh?" he asked, playing with her hair.

"I wasn't disciplined if I messed up, but I was made to feel like the world's biggest failure." She steepled her hands and propped her cheek atop them. "Tell me you killed your instructors."

"I did. Violently." The memory pleased him to this day. "Chaos purchased and trained me alongside the other Astra. They showed me how to rely on someone other than myself. Eventually trust grew. A bond formed. Together, we returned to the Order and gifted pieces of the instructors to their students as trophies." He turned the spotlight on her. "What do you know of your father?"

"Oh. Well." She appeared startled that he'd asked. "I've never met him. I don't even know his name, which is often the case for harpies born outside of a consort."

His chest clenched. His harpy daughters would know him; he'd make sure of it.

Halo blinked. His daughters? As if making a family with his *gravita* was a done deal. As if he craved it deep, deep inside.

Was it? Did he?

His chest clenched harder, bones seeming to crack.

She scooted a little closer, as if she hoped to soothe him. "As second-in-command of the entire army, you wield a ton of power. And as someone who has been on the receiving end of your authority, you wield that power well. Obviously, you love control. But do you ever want to throw your hat in the ring and fight to be the big boss man?"

"I agreed to assume the title if necessary, but I've never desired to wear the Commander's helmet. I deal with enough strain. There's no reason to add more now that I have other endeavors." Gaining more moments like this. Getting his woman naked and in his arms every morning, every evening. And any yearning to dominate, he could now exercise with his harpymph, who loved breaking and heeding his orders, orchestrating his sexual torment either way.

She scooted closer still. "What do you plan to do after you ascend and kill Erebus? Find another enemy? Have fun?"

He believed he might like to spend the next few decades in bed with his *gravita*. A promisingly sweet future indeed. In fact, a strange warmth spread through him at the thought. Strange, and yet he thought he might recognize it, as if remnants of it had somehow survived the ages.

Hope.

Rather than looking ahead and seeing eons of old and new burdens to bear between repeated trials and tribulations, he beheld a feast of pleasures and contentment, his for the taking.

"I'm not sure I've ever had fun outside of my time with you," he said.

"Really?" She jolted to her knees, plump breasts bobbing. Tussled dark hair shimmered in the light. She grinned. "You know what this means, right? I'm the best thing to ever happen to you."

She just might be. "Before you, I despised being touched. With you, I seek only more, but it's never enough. Before you, I took my lovers from behind and struggled to climax. With you, I struggle to *stop* from climaxing."

Her brow knit in confusion. "If you hated being touched, why did you keep a concubine?"

"A momentary release is better than no release at all."

Rubbing against him… "Well. I'm gonna make you so happy you copped to your deep and abiding obsession with me, Astra. I'm gonna show you supergood times today. The best! By tomorrow, you're not even going to remember a moment you lived without satisfaction."

Yes! He wanted this. Satisfaction. Contentment. More. He— A chill dusted him, and he stiffened. *Danger!*

"Phantoms." Halo flashed to his feet beside the bed, donned pants, summoned a T-shirt for Ophelia, and gripped a three-blade.

Three phantoms ghosted through the wall, one after the other. Near the foot of the bed, they walked in a circle, oblivious to the world around them as they chanted. "Go to Halo, give him message, eat the girl. Go to Halo, give him message, eat the girl. Go to Halo, give him message, eat the girl."

Hate the god. Erebus had sent in his minions the second the promise of pure merriment edged within Halo's clasp.

He glanced at Ophelia. She wore the shirt and sat on her knees, holding a three-blade she must have pilfered from his closet without his knowledge while gazing longingly at the phantoms.

An ache erupted in the center of his chest. "Do you want your first kill, Elia?" He was here; he could guard her. There'd be no real danger.

"Are you kidding? Yes!" She scrambled to his side as fast as harpily possible, her wings buzzing. "Not to complain about your whiplash personality changes or whatever, but what happened to me needing to train before I took on the advanced phantoms Erebus sends your way?"

His whiplash personality? His? "I've been assured you are fierce and determined on the battlefield."

The look she gave him. Halo willed the phantoms to die quickly, just to grab the harpy and throw her back onto the bed. Her emerald eyes were dreamy, as if he'd presented her with the world's most priceless jewels. A male could get used to a look like that.

He flashed behind her and clasped her by the waist, ready to issue instructions. "Be ready. As soon as they deliver their message, they'll fly over. You'll need to strike them one after the other with a single strike."

"I can do it."

The phantoms went still. In unison, their milky white gazes shot to him over the harpy's shoulder. "You are welcome, Halo." Their monotone voices flowed together. "I know you enjoyed your break from battle. And let's not forget your woman's survival. You grow closer to her every day. That is wonderful. For me. I'm sorry to say, it is going to make the next challenge so much worse for you. Ha ha. Ha ha ha. Ha ha ha."

Fury boiled up, but he ignored it, concentrating only on Ophelia's safety. "Be ready. They'll attack in three, two—"

Too late. *Ophelia* stormed forward. Halo observed, poised to assist at a moment's notice. She went low, stabbing—argh! Only air. The trio of phantoms disembodied and fled through the wall, taking their chill with them.

Had they sensed Erebus's mark on the harpy, making her off-limits?

"Argh! Why does this keep happening to me? Am I phantom repellant?"

He frowned. "This happened to you before the task?"

"Yes. Why do you think I'm without a kill?"

His frowned deepened. If the mark were responsible, and she'd been unable to approach phantoms before this...she had borne the mark before the task had ever begun. Which meant she'd had contact with the god before the task had ever begun. Information she had failed to disclose to Halo or her General. But...no. If the two had any kind of contact, Ophelia hadn't known it. She was secretive about her past, but not about the things affecting his task.

The harpy stomped her bare foot, delectable in his T-shirt. The material swallowed her lush curves. "I just want to kill someone. Anyone! Is that too much to ask?"

"I have no doubt the phantoms will attack you en masse once the brand is removed." A reason to leave the mark on her. No phantoms, no danger. Except, suddenly Halo wanted Erebus's claim off her, whatever the consequences.

The link between the god and Ophelia would be severed *today*.

Halo never should have left the mark on her. So he was going to hemorrhage power when he removed it? So what. "No more waiting. Off it comes." Fun could wait. He stalked closer.

"Now? But—"

"Now." Halo flattened his palm between her breasts to begin the long, draining process of— Boom! His power butted up against hers, and a high electrical charge punched him. He flew backward, slamming into the mantel above the blazing hearth. Broken wood and crumbled plaster rained around him.

"Astra!" Ophelia cried, seemingly unaffected by the blast. She raced over to crouch at his side, her emerald eyes glimmering with a cocktail of guilt and shame. "Are you okay?"

"I will be," he wheezed from a supine position. He thought every bone in his body might be broken. As he healed, searing pains amplified and died. Suspicions blazed, unleashing an inferno of distrust. That wall of defensive power hadn't come from Erebus or an ancient blade of untold origins but Ophelia herself.

All power carried the signature of its creator. A piece of their essence. Ophelia's signature didn't register as harpy or nymph, however, but primordial.

Proof that her blood had been used to summon the beasts?

Or had Erebus done something worse to her? The god had *dared*?

Rage charred the edges of Halo's calm. His instincts shouted, *Right. And wrong.*

Both? How could it be? What was he missing?

Stumped, he scrutinized the harpy's firelit features. Oh, yes. She did indeed project guilt and shame. Gaze darting away from him. Color blooming in her cheeks. Pearly whites nibbled on her bottom lip.

She hides more than I realized.

Other suspicions rose, crashed, then rose again, like torrents and tides in an ocean. Was there a deeper connection between

Ophelia and Erebus? Something Halo wasn't seeing? Something he maybe didn't want to believe?

Unease built inside him even as fury stirred anew, focusing on another target. If the harpy had betrayed him...

No. She hadn't. She wouldn't. Harpy loyalty never wavered. But...

He would watch her. Would decipher the truth, one way or another.

"What happened?" she asked.

Did she know or didn't she? Halo stood and pulled Ophelia to her feet. "Forget fun," he told her, already stalking toward the bedroom door. "We have some studying to do."

20

Five days later, Ophelia woke with a whimper in her heart and two certainties burning her brain.

The first: *Erebus is coming for me today.* He planned to morph her into a boar, the next animal Hercules fought.

Second: *I'm losing Halo.*

How she sensed Erebus's exact intentions, she wasn't sure. Well, she kind of had an idea. The mark and her evolving intuition.

How she sensed Halo's waning interest in her was much easier—common sense.

She lay in bed, awake and aware before Vivi ever entered the bunkroom. Ophelia stared up at the ceiling. Without the Astra nearby, she shivered with cold. But more and more, she was staying cold in his presence too. They hadn't kissed since he'd attempted—and failed—to remove her brand. There'd been no chin pinches or cuddles either. No questions. Though he had oh, so romantically offered to let her kill the messenger phantoms, he hadn't shown any interest in bathing with her afterward. Instead, he'd been stoic and quiet, either glaring at her with accusation or nodding at her with relief.

Old fears constantly pinged with new life. Did Halo want less of her now that he'd experienced more? Had he decided she wasn't *gravita* material, after all? Did he suspect the truth? That she had panicked the moment he'd turned his focus to the brand's removal? A voice she hadn't recognized had screamed inside her head, *Mine!* A total shock but come on! No brand meant no transformations. No transformations, no added strength. No added strength, no advantage over Erebus. No advantage, no victory. But...Halo kind of deserved the truth. He must sense it.

Daily, the same dilemma raged within her, dredging up guilt and fear from the muddy rivers in her mind. Confess the full truth or never confess. Do it after the successful completion of the task or before. Take one or two or three more doses of power or risk being stopped now.

Didn't she have a *right* to that power? Halo fought to ascend—and so did she. Not to become General. No. To become the kind of harpy who didn't *need* an Astra to protect her. The kind of warrior who defended those weaker than herself.

Was she selfish? Greedy? Was she a coward? Diabolical genius? Both? To ascend, you had to grow. That, she knew. To grow, you had to stretch. To stretch, you had to hurt. But...

She didn't want to be a source of pain for Halo. Only a fountain of pleasure.

Whatever the answer to her dilemma, she knew one thing for certain: she should *not* make the big confession today. Distract him right before a battle, risking his loss? That, he for sure would never forgive. But then, he might not ever forgive her, anyway.

Why wouldn't he talk to her?

She knew the second Vivi tiptoed from their shared bathroom, sneaking closer to the bed. The lioness and the hydra snarled inside Ophelia's head, ready to mount a defense.

Oh yes. The two creatures had begun making themselves known, a part of her now. The batteries Erebus had mentioned. Though caged, her companions liked to rattle the bars.

It was a consequence she hadn't foreseen, and the reason she had new strength. Nothing she couldn't handle, however.

"Get your lazy butt out of bed. Operation Lady— Oh. You've already opened up the ole mind shops. Well. That's not horribly disappointing or anything."

"I don't need to go to the gym," she said. "I'm already racer ready. Oh, and I've already attended the meeting with Taliyah." Plenty of times. Too many. "She was planning on banishing me to Ation, only to change her mind when I agreed to help Halo successfully complete his mission."

"I...you...*what*? A mission? With an Astra? Why am I just now hearing about this? You *know* I prefer live action updates."

"You've heard it several—wait. I should have started my speech with the time loop."

"Time loop?"

"The same day is repeating over and over again." Yawning, she strolled into the bathroom, Vivi hot on her heels. "Also, I'm considering changing my moniker to Lady O-mazing." It wasn't exactly perfect, but she'd been unable to think up anything better. Lady Eternal? The She-beasts?

"*What?* Maybe start your speech with something that makes a wee bit more sense because my brain is about to explode."

Too late. The world's most confusing thought was already posed at the end of her tongue. "If time is circular rather than linear, the past sixteen days haven't happened. Technically speaking. Which means nothing has repeated, and I've done nothing wrong. I haven't even met Halo."

Vivi gaped as Ophelia brushed her hair and teeth. "Forget

the time loop. My perma-single friend did not just go dreamy eyed over an Astra Planeta."

"Your perma-single friend *might* have gone dreamy eyed," she said, dressing. Ophelia had a *raging* infatuation with the douchebag. His heat…his intensity…those rare moments he teased her. His kisses and touches. His commands. Their cuddle sessions. His *everything*.

I can't lose him.

As if her thoughts summoned him, he arrived in her bunkroom, right on schedule. She couldn't see him yet, but she felt him, a familiar charge arching through the air. Her heart raced, as it always raced whenever he neared.

"Come to me, Elia," he intoned, and warm shivers cascaded over her spine.

Vivi's eyes bugged. "The Astra *fetches* you?"

"Often." Ophelia fluffed her hair and exited the bathroom, ready for this morning's confrontation with her Astra. Lately, he had looked her over, frowned, and flashed her to the library for more hours of reading.

Today he stood with his arms crossed over his chest—the power pose she'd named Big Trouble. The pieces of the trinite collar dangled from his hand. He wore the usual black T-shirt and leathers, but he looked better than ever. More aggressive, sharper edged and highly motivated.

Flutters erupted in her belly, and she forgot the rest of the world. *Sexy Astra.* The stripes in his irises spun as she approached and lifted her hair.

"I like you this way," he said with a soft voice. Dangerously soft. He clamped the cold stone around her neck, the chill barely registering as his hot fingers brushed her skin.

"In my flannel pajamas?"

A corner of his mouth twitched. "Acquiescent."

Whoa. What was this? Her heart raced faster. Irresistible Halo was back! The only version of him to tease her. But…

Why now, the day she sensed Erebus's intention to act? "Perhaps I'm lulling you into a false sense of calm," she said and humphed. If he thought she would melt the moment he showed her an ounce of affection, he was right. Wrong! Definitely, unequivocally wrong.

"Are you planning to attack me then?" he asked, grazing his knuckle along her jaw.

"Darling," she rasped with her most cunning smile. "I've attacked your thoughts since the moment we met." Bold words. Prideful and flirty. But also seeking. How did he feel about her now?

He returned her smile slowly, his features lighting up. "True. I didn't stand a chance."

He still likes me!

"Kiss already! Make me a big, beautiful Astra baby," Vivi called from the bathroom doorway. She pumped her fist in the air.

Oops. Ophelia had lost track of their audience. "Excuse me a moment," she told Halo. "I have a best friend to annihilate."

"We stay together." He captured her wrist and flashed her to the coliseum.

Huh. Empty. Usually, harpies trained here at all hours of the day and night. At any given time before the freeze, groups could be spotted running up and down the stairs or brawling on the sandy battleground.

"Today, we spar," Halo announced. "You said you excel at maiming and pillaging. Now you'll prove it."

Really? Truly? He was giving her a real chance? "One teensy little problem," she said, spreading her arms to indicate her current attire. "I'm in my pajamas and bootless."

"That isn't a problem, teensy or otherwise. A good soldier can fight in all manner of clothing. Or lack of it."

Well. He wasn't wrong. "Why test me now? Aren't you afraid the delicate nymph will get an owie?"

The muscle jumped in his jaw. A tell she hadn't spotted in a while—huge mad. *Aw. Welcome back.* She hated to admit it, but she'd kind of missed his anger.

"When I said I wanted to keep you," he grated, "I meant it. This is a part of your life, so it will be a part of mine. We will be happy together."

Just like that, a geyser of guilt blew its top, spewing cold, hot, awful acid. He was making promises he shouldn't. Promises he might not make if he knew all the facts. She should tell him the truth. Yes. She should. And she would. Just as soon as the time was right.

When she averted her gaze, he pinched her chin. Oh! Not the chin pinch! "We will be loyal to each other. I will not bring harm to you, and you will not bring harm to me. Isn't that right, Ophelia?"

"Of course that's right. We're allies!" She slapped his hand away, annoyed with him. With herself. No matter what it seemed like, she had only their ultimate good in mind.

"That's what I am choosing to conclude, because I am tired of keeping my distance." He rolled his head, then his shoulders, then stepped a few feet back, settling into a battle-ready stance. With a wave of his fingers, he invited her to challenge him. "Attack me."

She didn't. She crossed her arms over her chest, mimicking his power pose. "Be honest." What did he mean, choosing to conclude? Had he kept his distance because he'd doubted her loyalty? "Is this a real test of my skills or an excuse to feel me up?"

"It can't be both?"

Well. Another solid response. "All right, then." This was actually happening? Going head-to-head with a *god*? "I'll train with you."

"Don't hold back," he instructed.

"I'll give you everything I've got, promise." Wings fluttering, she stripped off her flannels. Wearing only a tank top and panties, she approached him slowly, rolling her hips. "You try your best to do the same."

He roved his heated gaze over her. "I thought we agreed warriors can battle in flannel."

"No, we agreed warriors can battle in *anything*. Try not to let my near nakedness distract you."

"Too late. I am undone. You do not fight fair, beaut—"

Ophelia punched him in the throat, striking fast and sure.

His breath hitched, his sentence ended abruptly, but nothing more. He healed too swiftly.

"You're right," she said. "I don't fight fair."

"We are to have no rules, then," he said when he was able. His eyes sparkled in the morning sunlight. "Good to kno—"

She punched his throat again. "You were saying?"

Another hitch of his breath. His eyes narrowed on her. She smiled as sweet as sugar—then she attacked for real. They grappled across the field. Rolling together. Springing apart. Launching blows. Dodging, flinging sand. At first, he merely played defense, allowing her to land certain blows. Learning her, just as he'd done with the lioness and the hydra. But Ophelia used the time to learn him as well.

Observation #1: Her body distracted him. Anytime he pinned her, he neglected the fight entirely and focused on rubbing against her. She might neglect the fight for a moment too, but she always sometimes bounced back in a slow hurry.

#2: He would not, under any circumstances, wound her. No matter what moves he executed, he never once scraped her with his claws. Never bruised her or broke her skin.

"Who knew the Machine could be hornier than a nymph," she taunted when he kneaded her breasts before springing back. "Hey, Halo. Do you remember the time I sucked you off? I do." She bounded to her feet, unwilling to stay down. "I'm considering it right now…"

Growling, he turned up the heat. No more defense only. He

launched multiple assaults, but again, he always stopped short of wounding her.

"Not injuring me at every opportunity is dumb," she told him, swinging for his groin. At the last second, he jumped out of the way. "It's also your burden to bear. I won't be extending you the same courtesy."

She kept her word. Ophelia took advantage of his unwillingness to land a blow. Clawing. Punching. Kicking. He was fast, but he wasn't always fast enough.

With each drop of blood she drew, the beasts snarled louder, demanding more. Aggression pumped through her veins, burning, singeing. Her bones vibrated, as if…no, surely not. But… maybe? Was she about to morph outside of a task, without the aid of the Bloodmor?

Ophelia wheezed, combatting the change. She was unprepared when Halo drove her to the ground.

"Elia?" he asked, radiating concern as he loomed over her.

Impact jolted her from the panic, her insides cooling, her mind quieting. Okay. All right. "I'm fine," she said. In control now. Proof of her growing strength.

Master the beasts, master Erebus. *I can do this.*

Halo stood and helped her to her feet. Trembles coursed through her fatigued limbs, but she balanced well.

"You are sure you're fine?" he asked, his concern undiluted. "You appeared to be in great pain."

Ophelia punched him in the throat for a third time. "I'm. Fine."

He rasped, "Sheathe the murder mittens, harpy. Practice is over." His arm shot out, wrapping around her wrist and creating a shackle. He flashed her directly into his private shower stall, where he stripped them both.

They washed each other, lost in their own thoughts.

Her guilt flared anew, and she couldn't stay quiet. "Let's say you're one hundred percent correct, and my blood *is* being used to summon the beasts. That means you *need* Erebus to approach me to complete your labor. That means you need me to hurt."

Some of Halo's tension faded, his posture easing. "He didn't need your blood to summon the hind."

"Yes, but the hind wasn't a primordial."

"It might have been." He shook his head, flinging water droplets in every direction. "Erebus's champion, Erebus's problem. If he cannot get to you, the burden falls on him to provide one another way."

Which put the fate of Halo—and harpykind—in someone else's hands. No. Absolutely not. Not while Ophelia's instinct was singing, *I've got this.* Not while her strength continued to grow leaps and bounds. This battle *belonged* to Ophelia.

"What if there's a great reason I must be the one to work with Erebus? Me specifically?" she asked. "And what if that reason aids you, not him, while seeming to do the opposite?" *Careful. Go too far, no turning back.*

He maintained a blank expression, revealing nothing. His most annoying skill. "Is there? Does it?"

Was this the right time to admit the full truth? To blurt out, *I'm the hideous beasts! You've killed me twice. Today, you might have to do it again. But stay focused, okay? Only everyone is counting on us.*

In the end, she merely shrugged.

He pursed his lips. "My argument stands. The burden falls to Erebus. If he fails to supply a competitor, I'll win the match by default, and you'll stay safe."

"I don't want to stay safe," she snapped.

"And that is *your* burden to bear," he snapped back.

They finished the shower in uncomfortable silence. Just before he switched off the water, he pressed a brief kiss to her cheek. A gesture of affection. An apology?

Her chest clenched. *He only wishes to protect me.* That wasn't a bad thing. Actually, she appreciated and applauded his enthusiasm. He cared about her. And caring was wonderful. A positive step forward.

But was it enough?

They dressed in clean clothes. Holding his gaze, nose in the air, she sheathed a three-blade beneath the skirt of her uniform.

Halo sighed. "Come here." He sat at the edge of the bed, reached out and cupped her backside, urging her to stand between his legs. Pressing his forehead into her breastplate, he gruffly admitted, "You're a good fighter. Crafty. You enjoy kicking your opponent when he's down."

"Yes. Well. That's because it's double the reward." Trying not to puff up with pride or melt with vulnerability, she combed her nails through his hair. "You're not just being nice again, are you? I mean, you didn't utilize every opportunity to take me down, and I supplied you with plenty. I know that. But you really think I'm skilled?" Ugh! What was she doing? Begging for praise?

He lifted his head and smiled wryly. "You broke my jaw, harpy. Twice. I would have stopped you if I could have. You're skilled."

So she preened a bit after that? So what? She didn't need *anyone's* admiration, but there was nothing wrong with enjoying it. Or enjoying him. Which she would do. Today. Even though she and Halo *would* go head-to-head at some point—her certainty of that hadn't dimmed. She would use this labor to test her control against Erebus. Tomorrow, she would tell Halo the full truth, and they would go from there, whatever his reaction.

Yes. Decision made. Things changed, and plans must change with them. And maybe, just maybe, this had been her problem all along; the reason he hadn't bathed her with stardust. Until she was strong enough to tell Halo the truth, she wasn't strong enough for him, period.

"So what's on today's pre-freeze agenda?" she asked. "Because you owe me a day of fun, and if you're game, I've decided to cash in."

He rubbed his hands along her sides. Not in a sexual way. Not exactly. This struck her as…appreciative. The way a collector might polish a favorite coin. Her belly fluttered.

He peered up at her as if he cared for nothing else. "You want fun, you get fun. Tell me what to do, and I'll do it."

21

"This isn't what I had in mind," Halo muttered.

Ophelia paraded him through the palace, stopping any harpy they came across, making introductions, and giving him the great honor of singing her praises while she preened.

"They won't remember this," he told her, slightly baffled as they walked away from the latest group.

"True. But I'll forever remember their reactions, and that's enough. You'll see for yourself. Ready for some verbal reciprocation, Immortal?" she asked, practically bubbling over with giddiness as she guided him toward Ian, who currently worked on a fortification for a window.

As soon as Halo had awoken this morning, he'd sensed a new labor loomed. He'd briefed the Astra on the highlights. Now they worked to keep Erebus from making an impromptu visit while Halo advanced his relationship with his harpymph.

Ian glanced up from his task, his brows drawn. "Yes?"

"Introduce me to your friend, darling." Leering at Halo, melting on him as only she could do, Ophelia said, "I want to make sure he knows how lucky he is to work with the most brilliant, powerful warlord in all the realm."

Hmm. All right. Yes. He saw the appeal of this. Ecstasy and agony. "I'm sure Ian knows, now that he's heard the truth from the realm's most cunning temptress." Halo kissed her knuckles. "Ian, meet Ophelia the—what moniker did we decide to go with, sweetheart?"

"Sweetheart?" she squeaked.

"Yes, that's it. Ophelia the Sweetheart." Halo nodded, adoring her dawning realization and horror. "Ophelia the Sweetheart, meet Ian."

"Wait," she said, batting at Halo's chest. A flush deepened the color in her cheeks as she faced Ian. "That isn't my name. We're considering Lady O-mazing. Or Death Slayer. The Sweetheart isn't even in the running. I'm vicious, I swear!"

Ian gaped at him, and Halo inwardly snickered. He desperately wanted to kiss his harpymph right now.

"Come, the Sweetheart." He led a protesting Ophelia to the foyer, where a crowd of harpies had gathered.

Grappling with her had primed him in ways he hadn't expected. And also impressed him. She had displayed shocking speed and strength, her every punch threatening to fracture another bone. Her reflexes had definitely quickened since he'd chased her through the royal garden. Perhaps he didn't have to worry about her getting hurt in battle, after all.

She peered up at him, her face an intoxicating study of amusement, frustration, and excitement. "If Ophelia the Sweetheart sticks—"

"There will be great heck to pay?" he asked. How he loved teasing her. A time when everything felt right. "Do you understand my joke? Because your name is Sweetheart, you dish heck instead of hell?"

A laugh bubbled from her, and she pressed her fingers over her mouth. "Thank you for the explanation of your…joke, did you say?"

At the sound of her merriment, his gut tightened. "I want inside you." A growled statement. No stopping it.

Her lips parted.

As different harpies looked their way, Halo flashed Ophelia back to his—their—bedroom. No more waiting. He wanted to kiss her, so he would.

Catching her gaze, he sat at the edge of the bed and clasped her waist.

"So." She stood between his legs and combed trembling fingers through his hair. "You want inside me, Astra?"

"More than I've ever wanted anything." He smoothed his hands up and down her curves. Tendrils of satisfaction beckoned, once again within his reach. Tunneling a hand under her skirt, grazing his knuckles over her damp panties, he rasped, "Do *you* want me inside you, Elia?" Would she admit it?

"I…do." Eyes hooded, she stepped back and unstrapped her armor. "Should I strip for you?"

She was giving herself to him? "Yes! Strip for me." He leaned forward and rested his elbows on his knees to prevent himself from reaching for her as the breastplate fell. Suddenly she wore only the collar, crisscrossing bands of black leather and the skirt. *Will never get enough of those curves.*

Fingers on the fastener on her skirt, she paused. "Am I yours, Halo?"

"Only mine." *Temptation itself.* "You like making me crazed, don't you?"

"I really do." She twisted the button but didn't free it, teasing him with what could be. "But you like being crazed."

"I do," he echoed. "The skirt. Remove it." She had decided to give herself to him. To trust him with more and more of her body and her life. He would have her, and they would make this thing between them work.

She reached for the leather straps shielding her nipples instead, only to sway and grow pallid. Her air of playfulness ebbed as she rubbed the disk that hung from the collar. "Halo?"

"What is it?" he demanded, jumping to his feet, ready to kill any threat.

"Something's wrong. He's summoning me, I think." Agony twisted her expression as she panted her breaths and clutched her middle. "I... He... Argh!" She pulled at the collar. "It's only getting worse. I'm coming out of my skin. Get this thing off me!"

Erebus was attempting to access her brand from a distance? Before the freeze?

Halo's blood iced over. He checked his inner clock—yes, they were seconds away from the freeze, and the god was tearing the harpy apart from the inside. "Breathe through it, harpy. You can do this. It hurts, and I'm sorry. I'm so sorry, sweetheart, but he cannot succeed as.long as you wear the collar. Breathe!"

Tears streamed down her cheeks. No, not tears. Blood. Crimson poured from her eyes and nose. The sides of her mouth. Her ears.

"Erebus!" he roared. If the god kept this up, he would kill her. Would slay her right in front of Halo. Perhaps his goal.

Without the trinite, she might have a chance of survival, at least.

Frantic, desperate and not knowing what else to do, he ripped the piece from her throat. For better or worse.

"He's going to take you, Elia. But I'm coming for you. Fight him until I get there."

"No! Don't come for me. I'll be ok—" She disappeared.

Rage stampeded Halo, *anhilla* rising. How many times had he failed to protect this female? How much would she be forced to suffer in one day?

As he flew through the castle, checking different rooms, he summoned a multitude of weapons he might need.

No sign of his harpy or Erebus. No sign of them outside the palace, either. *Can't fail her again.*

But he did fail her again. The trumpet blasted, signaling the end of his hunt and the beginning of his next test.

He prayed for a second blast, but it never came. Another battle to the death then. "Halo Phaninon!"

Had another creature been activated with Ophelia's blood? Was she already dead?

To silence a cry, he bit a finger to the bone. *Focus. Win. Get to tomorrow.*

Blood hot, he palmed motorized axes. Today's battle should involve a mythological boar. He would go hard, and he would go fast.

A mystical tug drew him to the coliseum. He flashed to the sandy battleground, where he'd trained with Ophelia. Once again, phantoms filled the stands. Erebus occupied the royal platform, perched upon the General's throne. Pale curls and white skin proved a stark contrast to his black robe.

"Apologies for my timing." The god grinned, smug. As if he knew a secret Halo did not. "The Blade of Destiny assures me you're going to suffer mightily after this next battle."

Hatred gripped his throat and squeezed. "Where is the girl?"

"Do not worry. She's frothing at the mouth, eager to see you."

She lived? Acid infiltrated Halo's veins. Was she being tortured? Sobbing for him? "I will enjoy killing you when the time comes."

Erebus's grin only widened, all teeth. "Unfortunately for you, you're only allowed to kill the she-boar today."

The ground shook with so much vigor, Halo suspected a *pack* of boars was coming for him. Yet only one beast flew from the catacombs, flinging those bars across the sand. The size of a rhinoceros, with thick wiry quills. Foam leaked from the corners of her mouth. Two tusks protruded over her upper lip; two curled from the sides of her jaw.

Her beady gaze never veered from Halo as she charged his way...

Protect her. The instinct pulsed, stronger than before. So strong he tensed.

Roaring, she leaped for him. He darted, but not quickly enough. A tusk gouged his hip. That tusk vibrated, shattering every bone in his leg.

Halo collapsed but fought his way to his feet as he healed. Still the instinct to protect clambered.

When he sliced off one of her hooves, she thudded to the ground. Like him, she didn't stay down. As she righted, a new hoof grew. No, not a hoof, but a... Halo blinked. A head grew, with a face. Sharp teeth, tusks and all.

A head. On her foot. As if the boar were a hydra.

The she-beast charged him once again, that head-foot eating dirt. He struggled to tear his gaze from it. Those eyes. They were pale green. *Ophelia* green.

His body jerked with shock. A suspicion he'd dared not entertain suddenly seemed...likely. Was *Ophelia* the monster?

No. No! She couldn't be. He would have sensed it from the beginning. Would have recognized her long before this, no matter her state. He would not have coldly, cruelly killed an innocent harpy in battle. Not his own female, a potential *gravita*. Not even Halo was so cruel.

The assurance gave him little peace, however. In the ensuing minutes, he fought merely to defend, learn, and think. He took blow after blow, each hit worse than the last. The boar's quills leaked a sweet-smelling toxin, tinged with Ophelia's carnality. And the way the creature faked a left and swung her head right. A slight hesitation with the final step before a leap. Things the harpy had done in battle.

His instincts sang louder and louder, until a chorus filled his head. *My Ophelia.*

She lived—as the boar. The way she had avoided questions about her involvement and death. Evasions about the blade itself. Her reaction to the removal of the brand. The guilt she'd projected upon occasion. His trust? In tatters. Killing Five? Nothing compared to this. Ophelia had known the truth all along, and she'd chosen to leave him in the dark. Chosen to leave him ill-prepared while the fate of the Astra hung in the balance. To make Halo suffer the shame of what he'd done over and over again for the rest of eternity.

Betrayal scorched him, and he gave a bitter laugh. Ophelia was Erebus's champion. Well-chosen. Forcing Halo to fight her as well as his own protective instincts. No wonder he'd vomited after the previous battles.

How could he ever, for any reason, harm the sensual beauty who pleasured him? The insatiable vixen he wished to pleasure in turn.

How could he do it again?

Halo's stomach wrung bile into his throat. How could he *not* do it?

Either Ophelia fought for Erebus, betraying harpykind, which Halo doubted, or she was letting herself be used for another reason. Something she'd hinted at during their shower, he realized. But either way, she had lied to him. Because she had *wanted* this. The truth was so clear now.

So. Halo would do this with zero emotion. Just as he'd done as a child. He would do it because he must.

He forced a total shut down. His mind blanked, his thoughts homing in on his goal. *Tonight, I end her life. Tomorrow, her freedom.*

He stopped defending himself against her assaults and launched an attack of his own. The tusks—gone.

Her sharp cry of pain did not affect him. Didn't gut him to his core.

Huffing and puffing, she circled him. Calming? Or planning the day's dinner menu?

"Surrender, and you'll feel no more pain." A command.

She went still. He prowled closer...

Spooked, she bucked. Waging a war within herself?

He avoided her next series of strikes, hoping to tire her out, but she never fatigued.

Erebus laughed all the while.

Increasingly aware of the rawness inside him, Halo did the only thing he could. He broke her front legs, forced her to kneel, and pushed her snout into the dirt.

"I warned you, harpy."

As he held her down, her muscles strained and tendons pulled taut. Her strength was incredible, her determination unmatched.

Heart thundering, he grated, "Surrender, Ophelia, or it will be much worse for you. You have no other options here."

Still, she fought, bucking. Erebus's laughter acquired a maddened tinge as it echoed across the battleground.

Gnashing his molars, Halo fit a mystically enforced rope around her legs, binding her feet together.

And still his harpy bucked.

Ignore the rise of nausea. If she would just *stop.*

"Do not think you can save her, Halo," the god called. "The labor doesn't end until one of you delivers a fatal blow."

Exactly as he'd suspected. Halo debated his options. Kill her. Kill himself instead. Let her kill him. This was a test but grading mattered. He was supposed to learn something.

What, what? To sacrifice himself for others, the same lesson as Roc? To win, no matter the cost?

The fate of the Astra at stake...

He fortified his resolve and withdrew the self-cauterizing dagger. Inhale. Exhale. Halo drove the blade through her spinal cord, severing her neural pathways. She flopped to the ground.

He repositioned, crouching near her face. Their eyes met as

she struggled to breathe. Life was draining from her irises swiftly, her internal light dying. When blood leaked from the corners of her mouth, he nearly roared to the sky.

The trumpet blasted. Halo lurched away to vomit. *Ophelia is dying, and it's my fault. Playing with her one moment, killing her the next. Again.* To know he'd harmed her as brutally and often as he had... That she'd let him do it...

"Another victory for you," Erebus called with a delighted grin. "My sincerest congratulations, Astra. How proud you must be."

Halo spit in the sand to clean his mouth and returned to Ophelia's side. As he pet her, he glared at the god. "Your loopholes grow tiresome. You took her from me before the proper time."

"Incorrect. I issued an invitation, and she accepted. As for the timing, please, prove I acted before the *proper* time." Erebus's grin returned and widened. "There's no need to fret. I won't issue her another invitation. From now on, I won't even use your female...unless she asks me nicely."

Hate this male.

And Erebus wasn't done. "I must admit. I'm glad you've discovered the truth. I've been eagerly anticipating this look on your face. And such a smart little Halo, solving the mystery all on his own. Yes, the Bloodmor transforms her into the beast of my choosing. As I requested, our harpy didn't ruin the surprise. But why would she? She gains power every time she acts as my tool against you."

Fresh fury overtook him, the reminder of her crimes a punch to the gut. Ophelia, Erebus's champion. With her actions, she had jeopardized everything, removing Halo's right to choose his own path. She had stopped him from planning accurately. Had left him at a disadvantage with an enemy. And she'd done it all for power. He should have known.

Halo yearned to shake her. To scream in her face. No, he yearned to shake himself. *I did this.*

Laughing once again, Erebus and his minions faded from view, misting to the spirit realm. Halo remained on his knees, watching as Ophelia wrestled with her encroaching death.

He petted her neck. Slow, measured strokes, his hand unsteady. "You listen well, harpy. I know you're in there, and that you understand my words. You comprehend that I've discovered your secret, and you suspect I'm planning a reckoning. You aren't wrong. Had you only trusted me with the truth..." Inhale. Exhale. "Tomorrow, you'll be tempted to run from me. Don't. You'll only make this worse for yourself."

Her eyelids closed as she expelled her last breath.

His heart shuddered. Between one beat and the next, he felt as if a hot poker was stuck between two gears. He'd hurt someone he shouldn't. And she had let him. Had let him caress her one moment and kill her the next. He couldn't get over that fact. He had softened for her in ways he'd never done for another. Given her more. This was his reward?

Fury rose anew. Things could have been so different. He'd wanted them to be different. Connection. Fun. Sex. What kind of future did they have now?

Only the assassin of gods—the Immortal—was cold enough to murder his own mate.

No. She wasn't his. No stardust, no *gravita*. He'd ignored the truth for too long. Fate would not saddle him with such a treacherous female.

From the beginning, Halo had handled her wrong. He'd given her pleasure, choices, and leeway; she'd given him new memories to despise. Well, no more. They would do things the Machine's way now.

6:00 a.m.
Day 17

Halo's eyelids popped open. He stood in the doorway of his bathroom, information streaming through his mind at warp speed. The repeating day. A new one had dawned. Ophelia. Betrayal.

Consequences.

Get to the harpy.

"Go," he commanded Andromeda, not bothering to explain the situation to her yet again. As cold as ice inside, he strode into his closet, dressed in leathers, and flashed directly to the harpymph's bunkroom.

Her friend Vivian exited their shared bathroom. Neither female noticed him. Of course, they couldn't see him. He stood between their realm and a duplicate—a copy realm made by the Astra before their invasion.

According to the rules, Halo wasn't supposed to leave Harpina. And technically, he hadn't. He was there but not there. Like Erebus, he knew how to create loopholes.

"Get your lazy butt out of bed. Operation Lady O Be Good commences in thirty," Vivian said, ripping Ophelia's covers away.

She jolted upright with a gasp. "I… I need a minute to think," she said, appearing shell-shocked as she lifted an index finger.

Halo pressed his tongue to the roof of his mouth. What was she thinking about? The excuse to offer him for her actions? *It won't be good enough!* Nothing would.

Working quickly, he sliced into his palm and used his blood to etch symbols on the doorpost in the duplicate realm, linking it to the original world, creating an invisible doorway. Why not use the same strategy Ophelia had witnessed in his memory? A one-way entrance to the duplicate realm—her new home—for the remainder of the task.

Only the harpymph could activate the doorway, and only upon entry. If he must imprison her to end her interference with his task, he would imprison her. There would be no friends coming to her rescue. Oh no. Halo intended to brand her with a mystical symbol and *chain* her to the duplicate realm.

Every morning, she would return here, pulled through the

invisible doorway anew. No Erebus. No battles. If Erebus tried to tear her in two with another "invitation," so be it. She would awaken the next day whole, without forcing Halo to murder her on a battlefield. No horrendous death, no ill-gained power—the price she paid for her decisions. The price they both paid.

A muscle spasmed in his jaw. *She deserves this!*

She would hate Halo for it, but he didn't care. Little harpies who played with the affections of an Astra did not garner his mercy.

He would get her settled in and leave her there. She would be safe, but never his. The task would carry on.

He completed the doorway between realms just in time.

"Okay, I've decided." Ophelia leaped to her feet, raced to her closet and yanked garments from the rack, blurting out, "I'll hit you up with all the deets tomorrow. Right now, I gotta armor up."

Her willingness to stay and confront him roused all kinds of—nothing! Certainly not admiration. Or guilt for what was to come. The tightness in his chest was also nothing. She merited no coddling for this.

"I can sense him," she said. "He's close."

"Wrong. He's already here. Armor won't help you, anyway."

As she gasped and straightened, Halo flashed directly behind her. He forced her to spin, and she met his glare with one of her own.

She dares? He crossed his arms over his chest. What would she do next? Run into his trap, as suspected? Or strike at him? Which did he hope for most?

She jutted her chin. "Well. Since the team's all here, I'm ready to listen to your thanks."

"My *thanks*?" he stated with a low, flat tone.

"Accepted." She scrubbed a hand over her face. "Look. I understand your side of the story. I do. Your task, your rules. Do you think I liked keeping my involvement from you and feeling almost sometimes guilty?"

Almost. Sometimes. Guilty.

"I'm an asset you refuse to utilize," she continued. "Every time I transform, I grow in strength and knowledge. Soon, I'll be able to control the beast and take out Erebus."

"If you believe that, you are a fool." Another flat statement. "You know nothing of the god and his ways. He has already seen the end from the beginning. He will never allow your strength to overcome his."

"He can't miscalculate? I can't be a sucker punch he never sees coming?" She massaged her nape. "During yesterday's battle, I came close to beating the compulsion to kill you. Next time I'll succeed. I know it."

Next—time. His fury bubbled over. "I killed you, Ophelia. On three separate occasions."

"And you successfully completed the labors."

"Leaving me with memories of killing you."

"Do you think the memories of dying are any easier?"

He flinched, fisted his hands. Opened his fingers. Inhaled. Exhaled. Calm didn't come. "Your actions have made you my enemy. If I cannot trust you, I cannot work with you." *I cannot keep you.* "I hope the added strength was worth it."

She paled but held fast. "Yes. Well. New strength is worth everything. It never lets you down. Something you understand, considering you, too, are fighting to ascend and better protect your people. Or maybe you don't understand. You are the eliminator, never the obstacle."

Realization dawned, sparking anger. This. The reason Erebus had offered the beautiful hind as a willing sacrifice.

The god hadn't sought Halo's upset. He'd sought Ophelia's. She had received a firsthand view of the endless depths Halo would sink to handle an obstacle. Why would the harpymph trust him with *anything*, much less her secrets?

"Let me see if I'm understanding correctly. You *killed* my girl?" Vivian flicked a fang with the tip of her tongue. "Well. Someone's becoming a eunuch today. Guess who it is."

Halo ignored the harpire, his focus on Ophelia. He grated, "When you're ready to discuss this reasonably, come to the palace."

"Not so keen to guard me from the enemy today, huh?" she asked, sugary sweet and far more bitter.

"Why would I? You are not my *gravita*," he snapped.

She flinched as if he'd struck her, and his chest hurt as never before.

"I killed you, Ophelia, but *you* killed what could have been between us."

A smile that didn't reach her eyes. A nonchalant shrug. "Whatever you've got to tell yourself, sport." Syrupy tone.

He hardened his heart against her. "You have an hour to get yourself ready. Then I'll come get you. Trust me when I say you don't want me to come get you today, harpy."

Batting her lashes, she tossed her hair over a shoulder. "Right now, Astra, I don't want you coming to get me *ever*."

"Fifty-nine minutes, eighteen seconds," he told her. Knowing she was soon-to-be trapped exactly where he wanted her, Halo flashed to the throne room and called a meeting with the Astra. They had much to discuss before he handled the harpymph once and for all.

22

Okay, so, Ophelia might have taken a wrong turn with Halo. Before he'd ditched her, he'd treated her to an entire ballet of twitching muscles. Huge mad. Gargantuan. She couldn't blame him. She'd gone on the defensive right from the start, disregarding her own wrongdoing and making light of his understandable reaction.

"You want to talk about it?" Vivi asked.

"Tomorrow." A countdown clock ticked in the back of her mind. Halo wasn't wrong. Ophelia *really* didn't want him coming to get her.

Stomach churning, she shut herself in the bathroom, hurried through a shower and dressed in the tank top and jeans she'd blindly yanked from her closet.

Despite her trepidation, she crackled with energy. The newest infusion of strength packed a wonderful punch…but she kind of wanted to curl into a ball and sob.

Halo had broken up with her.

Well. No matter. She blinked rapidly to soothe her burning eyes. This was no time for a pity party. Only thirty-two minutes remained on the clock. Just enough time to walk to the palace while pondering her newest round of life-altering mistakes and ways to maybe, possibly, fix them. Could she?

She sniffled as she exited the bathroom. Vivi had already taken off. Ophelia entered the hallway— Whoa! Her gaze darted. What kind of wild sorcery was this?

While everything appeared normal—claw marks on the stone walls, a bra hanging from an overhead light, a sign on the nearest door blinking Targets Only Entrance—the hallway was empty. Silent. Never, in all her days, had she come upon an abandoned *anything* in this building.

Foreboding crept up her spine. Had Halo ordered everyone away?

She licked suddenly dry lips. As she made her way outside, through the garden and toward the palace, her bones felt somehow lighter and heavier at the same time, as if they were made of metal, but concrete muscles supported the added weight without problem. But, um, where was everyone?

Soft gold and lavender sunlight bathed lush green foliage, as usual, but again, no harpies. Her confusion only magnified. She didn't like this. How could Halo get rid of so many so quickly?

What did he plan to say to her? To do?

He had questions, no doubt. But would he believe anything she said? Though her newest transformation had amplified her instinct to kill him, making it more difficult to control the other beasts, she had kept everyone in check. She even managed to slow the speed of her attacks. Her plan was working. Surely he could be made to see—to accept—that.

But probably not.

The urge to sob increased. Until roars erupted in the back of her mind, distracting her. The lioness, hydra, and boar rattled their cages. Alerting her to a problem? This place smelled different. Wrong. But also, somehow, right.

Her ears twitched, catching a soft whistle of wind. An unusual arctic breeze swept in, chilling her in seconds, her cotton and denim no match. Not without a certain Astra by her side, anyway.

How should she proceed with him? The guy had recognized her in that beastly form, then worked to kill her as gently as possible. A miraculous feat. Now, he was upset with her, his trust in her beaten black and blue. And rightly so. Ophelia had done to him what Nissa had done to her.

Ouch. That one hurt.

If this whole situation had been an audition for the position of Astra partner, Ophelia had failed miserably. So Halo might have done his best to stop her from morphing into other beasts if he'd known the truth? So what? A good harpy found a way to overcome, no matter the situation or adversary.

How had she ever forgotten that?

Her shoulders drooped. Why did she always blow up her life? How could she make things right? And seriously, where had everyone gone? What was the deal with—wait! What was that noise?

Quickening her pace, she broke past a line of trees, coming upon the marble fountain depicting Nissa in battle—and countless harphantoms.

They stretched out before the fountain, training with swords, spears, and an assortment of other weapons. As they moved, they blinked in and out of focus, slipping between the natural and spirit realms with seamless precision.

She'd never been this close to a harphantom without having her Astrian shield, and she only knew the basics about their origins. Harpies transformed into phantoms by Erebus and his twin brother. Entombed underground in untold agony for thousands of years. Freed by Taliyah.

Taliyah's second, Dove, stood on the palace steps, dressed for war. With her white hair plaited and her alabaster skin bathed in sunlight, she appeared colder than ice. "Your enemy shows no mercy. Do you?"

Shouts of "No!" blended, becoming a song of malice.

The harphantoms preferred to train in the duplicate realm. But how—nope, no need to ponder that one. Ophelia huffed a breath. Halo. Of course. He must have created an invisible doorway. One of his specialties.

Well, well, well. A point to the Astra. In essence, he'd trapped her here, attempting to bench her from the task, as expected, perhaps putting her out of Erebus's reach. Not a bad move. Far more merciful than, say, imprisoning her in trinite—which might be more effective. Now, at least, she knew her new mission: Win back Halo's trust and get her strength the right way. In front of his face, not behind his back. No more working against him.

As if sensing her at the exact same moment, every harphantom pivoted, facing her. Ultra-creepy. Her harpy took it as a threat. Ophelia bowed up, ready to defend. The beasts roared in their cages.

When the females continued to stand in place, Ophelia settled. "If you'll excuse me. I'm late, I'm late, I'm late for a very important date." Head lifted high, she marched forward, weaving through them.

No one responded, but no one halted her either. She exited the masses, breathing easier, and soared past Dove. What Ophelia would do when she reached Halo, she didn't know.

She hit the top of the steps and crossed through the empty foyer to enter the throne room, where she paused. Uh... Nine Astra filled the space, and her heart drummed faster. A buffet of colors, muscles, and sex appeal was spread before her. Hair and skin tones ranged from the blackest jet to pearl white. Most topped seven feet. All wore shirts and leather pants, the team uniform. Some were beautiful, even mesmerizing, while others were wonderfully rough.

They stood silent, clearly engaging in a telepathic debate. No one was too distracted to miss her presence, however. Different reactions registered. Everything from curiosity to admiration to rage. Big surprise, the most intense rage came from Halo.

He stood in the center of the group, his arms crossed. Big Trouble.

Trouble. Her wings fluttered. Living only half a life. That was her trouble. As Vivi had said at the start of the task: the overachiever versus the self-destructor. For too long, Ophelia had rolled with the punches rather than fight for better.

How hard would she fight for Halo now?

Pre-Astra, she had let go of the two "loves" of her life without hesitation. They had let her go, too—but she'd never given them any reason to hang on.

As much as she had craved commitment, she had feared it too. Losing herself without ever proving herself. Losing *everything*, lost to a needing.

Even now, she risked everything. She had no guarantees with Halo. He could find his real *gravita* and ditch Ophelia in a nanosecond.

You are not my gravita.

That one still hurt. He might only see her as an obstacle from now on. *Remember the hind...*

But. Why not take the risk? Only yesterday, Halo had considered Ophelia Falconcrest his personal property. The male who struggled to interact with others had *relaxed* with her. He loved when she touched him. How could she not hope to keep him around?

So. Yes. She would fight for him—for them—with everything she had.

New goal, new game. Outwit, outplay, outlast. *I'm done hiding from my desires.*

"Ophelia," he stated in that flat tone she hated.

She blinked into focus. Their gazes clashed, and there was no looking away. His draw was too powerful. "I'm sorry, okay," she blurted out. "I should have told you the truth from the start but I got greedy for power."

A pause. Then, "Yes. You should have." He glared, fury, hurt and longing flashing over his expression. That was good, right? A win for her? She could deal with anything but his coldness. "Come here, harpy."

"May I have permission to seduce you with my eyes first, Astra?" Did he even know how sexy he was right now in his tight T-shirt and scuffed leathers, issuing orders? Muscles bulging with aggression.

Mmm. *Look at the gift waiting for me behind that zipper. It's growing right before my very eyes…*

"Ophelia! No seducing." He pushed the refusal through clenched teeth. "Come. Here."

The sizzling command in his voice whipped her to attention. Right.

Sauntering over, she didn't even try to mask her leer. Though his posture was as stiff as a board, he pulled at the crew neck of his shirt, as if *affected*.

"I missed you on my walk." She stepped straight into him, winding her body around his, disregarding the audience. This was war; she didn't mind appearing silly to others.

He stiffened but didn't push her away. Breathing in his heady scent, she petted his chest and basked in his heat, nuzzling closer. He stiffened further, keeping his arms at his sides, but she didn't lose heart. Not much, anyway—not when she detected the swift beat of his.

"Stop this, Ophelia."

"Sure thing. As soon as I hear the safe word you don't have."

Blink-blink. "This part of our relationship is over."

"Set me aside then." She ran the lobe of his ear between her teeth. "Go on. Do it."

Moments passed as he silently fumed, but he didn't set her aside.

He wants me! She tilted her face to his and traced her fingertips along his jawline. "I know you don't trust me right now, and that's fine. I get it. You'll be more understanding when you realize you made horrible mistakes too. And don't worry. You'll get there, darling, I promise. You're just a little slower than me. But until then, let's enjoy each other physically. You *did* agree to be my concubine."

He pursed his lips. "Be silent. No. Say nothing else. I'm in the middle of a meeting. Nod your head if you understand."

She saluted him. "Ten-four. And I'm not disobeying you," she said. "An explanation about an action never counts as words. Everyone knows that."

He worked his jaw, tore his attention away from her, and resumed his telepathic conversation with the other Astra.

Sensing a hotter than average gaze on her, she scanned the faces—him. Ian. The one with short black hair, shining black eyes, and smooth dark skin. He studied her, always the most curious of the bunch.

"Are you as bored with the meeting as I am?" she asked. "And don't worry. Stating facts doesn't count as words, either."

"Oh, I'm enjoying myself immensely, I assure you." Ian did the Astra head tilt. "You are causing problems among the troops. A debate rages. Some believe you aid Erebus willingly, and you must be interrogated properly. Others believe an interrogation isn't worth a war with the harpies."

"Smart."

Halo slung his arms around her. "Heed my next words, harpy," he said, motioning to Silver. "Silver will read your mind, and you will let him, without protest."

Her stomach pitched. Read her mind? Share her universe of

insecurities with a veritable stranger? "I'll die first," she hissed, ripping from Halo's embrace. She wanted him, yes, but she would *never* agree to this. "My thoughts belong to me and those I choose to share them with." For someone to take what she did not offer... "I will kill *him* first!"

He was unmoved. "Had you told me you become the beasts in the beginning, this would not be necessary. You didn't, so it is. Now you will prove your loyalty to your sisters and *do this*."

That cut swift, sure and deep. "I did the best I could with the circumstances presented to me. I hate what I did to you. Like I said, I made some mistakes, but so did you. Don't use mine as an excuse for yours."

She spun to leave, but he caught her wrist.

"Do not resist this, harpy. You'll only hurt yourself. This time, you won't find an ally in me."

"Shall we invite Vivi to poke around in *your* head? By the way, she won't use telepathy but an ice pick. At my request!"

If forced, Ophelia would play her ace: the boon Silver owed her. She could keep him out of her head with a single command—*Do not read my mind today or any other.* But then, that might be what her diabolical Astra wanted. Why not force her to burn through everyone's boon without a fuss?

Halo squeezed her wrist with bruising strength, wrenching a gasp from her. The striations in his eyes frosted over, no longer spinning. "What either of us does or doesn't want is irrelevant. You made sure of that. Now, you will pay the price."

Okay. So. Her confidence wavered. This wasn't Halo; this was the Immortal. The Machine. She hadn't gotten through to him at all. This male felt *nothing*.

He continued, "One way or another, we will verify everything Erebus has spoken to you and how the beasts are affecting you."

She had to get *her* Halo back. *Can give a little to get.* "Astra," she said, molding herself against him once again. "You don't have to use Silver. I *wish* to share with you. Let me." And she did. She told him everything.

Strain darkened his expression each time she mentioned strength. A bad sign? A good one? Was she reaching him, even a little?

The other Astra appeared to have a multitude of questions posed at the edge of their tongues, but no one interrupted her.

When she finished, Halo continued as if she'd never spoken. "Silver is able to read your mind without branding you. But he must put his hands on you to do it. Do not contend with him."

Reaching Halo? Big nope. "You are *so* wrong, darling. Silver is unable to read my mind because I have a boon that says he is forbidden, now and forever." He wanted her ace? Very well. *Take it.* "What's next? Does someone else wish to try?"

Both Halo and Silver looked to Roc, who shrugged. Translation: *Don't ask me.* Finally, Silver offered a rigid nod.

Halo refocused on Ophelia, his ice unthawed. "There will be no mind reading. But there will be a reckoning, as promised."

He clasped her hand and flashed her to his bedroom, remaining in the duplicate realm. Oh, wow. The place was a warrior's wet dream. He stored his weapons here. Everything lined up perfectly, nothing out of order. The only piece of furniture was the bed, and it was the only surface free of weaponry.

He released her and rumbled, "You want me, Ophelia? Knowing I do not, will not, trust you?"

As her gaze met his, her breath hitched. He didn't like her, but he wanted her too. He wanted her *bad*, despite everything. His irises spun faster and faster.

They had no guarantee of a happily-ever-after, but she wanted him bad, too. Every broody, darkly seductive inch of him.

"Ophelia?" he rasped, his body so, so, so close to hers…but not close enough.

"I want you," she croaked.

His nostrils flared. "It wouldn't change anything. Until the conclusion of my task, you will remain a prisoner here. If you show up on a battlefield, I will kill you. We'll never be partners."

She absorbed verbal blow after verbal blow, taking her medicine, unwilling to give up—then she smiled. Because she accepted what he hadn't: This would change everything.

"I want you still, Halo."

Faster than she could track, he grabbed and tossed her to the mattress, where she bounced, breathless.

"What is it you want from me?" He prowled at the side of the bed, a predator toying with prey. "Say it."

"I want to have sex with you." Rather than scramble upright, she stretched, getting comfortable. "Lots and lots of full penetration, fill me with every drop of your satisfaction sex."

Black flooded his eyes, there and gone. "Why here? Why now? What do you gain from this?"

Ouch. Another doozy of a blow. But she could take a licking and keep on ticking.

Ophelia allowed her deepest, most secret emotions to overtake her face. Longing. Desire. Hope. Why not put everything on the line? If a harpy went down, she went down swinging.

"I gain you," she said simply. "I might be, kind of, sort of falling for you. We mesh." And there it was, the truth laid bare. No going back now. "You're kind of wonderful sometimes. And if we can get past the whole you murdering me thing, I think we've really got a shot at something special."

His mouth opened and closed, unintelligible sounds leaving him. "You are...falling for me?"

"Why wouldn't I? You cuddle me and play games. Train me and recognize me. And you're warm. And you smell good. And the pleasure you give me is immeasurable. And you're intense and smart and you have so many muscles, and I want you so much, why are we even still talking right now? Put your hands on me, Halo. Touch me...and I'll touch you too."

23

Touch her? *I must.*

Halo brushed his fingertips along Ophelia's midriff, where her tank top had risen above her jeans. *Soft as silk.*

More.

Entranced, he lifted the hem of her shirt. He shouldn't instigate this contact—shouldn't seek more. He should walk away. Nothing good could come from getting inside her. Except him. When he came inside her. Which he wouldn't be doing.

But still he didn't walk away. A bounty of femininity lay before him. Ophelia reclined on the comforter, her dark locks splayed over the covers, her dusky skin flushed, and her red lips parted. Light green irises devoured him, filleting his control. The most intense desire of his life razored his nerves.

He would kill to sink inside this woman. He *had* killed for the privilege. Why deny himself any longer?

No. He *would* deny himself. After conversing with the other

Astra, he'd opted to encase Ophelia in a trinite coffin and put her in hibernation. Each warlord possessed the ability; to create entire realms, they'd learned to manipulate the atmosphere around them. His hope? Removing her from the task, rendering her unreachable to the Deathless, with no way to communicate with him or respond to an "invitation."

The coffin and forced sleep might not work. There were no sureties—except her reaction. She would not forgive him for it. In fact, she might hate him. He shouldn't care about her feelings. Their relationship was over. Her emotions had no bearing on the situation. But he cared.

Were they truly over? No more training at the coliseum? No providing food for her to earn or steal? No small hands constantly seeking him throughout the day, driving him mad?

He bit his tongue. Perhaps he didn't need to put her to sleep for days to come. The next labor might not even involve any kind of combat. Hercules had only had to clean a mystical stable filled with thousands of immortal cattle.

Halo could do that. He could do anything—except kill the harpy again.

"Please, Halo." She subtly thrust her hips, appearing starved. Dilated pupils. Panting breaths. A fever-flush he longed to feel pressed against his skin. His lips. "Touch me."

Could he leave her in this needy state? Surely he wasn't so cruel.

Welcoming your own defeat?

"Let me show you where I ache." She whipped off her tank top, revealing a lacy bra the same light green as her irises. "Do you want to see, Halo?"

"Yes. No. Absolutely not." He gritted his teeth. How could she want this? How could she want *him*? He'd done worse to her than he'd ever done to Five. "Put the tank back on. Now."

"You mean take my pants off too? Okay." She kicked off her boots and shimmied out of her jeans, revealing matching panties. Lacy and light green. A barely there scrap of material he could remove with a single claw. His fingers twitched involuntarily, his nail beds heating.

The sight of this female! Breath blistered his lungs, and his blood rushed hot. Tension vibrated from one limb to another. His shaft throbbed. Every. Desperate. Inch.

Resist! He prowled at the side of the bed once again. Answers, then hibernation. "Do you think to win my loyalty in case I must pick between you and the Astra in the end? Because you will not like the conclusion of such a battle." Best she understood that. He would not hesitate to kill her. Would he? He rubbed the center of his chest and grated, "You choose your strength over my torment. I choose my brothers' lives over yours."

"That would sting more if you didn't have a hard-on threatening to burst past your zipper." Unabashed, she slid a hand beneath her panties. "But you won't need to choose, darling. We'll find a way to ensure I'm not your final opponent. Simple. Easy. Problem solved."

Simple? Easy? He'd only ever experienced simple and easy when he'd held her in his arms.

Pacing... How was he supposed to go back to his former existence? No passion. No Ophelia. Why not have her? Why not take what he could, while he could?

"You're really gonna make me play dirty with you?" she asked. "Okay, then. Just remember, you brought this on yourself." With a hooded gaze, she cupped her breast while playing between her legs, tempting him as no other. "If you won't satisfy me, I'll have to settle for a fantasy of you. Mmm. The things I'm imagining you doing to me..."

He wiped his mouth. *Don't ask.* "What things?"

"Your hands are all over me...your mouth isn't far behind. Oh, the way you move against me... I'm undone."

Halo heaved his breaths, fighting her pull. *Soon to break.* Then, he did. His control shattered; jagged shards sharpened insatiable lusts and primal urges. *Master her—all of her.*

Her undergarments—reduced to confetti with a few swipes of his claws. Nothing blocked her from his touch.

He didn't let himself touch her, though. "There is no lovelier sight than you." Glorious breasts. Amber crests. Flat belly, flared hips. Magnificent legs.

"Let me show you more. The best is yet to come." Holding his gaze, wanton and wild, she spread her thighs for him, revealing a luscious, glistening core.

His next breath blistered his lungs, and he stroked himself through his leathers. A vow spilled from his lips, the sight sparking a madness like he'd never known. "I will give you so much pleasure, you will forget every twinge of pain I've ever caused you."

Get inside her. Let nothing stop you.

"Yes. Give me," she said, sounding drunk. "Please, Halo. I need you so much."

Thoughts dulled as he pulled his shirt overhead. Cool air against white-hot skin. He kicked off his boots and unfastened his pants. She watched hungrily, greedily as he pushed the material to the floor.

Naked, he gave his length a firmer stroke. "Is this what you want, Elia?"

"More than anything."

"I'm going to give it to you." He dove down, claiming her mouth in a heated tangle. He. Felt. Everything. Lash after lash of sensation, each preceded by a storm of emotion. Burning passion. Playful affection. Tender caring. Uncivilized yearning. A churning possessiveness he couldn't quash. *She is mine!*

They exchanged breaths. He filled his lungs with her before dipping to her breasts and sucking those beautiful amber buds, one after the other. She writhed beneath him, moaning his name. No sexier sound.

When she scraped her claws over his scalp, he grazed a nipple with his teeth. In a shadowed corner of his awareness, he knew he needed to slow down and prepare her. He cupped between her legs and slipped a finger deep inside her. Those hot wet inner walls clung to it, an exquisite torment.

A frenzy overtook his mind. Somehow, he remained calm on the outside.

Tracing her curves with his gaze, he commanded, "Tell me you want me more than anyone."

"I want you more than anyone, Halo."

He pumped the digit and added another, spreading them. More pumping. A bit more. Working the fingers in and out. Honey coated each one and wet his palm.

She writhed beneath him. "More. Give me more." Her tiny claws dug into his shoulders as she held her prey where she wanted him at long last. As if he had the power to deny this beauty her pleasure.

"Please, Halo! Inside me."

Yes. Claim her! The demand filled every cell, but still he resisted. He would pleasure her better than any other ever had, no matter the cost to his body. Or his sanity.

"Halo, Halo. I need…need…"

"That's right, sweetheart. You need me." He sucked one of her nipples at the same time he plunged a third finger deep, earning a mewl of lusty agony. "You'll always need me, won't you, Elia?"

"Always," she said and moaned. "Always, always, always."

She wasn't the only one becoming drunk on pleasure. Dizzy with desire, Halo shot to his knees between her legs and spread her thighs as wide as they would go, baring her sex to his probing gaze. *Think I can come from the sight of her alone.*

The frenzy intensified as he bent his head to lave her clit. Lost in the throes, she writhed and moaned, fisting the sheets, begging some more.

Harder than he'd ever been, he straightened. He pressed his erection against her core, rubbing but not entering her. Not yet.

She cried out, bucking against him. "Halo! I'm ready. So ready. Give me what I need. You don't…you don't have to worry. I'm not fertile."

Snarls rose from him. "Are you sure you're ready for me, Elia?" A command and question rolled into one. He didn't recognize the sound of his own voice. "Be certain."

"I'm certain, I'm certain, I'm certain," she chanted as she thrashed.

Fighting for at least a semblance of control, he fit his shaft right where he'd tongued her. A slight push, and he breached her opening. He let himself go an inch and no farther. Not yet. Instead, he hooked his arms under her knees and lifted her lower body to align it with his.

Sweat trickled from his temples. Beaded his straining muscles.

"Mmm. So hot," she moaned, rolling her hips and sending him deeper. Her sweet scent took on different notes, thickening the air, fogging his head. A drug. Addicted. Forever. "More."

He fed her another inch and began to pant. The pleasure… almost overwhelming. But he wouldn't come before he was fully seated—not until he'd brought her to orgasm. He refused.

"Halo, please." Plump red lips beseeched him, her voice ragged with pleasure and pain. "Don't stop. I want it. I want it so much."

The thought of her inner walls gloving the full length of his shaft…

Roaring, he plunged the rest of the way inside. The pleasure—more than before, scalding every inch of him. Too good. Too much. But stop? Impossible. He plunged in and out, in and out, overcome.

"Halo! Yes!" Her back bowed, a scream barreling from her. She raked her claws over the sheets, shredding the buttery soft material.

Just as he'd imagined, those slick inner walls squeezed him as she came. Hoarse growls spilled from his tongue. How had he ever lived without this?

By some miracle, he rallied the strength to stave off an immediate release. He wasn't done with her yet. Not even close.

Panting, every drag of air like razors in his nostrils, Halo hammered inside her. Riding her hard, thrusting, pounding, keeping her open and vulnerable to him. Her breasts bounced before his ravenous gaze.

"Look at me," he commanded. "Want to see your eyes."

Her lids parted, blazing green irises finding him. There was a clink of mental connection, his chest tightening.

Gasps left her. "I'm still coming. It's so good. Nothing better." She burrowed her fingers through her tiny thatch of curls to thrum her clit. Another scream ripped from her. "This! This is better! Halo!"

Not ready to come. Hold out a little longer. Never want this to end. But the sight of her like this, the sound of her—the *feel* of her. Halo could contain his climax no longer. With a final roar, he jetted lash after lash inside her body.

Ecstasy washed over him. For the first time in his life, he knew no tension.

This changed nothing?

Forever changed. Can't give this up. Won't.

As soon as he collapsed atop her, she expertly flipped him to his back. She rose above him and straddled his waist, ensuring he stayed buried within her. Lifting her mass of hair, letting the strands cascade, she began to move on him.

Groaning, hypersensitive, he urged her on, bucking up. He'd gotten a taste of her. Nothing would stop him from gorging. "Ride me, Elia."

With hooded lids and upthrust breasts, she obeyed. Slowly. Leisurely. She rode him until they both came. But even then, they weren't done.

He maneuvered her to her hands and knees.

"Don't stop," she said, glancing at him over her shoulder.

"Never." He bared his teeth as he slammed into her with all his strength. "We go until you can take no more. Try to keep up, nymph."

24

"No more," Ophelia rasped between panting breaths. She sagged against Halo, a boneless, sweaty, exhausted, satisfied mess. Scratches and bite marks marred his torso as if he'd come fresh from a battlefield. "No more."

"Are you certain?" He fisted a handful of her hair and kissed her brow. "Not one more time? Or perhaps two? Even numbers are better than odd."

"Quick nap first. Then a hot shower and maybe a seven-course meal. Oh, and I should probably learn to walk again. Then more sex."

He chuckled, the rusty sound the most beautiful music to Ophelia.

Her heartbeat hit warp speed; any faster, and she might blaze right out of the time loop. Limbs trembled from exertion, certain muscles continuing to spasm. Pleasure saturated every inch of her being. Never had she experienced anything like this. An endless stream of orgasms, one after the other, rolling on and on and on for hours, until she drowned in an ocean of fulfillment she'd never dreamed possible.

In bed, the usually stoic male had come alive. He'd been at times wild, playful at others, but his ferocity had never lessened. Barely banked power had remained evident in his every move. He'd been a warrior gripped by an irresistible battle heat, desperate for relief only she could give him.

Sometimes he'd pinned her wings, making her as weak as a mortal. And yet she'd never felt stronger. One of the most powerful beings in the universe had trembled for her.

I'm not falling anymore. I've already gone splat.

The guy warmed her from the inside out. With him, a needing always overpowered her, but she never failed to recover. His intensity thrilled her. Those earth-shaking orgasms? Perfection. She was keeping him, and that was that.

In the most secret parts of her heart, a part of Ophelia had always dreamed of finding her man. But nothing could have prepared her for Halo. The strongest, fiercest brute in town. Sure, they had their problems, but come on! She had only just started fighting for him. He didn't stand a chance…right?

She worried her bottom lip as she lifted her arm into a beam of sunlight that streamed through the bedroom window. No big deal, she refused to panic, but there was still no tell-tale sheen of glitter.

Maybe he needed to trust her again first? Possibly?

Her stomach churned. Okay, so, maybe she experienced a *little* panic. What if she *wasn't* Halo's *gravita*? He yearned for her in ways he'd never yearned for another, yes, but that meant nothing without stardust.

You are not my gravita.

"I was led to believe my nymph possessed more stamina." He rolled them to their sides, so that they faced each other. He was grinning, none of his earlier resignation in sight, and it was *devastating.*

He looked more relaxed than…ever. Almost boyish. His eyes—she gasped. They'd flooded with black, pinpricks of light scattered throughout, one streaking across the expanse like a falling star. What she saw in their depths…

Had the Tin Man gone and gotten himself a heart?

I can't be alone in this. "Halo?" she asked shyly.

"Yes, Ophelia."

"I really am sorry I caused you so much hurt. And I really did— and do—have the best intentions. I *know* I can defeat Erebus."

Well. There went his relaxation. He tossed her to her back and rose over her again, pinning her with his weight. Resting a hand on her throat, where she usually wore the trinite collar, he shackled her arms over her head with the other.

Why, why, why did she like this dominant side of him? "You will not give up your quest for strength, despite my feelings on the matter." He glared at her. "Will you?"

"No." *Please understand.* "I have to do what I think is right."

"As do I." He searched her gaze. It wasn't anger he projected but frustration. "After a second's worth of careful consideration, I've decided I won't trap you here, or put you in hibernation. If you influence the final labor, as the Commander believes, your cooperation is needed regardless of your motives."

Wait. "You won't stop me?" she asked, hopeful. "Do you trust me again?"

"Trust you? No. But I'm confident you told the truth about your involvement. For now, that is enough. We will continue as before, navigating each day and labor as they come."

Enough. The word echoed in her mind. She didn't want good enough. She wanted everything. The best. Which meant it was time to harpy-up and own her feelings. No more caving to fear. No more running. This was the fight of her life, remember?

"Admit it," she said with a little smile. "The sex changed everything."

He snorted, then kissed her brow and rolled to her side once again. "It might have changed *some* things."

Would he cop to the next part? "Do you at least *suspect* I'm your *gravita*, Halo?"

"You are mine, Elia." He soured a hand over his face. "That, I cannot doubt any longer. I'm certain I will produce the stardust for you at some point. It's only a matter of when. The reason it comes must be different for every Astra, just as the females are different."

His words should have overjoyed her. But hidden fears read between the lines and provided a translation: *You aren't good enough for immediate stardust, Ophelia. Stardust will come only when my instincts consider you worthy.*

No. No, no, no. She wasn't doing that, wasn't going there. They were making progress. Being grown-ups and talking openly with each other. Sharing stuff. He'd forgiven her for her mistakes (mostly). She'd forgiven him for his. They had agreed to work together (kind of). The beasts were under control, and her confidence was rock solid (nearly). Life was good.

Drawing her over his chest, encouraging her to mold against him, he said, "Never want to be without this again."

"Well, then." Swallowing a sudden lump in her throat, she replied, "You'll need my cooperation, won't you?" She kissed the pulse at the base of his neck, where his *alevala* napped, everyone's eyes closed. A sign of Halo's own inner peace? "Good news, Immortal. My cooperation can be bought. Today's price is information." Her curiosity about him had reached new heights. "Tell me about your favorite battle."

"There is a twenty-three-way tie between every time I killed Erebus."

"Twenty-three times? Seriously?" Although, why such a shock

over the extraordinary number? So far, Ophelia had rung in a solid four deaths. And the tally was climbing fast!

"He always returns." Halo stiffened. "Just as you return after your deaths."

Okay. All right. His anger was clearly making a resurgence. "Are you complaining about my extra lives?"

"You know it is the deaths I protest."

Yeah. She did. Why not discuss the big bad and get it out of the way? "I think I should continue to go to the battlefield as a willing sacrifice. Believe it or not, I *am* learning to control the beasts. I'm an asset to you. Use me. I *will* help you take down Erebus."

"To what end? You scheme to slay the god before the final battle. Let's say you gain the power to succeed. How will it matter? He'll revive through either the time loop or his phantom abilities. The task will toil on to its determined end. If you're chosen as the final combatant—and I must assume that's Erebus's goal—I'll be forced to kill you for good or condemn the Astra to five hundred years of defeat."

And he would choose the Astra, as claimed; and she couldn't blame him. It hurt but what could she do? He had warned her. "I admit the final battle thing seems a bit…alarming. But I still think our best chance for success is me, beasting out. I wish you could feel my instinct about it. Everything inside me is screaming that I can and will defeat the god. I mean, you do realize the blood of primordials is flowing through my veins, right? I'm a walking miracle. The way we all get out of this. We can dominate your task the way Taliyah and Roc dominated his."

"There's no easy way to say this, so I will just blurt it out. Erebus might be responsible for your instinct. A false confidence to lure you onto the field."

No. This was all Ophelia. "Let's reach for the stars instead of the mountain."

"The risk..." He rubbed the center of his chest, tension pulsing from him.

For the time being, she decided to steer the conversation to the coming test. "What is the next labor?"

"Cleaning an uncleanable stable that is filled with a never-ending parade of immortal cattle."

"Oh, that's right. Then comes the man-eating birds."

"Then a Cretan bull." He closed his eyes as if he couldn't bear the thought of the battles.

Ophelia opted not to mention the giant, flesh-eating horse and three-headed dog that followed. "It's really okay, Halo. I want you to kill me." Not words she'd ever thought to utter.

"Have you considered what *I* want?" His eyelids popped open, his irises blazing. "I want to *not* kill you again." Raw agony twisted his features. "With even the thought of being forced to do so, the worst of my tension clambers to return."

No. No tension allowed. Not here, not now. "Halo. Darling. The way to overcome your aversion to using me in the labors is practice. So, let's do it. Let's practice."

He narrowed his eyes. "You expect me to practice murdering you?"

"Hardly. But your next challenge must merely be inspired by an impossible situation, right? Well, in lieu of an uncleanable stable, you've got yourself an insatiable nymph whose stamina has already recharged. So. You are going to do your best to satisfy her in a single night." She petted his chest, then glided her fingers lower and lower, until she clasped his erection. "The clock starts now..."

Day 24
5:09 p.m.

The newest freeze had occurred an hour ago. Would Erebus attack today? Would he not?

For the first time in Halo's remembrance, he was losing track of his hours and days. Everything was blurring together in a wonderful collage of sex, cuddles, and chats.

Every morning he came to awareness in his private bedroom and flashed to Ophelia. They shared pleasures, held each other, and discussed everything but the coming labors.

One taste of climaxing without effort, and he'd become an addict, as feared.

He tried to keep part of himself distanced and unaffected, but everything she did, everything she said, only served to lure him closer. Her smiles. Her teasing. Her passion and zest. Her humor. He even liked her determination and stubbornness, how she let nothing deter her from her goals.

With imprisonment no longer his aim, he had dismantled the door to the duplicate realm. Its creation had been foolish, anyway. The circumstances hadn't changed. As he'd reminded them both, his victory could depend on Ophelia.

So how could Halo win the blessing task *and* keep Ophelia safe in the end? He *must* keep her safe.

He couldn't shake a sense that a labor would, in fact, occur today, the right time or not. Would Erebus summon her? Would Halo be forced to face another beast? Part of him hoped so. He had an idea. A theory he wished to test—a way to win…by purposely losing.

As suggested by Chaos, he had learned something during the other labors. Though Halo had won when he'd killed the beasts, he had inadvertently lost. He just hadn't known it. *But never again.*

Currently he and his harpymph occupied his closet. She was dressing in the armor he'd fetched for her, anchoring her lush breasts beneath the metal cups of her breastplate. The short skirt allowed prolonged glances at the gorgeous legs he preferred to have wrapped around his waist. Or draped over his shoulders.

Halo adored this part of their day. Preparing to face the world together. Today, though, his nerves were fried, his thoughts returning again and again to the stable labor. What would Erebus force him to do this time?

Guilt and regret singed Halo as memories of the past tests surfaced. Ophelia, dead and bloody.

"Uh-oh. What's our rule, Astra?" She molded her body to his the way he loved.

He kissed the tip of her nose. "No man-pouting unless I desire a real reason to man-pout."

"Master is pleased." Rising to her tiptoes, she kissed his chin.

"He is indeed."

She grinned and ghosted her fingertips over his cheek. "*I* am master, and well you know it. *You* are my precious concubine who earned a reward by remembering my words of wisdom."

"If I'm owed a reward, I will collect." Halo hefted her over his shoulder and, while she giggled and wiggled, he smacked her backside and carried her into the bedroom. "Looks like we got dressed for nothing, nymph. Someone needs a reminder of her own. You belong to me, and I'll prove it…"

He did. Twice.

Afterward, Halo ushered his harpy to the royal stable for a look around. Were they soon to do battle here?

He shuddered as he took stock of the building. Eighty thousand square feet. Twenty-four tack rooms. Multiple feed storages. Washrooms. Attached chambers for caregivers. Living and kitchen spaces. Three hundred stalls occupied by an array of creatures. Mostly horses, with a few winged horses and unicorns thrown into the mix.

During her reign, General Nissa had kept the place as clean as possible, the animals well cared for; Taliyah was no different.

Everywhere he walked, the scent of fresh hay and beast tinged the air.

"Nissa loved it here," Ophelia offered softly. They entered a training arena with a dirt floor, set in a large circle, blocked by metal bars. "She always had a special connection with her animals."

This was the first time she'd spoken of her mother without evincing pain. "What is your favorite memory of her?"

"Let's see." She skipped ahead, all sensual grace, and hopped on top of the fence. Her perfect balance persisted as she traipsed from one side of the bar to the other. "Probably the time she ambushed me to assess my reaction, and I knocked her flat. She patted my shoulder, almost proud of me."

He imagined Little Ophelia had been much the same then as she was today. A feral sweetheart, with a blustery outer shell that guarded a blazing inferno of affection. Something her mate was tasked with stoking. Though Halo was an emotionally stunted male known as the Machine, he accepted the duty gladly and continued adding logs to the flames.

"Survive the next labor, Ophelia," he said, "and I'll give you more than a pat on the shoulder."

"Um, I hate to love interrupting your coming speech, Haylow, but the pin in my truth bomb has been pulled. Boom! I can't be bribed, no matter how adorably sexy you are. If I gotta walk through your sword to die during a labor, imma walk through your sword."

Conflicts razed his calm by the thousands, each one waged by only two combatants. Right and wrong. "I think you might be the first person in this world or any other to *request* repeated deaths."

"What can I say?" She winked at him. "I'm one of a kind."

Lingering resentments brimmed over. "You are forcing me to relive and repeat my *worst* memory."

"Oh, dear. The happy couple is already at odds?" The smug voice of the Deathless filled the arena. He stood outside the training ground, at the edge of a high platform that hadn't been there moments ago, where two empty thrones waited. "How devastating for you both."

Knew it. Halo braced as hundreds of phantoms materialized around the fence. They hovered inches off the ground, silent, their heads bowed.

Ready for this or not... "What is it you'd like me to do this time, hmm?" he asked.

"We'll get to that." Dressed in his customary black robe, Erebus eased into the largest of the thrones and crooked his finger at Ophelia. "Come, harpy. You will sit beside me."

Denials exploded inside Halo's head.

To his surprise, she jutted her chin. "I'm not your pet. Go screw—"

The god flashed her to the dais, directly to his side.

Anhilla stirred within Halo. Inhale, exhale. *She'll be all right.* Whatever happened, she would survive.

Until she didn't.

A trumpet sounded. Then another. Only a feat of strength or cunning, not death. He breathed easier, calling, "Halo Phaninon."

Ophelia smiled at him encouragingly from his enemy's side, doing her best to offer comfort. In the smaller throne, she was a queen unfazed by what happened around her.

Erebus smirked, gleeful. "There were so many ways to twist this task. In the beginning, I considered a time-sensitive challenge. An impossible puzzle. But in the end, I opted to amuse myself. All you must do to win is shovel the stalls and haul your bounty here. We'll watch. I'll charm your female with my wit and candor, and you'll fume. Good times will be had."

"Well, if good times are to be had, I might as well kick things off." Ophelia struck without any other warning, clawing out the god's throat.

Halo's chest swelled with pride.

As the Deathless gasped and gurgled and healed, she lifted his bloody trachea like a war prize. "Well. I think it's safe to say some of us will be having a better time than others."

25

Ophelia fluctuated between fury, admiration, and more fury. In seconds, Erebus mended from his dethroating, leading to hours of manure shoveling for Halo. Back and forth between the stalls and the arena he went, his wheelbarrow either full or empty, depending on his direction. He was dirty, sweaty, and utterly hot, his huge muscles constantly flexing. He watched her as much as possible, gazing up, always ready to pounce if things got dicey.

She and Erebus observed from the dais, his phantoms continuing to float around the metal fence, encircling Halo.

"I'm glad we have this time together," he said, playing the part of delighted party host. He never shut up, his unwelcome commentary acting as a cattle prod to her nerves.

"That makes one of us."

He wasn't a handsome man, but he wasn't ugly, either. With his broad shoulders and powerful presence, there was something inherently sexual about him. The mop of pale curls might lend him a false air of innocence, but eyes as black as an abyss couldn't hide his arrogance.

An idea unfurled. Hmm. It was definitely dangerous and probably stupid, with a high likelihood of boomeranging back. If it worked, though…

She grinned. She had wiles not even a god could resist—the pheromone.

Should she test it on him, see how he reacted? What could she force him to do? Shouldn't she find out? She slid her gaze to Halo. What happened if Erebus became hyperfocused on sexing her? If she had to fight him off—or Halo did? What then?

"One of the upcoming challenges involves an Amazon." Erebus leaned closer. "Know of any Amazons in the area, harpy?"

She rolled her eyes. "Let me guess. I'm supposed to get jealous and make Halo miserable in between labors? Sorry, but I don't function that way."

To be honest, Ophelia was kind of excited to meet the Amazon and exchange notes. If the other woman had no romantic aspirations toward Halo, they had no problems. Maybe they'd even become friends. Amazons tended to be more stoic than harpies, and yeah, okay, a bit self-righteous, but they made awesome sidekicks.

"Worth a try," the god said, and shrugged. "Hercules had to convince an Amazon queen to part with a mystical girdle, and I'm considering my options. Decisions, decisions. You are learning our Halo better than anyone. Any recommendations? I could make him remove the heart that belongs to the queen who holds *his* heart. Put him through another battle to the death. Perhaps I should demand he satisfy his former Amazonian concubine sexually."

The very jealousy she'd denied decided to team up with fury and denial. The trio quickly slaughtered her inner calm. *My Halo!*

But. Allow the god to know he commanded her emotions with his taunts? No. "I've got a recommendation all right," she said, flashing him a sharp grin. "Make the prize your *internal girdle*. Prevent Halo from disemboweling you—if you can."

The god seemed to give her suggestion some thought. "If I believed the act would be distasteful to him in any way, I'd do it."

Wait. "You seek the Astra's misery more than your own victory?"

"I do." He appeared sincere. "Without his misery, a win is worthless to me. I owe the Astra *much*."

More evil than I realized. He didn't care who got hurt in his quest for "victory." So, yeah. Okay. He deserved to experience his own suffering. Which meant it was absolutely time to unleash her pheromone. He'd made the decision for her.

There were only two types of males when her pheromone came into play. The stalkers willing to commit any deed, fair or foul, no matter how dangerous or humiliating, if only to near her. And sociopaths determined to bed her, no matter her opinion about it. Either way, Erebus wouldn't be walking away from their encounter today; he was going to crawl.

She waited until Halo headed out of the arena to muck another stall, then turned her focus inward. Next to her Dumb-Dumb switch was a fragrant well of endless desires, aka the pheromone. As she turned a mental crank to draw a bucket up, up, up, straining more and more, she cursed her past self. Why hadn't she treated the pheromone as the weapon it was and learned to wield it as nature intended? Had she done her due diligence, she could've summoned the scent so easily, perhaps even controlling the potency of the dosage.

A rallying cry echoed inside her head. *For Halo! For harpies!* Still cranking.

The bucket rose, higher and higher, and the innermost parts of her belly heated. Yes! Warmth and the sweetest, most delicious power spread through her, so different from the might she had received from the beasts. Softer, yet also somehow sharper.

The pheromone seeped from her pores, a perfumed cloud enveloping the dais in seconds.

Erebus gripped the arms of his throne, his knuckles quickly leaching of color. "Knew you'd do this...thought I was prepared for it...but no matter. I will not give in to you, wench."

"Oh, you will give in. You really, really will." She smiled at him, languid and sure. "Even now, in the midst of your great turmoil, you long to please me. Admit it."

"I do...not." A vein bulged in his forehead. He panted. "I will...won't...do whatever you command. Tell me. What do you command?" The question ended with a snarl.

Her smile widened. "Where to start?"

Halo entered the arena once again, the wheelbarrow full. Immediately his gaze sought Ophelia; finding her unharmed, he turned his attention to Erebus, glaring...frowning...slowing his pace. The warlord stopped and sniffed the air; his entire body jerked. His focus swung back to her. Their eyes met across the distance.

Sweltering desire radiated from every inch of him, and shivers racked her. Longing deluged her.

Steady. Control.

"Turn it off, Elia." Halo clenched his teeth. The wheelbarrow's handles all but disintegrated in his grip. "I'm not sure I can keep myself away from you much longer."

"Forfeit the task," Erebus advised. He reclined, as if carefree, but sweat trickled from his temple. His good humor didn't quite reach his eyes.

Oh, no, no, no. Have Halo forfeit the task and lose to the god because of her? He wasn't the type to forgive *anyone* for a crime like that.

"Do your part, and I'll do mine," she called. Her new mantra. Finally, she had Erebus where she wanted him—under her metaphorical boot. "Let me show you what I can do."

"Yes, Halo," Erebus said with a drawl. "Let her show us what she can do. A demonstration will be good for both of us."

"I don't need your help convincing him," she snapped.

As Halo dumped the wheelbarrow's contents, he hurled different silent messages her way. She thought she caught a vow for retribution, a curse upon her head, and a demand to *mind him* for once.

Having trouble resisting her pheromone, was he?

Well, well. The most delicious power went straight to her head, and she cast Erebus a look of haughty disdain. "Your mistress thirsts. Fetch me wine. Only the finest red will do."

Lines of tension bracketed his eyes. "Your pheromone is potent, harpy, but not potent enough to force my hand." He shifted in his throne, grating, "However, I thirst as well."

"Sure you do." Ophelia flashed him a crude hand gesture. "Go ahead and get comfortable, Bus. You don't mind if I call you Bus, do you? We're gonna chat."

He clapped twice. An embodied phantom appeared from thin air, floating over with a goblet of wine clutched in each hand. Milky white eyes were unfocused as Ophelia accepted the glass. Her thoughts tangled. Could the god control the fiends without speaking? She'd thought he had needed to issue a verbal command.

"Tell me the truth." She sipped the sweet drink. "You've never encountered a more powerful nymph pheromone, have you?"

"Once. Long ago." Erebus drained his glass and wiped his mouth with the back of a trembling hand, fighting her appeal.

Maybe because she'd used so little of it throughout the years, the pheromone's potency had built up over time?

"Perhaps I'll keep you chained to my bed once Halo is defeated," he added. "The Astra can spend the next five hundred years dreaming of every filthy thing I'm doing to you. It is especially satisfying for me when he makes *himself* suffer."

"Sit on a spear," she told him, smiling sweetly, unleashing another tendril of the pheromone. "Do it. For me."

"I. Will. Not," he said, but it was clear he wasn't convinced.

At the exit, Halo paused, tossing a sizzling glance over his shoulder. She pressed a hand over her stomach, suddenly breathless. His ferocity was barely tethered. He was in *agony* with want for her.

She didn't mean to, but she dropped the mental bucket, everything inside her reaching for him. The pheromone faded. She scrambled to grab it, but alas. No go.

The god recovered quickly, smug as he said, "Your turn to be honest. Do you envision a happily-ever-after with the Astra?"

Yes. No. Maybe? She both was and wasn't Halo's *gravita*. They both did and didn't have a future. Even though he'd been attentive to her, he'd held a part of himself back. The trust she'd lost, as well as the ease he'd gained.

If he was forced to kill her again, he would grow to resent her. He might not mean to, but he would. His ease might not *ever* return. Could she really do that to him, simply for another dose of strength?

"You think you have options," Erebus continued. "You cling to the notion there's a chance you and Halo can both survive this. Maybe you even believe you can sacrifice yourself in the end, one last time, and return to life as Taliyah did. But I assure you, if either of you kills the other on the last day, you are gone forever. The rules forbid a resurrection. I made certain of it."

"And you intend to pit me against him in the final battle?" Knew it.

"Why wouldn't I? Could anything hurt him more? Your death will cut deeper than an affair between us ever could." He took another sip of his wine. "The poor male has had a terrible life. Forget his mother's murder and his father's rejection. To become the Machine, young Halo was forced to assassinate other children, even friends."

Reveal nothing. "Yes, he told me."

"He told you some, but not all. I highly recommend you mention Five. The memory he relives every time he slays you."

Five...what? She wanted to naysay him but couldn't. Halo himself had confirmed it. *You are forcing me to relive and repeat my worst memory.*

Was this "five" thing the "worst memory" of Halo's life? She gulped, hating that the enemy knew more about her male than she did.

"Thank you for the advice I won't be heeding." Maybe. Probably.

He shrugged. "Your loss. But I swear by all I hold sacred; I offer you wisdom from the ages. The memory threatens to decimate the foundation upon which your relationship stands. If you do not know the enemy you fight, you do not engage. Fail to engage and you lose by default."

He wasn't wrong. "Aw. It's almost as if you care about my well-being."

"I hope to draw you and Halo closer together, nothing more. If he loves you beyond reason, he'll betray his brothers. The only good thing in his life. They will die, one by one. Think of the blame he'll carry. I can already taste it. Though he adores you, he'll associate you with that blame and fall from the greatest peace to the worst torment. On the other hand, if he loves you beyond reason and *doesn't* betray his friends, he must live with your loss, understanding he could have saved you. This is a win-win for me."

Her stomach flip-flopped. *Doomed?*

No. No! Not doomed. Not in the slightest. "We will overcome." There was always a way; they had only to find it. "I already have an idea brewing."

"Ah, yes. Your idea. You think you'll gain enough strength to control the beasts and attack me. Let's say you do it. Nothing changes for Halo. The final battle won't end until one combatant is dead."

Yes, Halo had said the same. "We will overcome," she repeated, but this time her tone was hollow.

"Look at what Halo did to the hind. Such a beautiful creature. Birthed from Mother Nature herself. Yet, your Astra decapitated it without hesitation. What do you think he'll do to *you* during the last battle? Do you foolishly assume you'll fare any better?"

No. No, she didn't. Halo had made it clear. The Astra came first, and all obstacles got eliminated.

Though she wanted to slink in her chair, she forced her spine to remain ramrod straight as she craned her head to meet his gaze. "I think your days are numbered, and I greatly anticipate the last."

He grinned, as if enchanted with her, then extended his hand. With a voice as soft as silk, he said, "Twine your fingers with mine, or I'll cut them off one by one and force the Astra to watch, unable to do anything to aid you."

What, he hoped to entice Halo from his goal with jealousy?

Ignoring the offering, she reclined and placed her forearm on the arm of her throne, a willing sacrifice even outside a battlefield. "Go ahead. Cut them off." She had already died four heinous deaths. The loss of a few appendages? Yawn.

"You think I bluff?" He slowly withdrew a dagger from the pocket of his robe. *The* dagger. The Bloodmor. The one he'd once thrust into her chest—a chest now heating, burning, singeing.

The monsters beat at their cages, rattling her confidence.

Was she soon to turn? Sweat beaded on her brow.

"Let me tell you how the rest of Halo's labors will transpire," Erebus said, calm as he twirled the weapon in a loose grip. "A man-eating bird, a Cretan bull, and a giant flesh-eating horse. They—you—will attack Halo. You will not gain control of yourself in time. As the horse, you'll nearly succeed in killing him." Relish dripped from each word. "After the horse comes the Amazon, and the real fun begins. The three-bodied giant, golden apple and Cerberus. Perhaps Halo will produce stardust at some point…is what you'll think. But he won't. Between you and me, I believe he'll realize he can do so much better than a power-hungry harpymph."

Oh, that one stung. What if, what if, what if?

By strength of will, she forced the monsters to recede. "I believe we'll surprise you." They had to.

"You'll never be first for Halo. In the end, he'll go cold and kill you to save his brothers. Oh, and before I forget." Erebus swung the dagger in a chopping motion, intending to remove her hand as warned.

Just before contact, a tattooed arm shot out, capturing his wrist. Halo! He'd flashed over.

The god blinked in bewilderment. See! A surprise. The god couldn't predict everything.

"If you touch her again, even once, I'll kill you." The menace in the Astra's tone emptied her lungs. His attention stayed fixed on Erebus, his breaths steady. Frost glazed his eyes. He had *already* gone cold. "How many times have you died over the centuries— and how many times did I wield the blade?"

Had any male ever radiated such confidence? And oh wow, that was sexy. Ophelia had no doubt Halo had wielded the blade *every time*. "I know, I know! Twenty-three."

Erebus's lips peeled back from his teeth. Hey. What was that popping noise? Frowning, she tilted her head and listened… Her jaw slackened. Were his bones breaking thanks to the power of Halo's grip?

Panties—soaked.

"The rules are clear," Erebus said. Had a thread of panic entered his tone? "Attack me and I may attack the others."

"I'm willing to pay the price. Are you?" Now the Astra chuckled, and it was a terrifying sound, making Ophelia wetter. "You want me cold? You've got me cold. Are you happy with the results?"

"Kill me then," Erebus snarled. "You'll lose the entire task, and I'll ascend. I'll return as the victor."

"Yes, but you'll not return for days. By the time you regenerate, the Astra will be hidden and hibernating. You'll have to wait five hundred years to challenge us again."

Ophelia knew the Astra had lost to Erebus twice before. Knew they'd hibernated then, too. Mostly, she knew she wasn't ready for the task to end in a disqualification.

Do something! Nothing in the rules said she couldn't harm the god.

Wings fluttering, she knocked Halo out of the way before either male could sense her intentions, then threw her fists at Erebus, one after the other, again and again and again. Blood flung as his head whipped from side-to-side. Basically, she used his face as a punching bag. Kind of her signature move during hand-to-hand. The jackhammer.

Oh. Possible name material? Ophelia the Jackhammer?

"Yeah baby!" The pain in her knuckles barely registered. "I can do this all day."

With a roar of fury, Erebus vanished. His phantoms followed.

A trumpet blared as soon as Ophelia and Halo were alone. The task was over and…a success?

Halo scanned her, his eyes aglow with concern and anger. "You are unharmed?"

Oh, no he didn't. "Those are your first words to me? Seriously?" She vaulted to her feet, massively ticked off. "Did you not see me whale on a god? Where's my *thanks for the assist, Elia. The task would've tanked without you.* Am I the only one willing to pull her weight for this team? My pheromone test was a wild success, by the way. Not that you asked."

He eased back on his heels, appearing shell-shocked. "The nymph stays in the bedroom, except when she's slaying males with her pheromone, and the harpy rules on the battlefield.

Noted." He breathed deeply. "Speaking of that pheromone... You told the truth before. You hadn't used it on me."

Okay. This was more like it. "Face it, Halo. Your female is pretty incredible."

He slitted his eyes, his thick lashes nearly fusing. "You must never use your pheromone on another male. You merely guarantee the death of any who scent it."

He coveted it all for himself? Mmm. Both sides of her loved the idea of that.

Motions clipped, he clasped her hand and transported her to his private bathroom. Though he touched nothing but Ophelia, hot water immediately rained from the multitude of spouts, spraying them. Steam filled the entire enclosure.

After they stripped and soaped off the trials of the labor, they gravitated to each other.

His gaze was tormented. "Need me inside you, Elia."

A question...or a command? Both? "I do, Halo. I need you inside me so much."

Triumph flared in his expression. "You'll give me everything I want." He cupped her cheeks. "Even without stardust. Forever."

Forever? "One repeating day at a time, Astra." And why bring up the stardust unless it weighed on his mind?

"Too much is uncertain right now. This shouldn't be. I want this thing settled between us," he said, stubborn. "I want forever."

Frustration poked holes in her desire. "Well, I want assurances." *Won't set myself up for failure.*

You aren't my gravita.

Ophelia shuddered. If she promised forever, and he later stardusted another female... Her harpy screeched. Her nymph whimpered. "Pleasure now, potential pledges later. That's the best I can offer."

"Forever," he insisted. He forced her to walk backward until cool tile stopped her. "With or without stardust. Say it...or I'll give you no orgasms for the rest of the day."

Ohhh. Were they about to enter a heated negotiation? Bones going liquid, she told him, "Between the two of us, darling, I'm the only one with experience in orgasm denial. And let's not forget I wield a sweet-scented tool in my arsenal." The moment he failed to resist her—and he would, an Ophelia Falconcrest guarantee—she would prove her point. From the strongest to the weakest, feelings were fleeting and always subject to change. With the right provocation, anyone could change their mind about anything.

"I will *never* forget that pheromone."

Heart thundering, she straddled one of his thighs and poured herself over him. A favorite pastime for them both. Not even trying to hide her breathlessness, she asked, "Can I interest you in watching me give *myself* an orgasm?"

"Yes," he hissed, squeezing her hips. "I'm interested. And I will see you do this. One day very soon, I'll insist upon it. But not today. You will do nothing to your body unless I demand it. In case I haven't been clear, I won't be demanding it until I get my vow."

Why did that turn her on so desperately? "You think you can stop me from tending to myself?" *You might be right.* She began to undulate. To pant. Halo, in total control… Her breath caught.

"I won't have to stop you. You'll stop yourself. Because you want me to do this. Don't you, Elia?" He cupped her breasts and pinched her nipples before resting a palm on the side of her face. "You know I own your pleasure."

Dang him! She did know it. Still, she raised her chin and told him, "I won't promise you forever, Halo. You were right. Too much is uncertain."

His irises spun. "Understand you have brought this on yourself, nymph. Let the sexual standoff commence."

Most. Frustrating. Evening. Ever.

For hours, Ophelia tempted Halo with heated glances, illicit touches and spoken fantasies. He resisted *everything*. He never kissed her. Never caressed her. No, he suffered alongside her, equaling the playing field, making the game even more irresistible to her.

Just how hard was he willing to fight for "forever"?

After the shower, Halo settled in bed with her. Under the covers, his big body enfolded hers from behind. Every flutter of her wings against his chest sent a new shiver down her spine.

"I don't know how I feel about this," she groaned. *More.* How she ached. "You shouldn't get to enjoy the benefits of sex without putting out."

"And yet I will be doing so."

"Well, I'm not sleeping with you," she huffed.

He kissed her nape. "You may have the privilege of watching me sleep."

How could he be so calm with his hard-on wedged between her butt cheeks? "If I'm to be your guard, I should dress the part and lie here in armor."

"Hardly. We sleep naked, sweetheart. Resign yourself."

"Of course, we sleep naked," she grumbled even as she burrowed deeper into his heat. "If you aren't going to assuage my nymph—" She paused, giving him a chance to pipe up.

"I am not."

"—then I need to discuss something with you. Something Erebus said."

He stiffened behind her. "Why am I just now hearing about it?"

"Slow your roll. He confirmed your suspicions, that's all. He hopes we'll fall in love so that you'll suffer whether you win or lose. He advised me to mention…five. Something you consider when you slay me. Your worst memory, I'm guessing."

He went still, not even seeming to breathe. "You are correct." With a soft sigh that fanned her hair, he rearranged his arms around her, putting her in a light chokehold.

"You don't have to tell—" she began.

"No, I should." He sighed. "At the Order, the children were known by numbers. I was Four. Five was my friend. Or as close to one as possible, considering the circumstances. He sometimes shared his books and food with me. His heart was too innocent for the school, and the headmaster knew it. My heart was…" He cleared his throat. "Headmaster commanded me to kill Five, and I did it without hesitation."

Had he regretted his choice ever since? No wonder he'd balked so hard about Ophelia's numerous demises. "I'm sorry you were put in such a terrible position." Her chest squeezed. "I'm sorry for the agony you've endured. And I'm sorry I treated your concerns so cavalierly."

In response, he tightened his hold. A possessive embrace she cherished.

"But, Halo," she said, linking her fingers through his. "You didn't murder your friend. The headmaster wielded the blade— you. Just as Erebus has been my killer, not you."

A pause. Then, "I do not wish to speak of this anymore." He used his flat tone. The one she hated. "I will sleep now, and you will stay put."

In a nanosecond, Halo's breathing evened out. She could only marvel. He had powered down so completely, so quickly. *He really is a robot. The Machine.*

The thought resurrected her sense of doom. What if he ever shut her out that easily and quickly? *The worst rejection of my life.*

She tossed and turned in Halo's arms, wondering, wondering… Had the Deathless predicted the coming matches accurately? The lack of stardust? Ophelia's eventual demise? Halo's misery?

One minute bled into another. Chewing on her bottom lip, she shifted and gazed at the face she adored, so boyish in slumber. Once again, her chest squeezed. She'd decided he was hers for now, and that meant continuing to fight for him—for them.

If they had any chance at forging something long-term, they

had to defeat Erebus. Halo had made it clear he believed the best chance would come from Ophelia's hibernation. And if he was right?

Why not sacrifice for *Halo* when it mattered most? Maybe this was the way she helped him defeat Erebus.

From the beginning, she had insisted he be a team player—while she was anything but. He was a seasoned warlord, born from war itself. He kind of knew what he was doing.

But her instinct... *Take the strength. Win.*

Every fiber of her being knew she could do this. Could she trust herself? Had Erebus screwed with her intuitions or not?

Argh! She didn't know anything anymore, least of all what to do. For the time being, she would continue on her current course. She would not resist the next transformation.

Or the next.

Then, she would reevaluate.

26

8:03 p.m.
Day 32

Halo surveyed Ophelia as she stalked the other side of the coliseum—as a man-eating bird. Eight feet tall with the face of a fowl and the thin, lanky body of a human. Sharp metallic feathers protruded from her spine and her limbs. Wild black eyes gleamed as brightly as a beak made of bronze.

Less than half an hour ago, Erebus had summoned and transformed her, and she'd been gunning for Halo ever since. Another battle to the death. So far, she'd taken him down thrice.

Erebus watched it all from the royal dais, laughing.

Ophelia pawed at the dirt, gearing to charge Halo again. Then she was off, running. Slowing. Stopping. She shook her head.

Had she gained control of her actions? The moment he'd been waiting for.

She had wanted strength? Very well. She could build it. But from now on, the labors would end *his* way.

Halo had learned his lesson well. No match that resulted in the harpymph's death equaled a victory for him.

Determined, he withdrew a firstone blade Taliyah had made at his request, and pressed the tip against the top of his sternum.

A high-pitched shriek left Ophelia. Then she was running again.

He drove the blade home, the pain searing. If Halo had to die to win during these tests, so be it.

The world dimmed as icy cold spread over his body. Whatever happened after this—

He knew nothing more.

8:14 p.m.
Day 39

Halo faced off with the Cretan bull in the center of the coliseum. This version of Ophelia was at least nine-foot-tall with a muscle mass double the size of his own. Two ebony horns stretched from her skull. A gold hoop hung from each of her nostrils, the pieces clinking as she swiped a hoof over the dirt.

Mere feet apart, they circled each other. Erebus watched from the dais and laughed, as always. But he didn't laugh as exuberantly as usual.

Ophelia was indeed getting stronger, gaining control of her actions faster. That didn't make Halo's job any less difficult, however. Fending her off until she willingly surrendered, giving them both a chance to learn her limits, vulnerabilities, and weaknesses. Not to defeat her but to ensure her safety.

And condemn the Astra?

His chest tightened. He was a planner. A solver. Yet he couldn't figure out a way to save everyone. Was his task like Roc's or not, a sacrifice needed? Must Halo win Ophelia's love and accept her sacrifice during the final battle or make a sacrifice of his own? And if she died for him and his task *wasn't* like Roc's? If Halo died for her?

Damned if he did, damned if he didn't.

"Want another go at me," he asked her, "or are you ready to skip ahead to the end?"

Hoof through the dirt.

Taking that as a request to skip ahead, he withdrew a firstone dagger.

She lunged at him, attempting to headbutt the blade from his grip. The blow sent him flying, but he never lost his grip on the weapon.

Halo stabbed himself in the gut just before he crash-landed.

With a roar, Ophelia rushed over. She whimpered and grazed the side of a horn against his face.

"It was either me or you, sweetheart."

As cold washed over him, his skin was hardening into stone and crumbling, he thought he spied a tear sliding down her leathery cheek.

8:37 p.m.
Day 46

The harpymph might defeat Erebus, after all.

In the middle of the battlefield, Halo lay in blood-soaked dirt—in two pieces. His upper and lower halves were no longer connected.

The god wasn't laughing anymore.

Transformed into a monstrous horse, Ophelia sat a few feet away, attempting to gnaw *herself* into two pieces. To save Halo. If she proved successful, she would die. Unlike the Astra, she didn't need firstone to finish the deed.

Her strength flabbergasted Halo. She'd taken him down in a matter of minutes. Now his blade waited in the dirt, just out of his reach. Let her kill herself? No. She had fought to get on this battlefield; she could deal with the consequences.

While she was distracted, Halo used his elbows to drag his upper body across the dirt, to his weapon.

She noticed the movement and belted out a protest. But it was too late. Halo met her wild gaze and stabbed himself in the chest.

"Until next time."

9:28 a.m.
Day 53

"Put me in hibernation, I said!" Ophelia's lovely face scrunched with frustration and the most adorable fury. "I am a harpy unhinged, and I command it!"

"Our patience hasn't grown, I see." Halo secured the sides of her armor. He loved dressing her like this, no matter her mood.

They currently occupied her bunkroom, preparing for the new day. After his daily reassignment of Andromeda, he had quickly briefed Roc and raced to Ophelia. They'd spent hours in bed, merely holding each other in silence. Dreading what was to come. At least, he was.

How much longer must he wait to bed his harpymph? The fact that he'd lasted this long…it was a miracle. He was dying for another taste of her. Another hit of that pheromone. Something! Until she promised forever, he could do nothing.

Needless to say, he was…on edge. But so was she. Which made the sensual battle of wills the brightest spot in his life. And Halo needed any bright spot he could get. They were running out of days. Only four tasks remained.

"I won't be upset with you, I promise," she whined now, stomping her foot. "Just do it. Hibernate me already. I'll help to save harpykind from the comfort of a bed, *and* I'll get to rub it in the General's face. Trust me, babe. I'll be good with everything."

"Roux's newest intel suggests neither trinite or hibernation will affect the final battle. I like this compromise instead. You get your infusion of strength—" perhaps their only hope now "—and I don't have to murder you."

"Yes, but I've had to watch *you* die."

"Only the same number of times I had to watch *you* die. Fair is fair, sweetheart."

"Argh! Stop being logical. It's annoying." She rested her brow on his chest for a moment. "I just… I hate watching you die, okay? You were right. It's the worst. So make it stop."

He finished the last latch, then grazed his knuckles along her jawline. "Take your medicine, harpy. If I can get through this, you can too. Didn't you imply as much before?"

"Stop being reasonable on top of everything else. You don't wear it well." Batting his hand away, she grumbled, "Maybe I should pheromone you into seeing things my way."

A jolt of eagerness. "Yes. Do that."

"But I won't," she continued, haughty, flickering her hair over her shoulder. "You would enjoy it too much. If I must suffer, you must suffer. That is our new rule."

"Sorry, sweetheart, but that particular rule has been in effect from the beginning."

"Be serious! You get that the Amazon is next, right? You should be panicking. What you shouldn't do is lose more practice tests than you win. We gotta keep the numbers skewed in your favor."

"I have two goals. Victory for the Astra, and your continued well-being. I will do whatever I must to ensure both."

"You are *so* frustrating." She banged her fists against his shoulders. "You don't give me anything I want anymore. How can our relationship survive?"

He lightly pinched her chin the way she loved and pressed a tender kiss to her lips. "You know what you must do to get what we both know you *really* want, harpy." Countless times, he'd nearly surrendered to her intractable will. Anything to sink inside her. But he hadn't exaggerated. He would settle for nothing less than a vow of forever.

The lack of stardust no longer bothered him…much. Mostly

her reaction to its absence did him in. Sometimes she peered at his hands, her countenance swinging between infinite longing and soul-crushing disappointment. Soon after, he would catch her staring at nothing, lost in thought. The few times he'd questioned her about it, she'd shrugged him off and changed the subject. But he knew.

Would she tire of waiting for the stardust and leave him? The very idea tore at his insides.

"There's going to be another labor today," she said, her tone pointed.

"Yes." As usual, they both sensed its approach.

"For the good of our mission, we should get rid of this distracting sexual tension between us."

"Promise me forever then."

She tried another route instead. "How about this? For the good of our mission, we should keep me strong. Pleasure helps do that."

"I constantly examine you for the most minute signs of weakness. If ever you display one, I will relent. Until then…you know what you must do."

She glared at him. "Erebus wants us miserable. Why are we aiding him?"

"I'm not living for the moment." He stole another swift kiss. "I'm living for tomorrow. I want more, Elia."

"So?" She clutched his shirt, wrinkling the material, and pouted, "I want your body, but I'm not getting it."

"We have a busy day, anyway." Beginning with a tea party. The honored guest? His former concubine. Ophelia had insisted on a *get to know the Amazon* session.

"Fine," she grumbled. "Just know you are kind of the worst."

"Noted."

They finished dressing in silence. He couldn't wait to be out of this godsforsaken time loop, when Ophelia could move into his bedroom permanently, her things mixed with his, her scent infusing *everything*.

—*Halo, there's a problem.*— Ian's voice filled his head, snatching his attention. —*This morning you listed everything that's happened throughout the task, but you omitted a mention of Taliyah and Blythe's catfight. Roc isn't happy.*—

A fight between Taliyah and her half sister? That was new. But then, despite the repeating day, no two mornings had played out the same. Each time the Astra and harpies learned about the time loop and their memories erased, their tempers flared ten degrees hotter than ever before.

Another valuable lesson he'd learned. Just when he memorized everyone's routine, something changed. The slightest adjustment altered everything else. Even the smallest decision mattered, shaping the road ahead.

"What's wrong?" Ophelia asked, aware of his sudden unrest.

"There's been a development. We are needed." Halo flashed her to the palace foyer, where groups of harpies congregated before the mantel. Nothing unusual there. But those harpies now formed a growing, chanting circle around the General and Blythe. The blonde and the brunette. Both possessed slender frames, blue eyes—and no mercy.

"Fight, fight, fight," Ophelia called, shoving her way through the crowd.

He dogged her heels, unwilling to let her out of his range.

"Are you seeing this, Sweetheart?" a harpy called from the front line, waving her closer.

"How is that moniker sticking, despite the memory loss?" she muttered. Then she called, "That isn't my name. I'm Ophelia… something." Nothing struck her as "the one."

At the head of the throng, the battling harpies came into view. The ferocity of each strike staggered him. The females were family. Despite their love for each other, they did not temper their blows. Blood dripped from multiple wounds.

"Is this a challenge for leadership?" he asked.

"I honestly don't know," she replied.

Ian, Roc, and three other Astra also occupied the circle. Ian grinned. Roc seethed. Silver looked as though he was taking each harphantom's measurements for a cage, while Azar, the Astra memory keeper, observed with unshakable concentration, absorbing every detail. Sparrow, an uncompromising voice of peace, waited calmly for a chance to intervene.

Bleu, Vasili and Roux were missing. Made sense. Bleu, their spymaster, excelled in the shadows. Vasili never interacted well with others, especially females. And Roux avoided everything Blythe.

The warlord had done more than kill her consort during the invasion. He'd also unwittingly harbored Blythe and her daughter within himself. Fearing for Isla's life, and her own, Blythe had forced her daughter to disembody and hide within her own body. Then, she too had disembodied and slipped inside Roux without his knowledge. Like living nesting dolls.

The two females would have died if Taliyah hadn't extracted them. Blythe had yet to confront Roux about any of it, but her hatred for him was clear.

"Don't you dare do it," Taliyah spat as she punted her sister in the stomach. "Claiming a blood vendetta against Roux will only hurt harpykind."

Ah. A blood vendetta. Revenge. A death for a death. This was nothing new for harpies.

"Do you think he can't defend himself?" Blythe shouted with a brutal punch to the General's jaw.

Taliyah whipped to the side, blood spraying from her mouth. She recovered quickly, the sisters launching at each other, rolling over the floor. "Do *you* think Daddy Dearest won't use our strife to his advantage?"

"If I do something, I'm doomed. If I do nothing, I'm doomed.

I can't take it anymore! He screwed with my mind. The things I've seen..."

They grappled, broke apart, and prowled closer, then started all over again. The battle continued until Blythe stopped and dropped without receiving a blow. Flattening her hands on her temples, she curled into a ball.

Taliyah's anger instantly morphed into concern. "Not this again." She skidded to her sister's side. "Just breathe through it, B." Blue eyes blazing, she bellowed to the masses, "All harpies go! Now."

Soldiers sprang into action, rushing from the foyer. Only the Astra, the combatants, and Ophelia lingered.

"That's my cue." The harpymph peered up at him. "Stay and play with your friends. I'll attend tea."

Halo slung his arm around her waist, holding her body flush against his as he sent a message to Roc, who nodded. "Blythe isn't part of my task," he told Ophelia. "The Commander has this situation, whatever it is, under control. I will attend the tea, as expected."

Halo transported her to the proper sitting room. A spacious chamber with multiple round tables strategically placed throughout. Near the farthest corner, Andromeda sat next to Vivian, both females polishing a dagger.

"—see those heads in the foyer? That's my girl," Vivian said with obvious pride.

He tensed at the reminder. His own head hung from three different mounts, alongside the beasts. The entire display never failed to ruin his good mood. If ever he woke to find the harpy's head propped there... Halo thought he might raze the entire realm.

"Where is the tea?" he asked with a harsher tone than intended. He scanned the room, ready to fetch and carry as needed.

"Aw. It's so cute when you remind me how much my old man isn't hip to the times. The tea is already in our mouths,"

Ophelia explained. "Tea is gossip. I am tea. You really should learn your girlfriend's language. It's only fair since I'm learning Geezer. Come on." She led him forward.

At his approach, the guests went quiet. They watched him with unwavering curiosity.

He adopted his "in public with allies" face—a pasted on *I'm not planning to kill you* smile. He assisted Ophelia as she sat next to Vivian, then claimed the spot next to her and slung his arm over the back of her chair.

"That's, um, quite a smile, Astra," Vivian said, clearly trying not to laugh. "Worried because your girlfriend is meeting your concubine?"

"Andromeda isn't my concubine any longer." But yes. A bit. Just not for the reasons she might think. He expected Ophelia to note the lack of stardust on the Amazon's skin, remember the lack of stardust on her own, and project more soul-crushing disappointment. She might grow tired of waiting.

Sweat beaded on his upper lip. *When will I produce it? When, when?*

"By the way, I'm Ophelia. Not the Sweetheart. I don't care what rumors suggest." The harpymph withdrew a dagger of her own and began sharpening her claws on the blade. "Considering I've been going toe-to-toe with this guy—" she hiked a thumb at Halo "—I might change my designation to the Come Back From The Dead Kid. Too soon?" she asked when he scowled.

Just for that... "The *Not* is silent," he told the Amazon. "Her name is pronounced *the Sweetheart*."

"Good to know. Nice to meet you, the Sweetheart," the Amazon said with a wink. "I'm Andromeda. Meda to my friends."

"Meda?" Halo frowned. "Since when?"

She hiked her shoulders. "Since always, I guess."

"Wow." Vivian gaped at him. "You didn't even know your own concubine's name? Disgraceful!"

"Former concubine," he corrected. Perhaps he would be better off *not* addressing the harpire's question.

"You know who doesn't remember his concubine's name, Halo?" Vivian batted her lashes at him. "A bad lover."

Deserve this. "I *was* a bad lover." His cheeks burned. Why? "I'm not anymore."

"I can vouch for that." Ophelia kissed his cheek, then winced, stealing a quick glance at Andromeda—Meda. "Sorry. Didn't mean to rub the big guy's obsession with me in your face."

The Amazon gave another shrug, not the least bit concerned. "Guys. Honestly. I'm fond of Halo, but my emotions were never part of our relationship. No offense," she said with a wince of her own. "I needed a Get Out of Amazonia Free Card, and he provided it. Now I'm thinking about dating around. The army sometimes trains near my window, and I've had my eye on a few dozen or so shifters. And berserkers. And vampires."

"You know what I just realized?" Vivian examined her blade in the light. "I'm the only one at this table who hasn't boned the Machine. Maybe I should, I don't know…just thinking out loud here…have a go at him myself? Just to be fair to everyone at the table."

Ophelia tossed a rag at her. "Go get yourself a side slice of your own. *Then* we can discuss an overnight trade."

"Okay, okay." Vivian ducked. "In the meantime, your side slice has to set me up with three of his friends. Minimum."

"Deal." She winked at Halo. "I'm teasing, darling, only teasing. I would *never* trade you…for an entire night."

He pinched her chin and held her gaze. "Sorry, sweetheart, but you are stuck with me—forever." A promise as much as a warning.

After today's labor, he would turn up the heat. He would not stop until he'd won her total surrender.

Ophelia chatted with the girls. For a little while, she forgot her troubles. And she had big-time troubles.

Every minute of every day, she fell deeper into her infatuation with the Astra. Didn't help that her body maintained a constant state of desperation for his. They had grown closer mentally and emotionally, but not physically. She hadn't even managed to talk Halo into an innocent fingering!

No matter what wiles she applied—flirting, stripping, fondling, pouting, teasing—he had continued to resist her. Something he shouldn't have been able to do, especially while he was hard as stone. Which he was. Always. But he never broke, never went further than a peck.

At first, she'd feared she'd lost her touch. Then she'd realized the truth. She had lost nothing; his hunger for her was never hidden. He yearned for her. He yearned for her madly—but he wanted her pledge more.

Did he have any idea how sexy that was?

Holding out was growing increasingly difficult. Sometimes she imagined saying yes to a happily-forever-after without the promise of stardust, more and more of her resistance crumbling.

Once the girls took off, Halo escorted Ophelia to an empty entertainment room. The place she liked to relax and watch movies. The freeze wasn't due to occur until 8:00 p.m. The next labor would kick off soon after; that, she knew. Erebus wasted no time nowadays; he couldn't. They neared the end of the entire blessing task.

And she couldn't forget Erebus's claim that the "real fun" kicked off with this next labor. A time Ophelia and Halo would supposedly suffer untold agonies.

"Something upsets you," he said as he removed his shirt. He reclined on a couch and crocked his fingers at her.

She joined him, straddling his waist. Mmm. Her core rested atop his hard-on.

"Is it the stardust?" he asked, his *alevala* jumping faster than usual. He gripped her hips to prevent her from grinding down.

The beasts—*her* beasts—caught her attention every time they reappeared. But oh, how she hated seeing their battles. Witnessing Halo's agony... Now that she had watched him die on a battlefield, she understood his upset with her deaths.

She traced a fingertip over the lioness. The one who started it all. It jumped again, another image taking its place. A beautiful female with kind eyes snagged her attention...

27

A haze fell over Ophelia's mind, her present superseded by Halo's past...

A new world opened. Six moons set in a circle around a seventh. Those celestial bodies came in a variety of colors, from pink to blue to gold, a few streams of light bleeding into others. Even the stars twinkled in circular patterns, creating symbols. A magic realm? The land itself took her breath away.

A forest clearing, spotlighted by the moonlight. Trees with tops that appeared to be cotton-candy roses, the petals like fluff. Roots that swirled over azure grass, simulating waves washing over the ground. Large, glittering rocks.

A beautiful female clad in a flowing ruby dress hovered nearby—the one from the *alevala*. She floated over the grass, a ring of fire and smoke seeming to create a force field around her. The gown's hem flapped in a wind only she could feel. Long auburn hair whipped around a pale face. Eyes like an abyss. Lips the same shade as fresh blood. She had aligned her body perfectly with the moons.

Thirteen Astra surrounded the ring. They were silent and exuding concern. Halo fought his way closer to the female—Ophelia gaped as the smoke thinned. Not mere flames, after all, but a horde of small, horned creatures set ablaze. Halo shredded monster after monster. Black blood splattered him, the droplets eating through his skin. He didn't seem to notice.

Pure ice. Ophelia flattened her hands over her stomach. And she'd thought him cold before. This male felt *nothing.* He truly resembled a robot, his chiseled features fresh off the assembly line.

His gaze remained locked on his target. At first, Red was unafraid of the approaching predator. But the closer he came, the more fear she evinced, going from pale to pallid. Her eyes flickered from black to green.

"I have done nothing to you, warlord." She threw the words at him. "For weeks, you've chased me across galaxies, striking at me. I have never struck you back. Yet you think to end me?"

"Without hesitation." He slashed and shredded more creatures. Almost within reach...

"Please," she beseeched. "Don't do this. I dream only of a better life. Let me have it."

"Better is only an illusion, female." He swung at her, a sword appearing in his grip midway. As her head went flying from her body, his impassive expression never wavered.

He killed her as easily as he'd once killed the hind, with no regrets or guilt.

The body crashed to the ground, flaming creatures dropping from the air. They, too, died, their fires extinguished by the time they thudded to the grass. Smiles broke out among the Astra. Roux came forward to pat Halo on the shoulder. Ian raced over and ruffled his dark hair. Halo rolled back his shoulders, his chest swelling with pride.

An unfamiliar male joined the celebrating melee. "You served us well, Halo. Rest tonight. Tomorrow, we begin planning for the next task."

The former leader, Solar, who'd ruled before Roc? Whoa! His beauty was blinding.

"Thank you, Commander," Halo said, confirming her suspicions. "I have a strategy mapped out." Already back to business as usual.

The present yanked Ophelia from the memory, and she met Halo's spinning gaze.

"Who did you see?" he asked with a frown.

"A redhead and her blazing circle."

"Ah. Dreama. A goddess of wishes. My fifth task with the Astra."

"In many ways, you are the same now as you were then," she said, sliding a fingertip over his washboard abs. Something he'd said to the goddess stuck with Ophelia. *Better is only an illusion.* Did he still feel that way—hopeless? "In other ways, you have changed greatly."

His irises glinted with promise. "Do you like these changes?"

"Oh yes. Very much."

Light and shadow jockeyed for position over his rugged features. "The stardust means nothing to me. You know this, yes? What I feel for you is real and lasting."

"It's more than that." Why not say it? "I'm scared, okay? The two times I risked my heart on love, I crashed and burned. I lost so much more than I gained."

With a hand on her nape, he urged her forward and kissed her lips. "Those males were not me, sweetheart."

"They weren't, no. They didn't go cold. As you've proven, emotions changed."

"Connection is more than emotion. It is an intangible link between two people."

"Yes, but links can be cut."

"Not my links."

Dang him! "Okay. What about the fact that Erebus will monsterize me for the last battle? We both know it's going to happen. And yes, monsterize is a real word of my own creation. If
we are pitted against each other, what then?"

He opened his mouth.

"No, let me rephrase. When we are pitted against each other,
what then? If you don't kill me, everyone else is cursed. If you
die, we're all damned. I mean, how many harpies do you think
will die alongside our Astra allies who can't win anything? How
are we going to save everyone?" Could they?

He rubbed the top of her sternum, above her brand. "Erebus will have no more use for you if we remove your yoke to
the Bloodmor. Which I believe I can do, if you do not resist its
removal."

She jutted her chin. "I remember you saying your strength
drains when you remove a brand, and that the removal of mine
doesn't come with a money-back guarantee. And, okay, I'll be
honest. The brand is the sole bridge to the last vestiges of my
hope." A part of her clung to the assurance that she could take
out Erebus and save the day—that she *would* do it, even if they
made it down to the wire.

"Perhaps we should steal the Bloodmor," he said, stroking his
chin. "Nothing in the rules prevents it."

Stealing the Bloodmor. That wasn't a bad idea. To use Erebus's
own weapon against him... "Yes. Let's steal the Bloodmor." Today
if possible. What did Erebus have planned for the next labor?

Halo leaned in and kissed the base of her throat, where her
pulse suddenly slammed. "Until then...let's get this vow of forever settled. My body misses yours, Elia." Kiss. "And yours
misses mine." Lick. "The sweet scent of your arousal keeps me
hard all day."

The ache between her legs doubled. Tripled. A mewl escaped
as her nipples drew tight and her belly fluttered.

"You want me," she moaned, "you can have me. Why don't we call a daylong truce? You'll show me what I'm missing when I refuse to purchase your lifetime warranty, and I'll prove I'm worth leasing with a *chance* for purchase. I'll return you to the dealer in only slightly used condition, promise."

She whipped her hips, and his pupils flared and contracted, like a pulse—a heartbeat.

"You make sense." He ran the tip of his nose up her throat, inhaling sharply. "Your logic is bulletproof."

"It is bulletproof, isn't it?" Her lungs constricted. He was soon to cave? Perfect! Wonderful! *Not* disappointing. Not the teeniest bit. Joy pinged her chest. Surely it was joy. With the return of her intense lover, she would be deluged with pleasure and satisfaction. But, um, had joy always felt so blah?

"It is," he responded, his irises suddenly reminding her of flint. "However, what's right isn't always what's rational. My resistance to your charms is the only way to prove my intentions. With you, I will never settle for anything less than everything. You are too important to me. In this, you'll find I have no give."

The harpy—rendered speechless. The nymph—breathless. *Halo might be winning me over.*

What if they *could* make forever work?

Roux appeared near the couch, all pale hair, red eyes, and muscles. "I have news."

The two Astra engaged in a telepathic conversation. Whatever was said before Roux flashed off infuriated Halo.

"Tell me," she insisted, stomach already churning.

"Roux visited Nova, our home realm. Each Astra has his own territory and palace, but each palace is connected through a mystical hallway known as the Hall of Secrets. Whispers are collected there. Secrets spoken by immortals are collected there. Five hundred years ago, Erebus whispered a message to me. He said my female is eternally bound to the Bloodmor. Destroying the weapon will destroy her."

"Wait. How would he even know that back then?"

"He owns the Blade of Destiny. I'm unsure what it does, exactly, or how it works, but it allows him to see multiple futures for multiple decisions."

"If that's true, and I'm bound to the Bloodmor..." The ramifications were greater than she'd realized. How had she not comprehended this sooner?

"We will have that dagger in our possession. Nothing will stop us."

Us. Was there a more beautiful word in any language? Obtaining the weapon would not be easy. Obviously. The god knew they would make a play for it, since he'd oh, so clearly foreseen this.

"I knew I should have done a double major to include Theft as well as Murder. Come on." Ophelia popped to her feet and tugged Halo to his. "Let's spar and test out my thieving skills."

He teleported her to the coliseum, where they worked on her stealth. Halo kept his focus on her improvement, his hands rarely straying—even when hers did. Though her illicit touches ceased when the monsters rattled their cages, aggression mounting.

A cruel mistress, she brandished a mental cattle prod until calm descended. Ophelia poured herself into the training—she trained as if her life and future depended on it, pushing herself until the sun slipped from the sky. A few times, she debated letting a beast slip its cage, just to find out what would happen. Now wasn't the day to risk it, though.

"Whatever occurs today, we finish our earlier conversation after the labor." Halo cupped her cheeks. Despite the intensity and longevity of their workout, he showed no signs of fatigue. "Do you agree?"

"Yes," she rasped, clutching his wrists. "We'll talk."

Satisfaction seeped from him. "The freeze comes in three, two, one."

She held her breath. Would Erebus act as quickly as she suspected?

A trumpet blew, and she sighed.

"Halo Phaninon," he barked, not removing his gaze from her. When a second blast came, they both exhaled.

"This isn't a death match," she said. Thank goodness!

"No, it isn't." Erebus appeared, oozing glee. For once, his army of phantoms wasn't congregated in the stands or stretched out behind him.

"This is to be a feat of cunning," the god announced. "Hercules won a girdle from an Amazon queen. You, Halo, must win your female's heart. Metaphorically or literally, your choice. And there's no need to thank me. Your expression is thanks enough."

Rage burned through her, every monster in her internal zoo banging its cages, seeking freedom. Hand over her heart? He had *dared* to force her hand? "You steaming pile of—argh!"

"I'll leave you to it." A grinning Erebus vanished.

Ophelia paced. Either she accepted Halo's offer of forever, or she forced him to cut out her heart. Both paths sucked for her. Yeah, for him too. Had she verged on accepting his offer before Erebus made his announcement? Yes. But now? Leaning into her foe's battle plan, as if it were a heavenly gift? Foolish! For her *and* for Halo. Surely he saw that. He would never know if she'd caved to save herself or because she truly loved him.

She swung her gaze back to him. And oh, wow. Okay. He'd crossed his arms and upped his smolder.

"Well?" he asked.

"You can't be okay with this," she screeched. "He wants me to pledge forever, which must mean his next torment hinges on it. Maybe. Probably. That's why we should...resist?" Argh! She'd reached the state of being she most despised, when she didn't know anything about anything.

Halo hiked his shoulders. "His goal means nothing to me. *My* goal means everything. I'll use every weapon at my disposal."

Her heart flipped. That was almost sweet.

What was she going to do? "Give me a minute to think," she mumbled.

His pupils did that pulsing thing, and she pursed her lips.

He was obviously *manipulating* her and loving it. Was there any worse quality a forever mate could have? No, not really. Also, a winner didn't let herself be outwitted, outplayed, and outlasted. In fact, a smart girl would force him to cut out her heart rather than admit she had sunk low enough to catch feelings.

But. A smart girl also put her money on a Thoroughbred rather than a common stallion. What if she was *supposed* to take a risk, sacrificing her fear on the altar of love, rather than her life?

And if she was wrong?

Her wings fluttered. How could she *not* want forever with him? This Astra had fought for her. He'd fought *hard*. Deliciously so. She mattered to him. He desired her like air. Relaxed with her. Laughed with her. He needed her in ways he'd never needed another. Because she was his and he was hers.

Because she loved the douchebag with all her heart. The nymph in her could not get enough of him—and never would.

He is my entwine and consort. She could deny it no longer.

Ophelia's gaze flipped up to his, everything inside her soft and vulnerable. "Halo," she whispered.

A trumpet blasted through the night, and he stepped toward her.

Aggression thrummed from him, but he kept his arms at his sides, his hands fisted. "I won you?"

She chewed on her bottom lip and nodded.

"Say the words," he croaked.

Ophelia licked her lips and did it. She risked it all, putting everything on the line. "You win, Halo. I want forever with you. I…surrender."

28

A roar of triumph left Halo. He swooped down, claiming Ophelia's lips with his own. Claiming her. She had needed her male to prove himself worthy of her affections. Someone willing to fight for her, whatever the cost, the same way she fought for him. Halo had done it. He'd demonstrated patience, and he'd won his prize. The most sensual, playful female he'd never known to dream about. A stunning beauty beyond his wildest imaginations. A champion unwilling to stay down, no matter how often she fell. A conduit of emotion who added vibrant colors to his black-and-white world.

He flashed her to his—their—bedroom. High on victory, he walked her backward, heading for the bathroom. Along the way, he stopped to press her against a wall. The kiss never paused. They were both grimy from practice, smears of blood wetting his skin, but he didn't care. He couldn't not taste her.

He ripped off the harpy's armor and undergarments, removing each piece with the utmost haste. His heart stormed in his chest. Internal growls mimicked blasts of thunder as he gained a deep awareness of every pulse point in his body. Heat flooded his veins. No, not just heat. An inferno, his cells set ablaze. Smoke wafted, clouding his head. Desire obscured all other thoughts. *Take everything. Give more.*

Ophelia sank her claws in his shoulders and devoured his mouth. Moans flowed between them in a continuous stream as he ripped at his zipper, his throbbing length springing free.

"Give me your pheromone. When I said I wanted everything, I meant it." He ground his shaft against her core, spreading her wetness between them, and hissed. "I've been without you too long."

The incredible scent filled his nose. He inhaled deep and lifted his head. Their gazes locked. Mere inches separated their bodies. The knowledge stripped him of control yet somehow also strengthened him.

"Mmm. Never happened so easily before," she said between panting breaths. Pale green irises resembled polished glass as she swayed. "I think I'm pheromoneing *myself*."

"Or you are drunk with desire for your male." He flashed a possessive grin. "I like that you recognize me as yours, nymph. Love that you surrender to me." That surrender made this an act of promise for them both. Together forever. He would treat it as the honor it was.

"I do. I did." She nipped at his lower lip. "So don't make me wait a moment longer for you."

"Oh, sweetheart. You will wait. That, I promise you. You will do whatever I tell you. Isn't that right?" He ground into her with increasing pressure.

Gasping, she arched her back. "It's right, it's right."

"Do not forget." He transported her to the shower stall, where he hurriedly stripped, and they cleaned up.

She stroked his shaft whenever she got the chance. Every sec-

ond he failed to bend her over and thrust into her torched another layer of his sanity. When he could take it no more, he fisted
her hair, angling her head, and pressed her against the tiles. Hot
water rained, every sluicing droplet a tiny caress.

He cupped between her legs and rubbed her clit. Her lips
parted on a gasp-moan before she poured herself over him the
way he adored. Rolling her hips and undulating as he stroked
her.

Steam thickened the air. A soft pitter-patter provided the perfect background chorus for each rasp, groan, and plea.

He nipped her bottom lip and unveiled what was surely a ferocious grin. "You please me, Elia."

"I'm truly yours forever?" She bared her throat to him. "You'll
always desire me?"

"Mmm-hmm." He licked her carotid. "I need more fun in
my life, and you will provide it. Every inch of you is now considered my personal playground. I think my first claim will go
here." He stirred his finger inside her, wrenching another groan
from them both.

Her breath hitched, and her nipples drew tighter. "And your
second?"

Holding her gaze, he slid his other hand to her breast and
kneaded. "Here." He grazed his thumb over the amber crest.

She cried out, a needy plea. "Guess what I just realized. You
won me, but I won you too. That means I'm stronger than you.
I took down the big, bad immortal. My courage is off the charts.
Something you will be sure to note in your killer recommendation letter."

A corner of his mouth quirked. He kissed her lips. "There
is *no one* stronger or braver than my Elia. No matter the odds
stacked against you, you forge ahead. If a path hits a dead end,
you carve out a new one. When you fall, you fight your way
back up. Time and time again, you've faced death head-on, even
eagerly. To defend those you love, you stop at nothing."

"Mmm, I sound amazing," she teased.

"You are." Naked and wet, Halo returned her to the bed, stretched her out on her belly, and paid homage to her delicate wings. To the elegant line of her spine. To the world's most perfect backside. He imagined her skin marked in his stardust, and raw longing nearly overwhelmed him. Flipping her over, sucking her nipples, fingering her deep, he growled, "You like being claimed by your male, don't you, Elia?"

"I do. I really, really do." She thrashed, pulled his hair. Squeezed his shoulders. Pricked him with her claws, putting her mark on *him*.

"For your honesty, I'm giving you a reward." More and more of his calm facade disintegrated. "Come hard for me." He pressed his thumb against her swollen bud.

She screamed his name, as her inner walls clamped around his fingers. He let her thrash and ride it out. By the time she sagged against the mattress, his longing had sharpened into lust.

Spasms subsiding, she moaned, "More, Halo."

Gladly.

He propped his upper body on one elbow, and positioned his erection at her entrance, sliding in just enough to madden himself.

Slowly she undulated, forcing him deeper. With each inch she gained, his pleasure escalated. Sweat sheened his brow. His heartbeat like a war drum.

When he could stand it no longer, he plunged the rest of the way. Crying out, she arched her back, then wound her limbs around him, clinging.

He pulled out. Pushed in. Lifted his head and held her gaze. In. Out. Long locks of damp, dark hair framed a flushed face. Those lust-drunk irises were shielded by heavy lids as he eased into a languid grind. *No lovelier female.* Lamplight cast a golden glow over her dusky skin. Plump breasts with those amber nipples razed more of his control. Scarlet lips bore little puncture marks from her fangs. Judging by her hungry stare, she longed to bury those fangs in his neck before they climbed from this bed. A harpy's claim on her consort?

Must have this! Halo clasped her by the nape and yanked her face to his throat. "Bite," he commanded. "Drink me."

"Are you sure?" She hesitated, merely licking his fevered skin.

He hammered into her once, twice. Again. "Bite and suck like you mean it." Again. Harder. Faster. "Give me what's mine, Elia."

"Yes…" With a whimper, she sank her fangs deep.

He loosened his grip until he was petting her hair.

"That's the way. Fill yourself with me." With his power. Was she right? Was this what Erebus had wanted all along? For Halo to cede his strength to a challenger, bit by bit? To aid in his own downfall? In the moment, he couldn't make it matter. "Come on me. Squeeze my length. Steal my climax from me."

He reached between them, grazing her clit. Her back arched again, her fangs withdrawing from his vein as her head fell back. A loud moan pierced his ears. Like music. Those tight inner walls clenched again and again as she came, searing his shaft.

Any lingering tension coiled in his chest until it finally, blessedly just…shattered. Halo roared and came, came and roared. The fragments of what had plagued him for so long—gone. It was the most incredible sensation he'd ever experienced.

For this, for her, he would have endured anything. Countless other centuries of misery? *In a heartbeat.* This was right. This was *his* right.

When he collapsed and rolled to his side, Ophelia fit over him. They panted in time, their hearts racing in sync. He wound his arms around her. His future had never been brighter—or worse.

If he could win the final labor without battling her, he could keep her. What could be better? But if he won the battle and lost her?

His chest stung. No. No! He'd lost too much already. He refused to lose his harpymph. They had another option. Possibly. The trinite cage and hibernation. Maybe he'd dismissed the idea too quickly. If that failed, he'd go another route—he just had to figure out what another route entailed.

If nothing came to him, perhaps they could all hibernate. The Astra had been willing to sleep for the next five hundred years to save Roc and Taliyah. Only fair they do the same for Halo and Ophelia.

Except, the success of this test led to ascension. Would the Astra receive another opportunity like it? With the ascension, they would gain the power to eliminate Erebus for good.

Ophelia yawned and stretched. Halo kissed her temple and eased out of bed. But only to gather the necessary materials. After he cleaned them both, he returned to her side.

"Am I your entwine and consort?" he asked, gathering her close. "I want to hear you say the words."

"Yes, okay? Yes. I'll admit it out loud. You are my entwine as well as my consort. What can I say? I'm a sucker for your obsession with me." She lifted her face to smother his with kisses before she folded her hands on his breastbone and gazed up at him, vulnerable once again. "Am I your *gravita*?"

He pinched a lock of her hair. "You are absolutely my *gravita*. No matter what. So we won't worry about the what-ifs, will we, harpy? We won't serve Erebus's purpose and allow doubt to grow between us."

"What do you consider his purpose, exactly?"

"To keep me miserable as long as possible and garrison your resistance to my charms."

She snorted, then blinked at him. "Oh, you're serious. Okay then. So, you believe you have charms now? Kindly tell me when this miracle supposedly occurred?"

The corners of his mouth kicked up. "The first time we had sex, my software received an automatic update."

She barked out a laugh. "Dang, I like you. But just to be clear, your software update understands that you can boss me around in the bedroom, but not on the battlefield, yes? Because I *will* fight alongside harpykind in combat."

"I do understand." Her skill and ferocity amazed him. If she was correct and learned how to fully control the beasts—some of the worst monsters in mythology—she would be a formidable opponent for anyone, including the Astra. "I won't stand in the way of your desire to challenge Erebus or steal the Bloodmor."

A familiar sense of foreboding pricked him, rousing dread. The next task involved a three-bodied giant with cattle. Another death match, he'd bet. But when? Erebus wasn't supposed to act for another seven days, but the god did love his loopholes.

Halo scoured a hand through his hair. The Deathless was spiteful enough to provoke a fight between Halo and Ophelia immediately after they'd pledged their futures to each other. *My nightmare. The ultimate misery.*

"Hey! Stop jumping ahead to the next battle," she said, reading him so well. "Whatever happens, we'll get through it. We won't mention the stardust again, either. If you say it's a non-issue, it's a non-issue." She trailed a fingertip to his groin. "Agreed? Or maybe you require a little motivation first?"

His thoughts centered on her next actions in a hurry. "I *must* be motivated," he rushed to tell her, threading his fingers through her hair.

"In that case…" Eyes hooded, she bent her head and flicked her tongue over his nipples, one after the other. "I think I'm going to drink straight from your tap."

His body jerked. *Yes! Want this.* "I will graciously allow you to do this," he said, his voice hoarse, "but you will owe me big."

"Huge," she replied, and licked her lips. "Tell me your demands."

"You will give me another day of fun and allow me to introduce you to the Astra. As my *gravita*."

All wicked carnality, she gave her lips another lick. "You want to show me off?"

"I'm desperate to."

Excitement glittered in her emerald irises, only to dull a second later. "Will they doubt you? Without the...you know. The powder that shall no longer be named."

"They might." Truth was truth. "But there's another way to irrevocably bond us together. A way that will let us communicate telepathically, as I do with the Astra."

The excitement intensified, only to ebb again. "I'll be able to speak to you always, in your head?"

"If I brand you with my insignia, yes." The link would let him flash her to and fro without contact, as well as converse inside her head, no matter the distance between them. "Will you bear it?"

"I will...one day. Maybe." She smiled and inched down his body. "But first you'll bear my insignia. Two fang marks..."

29

Day 61-ish
7:04 p.m.

Ophelia and Halo. An official couple. So far, their forever commitment had lasted a week—or so—mostly spent in bed. Her longest romantic relationship to date and his first.

Tonight, they intended to celebrate their incredible accomplishment with an anniversary party o' fun that he had kind of sort of requested. No better time for it. Neither of them felt the urgency of an upcoming labor.

Primping in a full-length mirror, Ophelia had to admit she looked pretty snazzy. After an amazing marathon of sex and a superquick six-hour power nap in Halo's arms, she'd kicked him out of her bunk. Despite his man-pouting, thank you. She'd cleaned up and donned an ivory sheath dress with cutouts between her breasts and around her navel. The flowing, slitted skirt reached the floor, playing peekaboo with towering stilettos.

It wasn't a dress she would have chosen pre-Halo. Now, however, she expected his furnace of a body to keep her warm.

She'd braided her hair in a dark crown, baring her neck and the spiked collar Halo had gifted to her this morning.

The only thing she was missing? His brand. She'd pumped the brakes on the idea—not forever, just for now. Halo wasn't happy about the lack, but oh, did she like his method of persuasion.

No more withholding orgasms. Now, he *lavished* her with pleasure. It was just, so much had changed so quickly. Admitting she wanted to keep him. Promising to spend her eternity with him. Experiencing true sexual satisfaction for the first time. Sleeping tucked up against another person.

She was stretched to the limit. Having a literal brand burned into her skin, establishing a mental link with her guy, perhaps even inadvertently sharing the thoughts and insecurities and worries she was fighting so, so, so hard to overcome…it was almost more than she could handle.

Ophelia pressed a hand over her twisting stomach and breathed. Calm came gradually. She wouldn't think about tomorrow. Or the final labors. Or the mental zoo, overflowing with beasts who never stopped clanging around in their cages, making her wonder what would happen if ever they escaped at the same time. She would keep her thoughts centered on now. The night was teeing up to be her favorite memory. A cherry on top of an already wonderful day, spent with the guy she'd chosen as her very own.

How could she not fall for the Astra? The way he responded to her, and only her. His utter worship of her body. That lust-inducing intensity. His droll sense of humor. His strength!

During three of the labors, he'd run himself through with a firstone sword, turned to stone and crumbled, simply to preserve her life. And how could she forget his heat?

Ophelia was happier than she'd ever been. Which made her panicky. *Bye-bye calm.* Obviously, something had to give, and soon. The other shoe had to drop, leading to the moment she lost absolutely everything she'd come to adore. Right? That was her life's pattern.

"The party has started." Halo's reflection appeared behind hers in the mirror, and her heart leaped at the sight. His eyes widened as he scanned the glass. His pupils pulsed. "There is *nothing* lovelier than you."

"You aren't wrong. But your loveliness is a close second," she teased. He looked good. He wore the usual T-shirt and leathers, but he'd added an adoring gaze to the ensemble and, well, he stole her breath. "You are magnificent," she told him, spinning to wrap her arms around his neck.

"I'd rather you *scream* how magnificent I am." He kissed her brow, the tip of her nose, the rise of her cheek. "Everyone will understand if we're late."

Shivers raced over her limbs, and she laughed. Why had she ever feared having a consort or entwine? For the first time in her life, she was free to be a harpy *and* a nymph. The two sides of her might be opposites—the lover and the fighter—but they were no longer at odds. They worked together, strengthening her *without* the help of the beasts.

But did they strengthen her *enough*? Could she combat the beasts if ever they broke loose in unison? What if *Halo* couldn't subdue her then? What if she...killed him? Had she allowed herself to become *too* strong? Erebus's plan all along?

She hurried to blank her thoughts. Now wasn't the time. Halo always sensed the slightest change in her demeanor. Apparently, the big, bad wolf's moods were now dependent on Little Brunette Riding Hood.

"Party first," she told him with a bright smile. He had specifically requested fun, so, he was getting fun one way or another.

He frowned at her, because yes, he'd sensed the change, but he also nodded. "Very well. I will do this for you, but you will owe me."

She snickered as he flashed her to the throne room now jam-packed with beings dressed to kill. Metaphorically as well as literally. Small round tables were adorned with an array of finger foods. Cue cards read Do Not Eat. Soft music played in the background. Candlelight glowed softly, glinting from chandeliers twined with chains of crystal.

Roc and Taliyah observed from a dais, seated upon their thrones. Mingling throughout were the highest ranked harpies and harphantoms plus Vivi, Meda, the other Astra concubines, an oracle Ophelia had never met, the General's family, and the remaining Astra.

The warlords were spread out throughout the room, though none actively participated in the festivities; they only watched as harpies downed shots and sang badly—some watched more intently than others.

Harphantoms had taken up posts near the walls, clearly uncomfortable and ready to ghost ASAP. Vivi, Meda, and three of the General's sisters pretended to be bartenders, manning a makeshift wet bar, arguing over who served the best cocktails and cockteasers.

Grinning, Ophelia linked an arm through Halo's, clutched his biceps, and leaned her head against his shoulder. This was the kind of event her...mother had thrown but never invited her to attend. *Never important enough.*

Her grin faded, but she quickly rallied. Halo considered her a VIP, and that was what mattered.

"I'm ready for my introduction to society," she told him.

"Be silent," Halo commanded the masses—and they obeyed. Conversations ceased, everyone peering at him with expectation.

She fought a laugh.

With pride stamped into every line of his being, he announced, "I present my *gravita*, Ophelia Falconcrest."

She executed her best curtsy without releasing his arm.

"All hail the Sweetheart," everyone called in unison, toasting her with their drinks.

"You've got to be kidding me," she muttered.

"That's not her name," Vivi called before downing two shots. She stood on the bar and winked at Ophelia, all *I've got you, girl. No worries.* "It's Mrs. Immortal."

A new greeting rang out. "All hail Mrs. Immortal, the Sweetheart!"

"We can definitely leave now," she grumbled.

Halo's eyes glittered with wicked delight.

Ian flashed over, surprising Ophelia with a nod of deference that fused a steel rod to her spine. "A pleasure to meet you, Ophelia."

"Well, maybe we can stay a bit longer," she told her male. With that one nod, Ian told her how much he respected her position as Halo's chosen mate. He also acknowledged her role as a soldier fighting—and dying—to keep everyone safe. Like Halo, he recognized her incredible worth. Because she had some. And oh, wow, what an amazing pick up. "It's a pleasure to remeet you, too, Ian."

If only Nissa could see her now.

A pang of sadness ripped through Ophelia, but it wasn't painful. Not anymore. The sharpest edges had dulled. But, um, why was Ian staring at her as if she'd sprouted another head?

Oh, crap. Had she?

Halo noticed the unwavering attention too. "You may look away from her, Ian. In fact, I suggest you do so. Now."

She rolled her lips between her teeth as she fought another grin. As more and more of her Astra's emotions bubbled to the surface, he displayed more and more of his reactions.

Ian seemed to fight off a grin as well. Dark eyes lively, he asked, "Why haven't you covered your female in stardust?"

Halo floundered for a response, discomfort and fury warring for control of his features, and Ophelia snickered.

"He's only teasing you, sport." She slapped playfully at his chest, stunned to find the stardust scarcity bothered her less and less. Halo was a stone-cold immortal able to create worlds. He knew his mind—and his heart. If he believed Ophelia was his forever, who was she to argue?

"Teasing," he echoed, as if the concept were foreign to him.

He would learn. Their new motto? No stardust, no problem. Maybe the powder would appear one day, maybe it wouldn't. Why base her happiness—or her misery—on a force outside her control?

He must have responded telepathically to his buddy. Something along the lines of *This is no joke—my female, back off.* Ian's grin broke free as he held up his hands in a gesture of innocence.

Halo's claim of possession never failed to thrill her. "Stick a pin in it, you two. Play nice. This adored female sees a dozen shots of vodka in need of thieving." Ophelia slid her hands under his shirt to flatten her palms on his washboard abs. Skin to skin, her favorite. "While I'm gone, you aren't allowed to worry, pout, or brood. You do, and I'll cancel the afterparty in my panties. But don't let that stop you from undressing me with your gaze…"

She winked at a gaping Halo. Pleased with herself, her male, and life in general, she sauntered off, exaggerating the roll of her hips.

"Who *are* you?" Ian demanded.

Though the warlord stood at Halo's side, he barely heard the words, his attention glued to the temptress who starred in his most fevered dreams. Did she feel his eyes upon her as she walked away?

The way she moved…a sensual feast. Halo stifled a groan.

Roux appeared beside Ian and crossed his arms over his chest. "Did you ask him?" he inquired of the other male.

"About the stardust or his new personality?" Ian waved a hand in dismissal. "Never mind. Yes. I asked him. I'm still awaiting a response."

Had Ophelia just shivered? *Should he go to her? Warm her?*

The warlords moved in front of Halo, blocking his view. The urge to knock their heads together and toss their bodies aside barraged him, but he breathed deep. *Shouldn't harm my friends.*

In their minds, he'd been an emotionless husk only yesterday. Today, he seethed with desire for a specific female.

He maneuvered the two to different angles. There. "I'm... me," he said, watching as Ophelia joined her friends at the bar. "Mostly. I'm the same male. Determined to defeat Erebus, no matter the cost." The enemy could not be allowed to win. Not this time.

"Speaking of Erebus. I have an idea..." Roux trailed off as his gaze flipped to the chandelier, as if drawn by an invisible force.

A harpy was crouched there. Blythe the Undoing. The lithe beauty glared at Roux.

As the warlord bowed up, Halo finally understood the woman's moniker. With zero effort, she was undoing centuries of Roux's civility, her hatred battering at his hard-won calm.

Did the male desire her the way Halo desired Ophelia?

And I thought my courtship was ripe with hardships. Theirs might get...rocky.

"Your idea?" he prompted absently. The harpymph was laughing at something someone said. She swiped a shot from another female and drained the contents. Others cheered as she raised the empty glass.

"We have the power to be our own worst—and most powerful—enemy," Roux said. "Do you think Erebus decided to pit you against *yourself*?"

He worked his jaw. "It's possible. In theory."

In the beginning, Chaos had mentioned the lessons Halo must learn. So. What had he learned so far? That, just as soon as he decided he understood something, new information came to light, proving he knew nothing. He'd discovered he had limits. Lines he wouldn't cross, no matter the provocation. He had discovered old desires, passions, and yearnings buried deep. He'd uncovered a shocking goal—a life with Ophelia, doing what he was born to do. Protecting and pleasuring her. He wasn't a machine, after all. He owned a heart, battered though it was, and it required his *gravita* to function properly.

But what would fighting against himself entail on a battlefield? What would it mean in the end?

Ian thought for a moment, frowned. "If you are your own opponent, Halo, one side of you will win. But the other side will lose."

Yes, and either way, Halo would have only half a life. Victory for the Astra meant defeat for Ophelia. Victory for Ophelia meant defeat for the Astra.

"I have much to consider," he muttered. But not here. Not now. Not until he'd taken every "test." Only then could he have a complete picture of his "lessons."

Magical laughter drew his gaze to his female. His mouth curved up and things loosened in his chest. Ears twitching, he homed in on her current conversation with Vivian.

"He can't take his eyes off you," the harpire whispered. "Be honest. You do weird tricks in bed to keep him this way, don't you?"

"Probably the weirdest," she whispered back.

"You're smiling. And smug!" Ian burst out, stealing his focus yet again. "You couldn't be prouder of your female."

No, he really couldn't.

Waiting for the freeze—the end of the party—to whisk her to their bedroom proved difficult. Somehow, he managed it. Let her enjoy this time without worries.

Finally, the freeze came. Ophelia wove through the stationary bodies, racing toward him.

He opened his arms and she jumped onto him, winding her legs around his waist. "I missed you."

"So much." He clasped her tight.

She framed his face with her hands. "Give me your mou—" Her brows drew together. The color drained from her cheeks. "My chest. The brand thingy. It's burning as if Erebus and the Bloodmor are nearby."

He frowned. A labor tonight, though they hadn't sensed it?

"I don't want to fight you, Halo," she said, nearing panic. "And I don't want to watch you kill yourself to save me. Put me in hibernation. Please! I'll steal the dagger next time."

Not if Halo stole it first. "Be at ease. I will do as you wish." He flashed her to his bedroom in the duplicate realm and willed her to sleep. Gently laying her upon the mattress, he whispered, "Dream of me, sweetheart. I'll return shortly."

Her eyes remained closed, her head lulled to the side.

Tension coiled in him but he hardened his heart and summoned the trinite case, trapping the harpy within. Without his brand. No way to communicate. A worry for later.

The black stone slab reminded him of a coffin. He didn't like the thought.

He forced himself to return to Harpina, to the coliseum, and took stock. Dark sky, no stars. Bright moonlight. Inhale deep. Slowly exhale.

A trumpet blasted once. Twice. A test of cunning then.

He breathed a bit easier, calling, "Halo Phaninon."

Erebus appeared at the far end of the field, already strolling toward Halo. The hem of his black robe dragged over sand.

Three dark-haired harpies flanked his sides.

Systems overload. Halo's mind was unable to compute what his eyes claimed to behold. He did *not* see three versions of Ophelia, each wearing the same white gown, eyeing Halo as if he were a banquet of sensual delights. Unless…

They were illusions? Transformations courtesy of the Bloodmor? One real, two fake? All fake? All real? Had the trinite case failed to do its job?

No, no. Surely not.

"Quite remarkable, aren't they?" the god boasted. "The original and the carbon copies, each bespelled to notice you alone."

The original? A lie. *Please be a lie.* Ophelia remained in hibernation, safe.

"Although, really, they are all originals, I suppose, considering the copies are her in every way that matters." Erebus grinned as he stopped twenty feet away. "They feel what she feels and thinks what she thinks. My apologies, Immortal, but this match is lose-lose for you."

Halo balled his hands as the three females fanned out behind the god.

Erebus spread his arms. "Hercules stole cattle from a three-bodied giant. I present you with your female, plus two. You must simply choose the Ophelia you wish to save. I'll keep the others. And please, take your time. They are in relatively no danger from me...at the moment."

He bit back a vile curse. *Reveal nothing.*

Oblivious to the god, the trio beckoned Halo closer, their motions perfectly timed.

Bile blistered his chest. Leave any version of his harpymph with Erebus—no! But if he chose wrong...

"The Bloodmor is truly a marvel." Erebus wound through the females, tracing a fingertip over their throats as he passed. "It morphs select individuals into anyone or anything else completely. They become the other being in every way, and there's no going back. Two versions of your female *will* become my pets. For a little while." He tilted his head. "Will it help you to know I replicated her with my phantoms?"

Halo huffed his breaths. *Must acquire that blade.*

Erebus nuzzled an Ophelia's cheek, and the sight sickened Halo. How much more must the harpymph despise the contact?

Get this done. "Release them so I may make my selection."

"Perhaps it doesn't matter to you, who lives and who dies," Erebus continued, ignoring his command as he moved on to the next female. "They look the same. Feel the same." He ran his nose up one's neck. "Smell the same. I admit, I'm eager to train my pets to enjoy my particular...needs."

Just like that, *anhilla* threatened, tearing through Halo's control.

He tuned out the despised male and concentrated fully on the females. A thorough inspection revealed zero differences between them, both outside and in. They even carried the internal brand in the same location.

"You can't tell?" they shrieked in unison. "Halo? I'm your *gravita*. How can you not pick me from a lineup of thousands?"

How was he supposed to do this? How could he not?

What did he know beyond any doubt? Hurting her pained him, and touching her never failed to affect him.

The trio glared as he strode forward. He stopped in front of the first, trembling as he cupped the side of her face. Her skin warmed...but it didn't feel right. He blinked with realization. *Not an exact copy, after all.*

Calm and relief washed over him, the answer suddenly so clear. He touched the middle female. Wrong again. The third. Well, well. Wily Erebus.

Returning to the first harpy, he met the god's cocky grin with one of his own. "This isn't her." Without pause, Halo withdrew a three-blade and stabbed her in the heart.

The god's amusement dulled the slightest bit. "This isn't a death match."

"Loophole," Halo deadpanned. The other two females hurled insults at him, cursing his familial line up to a thousand generations. He ignored the kink in his gut. "Not her, either." He stabbed the next, and new curses rang out.

The god's amusement dulled a bit more.

He stopped in front of the final female—and rammed the blade into her chest. "Or her." Quick but not easy.

The curses died with the duplicates, the trumpet sounding. Yet his stomach twisted even harder.

"I won the test." Of that, he had no doubt.

Erebus glowered at him. Had he not expected this? It was possible. He might own the Blade of Destiny, but he didn't know everything, as proven by his shock when Taliyah had sacrificed herself for Roc.

Had the General's last-minute decision redirected her fate? Had Halo somehow redirected his? But what had he done, exactly? What choice had he made to bring a change? How could he *do it more*?

"You won't win this in the end," Erebus said, his tone flat. "You don't see the truth yet. But you will." He vanished as quickly as he'd appeared, taking his hostility with him.

Halo returned to the duplicate realm, finding the trinite case exactly where he'd left it. With a thought, he flashed the stone away...

She remained inside, at ease, sleeping soundly, and his worry deflated. Hope prevailed. Until a question sparked.

Had the god attempted to summon her and failed, or had he *not* summoned her, thinking to lure Halo into another false sense of security?

He ground his molars. He required a plan B. The brand. Tomorrow, he would stop at nothing to get it done.

30

The next day dawned the same as any other, yet completely different. Ophelia's thoughts churned right from the start. Only two labors remained, the repeats set to end. Which kind of sucked. She'd gotten used to having a guaranteed do-over. It took the pressure off. But soon, she'd get no more fresh starts. What if she screwed up?

Halo picked her up and flashed her to the balcony outside his suite. "Anything you'd like to do today?"

"Let me think." She stood at the metal railing, soaking in a perfect view of the market and trinite wall. Sunlight glowed over a hilly landscape. An array of buildings and the Tree of Skulls cast long shadows over empty streets.

Those streets would remain empty throughout the day. At

the start of each morning, Halo always issued a stay-at-home order for the masses.

He gripped the bars at her sides and pressed against her, his big body caging her in. "Tell me another favorite place in Harpina, even if it's behind the wall."

Easy. "The Forest of—" The balcony disappeared, trees appearing around her. "Learnings."

"Why this place?" he asked, taking her hand and leading her forward.

"Why not?" She motioned to a pile of different size stones. "Anything can explode at any moment. Leaves look as soft as clouds but possess razor-sharp tips. Flower petals change colors like Christmas lights, tempting viewers to stare. Peer too long, and you'll be blinded for hours." She grinned, explaining, "This is where harpy children are trained. A land of stunning beauty capable of shocking horrors."

Exactly how she'd once cataloged romantic relationships. Now she saw the truth. Those "horrors" came with unbeatable benefits. Protection. Support. Affection.

"I've always felt comfortable here." Oops. Not something she should've said. He was a smart guy and might realize she wasn't feeling so comfortable. Those beasts...

He nuzzled her cheek, letting her know he *had* realized it, but he wasn't going to press. "Makes sense that you found comfort here. You are the embodiment of the terrain. Exquisitely treacherous. Deceptively soft. Very much like Nova."

Her toes curled. "After your ascension, I'd like to visit your world."

He appeared pleased. "You will enjoy Nova, I think. Each Astra rules his own territory. Mine is a blank canvas ready for your most explicit demands. In a matter of days, I can remake the land however you desire."

"You can redecorate *land*? Adding trees and lakes and stuff?" Wow! "Can we give Vivi her own island? Please, please, please."

She threw herself in front of him, stopping him in his tracks. A pink petal curled past, dancing in the breeze. "She'll demand beach weather always."

His lips quirked as he looped his arms around her. "You in a bikini...yes, I'm liking this plan. We can give Vivi a thousand islands." He kissed her mouth. "Tell me what is bothering you." Okay, so he was going to push. Guilt shadowed his irises. "Am I failing to fulfill one of your needs?"

"You are fulfilling me plenty, I promise."

He tightened his hold. "But?"

"It's the beasts, okay? They're agitated all the time. And they're strong. I can control one at a time, but all? The worst part is, you might have been right, and I might—might!—have been a tad bit foolish to continue accepting my transformations. I might have welcomed our doom." If he lost everything because of her...

You ruin whatever you touch, Ophelia.

No. No! She didn't. Halo had learned how to juggle his emotions thanks to her. And, you know, to feel them. Those were good things. Beyond good! His deepest strains had been vanquished.

"I believe I can aid you with the beasts." He lifted her off her feet, walked her backward the way they both liked and seated her on a boulder, her legs open to him. "Remember how you owe me a boon? I wish you to let me help you."

"Be more specific."

"How is this for specific?" Eyes swirling in the sunlight, he lightly pinched her chin. "You've delayed your acceptance of my brand long enough."

She winced. "Oh, uh, you were serious about that?"

"I'll burn my royal crest on your nape. It will become a part of you and won't fade when the day repeats." He turned, revealing the back of his neck and the circular scar with lines running through it. "This comes from Chaos, each line representing a different Astra. As I explained before, this is how we are able to speak telepathically."

With her claws curling on his shoulders, she leaned forward to kiss the brand. "You think to do more than communicate during hibernation. You hope to communicate this way when I'm in beast form?"

"I do," he confirmed, spinning around. "You'll calm for me. I know you will."

So confident. "Even though the beasts haven't listened to you outside my head?"

"Even though." He glided his fingers up her thighs. "The brand will allow me to flash you without touching you as well."

Ahhh. She thought she understood now. If firstone wasn't involved, he would be able to move her into or out of his path during battle—at *his* will and with only a thought. To control if she won or lost.

By doing this, she wasn't just placing her heart in his hands. She was placing her life there too. But hadn't she promised him forever? And what if he could do it? What if he calmed her?

Why fear this final step between them? Either she'd meant forever, or she hadn't.

"Won't a branding require energy or something?" Energy he needed to maintain considering the trials in their future. "Erebus might kick off another labor. I don't sense anything, but I didn't sense anything last time, either."

"Hardly any energy. It's far easier to open the door than to close it."

"Okay. All right. I'll do this. For you," she said with a nod. "But in return, you'll tattoo my name somewhere on your body. My *full* name. *Ophelia Falconcrest Formerly Known as the Flunk Out and Mistakenly Referred to as the Sweetheart.* I'm betting there's only one spot long enough."

"Deal," he replied with a grin. He kissed her breathless, then tugged her to her feet. "Turn around and hold up your hair."

He didn't wait for her to act but maneuvered her into the desired position with a flick of his wrists. She braced, expecting searing pain, but she perceived only a delicious warmth as he worked, tracing a fingertip over her nape. That warmth spread through the rest of her. Her veins tingled, her blood swiftly morphing into fuel, as if she'd plugged into a fully charged battery. Wow! A total rush! The beasts quieted, as if they'd just been hit by a tranquilizer dart.

How soon could she cast her thoughts into his mind? —*Halo? Halo! Yo, yo, yo. Want to get ravished?*—

He clasped her waist and tugged her closer to kiss her brand. The barest caress, and the sweetest tickle. "Finished, love. You wear my brand, our connection eternal." —*And yes, I do. Immediately.*—

Gasp! "I heard your voice inside my head." A shockingly intimate caress she liked very, very much indeed.

He cupped her backside through the pleats in her skirt. —*Let's see what else I can get inside you.*—

Halo awoke at 10:00 p.m. sharp. He remained in the Forest of Learnings. He lay upon a boulder, naked and bathed in moonlight, with a naked Ophelia draped over his chest. The contentment he felt...

Will kill to keep it.

He cast his awareness over the terrain, on the hunt for any threats. A stream rushed farther south. Cool air scented with foliage and dew carried a charge, as if a storm approached. Nothing odd caught his attention, and he relaxed against the stone.

Two labors remained. The final test followed by the deciding battle. Victory, or defeat. The start or end of their union. They— were not alone. The knowledge hit, and he cursed. Someone approached.

A flock of birds took flight, and Ophelia's eyes popped open. "Danger."

"Yes," he said, flashing them to their feet. It wasn't the proper time for a labor, but when had that ever stopped Erebus?

Halo summoned the easiest clothing to don. Robes. He always kept some at the ready, the pockets fully loaded with weapons, just as the headmaster had coached him. They dressed in silence. She worked fastest, moving at a speed triple any she had displayed before, then she patted the material and withdrew a three-blade stored inside a pocket.

A trumpet blared once, twice, announcing a nondeath match. Halo breathed easier and shouted his name, proclaiming his intention to be his own champion.

"If you can take the blade from him," Ophelia muttered, "do it."

Erebus appeared mere feet away. Smug delight replaced yesterday's shock. He wore a tunic and leathers to better display his lack of weapons. Meaning, there was no Bloodmor in sight. "Oh, how I've waited for this moment."

Halo's mind tossed out facts. He hadn't perceived the previous battle. Now this one. The truth was suddenly so clear. *Outmaneuvered from the start.*

"You purposely warned us about the prior labors, luring us into a false sense of expectation," he grated. The god must have purposely alerted Ophelia through the brand, allowing Halo to detect it through her. No alert, no detecting.

"Or did she do the luring for me?" Erebus asked. "As my champion, it is her duty, after all."

Aggression electrified the air around her. "I'm not betraying Halo, you—" She pressed her lips together. —*You know I'm not betraying you, right?*—

—*I do.*— Like the Astra, she had become a trusted constant in his life.

"Although," Erebus continued, "that *does* sound like me. I can be such a rapscallion at times." Though his hand was empty, he mimicked throwing something Halo's way. A golden apple appeared midair. "To win this labor, you have only to take a bite of this. Or feed it to the girl. Refuse to do either, and I shall be declared the victor of this round."

Halo caught the fruit and frowned. He discerned no poison, no toxin. Chaos had stamped a small brand in the center, authenticating its use. "What do you hope to accomplish with this?"

"The apple will show you the truth. Nothing more, nothing less. I want you to see. To know. But the longer you wait, the faster the fruit will rot. The more it rots, the cloudier that truth will become. Trust me. You wish to know what I know, too." Erebus disappeared a moment later.

Let the apple rot, even the minutest bit? Halo didn't hesitate to take a bite. He *did* wish to know what Erebus knew. Too many unidentified puzzle pieces remained.

"You fool! Have you never read *Snow White*?" Ophelia slapped the fruit from his hand. "We don't eat weird apples."

He swallowed. "Too late." He'd never been more ready to see the truth. Had never been so eager for anything, really.

They waited in silence for the effects to emerge. Minutes passed, but he felt no different.

Then a full-blown laugh barked from him, and he frowned. Why had he done that?

"What was that sound?" Ophelia demanded, looking here, there.

Another laugh escaped. Then another and another. They flowed from him continuously, creating a joyous stream. The kind of merriment he'd never experienced. No, not true. He'd laughed like this as a child with his mother when they'd played games. He'd toddled around, and she had chased and tickled him.

"Halo?"

He clutched his stomach and bent over, laughing, laughing. Tears poured down his cheeks. This was true ecstasy. Total ease. Possibilities. Connection. The kind of bliss he would've experienced on a regular basis if his mother had lived. The kind of elation so many took for granted.

"You are freaking me the freak *out*," Ophelia exclaimed. Except, a laugh burst from her, too. Amusement glittered in her eyes. "Seriously. Stop that. It's contagious."

"Deep down, you don't want me to stop." Moving faster than anyone could track, he gripped her waist and twirled her. "You yearn to play, and I yearn to play with you."

He took her to the ground—and tickled her the way he remembered being tickled.

"Stop, stop, stop! Halo!" She squealed and squirmed and thrashed, and he soaked up every second. Breaking free, she bolted through the forest, calling, "Catch me if you can, Immortal."

Oh, he would catch her all right. Halo gave chase. Flashed closer. Reached for her...she darted to the left, avoiding capture.

She giggled and said, "Some all-powerful assassin you are." A quick glance over her shoulder. "What's the matter, darling? Did your nymph wear you out earlier? Poor boy."

"I'll have you begging for me in a matter of minutes."

He flashed. Again, she evaded him. Halo throbbed for her. Throbbed and laughed and chased and dove and throbbed some more. Contact! He plowed into her, wrapping her in his arms and taking her to the ground once again, twisting midair to absorb the impact. They skidded, chunks of dirt and grass flying. Two trees uprooted as they plowed into them.

As soon as they stopped, Halo rolled, pinning his prize to a bed of moss. They had reached the babbling brook. Delicate flowers grew at the edges, where foam frothed. A glockfish broke the water and spit out a smaller fish like a bullet before crashing below the surface.

He summoned a shield faster than most warriors could raise one. As soon as the little fish bounced off the metal, he tossed the shield aside and grinned down at Ophelia. She glowed with passion, locks of sable hair clinging to her damp face. Her irises blazed with lust and good humor. Her lips were parted, ready to receive his kiss.

He rubbed against her. Tone silken, he asked, "Would you care to apologize to your male before he oversees your punishment?"

"Punishment?" Her eyelids hooded as she melted beneath him. "Do tell. What's my crime?"

"You've taunted me mercilessly without cease."

"If you don't want to be taunted, you should try not to be the most irresistible male in all the worlds." She undulated against him, meeting his soft thrusts with harder bucks. "How is Erebus enjoying this? We are far from miserable. I'm not sure I've ever been so happy."

"Don't know, don't care." He laughed as he bent his head for another kiss. Was this the kind of male he was meant to be? The one he should have been...but not who he was?

His laughter faded to nothing as his future crystalized. *Doomed from the start.* Erebus had indeed played the long game, using the tests to elicit Halo's misery and set him up for a crash. The god had kept his focus on the labor's conclusion—overseeing Halo's demise. The god had chosen Ophelia as his champion but in the end, he would name Halo, as Roux had suggested.

Halo would have to die to win.

Erebus hadn't cared if he himself won or lost the practice rounds because he himself didn't care if he won or lost the final match. As the god's champion, Halo could only win the final battle by dying—worse, he would have to name someone to act as the executioner. Whoever Halo chose as *his* champion. There was no other way. He refused to name Ophelia, which meant he'd have to name one of the Astra.

One of his brothers would be forced to do the deed.

How sweet the apple had tasted, but how bitter its truth. The Astra would be left in shambles, mourning the loss of their brother in arms. They would be ill-prepared for the third blessing task.

Halo must die. He must die *after* he'd tasted of life for the first time. He must leave his *gravita*, after he'd promised her forever.

For her sake, he must leave her even before he died.

Both consorts and entwines followed their mates in death, one way or another. If they survived it, they became the living dead. Like Blythe. The only way to ensure Ophelia survived Halo's loss—teach her to do so now, before his death.

Her smile faded. "Halo? What's wrong?"

Erebus had used the apple as a weapon. A cruelty meant to taunt Halo with the life he should have, could have, would have had. Centuries of laughter and peace. Pleasure. Contentment. Connection. But Halo would do it. When the time came, he would sacrifice himself, saving both the Astra and Ophelia.

31

Day Whatever
8:46 a.m.

He's not coming for me.

Ophelia spent the first part of her morning rushing around the bunkroom, cleaning up, dressing in her uniform, and explaining the situation to Vivi. The harpire listened, rapt. As always, she voiced no doubts.

"This kind of sounds familiar to me. Like there's a memory lodged somewhere in my brain." Her gaze took on a faraway glaze. "If I could just find it..."

Interesting. Were the others remembering, now that only a lone task remained?

Ophelia plopped beside her friend at the edge of the bed and returned to the subject that mattered. "What did the apple show Halo, V?" Because dang. He'd gone from a playful lover to a cold prick in a matter of minutes. And the attitude had lingered for the past six days! He'd barely spoken to Ophelia since, joining her a little later each morning.

"I snuck over and stole my own bite of the apple before the reset," she continued, "but the stupid thing evaporated." Ophelia glanced at the door. "Where is he?" Had he gotten caught up with Roc?

"Wherever he is, whatever he's doing, there's a silver lining," Vivi said, rubbing her hands together. "You get to punish him."

"True." And really, with the final labor on the horizon, he had more people to command than usual. More things to do.

Except, shouldn't Ophelia be a top priority too? They were linked now. An official couple. #Halophelia. #Ophelio. Even their names were cute together!

Another ten minutes passed. Twenty.

Old fears came out of hiding. The trash pandas of the mind. They reminded her of every insult Nissa had ever lobbed her way. The total rejection of her mother. The absence of stardust. Because yes, it had started bugging her again.

Come on, Halo! He wasn't ditching her right when they approached the finish line. Just because they hadn't stolen the dagger or discovered a path to happily-forever-after, well, it didn't mean they wouldn't. Last-second saves happened all the time.

Besides, he'd fought too hard to win her to ditch her now. Keeping her topped his agenda. Unless he'd seen a truth she refused to grasp? That maybe, possibly, they weren't actually... fated.

No stardust, no gravita.

Her stomach flip-flopped. The past few weeks, she had enjoyed more pleasure than she'd ever dreamed possible. She had no regrets.

Did he?

He might...if he'd foreseen her death. Or even his own. But why believe a vision given by a so-called "truth apple"? Just because Erebus asserted the apple showed only the truth? What if he'd utilized another loophole?

A few times throughout the week, Ophelia had reached out through the brand. Halo's replies had been sharp, so she'd stopped, too afraid she would resemble a beggar willing to accept the smallest crumb of affection. But…

What if she came across as a warrior woman determined to get what she wanted?

Wings rippling, she focused her inward attention on the scar he had so tenderly and painlessly burned into her flesh. As the raised mark heated, she pushed a message into his mind.—*Where are you? What's going on?*—

A minute passed. Crickets.

"I hear a commotion in the hall." Vivi popped to her feet. "I'll be right back."

"No need. I'll save you the trouble. Everyone's abuzz because multiple heads are hanging in the palace foyer, and mine and Halo's are among them." Seeing her replica mounted on the wall of victory and defeat had been a shock. Halo had stared at it for hours, his expression blank.

"Your head is mounted on a wall and mine isn't? No fair!"

Ophelia concentrated, letting her inner voice build into a shout. —*Halo!*—

—*Harpy.*—

Frost accompanied his overly harsh timbre, and she shuddered. Cold before, frigid now. —*I miss you, Immortal.*— The words left her without thought.

—*You shouldn't. I'm told the final labor will occur sometime today. The freeze is over, and the day will repeat no longer.*—

They'd run out of time? —*What did the apple show you? Please, Halo. Help me understand what's going on.*—

—*What's going on is this. The task is set to conclude and so is our relationship. Get used to being without me, harpy.*— He went quiet then. Not just quiet, removed. As if he'd erected a mental block between them.

A block of ice.

Ophelia blinked rapidly, her eyes stinging. "I think the Astra...dumped me." He'd gone cold. Arctic. He felt nothing.

"He did *what*?" Vivi demanded, fangs lengthening.

The labor hadn't even started yet. Why give up now?

The stinging worsened, and her chin trembled. "I think he's given up hope. He's certain I'm dying—or he is." The beasts agreed, going stationary and silent inside their cages. Helping her?

Instinct sharpened. Kill or be killed. A reminder. Halo had died for her on the battlefield—not something he would do for someone he expected to toss aside. What if he planned to do it again? Only, this time there would be no do-over.

Get used to being without me, harpy.

"That...that...*douchebag!* He doesn't get to convince me I'm his heartbeat, then immediately power down. No. No! His software is getting another update. I'll hack in, if necessary, but I will make him rue the day he decided to go this route!"

"Make him rue!" The harpire pumped her fist. "I don't even know what we're discussing right now, but I am *loving* the energy. Mistress O is in the house, yo."

"Call me the Sweetheart." Oh. Gross. "No. Don't. That's a more horrible name than expected." Halo would not be dying today, if they were pitted against each other. She would. So the slain one wouldn't resurrect, as Taliyah had? So what. There were other ways to revive. And if Ophelia didn't awaken? Again, so what? Live as a warrior, die as a warrior. What would be better?

"Are you with me?" she demanded of Vivi.

"I'm with you!"

"To battle we go!" Ophelia bolted for the door.

Vivi ran with her. Side by side, they plowed through anyone in their path.

More harpies congregated in the hallway than usual, discussing the "wall of heads and horrors." They peppered the gardens and wrestled over disagreements around Nissa's fountain. Anyone who noticed Ophelia crowded behind her, following her every step.

Ophelia and Vivi flew up the stairs. For the first time, two Astra guarded the palace entrance. Ian and Roux. The massive brutes stared straight ahead as other harpies marched inside the foyer. Or seemed to. She'd bet good money they clocked everyone who approached.

Proof: they blocked her and Vivi from entering, becoming a wall of muscle. Harpies bumped into them—until Ophelia started throwing elbows and snarling and everyone backed off.

Whoa! Had that animalistic sound just come from *her*? Cage locks were melting, a breakout imminent. Though uneasy, she forged onward. *No surrender!*

"You aren't to go past this point," Ian informed her. "Halo doesn't wish to see you."

They think to keep me from my male? Heat spread through her chest, burned a path up her throat, and exploded from her mouth in a roar. A blending of roars, courtesy of her beasts.

Both Astra canted their heads, as if they'd just discovered a new hybrid species—bunny-dragons. Seconds passed without a word. Conversing among themselves?

Enough waiting. Nothing had ever been so important to her. She flared her claws. This was a time for action.

As Vivi and the others chanted, "Fight, fight, fight," Ophelia the Astra Slayer attacked.

Now there was a name she could get behind.

Halo, Roc, and Taliyah occupied the usual conference room. He had explained the situation and what had transpired. They had protested his prediction for the final battle, their main argument sound. What if he was wrong?

But he wasn't. He knew this was right just as he knew Ophelia could change his mind. Exactly why he must avoid her. He couldn't enjoy a life with her, but he could do everything in his power to ensure she enjoyed her time without him. If he neared her, he might not retain the necessary fortitude to leave her. He must remain in an emotionless void, so strained he barely functioned. Something he'd never wished to experience again.

But he did it; he endured. Anything to keep his harpymph safe. What he must do next…what he must convince the Commander to do…

"There must be another approach," Roc said. "You cannot be asking me to do what I think you are."

"You suggest I haven't considered this from every angle?" He had. "Erebus will select me as his champion." There was no way around it. "His goal is clear. Pit me against myself, only in the guise of another." Halo's champion couldn't be Erebus himself. The god would only kill himself, making Halo the loser, and bringing the curse upon the Astra. Then, Erebus would resurrect on his own, as he always resurrected, with no outside aid needed. A loophole.

No, the god had to be kept off the field of battle entirely. "I'll be picking you, Roc." The one good thing to come from this end? Halo got to eliminate Ophelia from the equation entirely.

"I won't kill you," Roc snapped.

"I'll take care of the deed myself. You need only stand on the field."

"No."

He slid his gaze to Taliyah.

"I'm happy to jump in the ring and do the deed myself," she said with a firm nod. "But I won't. Do you know the mantrums I'll have to tolerate from Commander Drama Queen if I mercilessly slaughter his soldier? No thanks."

And we're back to Roc. He grated, "You would force me to select another to perform your duty to the Astra?"

Roc's eyes narrowed.

"In this, you are not the Commander," Halo stated. "I am. I won't choose another, and you won't ask me to do so. You owe me. Think back to your last blessing task. To bed your *gravita*, you agreed to willingly abdicate at the conclusion of the final one. Keep your rank and kill me. That is what I want from you. Then, you will do everything in your power to retrieve the Bloodmor from Erebus. You will stop at nothing." Only then would Ophelia be completely free of the Deathless.

Not being able to leave Harpina to hunt the blade ate at Halo.

His hands curled into fists. Uh-oh. Not so unemotional now, fury and frustration bubbling up.

"And if Erebus chooses your *gravita* as his champion?" Roc demanded.

"He won't." He shouldn't. But if he did, there was a good chance Ophelia would be transformed into Cerberus, Hercules's last challenge. Once a hellhound selected prey, nothing dissuaded the creature from its path. And the primordial hellhound at that? He nodded. She would attack—and Halo would let her.

He hoped the god decided to go the other route, however. The thought of abandoning her with such a horrendous memory left a foul taste in his mouth.

An uproar outside the conference room drew his gaze toward the arching double doors—doors now bursting open. Ophelia strode inside the chamber, dressed for war with a group of similarly garbed harpies collected behind her.

Dark hair hung in waves around her delicate features. Slitted green eyes crackled. She was magnificent.

"You want to break up with me?" She picked up a chair and hurled it at him. "Fine. Go ahead. At least have the balls to do it in person." Another chair.

Halo ducked both missiles, his chest clenching. More fury and frustration bubbled up. Where was his iron control? He used to wield it so easily.

"I'll do what I must, when I must," he stated.

Another chair. "I wasn't done talking!" she shouted. "You're just giving up? Because a quitter isn't worthy of being my male!"

—*You can take your brand and shove it.*—

The words filled his head, and he scowled. *Remember the goal. Ophelia's survival, the Astra's victory.* "You will find another male. It is possible for both harpies and nymphs. Upon occasion. Under the right circumstances." A shout of denial rushed up his throat. He clamped his lips shut.

She flinched a little. Then she stopped, merely dragging her claws over the next chair. "You know what? You're right. I *will* find another."

I will tear out his heart!

"I'm not giving up," he informed her as calmly as he was able. "I'm doing what is necessary." Chaos had told him to learn from the test rounds. Finally, he had. The right lessons.

With the lioness, he'd discovered he might not be fighting who he thought he was fighting. Or rather, he should have learned it. He hadn't. So he'd gotten schooled again with the hydra. But he'd failed to learn a second time.

The next test had taught the same lesson from a different perspective, showing him how his past could be used as a weapon against him. Then came the boar. Another reminder that he wasn't fighting who he thought he was fighting—and his opponent mattered *greatly*.

With the stables, he'd learned to never underestimate how low Erebus could sink. The man-eating bird, bull and flesh-eating horse proved sacrifice treated him far better than vengeance. By winning Ophelia's heart, Halo grew to understand the true prize in any war. When forced to pick between the trio of Ophelias, he'd learned to trust his instincts. They never steered him wrong.

The apple taught him that he could withstand anything—except his female's harm.

You harm her now, pushing her away.

I save her now.

"Well, isn't this just great? I pledged myself to a quitter *and* a fool." She hurled another chair at him. The other harpies spread out through the room and cheered. "You do not leave the woman who loves you hanging. Especially on the day you think you're going to die."

Sweat beaded on his brow, emotions fighting their way to the surface. "I *will* die. If Erebus doesn't choose me as his champion, he'll choose you. If I kill you, I'll lose more than my life." He *couldn't* continue without her. If something went wrong and she died, he planned to see the Astra through their tasks and follow her. But it wouldn't come to that. A good future awaited her. In his absence, the Astra would attend to her care.

Another chair flew. "Ohhhh. Something more than your life. Do tell."

He scrubbed a hand over his face. A suddenly burning hand. Perhaps he'd handled this poorly. There were other ways to gain her cooperation. He'd learned that, too.

"Well?" she demanded, throwing another chair.

"I'll lose everything I've come to love," he told her. "There's no need for you to lose everything too. So you will let me do this for you. For me!"

"Love?" she squeaked, her eyes wide. "You love me?"

She hadn't realized the truth? How could he leave her without sharing everything she meant to him?

"How else would I have the strength to keep you at a distance today?" He raised his chin. "Enjoying one more day with you is a treasure beyond measure, but it pales in comparison to your future happiness. So I will stay cold, and you *will* let me. I will do what must be done."

Chair. "Oh, I will, will—"

A trumpet sounded in the distance, and his brow furrowed. So soon?

He wasn't ready.

The conference room vanished. Suddenly, Halo stood in the center of the coliseum. He scanned the area. Most of the Astra and an army of harpies filled the stands, their confusion rampant. No sign of Ophelia. Where was she?

Chaos stood on the royal dais, with Roc, Taliyah, and Erebus at his sides. The Commander appeared unfazed by the change in scenery. He stared straight ahead, with his hands clamped behind his back, pretending a male he longed to murder wasn't within striking distance. To attack now would be an act of war against Chaos himself. A foolish move while in the midst of a war with Erebus.

"The final battle is set to commence," Chaos called to one and all, spurring cheers. "The two combatants are the only ones allowed on the field. Anyone who joins the fray will die. Erebus, as challenger, you will select first. Name your champion."

32

"I choose Halo Phaninon," Erebus called, and a collective gasp rose from the crowd.

Knew it.

Boos provided a nice chorus for a plethora of jeers and insults. "Cheater!" "He can't do that!" "Suck a hairy nut sack!" "Take off your robe!"

The god remained unmoved by the commentary, clearly gleeful over his choice.

Fool. Halo notched his chin and fixed his attention on Chaos. This was the outcome he'd preferred. Now Ophelia's part was done, their association over. She would live. At some point in the future, some other male would come along and win her heart—and Halo would return from the dead to do murder!

Deep breath in. *Stay cold.* He wanted Ophelia happy after this. What he did now was for the best. She'd given him everything. Now, he would do the same for her.

Where was she?

"And you, Halo?" Chaos called. "Who fights for you?"

He jerked his gaze to Roc. The Commander maintained his hard stance, clearly doing his best to go cold, so he could do the deed Halo demanded—stand there and do nothing while he ended his own life. Not a fate Halo would have ever chosen for either of them. The memories would haunt Roc for the rest of eternity. But what else could Halo do?

A tremor shook the coliseum, the very ground he stood upon, and he frowned. He recognized the sensation. Had felt it every time he'd battled a beast...

Foreboding prickled his nape. If Erebus had turned Ophelia...

Anyone who enters the fray will die.

Suspicions kept Halo silent. If the god had turned Ophelia into a mystical hellhound, if she burst onto the field, entering the ring of sand, and she *wasn't* named as Halo's champion, Chaos would kill her, no matter the outcome of the battle.

What if the creature *wasn't* Ophelia? Merely a trick?

Hope bloomed.

But he knew better. Erebus had turned her and no other.

Hope withered, despair rising in its place. *Not so cold anymore.*

The ground shook with more vigor, and Halo's heart thudded. Metal bars exploded from the entrance to the catacombs, a three-headed dog flying out. No, the lioness. No, the hydra. The bird. Bull. Horse. She morphed again and again, until various parts of her solidified into different beasts, creating a monstrous amalgamation.

"Ophelia Falconcrest," Halo shouted in a rush. "I choose Ophelia Falconcrest." Now Chaos couldn't kill her for interfering. She could survive. She *would* survive. Halo would make sure of it.

The course was now set in stone, the ending clearer than ever. But oh, how he despised this. Detested the guilt she would carry for the rest of her life. The killing of her consort and entwine.

Mostly, he hated that he hadn't spent their last hours together in bed, loving each other.

He was the fool.

As the beastly Ophelia charged for him, Erebus boomed with his customary laughter. Three heads, three sets of metal teeth coated with firstone. Foam formed at the corners of each mouth. Crazed black eyes locked on him.

She stumbled and shook her head, her mishmashed face seeming to frown. But still she charged forward...

"That's our Lady O?" someone shouted. "So jealous!"

Halo tuned out everyone but his harpy. Closing in...

He lifted his sword, intending to strike himself after the first contact. Quick and easy. Halo would turn to stone and crumble for the last time.

She dove, soaring the distance between them. Her momentum slammed her into Halo with such incredible force, he flew across the field. Bones broke, the sword falling from his grip. He hit and skidded a good stretch, enveloped by a sand cloud.

The second he stopped, she was there, slamming a paw into his chest, thick claws embedding throughout his torso. Her massive bulk snapped numerous ribs. Just as soon as he healed, the pressure ravaged him once again. Pain ebbed and flowed in ceaseless waves.

He could have thrown her off—maybe. He glared up at her instead. When he'd originally branded her, he'd thought to use the bridge between them to calm her in battle. Now...

—*Do it!*—

But she didn't. She heaved her breaths, her visage once again changing from one creature to another. Her eyes darted. Throwing back her heads, she roared. The roar tapered into a howl, the howl into a grunt.

"Why do you hesitate?" He wrapped his hands around her paw, holding them together.

—*Do it.*— The burn he'd experienced earlier. It reignited,

his palms so hot he expected to see flames. —*Tear into me, harpy. I'm the male who abandoned you at the end.*—

She wrenched backward, severing contact. As she huffed and puffed, spittle sprayed from the corners of her snouts.

Each set of eyes continued to dart. What did she search for?

A stream of her thoughts suddenly trickled into his head. —*Kill… won't kill…think, think.*—

His entire body jerked with a massive spike of emotion—her emotion. Something she felt so strongly, she had pushed it across their link. *Nigh mindless rage.* But she was fighting the all-consuming drive to attack him…and she was winning.

He stayed on his back, splayed before her. An all-you-can-eat buffet, with his hands lifted in a sign of innocence. Perhaps he'd handled her wrongly, by issuing commands. He'd thought he battled the harpy beneath those monsters. But he now suspected he contended with the nymph. The lover. The one who empowered the harpy, the two forever intertwined.

The nymph didn't respond well to cold, only warmth. And in that moment, he knew what he must do. Halo let go of the cold wholly, once and for all, embracing his love for this female. Letting himself feel everything without reservation.

Slowly he reached for her. Though stiff and leery, she didn't bite him. He lightly pinched one of her chins. All three sets of eyes flared wide.

"Do the right thing, love. Please." He smiled sadly. "Win. Pad your résumé."

She shook her head, dislodging his fingers. He frowned. He couldn't be seeing what he thought he was seeing. But…he was.

There, in the middle of her chin, on the hide of the lioness, was a glittering thumbprint.

Stardust. Of Halo's creation.

His eyes widened, and he examined his hands. Yes! Stardust coated his skin, dazzling in the light.

Primitive satisfaction warred with crushing sadness. Finally, he had provided his female with what she'd craved most. A reason to celebrate. And yet, he must convince her to kill him.

—*Elia, I know you can hear me. I know you're fighting your instinct, love, and I need you to stop. All right? Yes? Bite me and don't let go. Do it because you love me. This is the only way to save everyone.*—

Kill. Won't kill. Kill. Kill! THINK! Ophelia breathed in. Out. With a plethora of eyes, she saw So. Many. Things. Each set viewed the world from a different angle, sending streams of information to the various minds vying for dominion.

There was Halo, her love. A crowd of cheering harpies. The stoic Commander. A grinning Erebus. A bored stranger.

Think. Halo had spoken words to her. He'd commanded. No, he'd explained. Save everyone…but not him? For Halo to win and rescue his brothers, Ophelia had to kill him?

Make it make sense! Halo was part of everyone, and she was supposed to save everyone.

The beasts understood him perfectly, however, and demanded she do it, sink her teeth deep. *Devour him!* There, there and there. Such tender meat. But a light of sanity refused to dim as white-hot heat spread over her skin. Ophelia clung to it, fighting the instinct as she fought everything—with everything she had.

The strangest thing happened. The beasts began to bow to her will. To surrender to the queen of the jungle.

Without their interference, her greatest desire crystalized, growing, strengthening. *A life with Halo. And I can have it.*

She couldn't kill him. The first victim to grace her résumé would not be her consort.

He'd tried to warn her; the mental anguish would be unbearable. Because she loved him and he loved her. She wouldn't give up her family.

But how was she to achieve this goal? He thought he needed to die by her hand—or teeth—to win. And if he was right?

There were many ways to die, and not all of them permanent.

She didn't wish to kill him. However, she had demanded this Astra take one for the team time and time again. *It's my turn now.*

Decision made. Ophelia *would* murder her consort-entwine. His name *would* grace the top of her kill list. The terms of the battle *would* be met, and Halo *would* revive on his own, no mystical resurrection required. A loophole.

Too easy? Maybe. But he'd mended and regrown organs on the battlefield before. And he hadn't expected Erebus's natural abilities to be negated at the end. So why would *Halo's* be negated?

If she were wrong about this? Had it been a viable option, Halo would have suggested it, yes? Would only a true and final death count?

Trepidation perforated her calm, but she shook it off. Instinct said: *You can have it all.* She had to take a leap of faith—in herself. Either she believed in herself and her abilities or she gave up and accepted whatever happened.

I will never give up!

A monster of indescribable power, Ophelia repositioned her bulky body. No using her firstone teeth. She needed to stop his heart another, less permanent way. And there was only one way available to her right now…

With a snarl, she lunged at Halo. He made no move against her as she swiped a paw at him, shredding his chest with her claws. Blood rained.

"That's my good girl." He smiled tenderly, so proud and pleased. Blood wet his perfect pearly whites. "Don't stop now, sweetheart."

Her mind screamed and her insides churned, the sight gutwrenching. Another slash, and bone no longer blocked her path to his beating heart. Beat. Beat. Beat. She whimpered. The moment of truth.

No going back.

"Good girl." He winced but still he smiled. "Now bite me,

love." Pain coated his broken voice, but so did affection, and it nearly broke her. "Bite me hard."

With a roar, she severed the organ with a claw, ending his life. For a moment, only a moment.

Please be only a moment.

Death was death, and the blare of the trumpet proved it. The match was over. Why hadn't Halo awakened? She huffed her breaths as she peered down at her consort. He lay in the sand, still and bloody. His wound hadn't closed. His heart hadn't yet regenerated.

The crowd remained silent, everyone poised at the edge of their seat, waiting. Erebus stood at the rail of the royal box, seemingly disappointed. Because playtime was over?

Come on, Halo!

Ophelia bellowed his name, demanding he awaken. Or she tried. One head howled. Another whimpered and the third snarled. She slammed her paw onto the Astra's chest, pumping his heart for him. Wham, wham. Wham, wham, wham.

She bent a head and licked his face.

Halo sucked in a breath, his heart and ribs healing as the flesh wove back together. Ophelia nearly collapsed with relief. *We won, and we live!* Then she remembered. The god.

Slowly she turned toward the royal box. Toward him. The pale-haired one. Erebus. Enemy. The time had come for a reckoning. She had an impenetrable hide, the ability to regenerate limbs in spades, an assortment of venoms and antivenoms at her disposal. The beasts had slipped free of their cages, yes, but she held their leashes. Ophelia was super *everything*, and she would have her revenge.

Attack! She shot into a warp speed run.

He shouted a demand at the male beside him. "The task is over, Chaos. Allow me to leave."

That male—Chaos—grinned and clapped, watching her. "Magnificent. Simply magnificent."

She leaped and snagged different parts of Erebus between different sets of her teeth. Firstone pierced his muscle. No matter what he attempted, he failed to escape her jaws of death.

Erebus shook—until he didn't. Ophelia dropped him at his father's feet.

Chaos peered at his son's bloody remains. "He'll only return to life stronger."

Ophelia didn't care. Dark gray lines spread over the god's skin, the firstone affecting him as strongly as it affected the Astra. Pieces of him crumbled. Were her friends seeing this?

Ophelia had made two kills in one day. An Astra and a god. This must be a record. Surely all of harpykind would sing tales of her feats.

Look at me! Look at me! Oh! She bet Halo would love to praise her right this second. Ophelia snatched off Erebus's head and zoomed back to the battlefield, then ran circles around the Astra. He sat on the ground, fully healed, watching her with an adoring expression. She spit the stone head at his feet. An offering.

The head rolled a little, reminding her of a ball. Oh! Oh! She really, really, really, probably should follow it.

Focus! She panted, her tongues hanging out of her mouths.

"Roc?" Halo called, though his gaze remained glued on Ophelia.

"I have it," the Commander shouted, lifting a dagger. The dagger. The Bloodmor. Metal and jewels glinted in sunlight. "I'm told you have only to press the hilt against the brand and say her name to change her back." He tossed the weapon, the tip soaring straight for Halo, who caught it by the blade.

Blood dripped from his hand, satisfaction radiating from him. "Elia," he said, crooking his finger as she jerked to attention. "Come. Sit."

He was treating her like a dog. And yet, she was so eager to obey him. Ophelia bounded over and sniffed him. Familiar.

Mmm. Delicious. And his heat. That was nice. She settled in beside him.

He petted her, each stroke adding fuel to the heat, warming her inside and out. And oh, wow. The heat was better than ever. She leaned into his touch.

"We have the Bloodmor now, and we will protect it as we see fit. No one will use the blade against you ever again." He tapped the hilt against her chest, saying, "Ophelia the Sweetheart."

In seconds, bones shrank, and hide receded, welcoming flesh. Of course, when the transformation completed, she was 100 percent naked for all to see. Or she would have been, if his body hadn't shielded her. He never stopped petting her, and the heat never stopped spreading.

"I've always loved Lady O and now I know why!" someone called.

Cheers broke out. She thought she heard Vivian's voice rise above the others. "That's my best friend! Did you see her? Did you see my best friend beast out? I'm her favorite, never forget."

Ian shouted, "Where might I find a nymph of my own?"

Halo growled, all hint of frost gone as a sheet appeared in his hand. He wrapped the material around Ophelia from shoulder to ankle, then pulled her onto his lap.

She burrowed into his powerful, bloodstained body. *He's marked by me in every way.*

Wait. What was that on her sweat-glistened wrist? She gasped. "Halo! I have stars." The stars of a General. "Four out of ten. I sacrificed something I dearly loved and oversaw a victorious military campaign. Let's face it, I was totally the brains of this operation. I convinced the reigning General to do something she didn't want to do. Finally, I won a battle with my wits alone— against you."

"I'm proud of you, sweetheart. And I'm so sorry for how I treated you these past six days. Today especially. I swear to you,

Elia, I will never treat you in such a way again. I feared I couldn't leave you without going cold."

"I know, darling." She petted his chest. "But you're right. You won't ever do that again. If you do, I'm gone."

"There is no worse punishment," he told her with a shudder.

"In that case, you're already forgiven. I mean, how can I doubt your affections for me? You have died for—Halo!" She straightened with a snap, studying her arms. "I'm not glistening with sweat, I'm glittering. You stardusted me? Even though I beasted-out all over you?"

His lips twitched. "I did. And you wear it well. Now to settle official business so that we can move on to our make-up sex." He cast his attention to the dais, shouting, "Well? The trumpet sounded, but you are the final judge. Render your verdict."

Chaos spread his arms. "The twelfth round has ended with your victory through Ophelia, as well as your loss as Erebus's champion. Technically, you should not be allowed to revive. But because you are also the winner, you shouldn't be punished. A loophole."

The final battle was over then, with Halo the official victor. The Astra would continue on, another step closer to ascension. As Chaos had said, Erebus would return soon. Stronger even. Here, now, Ophelia didn't exactly care. Bring it. She and her consort-entwine had survived, and a bright future awaited them.

Halo climbed to his feet and lifted her arm in triumph. "To the Sweetheart."

The crowd erupted into cheers, and she preened. She also blushed.

"I cannot get over the sight of you in my stardust," Halo said, kissing her knuckles. "I plan to mark every inch of you in stardust."

"I'll never be without it again." A vow of her own. "Maybe we should have named me the Glitter Bomb."

He laughed, pleased beyond measure with her. Every Astra in

the stands quieted, causing the harpies to go quiet too. Silence stretched, and Halo gazed here and there. "What's happening?"

"You laughed. Out loud," Ophelia explained. "That isn't something they remember you ever doing. To them, you were the same emotionless robot as usual just yesterday. Now, I'm a fierce, all-powerful miracle worker who amused the Machine in less than twenty-four hours."

The Astra flashed around them, staring down at Halo, still shell-shocked.

"What was that awful sound?" Silver demanded.

"Do I sense…enjoyment?" Roux asked, as if suddenly presented with the world's greatest mystery.

"I meant what I said," Ian muttered. "I wouldn't mind a nymph of my own."

"Halo?" Ophelia purred.

"Yes." He flashed her to their bedroom and tossed her onto the mattress. As she bounced, she wiggled out of the sheet, revealing her naked body to him. "All those delicious, dusky curves. The way those eyes watch me with excitement…" He unbuckled his belt. "Do you crave your male, Elia?"

"I do, I do," she assured him. "Am I going to get him?"

"Oh, you get him. Often."

"That's not enough. I demand more."

He grinned. "Then more you'll get." He crawled up the bed, kissed up her body, and gave her more.

Halo gave her everything.

EPILOGUE

"Get your lazy butt out of bed. Operation Lady O Be Good commences in thirty."

Ophelia groaned, her mind slowly rousing from the most amazing slumber of her life. A pleasure drunk slumber, not a vodka drunk one. "That's not funny." Blinking open her eyes, she slapped at Halo's bare chest and muttered, "Is this how it's gonna be every morning from now on?"

"Probably. I do like my routines." He chuckled and brought her hand to his mouth to kiss her knuckles. A real chuckle! "We slept in the same bed the entire night and awoke together. A first for us. And for me."

His delight was too cute, and she grinned. She lay on her stomach, naked and facing him. Even though she knew the answer, she asked, "And what's the final verdict on the all-nighter?"

Expression fierce, he told her, "I will destroy worlds to have this for the rest of forever." He rolled closer and kissed her forehead. "My female makes me greedy for more of everything."

She beamed at him. He'd kept his word and covered every inch of her in stardust. Many, many times, all night long. He'd done his X-ray vision thing a few hours ago and discovered she still bore the mark of the Bloodmor. Which made sense, since the creatures remained inside her head, caged once again. Halo could remove the mark...but she had to let him do it.

After much deliberation, they'd agreed she should keep the beasts. The defense aspects couldn't be beat. She was able to morph into anything or anyone, then return to herself. The Bloodmor belonged to her, after all, and only she and Halo knew its current location. In between bouts of lovemaking, they'd hidden it.

"The next task will soon begin," he said, smoothing a lock of her hair behind her ear.

Another Astra destined to find his *gravita*? "Who do you think is up to bat?"

"I have absolutely no idea. We're only to expect the unexpected."

"Well, whoever he is, I feel sorry for him. You got the best task, and the best girl."

"I did indeed." Grinning, he flipped her to her back, pinning her to the mattress with his weight. "She is insatiable for me. Beautiful beyond imagining. Brilliant and crafty. Filled with enough energy to bring a dead machine back to life. A prize worth any cost."

"Someone's software got another update, I see. This one is all about romance," she said, curling her body around his. When he said such sweet things, Ophelia had no defenses. But then, she didn't need defenses with him. She enjoyed being laid bare before him in every way.

The striations in his eyes twirled. "Be aware. The update can't be completed until I'm plugged in and powered down."

She snorted, adoring this teasing side of him. "Kiss me like you'll die without me, Astra."

He lightly pinched her chin and angled her lips to his. "The same as always then?" he quipped before claiming her mouth and making the rest of the world disappear.

★ ★ ★ ★ ★

Turn the page for a very special second epilogue for
The Immortal,
exclusively yours in this Walmart edition!

Erebus ghosted through the harpy palace, going from room to room, observing. A celebration raged, multiple females spraying champagne from chandeliers, raining the droplets all over friends and furniture. Others threw clothing at Astra warriors while shouting lewd suggestions.

No one noticed Erebus. No one sensed him. They couldn't. He traversed a plane beyond their comprehension. A realm between past, present, and future, each stacked upon the other, all playing together at once. Making sense of the chaos always proved challenging, and today was no different. Though he required great focus to keep the celebration in his sights and cull the rest, his mind whirled.

He had lost the battle against Halo, as he'd known he would. The Blade of Destiny—the key to the doorway that led to his land—had offered many versions of the task, born from a multitude of fates and altering decisions. Few had led to Halo's defeat. In the end, Erebus had followed the most painful path for the Astra. And what fun it had been.

A slow smile bloomed. He rubbed the bite marks still healing along his collarbone. Oh yes. *Worth it.*

The next blessing task loomed, and he knew the identity of the Astra soon to step up to the plate. Unlike with Halo, most pathways led to this warrior's defeat.

The most sublime satisfaction filled Erebus.

He entered the throne room, his final destination for the day. The reason for his visit perched on the largest chandelier, alone, no other harpy willing to go near her. He took a moment to admire her finer qualities. Ice-blue eyes. Jet-black hair. Delicate bone structure. A devoted mother. A royal harpy-phantom hybrid.

His eldest daughter, Blythe.

Unlike everyone else, she noticed him. But then, she wielded abilities unlike any other harpy or phantom.

Her eyes narrowed and she vanished, only to appear at his side. They stood in silence for a long while, peering through the mists of time.

Finally, she spoke. "You came back from the dead sooner than usual."

Erebus clasped his hands behind his back. "I grow stronger."

This was not their first conversation, and it would not be their last. Like his other daughter, she despised him for the things he'd done to her family. But unlike Taliyah, Blythe hated the Astra far more. They had killed her consort. The warlock husband she'd loved and adored. The father of her only child and the sole male in existence able to soothe the worst of her temper. Now she would be forever worked into a cold rage bent on revenge, just the way Erebus needed her to be.

"Roux is next, isn't he?" she asked.

"He is. He will be tasked with the conquering of a planet.

Ation." A prison realm filled with harpies, Amazons, and many other predatory females of myth.

"He will lose his task because of me?"

"He will indeed. You have your pick of methods."

From the mist, he watched as her daughter entered the throne room. Little Isla Skyhawk. A miniature of her mother. Extremely powerful. Untapped potential. A shame Isla was going to die, too. He might have liked having a granddaughter. Instead, she was to be a sacrifice for the greater good—the downfall of the remaining Astra.

They deserved everything they had coming.

Blythe watched the party a bit longer. She stiffened when Roux entered the room. Hatred radiated from her, and Erebus smiled again.

"Will you kill him or let him live with his loss?" he asked. The futures he'd beheld promised either outcome would result in his victory.

"What do you think?"

He chuckled. "I think you wish him to suffer." Which made her a daughter after his own heart. If he'd had a heart. "You understand you will destroy your sister's consort in the process, yes?"

"Roc will survive with Taliyah's help. But more importantly, you'll be unable to harm the couple. Once Roux is dealt with, I'll turn my attention to you. You won't live long enough to cause them any more problems."

He snorted. "You think I haven't foreseen your moves against me? You fail like the Astra, I promise you. I take you down."

"You think that will stop me? I know the part you played in my husband's death. You planned for him to die. You wanted me consumed with this hatred so you could use me to do your dirty work."

All true. However. "I am not the one to blame. You are. Had you not been capable of this, I would have chosen someone else."

Erebus knew she wasn't setting him up, intending to turn on him as soon as the next task began, because he knew the ins and outs of the coming fates and fortunes. Everything leading to the death of his victims—everything but the reasons for each decision.

Curiosity got the better of him. "Why do it? Why aid me while plotting my end?"

Slowly she turned her face toward his and focused those icy blues on him with such pure, undiluted malice, he felt ice spread over him. "Because I am everything my name promises. I am the Undoing."

Can't get enough of New York Times *bestselling author Gena Showalter? Check out this sneak peek at* Ruthless, *the second book in her captivating and unforgettable Immortal Enemies series.*

THE STORY:

Micah the Unwilling, fae King of the Forgotten, can tame even the most violent of beasts. Gearing for war with a sadistic enemy, he is disciplined and focused—until a feral beauty he encountered long ago wanders into his camp.

Viori de Aoibheall is ill prepared for Micah's fearsome brutality. Not to mention the ferocity of their connection and the carnality of his touch. But the real problem? Her brother is Micah's greatest foe. And though the sensual king makes her burn, she must stop him, whatever the cost.

Forbidden. Powerful. Ruthless.

AN EXCERPT:

Micah glared down at the feral beauty who had become a fever in his veins. He wanted her. He wanted her so badly, he could barely think of anything else. *Remember her crimes against you.*

Remembering wasn't the problem. He struggled to make those crimes matter. His resistance to her? Gone. Shattered. Inside him, pressure mounted. Scraped raw.

As they continued to stare at each other, awareness crackled in the air between them. His breath turned shallow. Hers did, too. Beneath his palm, her pulse raced.

Perhaps she suffered with the same problem, craving what she shouldn't? Perhaps he could have what she'd nearly given him before. It didn't have to mean anything. She could be nothing but a receptacle to him. Exactly what he'd had with each of his mistresses. A release. Satisfaction that would be wiped away within minutes, replaced by a deeper discontent.

The thought tossed fuel on the fires of his fury, and suddenly he wasn't struggling to make her crimes matter. They mattered greatly. She had given him hope for a bright future. Had made him long for what he'd never had, resurrecting old dreams that refused to die a second time. He hated her. And yet…the view…

The view yanked him right back under her spell. All that creamy skin now flushed from sunlight, damp with water droplets and glistening. Hair almost black when wet, the change in color highlighting her delicacy. Her vulnerability. Bright emerald irises, nearly overshadowed by her pupils. Red lips parted, all but pleading. The rise of her breasts every time she inhaled, puckered crests visible over the surface of the pond. The sight of her bound wrists, floating in front of her…

"Maybe I'll keep you chained to my bed for the rest of eternity," he rasped, tracing his thumb along her jugular.

"Maybe I'll enjoy it," she rasped back.

Need to know what happens next?
Preorder your copy of Ruthless *today!*